RED ADAM'S LADY

RED ADAM'S LADY

GRACE INGRAM

Foreword by Elizabeth Chadwick

CHICAGO REVIEW PRESS

This edition republished in 2018 by arrangement with the Estate of
Doris Sutcliffe Adams

Chicago Review Press Incorporated
814 North Franklin Street
Chicago, Illinois 60610

ISBN 978-1-61373-967-9

Cover design: Sarah Olson
Cover image: Talik Myrgorods'kyy
Interior design: David Miller

Printed in the United States of America
5 4 3 2 1

FOREWORD

Aged 16, I was browsing the shelves of my village library when I came to the stand where the new fiction books had been arranged for borrowing. Among them was *Red Adam's Lady* by Grace Ingram. The front cover depicted a sword hilt entwined with a chain of marigolds. I had recently fallen in love with the medieval period, especially the twelfth century, and so this book was an auto-grab for me. Once home I disappeared to my room to read, and from the first page, I was sucked into the story by the immediate, atmospheric sense of time and place, by the lively language, and by the determined heroine Julitta de Montrigord who finds herself in a minor but annoying predicament but by page six is involved in a situation that will change her life forever when she encounters Red Adam de Lorismond, the new Lord of Brentborough Castle. He is drunk and bent on debauchery until she puts an end to his intentions by felling him with a stool. The next morning, amid a welter of disapproval from all concerned, Red Adam does the decent thing and marries Julitta. For better or worse they are now bound together, although how long they will live is debatable given the hostility from immediate neighbors, the wider political unrest caused by the rebellion of King Henry II's sons, and Scottish incursions over the border.

Grace Ingram had the knack of assembling a feel for time and place in a few well-chosen words. The reader is immediately immersed in the sights, sounds, and smells of the twelfth century, never more than when Julitta is dealing with the slovenly habits of her predecessors at Brentborough and attempting to undo years of neglect. It's a visual, visceral delight. I felt tremendous satisfaction in watching Julitta at work, and I empathized with her bravery and determination. I often chuckled too. Grace Ingram had a mischievous sense of humor and comic timing and knew exactly when to turn the moment. She also knew how to tug at the heartstrings and instill sympathy and warmth in the reader, but she was never mawkish with her characters. Their personalities, traits, and behaviors are always believable and three-dimensional. Well ahead of George R. R. Martin, Grace Ingram also understood the shock value of the unexpected, and this helps to ground the work and bring the light and shadow into perfect alignment. The reader is well reminded that Julitta and Adam are fighting for their lives.

Red Adam's Lady is quietly groundbreaking in other ways. As well as being a romance in the wider sense of the word, it is also a medieval murder mystery. Four years before Ellis Peters produced her first Brother Cadfael novel, *A Morbid Taste for Bones, Red Adam's Lady* preempted the genre by weaving a murder mystery into the wider plot: Red Adam's uncle was purported to have murdered his pregnant wife, but it was never proven. So what really happened to her?

I have read and reread *Red Adam's Lady* over the years, and I always derive great pleasure from it. The first time, I galloped through the novel and then had to go back and read it all over again more slowly in order to savor the characters and the story. I had to take it back to the library, but I borrowed it again and again, and when it came out in paperback in 1973, I bought my own copy. It's a treasured work on my keeper shelf as one of my curl-up comfort reads. It never fails to entertain and satisfy, even though I know the story by heart. I am so delighted to see it back in print and available to readers once more. For those who have never had the opportunity to delight in *Red Adam's Lady* before, I hope it will enter their hearts too and become a keeper.

ELIZABETH CHADWICK

1

Within sight of Brentborough village and the castle lowering over it, and five miles from home, the lady's palfrey cast a shoe. Pronouncing maledictions on the cross-eyed sot who had shod her, the groom swung down, set his mistress in his own saddle, recovered the shoe and started to lead the limping mare.

"Could ha' been worse, Lady Julitta. Handy enough to a forge, and if t' smith's not sober he soon will be."

"A little early for him to be incapable," she replied drily.

"Who's to say these days, wi' t' new lord setting such a rare fine fashion in tippling? And mind you, m' lady, while I deals wi' t' smith, you sets mum as a mouse in t' priest's house outa sight."

The lady grinned. "So desperate a ravisher?"

"Best put no temptation in his road, m' lady," the groom answered austerely, and as they squelched into Brentborough through the drizzle he steered her firmly for the church on their right hand. A man standing in the doorway of the alehouse, whose green bush proclaimed a fresh brewing, recognized their plight and called over his shoulder. One fellow came running to take the nervous mare, and the smith appeared, no more than amiably moistened, and ambled towards his forge. Then the alewife herself emerged and trotted heavily across the miry green, her bosom surging with the effort, and dropped a curtsey.

"If you seeks Father Simon, m' lady, he's up at t' castle shriving some poor sinner, God rest him," she panted, crossing herself. "'Twouldn't be seemly, for sure, for you to set foot beyond t' gate, and a stiffish climb too. But if you're wishful to rest out o' t' rain while Edgar shoes your mare, Lady Julitta, I'd be honored, though 'tisn't fitting I knows—"

"Right gladly, and I thank you," The lady accepted, dismounted and shook out the damp-spangled skirts of her shabby riding dress. On so wet an evening she was grateful for any shelter. Ignoring her groom's disapproving eye, she accompanied her hostess to the alehouse, where the customers were summarily shooed out.

"Off home, ye slummocky gawks—off ye gets to your wives, trying to keep your suppers from scorching while you swills! Mend your manners, goggling like codfish at the noble lady!" She flapped her apron at them, and they scuttled, laughing, all save one old woman sharply regarding them over a wooden piggin. Her wizened face disappeared behind it, and she swallowed like a veteran. "Aye, you too, gran'mother! Time all honest women was inside their own doors!"

The old woman smacked the piggin down on the bench with a jar that demonstrated its emptiness. "If I was your gran'dam you'd ha' been born wi' more wit nor you've got now, Gunhild," she declared belligerently, "an' as for honest, I'm past being owt else an' so are you!" She bounced from the bench, a bundle of bones in withered skin, and past them to the door. Outside, she poked her head round its frame. "Put less water to your malt if you'd have a brew worth drinking," she recommended, winked alarmingly at the girl, and vanished.

"Tippling owd besom—never heed her! Come sit you down, my pretty dear—m' lady. A horn o' new ale, now? And what's your fancy? There's green cheese, and eggs, and fresh-baked bread, or shall I toss you up a fry o' bacon? You'll be sharp-set riding from t' nunnery, and likely not much to your dinner, the Reverend Abbess being too holy-minded to set much thought on folk's bellies."

Holy was not the word the girl would have applied to the Reverend Abbess' mind, but she laughed, accepted the horn of ale, coarse bread warm from the hearth and soft cheese, declining all else the widow's bounty pressed on her. She warmed to a kindness seldom hers, even though she knew that Brentborough would be wearied for weeks to come by the honor done Gunhild's house by young Lady Julitta of Chivingham. She looked about her in the twilight that came through the open door. The single log, flat on its bed of ash, smouldered sullenly, eddying a blue haze about the blackened side of bacon, the half mutton-ham, the dried fish, strings of onions, and bunches of herbs that hung from the rafters. In a corner a shaggy bitch suckled a tumble of pups, and the earthen floor, smooth and hard as polished wood, had been newly swept and strewn with green rushes. The air reeked of the sweet-sour scent of brewing.

"Let me fill up, m' lady. Dismal riding today, and your gown all mired. A rough road for a lady, and on a bootless errand too, for o' course you're about Lord William's business, and everyone knows as t' holy Abbess isn't t' lady to abate a scrap o' her house's rights, and all Holy Church to her back. But 'tis your uncle's affair." She cocked a knowing brown eye at the girl, who retired prudently behind the ale-horn, marveling afresh that the peasants knew every secret of hall and bower. Not that her uncle had any secrets, since he loudly proclaimed his mind on all matters that engaged it.

The alewife bustled about the hearth, pulling the iron firedogs closer, setting a couple of fresh logs against them, sweeping in the ashes. The girl munched with healthy hunger, reflecting on an unpleasant errand whose fruitless outcome she would have to explain to her uncle, though why he should expect her to prevail when his lawyer, his chaplain, and he himself had failed to budge the Abbess a hair's breadth from her stand, was past her comprehension. Whatever flaws his lawyer had discovered in his grandsire's charter making over the disputed acres, the nunnery had been in possession these thirty years, and his suggested compromise that it restore half, to avoid the mutually ruinous costs of a lawsuit, had been rejected with the contempt it merited. Nor was it easy to plead a hopeless cause with a detestable woman. The girl shrugged incautiously, and regretted it; her shoulders still ached from the beating her protests had brought her.

A steady ring of hammer on iron proclaimed the smith's industry. She had not a penny on her for payment, and her uncle, applied to, would blame her again. She would not be back before dark, incurring further censure. She swallowed the last morsels, drained the horn, and thanked her hostess. She moved to the door. The sky was darkening fast. The castle's black bulk was already pricked out with lights, gathering strength as the night thickened. A raucous yowling, rapidly approaching, jerked her head round.

Four men were trampling up the track on lathered stallions, affronting the evening with their variant versions of a lewd song. They reeled every way as they rode, reins loose and heads thrown back, but their high-peaked saddles and horseman's instinct kept them astride their mounts. The girl stepped back from the doorway with a snort of mingled amusement and disgust, knowing them for the new lord of Brentborough and his pot comrades, returned a fortnight ago to scandalize the neighborhood, this rainy harvest-time of 1173. Opposite the alehouse the leader suddenly flung up a hand and wrenched on the reins, halting song and mount together in a splatter of mud and foam.

"*Come, you gallant*—hey, the bush! New ale!"

The other three overshot him and swung plunging horses about. "New ale!" Moved by that stimulus, they pounded across, tumbled from their saddles, and surged for the doorway.

The alewife already blocked it, hissing over her shoulder, "T' back room, m' lady!"

10

The lady had needed no telling, but by mischance she was on the wrong side of the doorway. The men's rush spun even Gunhild's bulk from their way, and as she staggered the foremost exultantly gave tongue.

"Hey, a wench! Hell's Teeth, she's found us a new wench!"

He lunged at her, his face split by reckless laughter under the fire-red crest of hair. She backed to the wall, too furious to be afraid.

"Hold off!" she cried in French, as they deployed about her. "I am Julitta de Montrigord, no peasant for ravishing!"

They were past heeding or understanding; yelping gleefully, they closed in. She eluded one man's wavering grasp, to be grabbed by the redhead, whose eyes functioned less independently of each other. A third clawed the kerchief from her head, and her braids tumbled free. "A match!" he howled. "A red match—for Red Adam!" As she dragged against the hold on her wrist, he flung his arms about her and planted a slobbery kiss awry on her eyebrow. His breath reeked of wine and ale.

The girl clouted him across the mouth. The redhead hauled her to him, twisting aside barely in time to evade her upjerked knee. The alewife, on all fours with her broad buttocks uplifted like a rising cow's, heaved erect, snatched a piggin from the bench and lumbered round the scrimmage's fringe, thwacking at every head in reach and yelling abuse at her liege lord and his friends. The mongrel bitch shot snarling from her corner into the tangle of legs, and snapped at any unprotected by skirts. The pups squeaked, the bitch worried, the bench and ale-barrel crashed over, the piggin cracked and Gunhild cursed, and the flurry swirled rushes and ash underfoot and gushed the murk full of smoke and sparks.

The lady's groom came on the run shouting to his mistress, and dived dagger-first through the door. The glint of steel cleared fighting men's wits. His dagger spun from a numbed hand, a kick struck his legs from under him, and he fell backwards across the overset bench and rammed the

11

flimsy wall so that the cottage reeled. Gunhild, stepping back to clear her aim, tripped over the dog, caught her heel in her gown and sat backwards in the fire.

She rebounded screeching and rolled across the floor in a throat-catching stink of scorched wool. A foot hurled the bitch tail over teeth through the doorway. The groom scrambled up and grabbed for the dagger winking in the rushes. The only man of the four drunkards to wear a sword fumbled for it, twisted round at his back, and began to haul it clear. The lady, held by the redhead and his comrade, screamed warning, but the last man kicked at the groom's head. He went down, blood spattering from his broken mouth, and as he lurched to hands and knees, the last man caught up a trestle and stretched him senseless.

"Murderers! Ivar—you've killed him!"

The attacker spun round, lost the trestle, crossed his legs and sat on the alewife. He stared vaguely at the rivulet of ale from the overturned barrel. "Waste 'f ale," he pronounced, groped for the piggin between his feet and held it more or less under the bung hole. "Mus'n' washe good ale." His comrade had at last drawn his sword and brandished it aimlessly. "Gone 'way," he mumbled, peering about him. He observed his friend's preoccupation and conjured a piggin into his own hand.

The redhead and the other grinned across the struggling girl, who fought again to wrench free and reach her groom. "You've killed him!"

"Y'r hushban?" asked the brown man. "Nev' min'—not mish him tonight."

"Not dead," the redhead assured her, still grinning. "Broke head—salve in morning—hish price. Don' fight—more fun with me." He tugged her towards him.

"No!" his companion objected. "My wench—you had lash one—thish mine."

"Who's lord of Bren—Bren'b'rough—me or you?"

The girl braced herself against their tugging and spoke with icy clearness. "I tell you, I am William de Montrigord's niece, no peasant!"

Despairingly she realized that even had they been sober

enough to understand her and appreciate the quality of her French, they would not have believed her; William de Montrigord's niece should not be found in a village alehouse, attired like a peasant girl and attended by only one groom.

"'S my turn!" the brown man was arguing with drunken tenacity. "You had yellowhead—thish one mine." He hauled at the lady's arm as though to tear her asunder, and she kicked him fiercely on the kneecap. He staggered. The redhead, who had either imbibed less or owned a harder head, jerked at her other wrist, and as he stumbled within reach smote him under the ribs' arch with his clenched fist. He reeled back, fetched up against the wall, slid down it and spewed all that was within him.

The redhead hooted gleefully and grappled the girl to him, spinning her round adroitly so that she could only kick back at his legs. He heaved her from her feet and slung her over his shoulder. "Alwaysh liked—sh-spirit," he declared with satisfaction, and shouldered out of the doorway into the sodden twilight. Hanging upside down, the girl pounded fists against a hard back and kicked ineffectively. He slapped her bottom. "No need—kick 'n claw—out o' hushban's sight," he told her cheerfully. She felt him squirm and fumble under her waist, and then she was swung back on to her feet, his cloak bundled her into a cocoon, and he heaved her on to a saddlebow that drove out what breath remained in her. Then he was up too, gripping her to him, urging his tired beast into a run. The rain driving into his face seemed to clear some of his wits, for he continued his tavern song to the disapproving sky.

He finished on a note more becoming to a hunting wolf, and tightened his hold on the girl, who had ceased struggling and was praying desperately to God and His Mother and the Saints for succor. He tried to kiss her, and she ducked her head into the cloak so that her crown caught his chin and made his teeth clack. He yelped. She twisted to slide through his slackened grip and over his horse's withers, and he tightened it ruthlessly. "Wan' to break silly neck?" he demanded. "Have fun—shan't hurt you."

The horse slowed for rising ground. The girl turned her

head and saw the mass of a gatetower loopholed with yellow light. "Let me go!" she gasped. "Indeed I am no harlot! My uncle is lord of Chivingham—"

He did not heed her. There had been a hail, the drawbridge was creaking down, and then its planks rang hollow under the horse's hooves, the ditch's gulf gaped black below, and the portcullis' spikes hung over the gateway like the fangs of Hell's Mouth. Torchlight flared at the tunnel's further end, completing the illusion; the girl cried out to the waiting fiends that crowded forward.

"In God's Name, help me!"

"She's bashful!" Red Adam exclaimed. "Who — whoever heard of a shy whore?" He rode forward into rainy darkness, the torches spluttering along with him, and then reined in. A shape, more like an upright bear than anything human, caught the reins. He was suddenly out of the saddle, and before the girl could struggle had slung her again over his shoulder and was climbing a flight of steps, to the sound of devils' laughter below.

Candlelight glimmered on matted rushes, shifting legs and tunic hems; bawdy jests and sniggers were about her, and then her captor was mounting unlit spiral stairs. Once he stumbled, and gripped harshly as she writhed. The blood was drumming in her ears and darkening her eyeballs, she could scarcely breathe, and such terror filled her that only Red Adam's solid bones and gripping arms had reality. She kicked futilely, and he lurched against the wall and then recovered. Six strides took him to an open door, from which a pair of feet skipped nimbly aside, and he thrust through it.

For a moment he stood jerking breath into his lungs; then he grunted and kicked shut the door behind him. Sobbing in desperation as she glimpsed the bed filling most of the space, she fought frantically. He stumbled. Somehow she hooked a foot inside his knee, and they fell sideways across the bed, still locked fast. His hand fumbled at her breast, and she wrenched one arm free of the cloak, gripped a fistful of hair and tore his head back with all the strength she possessed.

14

He yelped and rolled from her, clutching again at her wrist. "Whash amiss?" he demanded with sottish indignation. "Don' be 'fraid — shan't hurt you. Have fun, you'n me. Shan't be mean, either." He grinned at her, his teeth gleaming in the dim light, as the crushing hold forced open her fingers and he jerked his head free. "Hushban' won' inner — interfere — shan't be mean with him either." He heaved up on his elbow, jerked her wrists together to grasp them in one long hand, and reached for the neck-lacing of her gown.

She ducked her head, sank teeth into the fleshy base of his thumb and bit until the tough skin burst and her mouth filled with salty blood. He yelped again, his hold involuntarily slackening, and she writhed free, rolled out of his cloak, off the bed and to her feet in one frantic surge of effort, wild-eyed and claw-fingered.

"Vixen!" he exclaimed reproachfully, and sprang up, still terrifyingly sure of hand and foot. The girl retreated along the bedside, casting about for a weapon. He was between her and the door, and there was no space to dodge him. He started towards her, extending arms that seemed to reach forth like a tree's branches. She backed round the bed foot, and almost tripped over a stool.

"Don' you *wan'* fun with me?" he asked, incredulously reproachful. "Li'l vic — vix —" He followed close, and she snatched up the stool by one leg and swung it with all her strength.

The impact jarred her arm to the shoulder. He went down sideways against the bed, rolled on to his face and lay unstirring, blood bursting through his hair and puddling black in the rushes. The girl watched narrowly, the heavy stool hanging from her hand, for the space of half a dozen breaths, until his stillness convinced her that he was truly no menace. Then another terror drove her to lay a flinching hand on his back, and jerk it away in relieved loathing as soon as it lifted to a breath. She glanced wildly about her and leaped to the door.

She clawed at it, then suddenly recollected herself and drew it open enough to set an eye to the gap, peering cauti-

15

ously into dusky space full of flickering shadow. Fires were banked for the night, but the glow upwelling from a few candles and torches outlined the gallery and its rail. A scuffle of movement and a drone of talk below broke to a hoarse guffaw that made her start.

She thrust the door shut on it. She was as fast a prisoner of Red Adam as ever, and she knew well what would befall her if she ventured forth from this room to be seized by the guards below, after she had cracked their lord's head for him.

She set her back to the door, then gulped resolutely and turned to see if it could be made fast. Luck was with her. This must be a strongroom diverted from its rightful purpose to have a door at all, and a new wooden bar had been fixed, presumably to ensure privacy for Red Adam's dubious amusements. She slammed it down with a clatter that made her catch a harsh breath, but the sprawled body by the bed had not shifted. A wall pricket above two padlocked chests bore a candle, flaring and smoking in the draft from an ill-fitting shutter.

The girl glanced about her at bed, chests, stool and candle, and then contemplated the man breathing stertorously in the filthy rushes. Her sharp chin lifted, her wide mouth tightened. She twitched the dagger from its sheath and slid it point first up her left sleeve, which marked her as a young woman of uncommon education. Still he did not stir, so next she dragged his belt from under him, passed it round the bedpost, heaved his weight on to its side so that she could bring both wrists to the post at his back, wound the leather over and under and buckled it fast, yanking the prong up to the furthest hole with vindictive fierceness. Then she plumped down on the bed and wept.

She was scrubbing the tears from her face with the skirt of her wet gown when the gallery reverberated under ill-managed feet. They halted at the door. "Hey, Adam!" an aggrieved voice bawled. "My turn — don' take all night shwive a wench!"

"He'sh ashleep," suggested another voice, after a hard-breathing pause.

"He'sh greedy shwine. New wench — fair sharesh. Adam! Lemme in! Fair share!" Fists pounded heavily. The bar rattled, but held.

"Ashleep," pronounced the second voice.

A heavier thud, lower down, was followed by a squall that suggested the oak was harder than the toe assailing it. "Not fair! Greedy —"

"Fin' 'nother wench," the other suggested reasonably, and the feet and grumbling reeled away. The girl loosed her breath and thrust back the dagger she had shaken down her sleeve. Her heartbeats steadied. Presently she moved from the door to sit again on the bed, stiffly upright, listening fearfully. The keep settled to quiet. The candle guttered lower. Rain beat against the window shutter. Drafts probed round it, chilling her in her clammy gown so that she huddled Red Adam's cloak about her, curling up on the embroidery-crusted scarlet bedcover. Once an over-active conscience drove her from it to lift her victim's head, but the blood had clotted and he was breathing steadily, so she sat down again and considered more urgent matters.

Ivar was hurt. There was no knowing how badly, and she said an earnest prayer for him and another for the alewife who had defended the guest under her roof. Yet if Ivar could crawl to a horse he would be at Chivingham gate within the hour. She flinched as she imagined her uncle's reaction to his tale and the need to rescue her, a contemplation so dismaying that she forgot she had still to be rescued. Neither sympathy nor consideration had come her way since William de Montrigord had been obliged to receive his orphan niece into his household, an obligation which, as he informed her and all within reach of his voice whenever he set eyes on her, he reckoned an intolerable imposition upon his justly-famed charity. Moreover he had openly given thanks, when Red Adam inherited Brentborough from a distant cousin, that his youngest child Sibylla was unpledged. He had even made the first advances when the young man returned north a fortnight ago. His plans were now disastrously overset, and she knew where the blame would fall, and quailed.

The rushes stirred. The heavy breathing checked. A grunt,

17

another rustle, and a thick voice proclaimed, "Hell's Teeth! My skull's split!"

Julitta held her breath, her heart thudding against her ribs. The man moved more purposefully. A half-stifled groan gratified her heart. She leaned to peer at him. He blinked through the mess of hair clotted to his brow, screwed up his eyes in bewilderment, looked about him and back to her.

"How did you come here?"

"Over your shoulder," she answered tartly. "Have you forgotten?"

He shook his head as though to clear it, winced and desisted. "I must have been soused as a pickled herring," he commented ruefully.

"You were vilely drunk."

"Did you crack my skull?"

"Yes."

"With what?"

"The stool."

"Why?"

"To save my virtue."

"Did you really need to be so drastic?"

"Yes."

He tried to sit up, and could not, pulling briefly against the tether. "And then you trussed me to the bedpost." He grinned through the crusted blood. "I concede you the victory, lass. Loose me and I'll take you home."

"No."

"I'm harmless when sober, I assure you — and I'm most uncomfortably sober now."

She scowled at him and hugged the cloak closer. The guttering candle, at its last inch, turned his streaked face into a devil's mask, and she flinched from him. He shrugged, and grimaced.

"No woman ever could tie fast," he declared, and fought the belt so that the bedframe shuddered. Suddenly he desisted and fell slack. "Hell's Teeth, I've met her!" he gasped. Breathing jerkily, he shut his eyes, obviously assailed by the shattering headache he deserved. She hugged her knees and watched him somberly.

18

His eyes flicked open, staring at her in something like alarm. "You've addled my brains with that stool! No peasant speaks such French! Who are you?"

"Julitta de Montrigord."

"Montrigord — Lord William's kin? Not his daughter; that's a rabbit-nosed yellowhead called Sibylla. The niece?"

"Yes."

"The one the Lady Abbess tossed back to him for lack of a dower?"

"Yes."

"The most sanctimonious she-weasel north of Humber from all I've heard." He hitched himself up against the bed-post and endeavored to focus his gaze. "I own I've no clear recollection of what occurred, but didn't we find you in the alehouse?"

She flushed painfully. "Yes."

"What business had a girl of your quality there?"

"Gunhild offered me shelter while my horse was shod."

"Didn't some fellow — your groom, that would be — yes, I remember now." He had the grace to flush. "We mistook you for a peasant wench."

"And it is a noble lord's prerogative to ravish peasant maids."

He grinned. "My dear girl, peasant wenches of your age are never maids. They go at first flowering to some churl's straw. Nor, when I got one to bed, did I ever find her unwilling."

"How lavishly you must pay for their accommodation!"

"You've a well-filed tongue," he commented. "But you're dressed like a peasant. What was your uncle about, permitting you to go abroad so ill-clad and attended?"

"Particularly when he knew you were ravaging the neighborhood," she completed sourly. "That you had better ask him when the reckoning is made. He sent me."

With no remnant of levity he looked up into her eyes and said, "I doubt not you would sooner spit in my face than hear my apologies, demoiselle, but I offer them."

"And account your conscience cleared?" she snapped.

"Whatever amends are possible I will make," he prom-

19

ised. She scowled at him, knowing his words worthless; nothing he could do would avert her ruin. "And now, girl, do you propose to keep me all night tethered to this post like a billygoat?"

"Why not?"

He smiled wryly at that. "We'd both be more comfortably bestowed apart. Let me go, lass. I yield me captive; you have my knightly oath. Moreover I'm in no state to ravish anyone; my skull's cleaving apart —"

"That gratifies me!"

"Vixen — And by the turmoil in my inwards I shall soon be vilely sick, which will make me even less agreeable company."

That argument moved her more powerfully than appeal or oath. She regarded him narrowly, and judged that he spoke truth by the sheen of sweat over his brow and the greenish pallor about his mouth. Abruptly she hopped from the bed, circled warily round his legs, and wrestled with the buckle until it slipped from his wealed wrists. Then she stepped away behind the bed, her hands together at her breast in what appeared an attitude of prayer.

Red Adam sat up and rubbed his wrists. He leaned forward a moment and propped his head in his hands. Then he climbed unsteadily to his feet, with the bedpost's help. He towered in the candlelight. He wavered to the door, and with his hand on the bar looked back at her. "You won't need my dagger," he told her, faintly smiling. "Bar the door and go to bed. I'll marry you tomorrow."

2

Julitta jerked up, roused from unexpectedly sound sleep in the most comfortable bed she had ever occupied. Someone was at the door. She twisted over in alarm, and found reassurance at sight of the bar, firm in its sockets. A repeated tapping on the other side of those admirable boards brought her from the bed. Daylight, leaking round the shutter's edges, showed her Red Adam's belt still looped about the bedpost. Nightmare was reality. Her garments were spread to dry over the chests. She scrambled into them.

"Lady Julitta!" A woman's voice, softly solicitous, supplemented the tapping. At its sound all the night's lonely terror rose from the girl's breast in a gulping sob. She dropped back on to the bed, tears flooding. "Lady Julitta, there is nothing to fear. Will you open the door?"

She choked back the tears. She dared not trust a Brentborough woman; Red Adam might be standing by her side. Yet he had, once sober, been perversely reasonable. He had given his knightly word. Also, even those planks would not keep him out if he determined to hew them down. That resolved her. Her flesh cringed from another encounter, but she would not cower in a corner while the door was forced

21

and be dragged out shrieking. She withdrew the dagger from under her pillow, sleeved it, clenched her teeth and jerked out the bar.

She stepped back involuntarily from a billowing blue and white embrace, and stared at a very lovely lady. "Ah, poor sweet child! Come, let me comfort you!"

She dodged ungratefully from the reaching arms. "Who are you?"

"I am chatelaine of Brentborough—Constance, the seneschal's wife. Trust me, my child; I will keep you safe."

Julitta wondered rather grimly how this lovely lady would fend off Red Adam if he were set on rapine; obviously last night she and all other prudent souls had retired and left their lord to his pleasures.

"You are stunned, poor child," Lady Constance crooned, regarding her with concern. "A convent-bred innocent, so outraged!" She cast an experienced glance over the bed, whose state seemed to disconcert her. "If only he has not got you with child! You must pray to the Holy Virgin, and drink pennyroyal to promote your courses —"

"I am virgin," Julitta declared. Lady Constance stared in amused disbelief. "I stunned him with the stool." The skeptic smile widened. "Do you not believe me?"

"If I did, no other will," Lady Constance said. "Think of a more likely story, child."

"You know it's truth! How else was his head broken?"

"A tourney champion overthrown by a maid with a stool?"

Julitta chilled. This mockery accorded ill with the lady's protested concern. "He was drunk," she stated.

"Drunker than ever I have seen him, if it made him clumsy." She set a hand on Julitta's shoulder and spoke earnestly. "Poor child, you must reconcile yourself. Naught can mend a broken maidenhead. But Lord Adam is not ungenerous, and has interest at the convent, where you must long to return. Where else but in Holy Church's arms can your shame be covered?"

"I have no shame to cover."

"After this outrage, surely you must wish never again to set eyes on a man. You must desire only the peace of—"

"Of the tomb?" Red Adam suggested from the doorway. "And a very fair imitation you provide, Lady Constance; so much gloom one doesn't miss the bier."

The lady swung about, her face darkened alarmingly.

"In with you, girl!" He shoved forward a sluttish serving wench, gaping over basin, ewer and towels, and strode to the window. The bandage about his head flashed in a streak of dusty sunlight. He heaved at the shutter. "Half the woodwork in this hold is rotten," he commented disparagingly as it suddenly yielded, powdering him with worm-frass. Sun and wind leaped in. The rushes fluttered, the one wretched hanging flapped, and every stain on the discolored plaster showed stark.

Julitta took her first daylight look at her abductor, and surprise widened her eyes. He was neither a sodden lout nor a ravening brute, but a boy; a long-shanked lad with fiery hair awry under the bandage and disarming freckles spattered across nose and cheekbones. She was not disarmed. It was less tolerable to owe her ruin to a lad's frolic than to a scoundrel's villainy. She scowled, resentful of his critical gaze. She was no beauty, and at this moment must appear at a deal less than her best, but that gave him no right to assess her like a horsecoper surveying a doubtful nag at Smithfield Market.

"My lord," began Lady Constance, "if you dare jest over the outrage you have done an innocent maid —"

"The only outrage was done to my skull with a stool," he retorted, "and I'll amend my fault by marriage."

"You expect this ravished child to *marry* such a monster, when the cloister offers her safe haven?"

"You'll have hard work making a lass of sense refuge herself with the she-weasel. Moreover, I haven't offered her the choice. Heart up, girl! You've hope of a well-dowered widowhood to sustain you, and no convent could offer that."

"It's a cruel jest!" Lady Constance exclaimed as he left them. She set her arm about the girl's rigid body, offering

23

a shoulder for her comforting. "Great lords marry lands and power, not the maids they have ravished. But depend on me to find you safety in the convent, your only shelter."

"He meant it," Julitta said bleakly, twisting from the maternal embrace. The ruthless daylight showed the lady was indeed of an age to be her mother; lovely yet, but twenty years past her flowering. The gold was faintly tarnished, clear lines blurring, rich curves sagging. Her solicitude somehow jarred like a misstruck string. Julitta was put in mind of those of her father's strumpets who had made much of her, after her mother's elopement with an Angevin knight.

"My dear child —"

"I'll not marry him!" Julitta said violently. The serving girl was still gaping by the door, and she signaled her to set down her burdens on a chest. The water was warm, a luxury seldom vouchsafed her; Julitta washed with vicious thoroughness to remove the taint of Red Adam's hands and lips. The dagger was reassurance inside her sleeve, a deal more comforting than Lady Constance, fussing over her muddy gown that had never enhanced even its original owner's looks. Her kerchief was gone. Lady Constance produced a comb, and she braided her hair as rigorously as its unruliness allowed. Then she braced back her shoulders, lifted her chin, ignored the qualms churning in her belly and stalked through the doorway.

Red Adam lounged against the gallery rail, which creaked protest as he straightened. His gaze flicked over her. "I thought your hair was red," he said irrelevantly.

She stiffened and scowled defiance, her heart thumping at her ribs. He grinned, glanced past her at Lady Constance, and remarked, "A lass of discrimination as well as spirit. A cracked head's a cheap price to pay."

"I wish I'd split your skull!"

"I'm well aware you did your utmost, vixen." He smiled wryly. "I'm resolved to remain sober henceforth. A man should reform his way of life when he weds." He moved closer, and for all her defiance her flesh flinched. His voice softened. "I had less than my deserts, demoiselle, and I honor you."

24

That she had never anticipated, and her composure came near cracking. She bit at her lip to steady it, blinking against the tears that pricked under her lids. A hard hand caught hers, turned her about and drew her back into the room.

Out of spinning fog the hated voice said, "Here's food and wine to hearten you, my lady."

She looked up, her sight clearing. Last night's bear bowed clumsily and offered her a silver cup and platter. The resemblance was startling enough, emphasized by a rough dark tunic, but the brown eyes regarding her between shaggy hair and beard were amiably bovine.

"My body-servant Odo, at your command." Red Adam presented him, and took cup and platter to serve her himself. For a moment she was tempted to cast them in his face, then compelled herself to match his courtesy. The unwatered wine burned into her innards and woke appetite; the wheaten bread and cold boiled bacon were a more substantial meal than the usual crust that broke one's fast. She looked up belligerently.

"Fortified now to confront your uncle?" her tormentor inquired.

"My — Is he here?"

"Sighted at sun-up. We'll hear the horn any moment. Come, greet him with me." He gripped her hand and pulled her up. Like a sleepwalker, she followed him down turn after turn of stairs, across a guardroom as full of staring eyes as a basket of crabs, and out at the door. The wind swooped upon her, billowing her gown and tearing her hair into wild curls. The bright brown of it took fire from sun or torchlight, dulled to insignificance in gloom, but since she had scanty acquaintance with mirrors she did not guess why Red Adam eyed her in fresh appraisal. Pressing her skirts close against the wind's insolence, she hurried down the stair. After heavy rain the bailey's grass was churned to mire, and the rough paths of beach pebbles were slimy with mud. Every person in the court halted activity to gape.

Red Adam towed her briskly towards the gatetower. His ears and the back of his neck had reddened as though even he could feel embarrassment. A horn bellowed, and the

or so of riders were advancing up the track from the village. "No siege train?" he remarked, as she too looked out and confused fears battled in her. He missed no move she made; he had not forgotten the dagger. Suddenly his grin flashed. "A truce, lady, until your uncle is here. And enlighten me as to his company; I'm not as well acquainted with my neighbors as I should be."

"Whose fault is that?" she demanded waspishly; in his two brief visits to Brentborough since he inherited it he had avoided all social engagements.

"Prudence, though you might find that hard to credit. I'll dip no cup in this brew of treason that's bubbling against King Henry — and a washy brew of froth and wind it is, stirred by such fools." He leaned to scrutinize the company. "Lord William I've met, and his eldest son behind him — Gilbert, is it? Doleful as the prophet Jeremiah, but that's no marvel. The straw-thatched lout with the face full of teeth will be Gerald of Flackness, your betrothed. Faced with wedding *that*, you shy at *me*?"

"What difference is there?"

Her bitter query pierced every layer of arrogance, vanity and self-satisfaction, more hurtfully than a knife blade. Surprised, she watched the color drain from behind his freckles, his eyes widen in shock. He gazed almost blindly at her, while his brain accepted it; then he nodded. "That's — very just."

"There has been no formal betrothal. I have no dower. He will be glad to repudiate me," she informed him, as one nightmare ended another. "You need not fear his challenge."

"You reassure me. Who's the cub breaking line on the left?"

"My youngest cousin Gautier. He wishes to venture Outremer, but my uncle will not equip him."

"He should be thankful. He'd not last a month; I've been there. The lean badgerhead, falling back where the path narrows?"

"Everard FitzJordan of Digglewick."

"The fellow whose wife is with child after seventeen years

28

of barren wedlock? Has he roused out all his neighbors to support — oh no! Rejoice in the Lord, all ye righteous! I interrupted a plotters' convocation, and they've all trotted along to see the sport! Yes, there's old Ranulf of Hostby; be sure he'd lend his sheep's brain to any half-witted enterprise! And who is the miracle of manly beauty at your uncle's right stirrup?" Fire scorched up her neck and face. Instead of grinning, he twisted his mouth in a curious grimace. "Humphrey of Crossthwaite?"

She nodded, biting her lip for the betrayal, and dully wondering at his forbearance. She had betrayed herself months before when newly come, grudged and unwelcome, to her uncle's hold; when she plunged into a girl's first silly love for a handsome face and a casual smile. She had been rated and teased and mocked; but still she quivered with rapture at a smile, felt her heart quicken and her loins melt whenever he looked on her, and now was conscious with all her being of every move he made. Before Red Adam inherited Brentborough, her uncle had hoped to match his youngest child Sibylla with Humphrey, but their conceptions of an adequate dower had proved too wildly disparate. Julitta had dared to wish his new aim success, though she knew well that if Humphrey reckoned Sibylla's dower insufficient he would never consider one who possessed nothing. And now he "trotted along to see the sport... " as though her ruin were an entertainment.

She scowled at the man who had ruined her. He was looking beyond the cavalcade to another company appearing over the brow beyond. "If that's not a skirt fluttering, procure me a staff and begging bowl!" he exclaimed, and slapped the merlon beside him with delight. "Prepared for all contingencies! He's brought his womenfolk to take you in charge!"

William of Chivingham, half a length in the lead as he reached the ravine that served as ditch, lifted his scowl to the two above and champed visibly. His crimson face shone violently at odds with the scarlet tunic that should have made kitchen clouts years ago, and with the molting fox furs adorning it. He sat awkwardly, and Julitta's vitals cringed; yesterday's wet weather had set hell fire throughout his joints, and in such a state he spread his affliction lavishly on all about him.

"So much choler, not armed to avenge you?" Red Adam murmured.

"He'll make peace cheaply enough. He sets small value on me."

"His error. Don't be afraid." He seized her hand again to lead her down. "Saints, if ever he puts his face round the dairy door he'll curdle all within!"

She choked, but as she scuttled down the narrow spiral some oppression lifted from her, though she did not recognize the debt she owed his irreverence until the drawbridge began to creak down and her uncle's face hung preposterously over its further edge. She met his glare as she had never done before, a queer triumph leaping in her.

Red Adam stepped under the portcullis and bowed. "Save you, Lord William. Will it please you to enter, that I may answer for my conduct towards your niece?"

Lord William scowled at Julitta. He was not devoid of family feeling, and had she been pretty and meek would have reconciled himself long ago to her presence in his household, but his tyranny and her barbed tongue had left them nothing but rancor. "Save you, Lord Adam. A sorry affair, but it shan't stand between us and amity." He clopped over the timber and heaved himself painfully from his saddle. A groom darted from the bailey to take the reins.

"Very reasonable," Red Adam answered, anger edging his courtesy. He smiled unamiably at Lord William's advancing companions. "Since it seems you're not here to hew me into hounds' gobbets in my own bailey, enter. No challenge from the lady's avenging kinsmen, nor her betrothed?"

"There's no betrothal!" Gerald of Flackness made hasty denial. "I'll not fight over a scandal-blown wench who's naught to me."

"The lady must thank Heaven to hear you."

Gerald checked with his foot still in the stirrup, his lips

lifting from his formidable teeth, and Lord William said hurriedly, "We're not here to quarrel, and you know I'll not hold you to the match." He turned on Julitta. "By God's Blood, I've always known you'd shame my household!"

"Hell's Teeth! Dare you blame a guiltless maid for *my* sins?" Red Adam looked grimly into Lord William's congested face. "An accounting is your due as the lady's guardian." He drew hard breath, and his hands clenched. Julitta incredulously recognized that he did not find this easy. "Last night, being vilely drunk, I mistook your niece for a peasant wench and bore her here by force. She saved her maidenhead by stunning me with a stool." He touched the bandage.

"A likely tale!" Gerald jeered.

"Yet true."

The menace in his voice halted mockery. Lord William declared, "There's none here will deny any tale you testify to, Lord Adam. We've all been young and randy-drunk in our time."

"There's only one reparation I can make. I ask her hand in marriage."

As though he were a basilisk whose gaze turned men to stone, they gaped at him in unbelief. "But — she's dowerless!" Humphrey of Crossthwaite croaked at last, exposing their minds indecently naked. Red Adam's glance brought scarlet to his face.

"That's not *my* foremost consideration."

Gerald brayed coarse laughter. "Virtue for you, in a *Lorismond*!"

Red Adam ignored him, though his shoulders stiffened. He was waiting on Lord William, who was speechless with conflicting and ungratifying emotions. Julitta, knowing how vital an alliance with Brentborough was to his plotting against the King, could guess at them, and caught her breath in hope; it would not suit him in the least to marry his niece to its lord.

"Most nobly offered," he pronounced, "But there's no need of it. Your word suffices —"

31

"I'll not take damaged ware," Gerald hastily asserted.

Lord William shot him a glance of acute dislike, shifted painfully and winced as his joints twinged. "She can go back to the convent. If I withdraw my lawsuit the Abbess should be thankful enough to take her cheaply, and you're honorably quit of her. If not, I could give her to one of my sergeants."

"Your brother's daughter?" Red Adam protested.

"Of that I'm less sure than he was. She's daughter to the whore who destroyed him, and harlotry's in her blood." He glared at his niece, and plunged into his astounding offer. "It's been my dearest hope that you'd match within my family, Lord Adam. I'd bind alliance closer still. My girl Sibylla is virtuous and well-dowered. Send this wench to the convent and I'll gladly wed you to my daughter."

"It was not your daughter I wronged."

Lord William's head reared in affront. He encountered opposition so rarely that he had come to reckon his behests incontrovertible as the will of God. "You're daft!" he began, recognized inflexibility, gulped and assumed an unconvincing smile. "If your heart's set I'll not refuse you."

Julitta had been praying earnestly for the convent. She had no vocation, she reckoned the life dismal, she detested the Abbess, but it would be a haven from marriage to this raptor. "No!" she cried, starting away as Red Adam reached for her hand. "No!"

"What's this? You'll do as you are bidden, girl, and thank God your shame's covered."

"Let me take the veil, and never set eyes again on a man."

"I'll not dower you to spend forty years as a penitent whore, my vixen. Wed me, or the next unlovely oaf your uncle rakes from the midden," Red Adam told her grimly, heedless of Gerald's snarl.

She turned from one hard face to another, flinching from the brutes who disposed of her, from Ranulf of Hostby's embarrassment and Everard FitzJordan's shamed sympathy, in betraying appeal to Humphrey. There was no aid in him. He had less feeling for her than the neighbors. Despair filled her as he frowned and drew her uncle aside a pace to mutter urgently in his ear. Scarcely comprehending, she caught three words. "Mistake — not amenable —"

Red Adam came briskly to his point. "An immediate wedding, you'll agree, Lord William?"

"Aye, that's wisdom. Then none can point, however soon she pups."

In the silence which followed this infelicitous observation Humphrey's contrary advice was more audible than he had intended. "Delay! Keep her to bargain with!"

"Bargain?" Red Adam asked gently, and as he reddened furiously, turned to Lord William. "We've witnesses at hand. Summon your ladies, and we'll go to church straightway."

"Here — and now? It's against all custom — no time to prepare! A week — three days — at least time to provide bride clothes!"

"This afternoon. Your lady is here to order it, and assemble what state there's time for. Neighbors all, you'll honor my marriage feast?"

The half-dozen bewildered witnesses meekly surrendered their swords to the porter and their horses to the grooms. The women, waiting beyond the drawbridge, clattered in; Lady Matilda, Gilbert's wife Bertille, the wives of seneschal and marshall escorted by their husbands, Sibylla agape with curiosity, a dozen waiting-demoiselles and servants, and six men-at-arms for guard. Julitta, scanning all their censorious faces for that of the one who would surely not have failed her, roused suddenly.

"Ivar!" she exclaimed, interrupting the greetings. "Where is Ivar?"

"Hold your tongue!" her uncle bade her.

"Is he sorely hurt? What —"

"He's dismissed my service for offering me gross insolence, and I'll hear no more of him."

"Ivar — Ivar a masterless man!" she cried, and rounded on the man beside her. "Is there no end to the wrong you have wrought, monster?" His face and bandaged head swam in a blur of tears.

"It seems not," he agreed.

33

A white wimple came between them. "If you're to wed," snapped Lady Matilda, "it's unseemly and unlucky so much as to set eyes on each other this day until you stand before the priest, though there's been little enough that's seemly between you, and wedding will do no more than patch over your shame. So I'll trouble you to give this wretched girl into my care, Lord Adam, to take her in charge and make her ready while you set your marriage feast in hand, though it's asking a miracle of me to order a fitting ceremony at half a day's notice and you must be distempered in your wits to expect it. Not that that isn't plain to all when you choose to marry this graceless wench instead of Sibylla!"

"But we may surely expect the impossible from a lady of your repute?" Red Adam replied courteously.

The women closed on Julitta and hustled her in a scandalized flurry across the bailey, into the keep and up to the bower, vacated for their use. Lady Matilda as they went enumerated her requirements to the seneschal's wife. "Bride clothes she must have for very shame, and no time to make or alter. And wedding attire for all of us, and bring my tire woman and all the sewing maids; I'll not have Brentborough folk looking down their noses. Let me reckon; my second-best cendal smock and four linen ones from the chest by my bed. For the marriage, Sibylla's scarlet gown." Sibylla squawked dissent, and was smartly clouted. "We must all make sacrifices, and it becomes you not, so stop sniveling! My blue with the embroidered neck — no, she's too tall; we can't contrive four more inches. Sibylla's green riding cloak — one more whine from you, my girl, and I'll birch you so that you sleep on your belly for a week! Yes, and household linen; none shall sneer that she came from us empty-handed! Three pairs of sheets at least, and three of the good tablecloths —"

The seneschal's wife dismissed to deal with a formidable list, she pounced on Julitta to question, cross-question and requestion her about the night's events, and then condemn her as a contumelious liar.

Lady Constance billowed in, gracious enough to set one's

teeth on edge. "I am chatelaine of Brentborough, Lady Matilda, and would place all its resources at our bride's disposal."

"Chatelaine, is it? And fine resources this slut's domain offers, as anyone may see! Yes, and you connive at that randy young sot's abducting noble demoiselles —"

"And how should anyone have guessed her quality?" the fair woman retorted, and withdrew.

"Such insolence, and to her future lady! You've no light task there, my girl, to set that impudent strumpet in her place after she's queened it here ever since Lord Maurice's wife was lost. Yes, and now I've set eyes on her I know what to think of her place."

"Her husband *is* seneschal," Bertille, a professional peacemaker, pointed out.

"It's well known he's as blind as a mole, and when did a husband ever deter that lecher? Did you note the gown on her? Flanders broadcloth, no less, and her girdle of silk with silver clasp and tags! A slut she is; cast your eyes over those hangings, and the smuts and cobwebs everywhere, and that sewing tossed down like a dishclout, not to mention rushes never changed these two years at least. And the serving wenches —strumpets every one, and the hold no better than a brothel." She glared at Julitta. "Oh, yes, a splendid marriage you've achieved!"

"Lady of Brentborough!" said Sibylla resentfully.

"*No!* I will not!"

"What's that? You should be on your knees thanking God! Here you stand, cast off by Gerald of Flackness, dowerless and housed by our charity you've so shamelessly disgraced, and Red Adam — Saints keep his wits from him until the knot be safe tied — will make you Lady of Brentborough!" Lady Matilda sniffed disapproval of Heaven's decrees.

"It is rape!" Julitta protested in panic, her horror waking afresh.

"Rape? Nonsense! It's what befalls every girl on her marriage, and never let that insult come to Red Adam's ears when he has condescended so far. School yourself to be meek and

35

obedient and please your husband. However you mislike him, you will have a great estate to rule, and your children for consolation. Besides, he will soon weary of you and return to his low-born paramours."

Julitta had no wish to rule a great if disorderly estate, and the prospect of a string of brats in Red Adam's image appalled her, but the probability of a husband who would turn from her to peasant paramours she found, inconsistently enough, even less tolerable. She stared at the great bed set against the wall, clenched her fists until her nails cut into her palms, and fought revulsion that would set her shrieking if she gave way.

"Lechers and ravishers to a man, the Lorismonds," Lady Matilda yapped on, "and unchancy to marry, as old Maurice proved." She did not add the conventional "God rest his soul" to the dead's name, because no one had ever entertained any doubts as to that sinner's destination when he died unconfessed and unshriven nearly a year ago. "We'll not know what befell his poor wife until the dead rise up at Gabriel's trumpet, but I for one will never believe he didn't slay her, for it stands to reason she'd have gone to her kinsmen if she'd been alive —"

"And this cousin's another drunken lecher," said Sibylla spitefully, "and he's only wedding you to avenge his broken head."

Julitta backed from them. "No!"

"You'll do as you're bidden, and thank God —"

"I'll refuse at the altar!"

She held desperately to that resolve through all the clamor they raised about her. As a last resort Lady Matilda sent for her husband, and he limped into the bower. He had been drinking; wine temporarily deadened the pains in his joints but did nothing to ameliorate his temper. "God's Head! You're mad!" he bellowed at her. "Refuse such a match for some silly distemper?"

"I will not!"

"*Think*, you witless ninny! You'll rule a dozen rich estates, you'll wear fine clothes and jewels, and by God's Blood, Red

Adam will be an easier husband than Gerald! And who else would take his leavings?"

"No!"

"And what of your duty to me, your guardian, after I've housed you all these months? Let alone it's my right to dispose of you, is there no decent gratitude in your carcass? This match is God's answer to our prayers! We must have Brentborough with us if our righteous enterprise on behalf of the Young King is to prosper, and your part is to join your husband to us, so that we dispossess that tyrant the second Henry who oppresses England. There's the holy Saint Thomas, martyred at his own altar, to avenge, and our Young King to set on his throne! It is manifestly God's will; why else should Lord Adam set his crazy fancy on you?"

"I will not —"

"God's Head, you'll obey if I have to thrash you twice a day and lock you in the cellar on bread and water! It's not for you to say you will or you will not, but to wed where you're given and be thankful."

But dread had become an obsession in the girl; no normal fear could take root in her. She snarled at him. "No!"

"Wait until I have you home in Chivingham, and I'll flay the skin from you! You've shamed my household, brought scandal on my name, and defied me to my face. Honest wedlock's not for you? If you'd turn whore like your mother you'll do it beyond my boundaries."

The women, blasted into the furthest corner by his wrath, squeaked and cowered. Julitta confronted him, her legs quivering and her loins a jelly; she could not have budged had she tried, but that served for resolution. An icy-cold corner of her brain wondered how long he might indulge himself in meat, wine and fury before an apoplexy smote him. His voice reverberated through the keep. Words failing him, he lifted an arm to clout her headlong, and a voice behind him said sharply, "My lord!"

He turned heavily. "The wench defies me —"

"And you're so gently persuasive!" Lord Adam came swiftly between them, and Julitta involuntarily recoiled, to

37

"I am no man's whore!" she cried, and dodged aside, impeded by the press of astounded folk behind her.

"Up with you!" He seized her right arm and tried to haul her across his saddle bow, spurring his horse under the arch. Dragged from her feet, she struck out with her free hand, her gown flapping against the chestnut's legs. He squealed and reared, so that her arm seemed to be tearing from its socket, and Humphrey clutched his saddle bow and heaved again. The drawbridge thundered beneath them. A red head flashed on the edge of her sight. A startled howl blew from Humphrey's mouth, his right leg jerked high from a sharp thrust, his hand slipped from the saddle bow and he sprawled beside her, tumbling her to her knees.

She wrenched free and scrambled clear of the hooves and to her feet, surprised to find herself on the ravine's further brink. The chestnut plunged and snorted. Red Adam set a hand on the crupper and vaulted over, landing with both feet on Humphrey's spine. The remaining wind whooped out of him. The horse danced sideways from them. Red Adam caught Julitta before she could run a step, dropped a kiss awry on her eyebrow as she ducked, took a sharp crack under the chin as she flung her head up, and swung her round by the elbows and grappled her fast when she tried to stamp on his toes. She could feel the laughter shaking him.

Humphrey rolled over, crowing and squawking, sleeved mud from his face and fumbled for his sword.

"Hell's Teeth, can't you even heave a wench over your saddle?" Red Adam demanded unkindly. "Do you expect them to swoon under your boot soles for one smirk from your pretty face, Ladies' delight?"

Humphrey spat out mire and choked, "You'll meet me —"

"Oh, be off! You poor randy tup, you should thank me. If you tossed this one to your men she'd carve your liver out."

Humphrey pushed erect and cautiously straightened his backbone. He scowled at his enemy and limped to his mount,

40

which jibbed and flung up its head. He subdued it with a vicious jerk on the rein. "God's Blood, you'll hear from me!" he promised, and heaved himself up.

Julitta twisted round in a slackened hold to voice her own defiance, and past Red Adam's shoulder saw the gorse on the ravine's edge part, a hand grasp the drawbridge's planking and pull, a ragged body lift over its edge and hurtle, steel glinting, at Red Adam's back. One glimpse of a murderous face tore a screech from her.

"Ivar!"

She was flung sprawling, and rolled to her knees. Red Adam threw himself backward under the knife, which passed over his shoulder with a rip of cloth. He grabbed up at Ivar's wrist and dragged him down. They squelched side by side into the mire. Ivar wrenched round and lunged at Red Adam's throat as he rolled on to his back. Still grinning, the younger man brought up both knees, drove his feet into his foe's exposed midriff and hurled him across the track into the rough grass. The knife sparkled wide. Red Adam bounced up, swooped on it, seized Ivar and threw him back on to the planks. The knife glinted.

"Quick, girl, with me!" called Humphrey, reaching a hand as Julitta scrambled up. She struck it away, scarcely heeding, her horrified gaze on the other two.

"No, you butcher!"

Lord William's hangman's scowl loomed over them. "He attempted your life, Lord Adam? A priest and a rope, with all dispatch!"

"Why so much trouble?" he asked. He caught Ivar by the neckband and hauled him, oddly unresisting, to his knees. His head jolted forward, and a groan escaped him. His torn tunic pulled away, and the victor's grin vanished. Julitta also saw the bloody, half-scabbed stripes across his shoulders, and caught her breath. For a moment Red Adam hesitated; then the knife point pricked under Ivar's ear, and one eyebrow lifted at her. "It's for you to say, my lady."

"I will marry you." There had been no hope from the first; she had only deluded herself.

41

"You'll spare the knave?" demanded Lord William incredulously.

"I've use for him." He thrust the knife under his belt and hoisted the half-senseless man to his feet. "Odo! Tend and feed him and bestow him safely." He seized Julitta's cold hand, his face lighted with triumph. "Rejoice with me, my lords! This is my marriage day!"

3

Her marriage day passed for Julitta in a waking nightmare. In a trance of despair, dressed like a doll in scarlet hurriedly cobbled to her body, her hair, by Red Adam's order, blowing about her shoulders in token of her virginity, she rode and walked, repeated senseless words like a popinjay, gave her lifeless hand into a possessive grasp, and returned unseeing through lines of yelling peasants to her prison. In a blaze of heat and light and color, at the head of a table in a packed hall vague as mist, she sat paralyzed, neither eating nor drinking. The feast roared about her, voices droned speeches of which no word reached her, toast after toast was drunk. All the time an outraged voice insisted within her that this was not real, it was not happening, this girl at Hell's Mouth was not Julitta de Montrigord.

God and His Mother had deserted her. A throng of women, her aunt by marriage, Bertille, Sibylla, neighbors she should know and strangers she could not name, drew her by the hands between ranks of wine-flushed faces shouting lewdness, up dark stairs to the same chamber where last night she had stunned Red Adam. Laughing and bidding her take heart, they pulled off the gown, the golden circlet from her hair, and the shoes and hose from her feet, but when they would have stripped off the cendal smock reality touched her with their fingers, and she cried out and pulled away, huddling her arms about her breasts. Someone thrust a steaming cup at her tight lips, and the scent of wine, honey and spices filled her nostrils. She ducked her head aside from it, and Lady Matilda gripped her sore shoulders, hissing admonition in her ear.

"What conduct is this? The men will be bringing the bridegroom; will you shame him and your kin by resistance? It is woman's fate, and you must submit to it."

"Get you to bed and drink the wine," whispered Bertille in her other ear. "Will you have Brentborough folk mock your folly? Drink and take heart; this is soon done."

But she stood stiffly, and would neither drink nor let them take her smock. Nor would she lie in the sheets they drew back to enfold her. A horror of great darkness encompassed her, and a horror of these women who squawked and flapped and tugged at her like carrion crows over a carcass. They pushed her on to the bed by force and dragged the covers to her waist, and she sat against the pillows in a terror so great she could neither speak nor stir. The knife inside her silken sleeve pressed against her breast; she had concealed it among the rushes when they undressed her for the bath, and resumed it later. It was the one resource left her, to kill Red Adam and herself.

A quiet voice spoke from the doorway. "My ladies, will it please you leave my bride to me?"

The fowl-run cluckings stilled to whispers and giggles, but no one protested, and the flurry of gowns and wimples was suddenly banished. Red Adam closed the door.

"Under the circumstances I reckoned you would choose to forgo the ceremony of bedding us," he remarked, thrusting home the heavy bar. He had thrown a cloak over his scarlet, and held in his left hand the wine cup someone had passed to him. He moved from the door, and his shadow swooped across the bed and over her.

"Don't be afraid," he said in that quiet voice. "I shall not hurt you."

44

The same words had been uttered last night by the drunken brute who had despoiled her mouth with wine-fumed kisses and crushed her under him. Nausea rose in her. If he touched her she would vomit where she sat. With the light at his back he was a featureless shape of horror. Then he moved nearer, and the candlelight reached her face.

"Hell's Teeth, must you look at me like that?" he demanded violently. "Am I a monster?"

His anger broke the trance. "You would have murdered Ivar unshriven!"

"No."

"Your knife at his throat, and you deny —"

"To keep you from your uncle's wrath, or shame with the Ladies' Delight," he answered. "I'm no murderer."

"And I am no man's whore."

For a long moment he looked into her face, then nodded. "That I see."

"It was a lie — a heartless trick —" Again she huddled her arms about her breasts, shivering in sudden chill.

He moved closer, and she flinched involuntarily, fear an icy thrill along all her nerves. "Don't be afraid," he said gently, as though she were seven rather than seventeen. "I shall not force you. I'll not touch you against your will."

That was beyond her belief, beyond all she knew of men, beyond her memory of the ravisher who had implanted this horror in her. She stared at him, and unexpectedly he smiled; not the flashing grin she had come to detest, but a softening of his face to kindness, compunction, and a rueful amusement that reminded her again how young he was.

"I mean it, owlet. Here, drink your wine and take heart."

She took the cup from his hand, scarcely knowing what she did, and whispered over it, "Dare I believe you?"

"I'll not make ill worse. If I forced you now you'd hate me forever," he replied candidly, sitting down on the chest and linking his hands about one up-drawn knee. She sipped the wine, watching him over the cup's rim, and as its warmth spread outward from her belly she resolved that his forbearance should not cozen her into submitting to her woman's fate as his meek bedmate. Tears prickled at her lids from

45

reaction and the relaxation of immediate fear. "We've time before us," he said, echoing her thought with uncanny accuracy, and she repudiated it.

"Mary Mother, why could you not have sent me to the convent?"

"Have you reflected how any convent would have received you?" he asked soberly.

She had not, but a very brief consideration sufficed. An adequate dowry might induce some nunnery to admit her, to be treated as a penitent whore and live out her years in humiliation. He watched her from the chest. He had shrugged off the cloak, and flamed fire-red under the candle. She swallowed more wine, and its unaccustomed pungency caught at her throat and set her coughing. Angrily she mopped her eyes with the sheet's edge, and then stiffened lest he should think she weakened.

"Should I *thank* you? I shall pray for a speedy widowing!"

"I'll not quarrel with that so long as prayer suffices. Lie down and cover yourself, girl, for you are a sore temptation."

"You will doubtless find consolation among the kitchen wenches."

"I'll not put that affront on my wife in her own household," he told her bleakly.

It had been an unworthy jibe, but she would not retract; there was naught in her but hatred after all the day's bludgeonings. She scowled at him, drained the cup and relinquished it into his hand instead of yielding to the impulse to hurl it at his head, and sullenly slid down between the sheets as his wary look gave place to a grin. He stood up, stretching so that his shadow leaped over bed and wall.

"I suppose if I were nobly ninny-witted I'd leave you to your virgin rest, but Devil grill me if I proclaim myself a eunuch on my wedding night," he observed. Stooping, he hauled from under the bed a pallet of plaited straw, of the kind used by servants. He swung it beyond the bedfoot, under the window, and over it flashed her a rueful grin. "Some foreboding warned me to provide this. If I'd found you ready to leap into my bed, vixen, we might be very merry therein but we'd not be wedded." He pulled his tunic over his head while she sought for an answer, kicked off his shoes, swung the cloak about him and blew out the candle. She heard the rustle of his movements, and then the straw creaked faintly under his weight. His voice provoked her through the dark. "Dare I risk sleeping?"

She choked, flounced over in the admirable feather bed, submerged her head in the pillow and heaved the covers over her uppermost ear. Through sheet, blanket and coverlid his voice still reached her. "Fair dreams be yours, sweet wife!" She gulped, hoping he lay hard and cold but not trusting her voice to say so. Then a sudden recollection jerked her head out.

"What have you done with Ivar?"

"Naught, as yet."

"But — but what — you'll not hang him?"

"I've a better use for him."

"As a hold on me, you mean?"

"No need of a hostage now we're wedded."

"Then what do you intend?"

"That depends on him, but no hurt. Go to sleep, vixen. Your troubles will wear a fairer face in the morning — except my lord your uncle."

Sound advice it might have been, but it was half the night before she could follow it.

An irregular hammering roused her, and she lifted on one elbow to see Red Adam assaulting the shutter. It yielded with a noise of splitting, and he addressed it in foreign words and pulled a splinter from his palm with his teeth. He knelt in the window splay to thrust forth his nose, his tousled head dark against scurrying clouds, and then turned bright eyes upon her.

"Ruing your bargain?" she demanded acidly.

"Not yet," he answered equably. "I knew you'd teeth. But if you persist in snapping at me, vixen, all my forbearance will be wasted."

"If you seek to cozen me —"

"I merely suggest you use the wit you were born with."

"What do you mean?"

"We must show a decent amity in public or become the jest of the North Parts. Will you cry truce outside this chamber?"

Sourly she reflected upon that reasonable proposal. To humiliate him publicly would gratify her, but common sense warned her that such satisfaction would cost her more than its worth. She nodded sullenly.

"A bargain!" he announced briskly, and thrust the pallet under the big bed. "Get up, girl." She clutched the covers to her as he advanced, jerked them back and swung his long legs in beside her. She shot forth and over the low bedfoot, grabbing at the dagger as she went. He sprawled there, mocking her panic, and rolled across the bed and back, creating havoc among sheets and pillows. His own dagger flashed; as she gasped, he pushed up his left shirt-sleeve, nicked the inside of his forearm, and squeezed and smeared a little blood in the midst of the bed. "That will silence those who maligned your virtue," he said, suddenly sober. He picked up his tunic and dived into it, his next words coming muffled and jerky from within. "And now, Saints aid me, to show courtesy — to my new uncle." He tied the throat lacings, clasped his belt, settled his dagger in its sheath and stooped for his shoes. He glanced sharply up at her. "Do you never smile?"

"What cause have I?"

"It might become you." He unbarred the door, said over his shoulder, "I'll send the women to you," stepped out and shouted, "Odo!"

Odo must have been waiting close at hand, for she heard the rumble of his voice at once. She paid little heed until Red Adam's voice lifted in anger.

" . . . let the fellow get clear away?"

"Safest rid of a knife-minded knave like that, Master, so I thought it wisest to let him run."

"Hell's Teeth! You *can't* think. Whenever you try, you prove it. It's a compliment to call you beetle-witted."

"Now, Master Adam, you don't want a back-stabbing hound lurking —"

"I said I'd a use for him. Don't we need something better in the stables than that redhaired bastard? Hell's Teeth, Odo, you'll find *thinking* fatal some day!"

"Master Adam —"

"In fact, I'll most likely murder you myself."

Julitta waited, unconsciously holding her breath, for the order consigning Odo to dungeon, stocks or whipping post, but apparently those exasperated words were to be the end of the matter, for a moment later Red Adam put his head round the door.

"As you doubtless heard, my well-intentioned half-wit let your Ivar run. He's had the best part of a day's start. Has he kinsmen or friends where he might refuge, do you know?"

"Did you mean it — that you'd take him into your service?"

"How could I do less, when the blame's mine? And I'd rather have him peaceably occupied in my stables than prowling with a grudge. Gives me an itch between the blade-bones."

"By your leave, Lord Adam!" an imperative voice commanded, and his head disappeared.

"Always at your gracious bidding, Lady Matilda!"

With compressed lips and anger-heightened color she swept in, at the head of a procession that might make the boldest hero give way. Bertille, the seneschal's and marshal's wives, and a serving wench with towels, basin and ewer crammed the narrow space, twittering with excitement, examining and freely commenting upon the state of the bridal bed, assaulting her with explicit questions about Red Adam's conduct therein. Julitta, taking refuge in a dour silence which she hoped they would mistake for modesty, washed and dried herself, glad to turn her back. Even the servant goggled like a frog as she took the towel from her hand. Lady Matilda's voice beat insistently at her ears, demanding for the fifth or fifteenth time a reply to a query that scorched her cheeks.

"Are you smitten deaf or daft, girl? We are all wedded women here, so answer straightway."

It suddenly came to Julitta that she need never again heed Lady Matilda's bidding, that she was free of her carping for ever. "That concerns only my husband and me, my lady." The serving wench dropped a towel into the basin, Bertille clutched at her belly as though to guard the child within from hurt, and Lady Matilda's sallow face mottled red.

"Insolence!" she quacked like an affronted duck. "You *dare* —"

Julitta took the scarlet gown from palsied hands and hauled it over her head. Tugging it into place, she turned a challenging stare on her uncle's wife. "You were saying, my lady?"

Recognition of her status reached Lady Matilda. "Ungrateful girl, we are concerned for your welfare and the child you may have conceived, but if you set yourself up above your guardians who have tried to teach you seemliness, we will trouble you no more. Wench, what are you about, gaping like a zany? A comb and a mirror for your lady, at once! The service in this hold would disgrace a cowbyre, but what can be expected when it has lacked a mistress these eighteen years? Dolt, do you reckon you are currying a horse?"

Julitta seized the comb herself. "Take away that water, girl!" she bade briskly, doubly angry that she and her servant should be chided each in the other's presence. Only appreciation of gossip's power restrained her until the broad buttocks had switched round the door. "The service of Brentborough is for me to amend."

"What folly and pride is this? You are far too young, and what instruction have you ever had in ordering a household? Your uncle and I have decided that Gilbert and Bertille shall remain to school you in your duties, since Lord Adam has no elder kinswoman and there is in this hold no lady fit to take you in charge —"

"You mistake, Lady Matilda," said Lady Constance's voice from the doorway. "This household has been in my hands many years, and it is my privilege to take my lady in charge."

Julitta desired no overseer, and the thought of being governed yet by her uncle's emissaries gave her an acute griping of the guts. The fair woman was smiling invincibly, Lady Matilda drawing breath for battle. They might rend one another asunder and strew Brentborough with fragments for

50

all she cared, but a surer instinct bade her seize control. "That is for my lord to decide," she declared, and reflected, as she turned to the mirror and dragged the comb through tangles, that Red Adam would never tolerate Gilbert and Bertille in command of his household.

Lady Constance, her smile undimmed, pressed between the others, took the comb from Julitta's hand and set about ordering her hair. It was so unnatural to the Montrigord women to attend upon their kinswoman that no one thought to forestall her, and Julitta's toilet was completed in eloquent silence. She drew a deep breath, braced her shoulders, and stepped out into her frightening new life.

Stumbling feet rushed at her from the stairhead, knees thudded on the boards, a weight fell against her legs and hands clawed at her gown. She looked down into a face that had been pretty before much weeping swelled and blotched it.

"Oh, Avice, I am sorry!"

"My lady, my lady, help me!"

"What can I do?" Julitta asked bitterly, gripping her heaving shoulders. "Ivar has fled. I'll try to find him —"

"That'll be too late," the girl whimpered. "We'd have been wed if there'd been a hut free in the garth. But now Ivar's gone, and — and — oh, my lady, I'll have to take Cuthbert the smith! He's spoke for me — soon's they put Ivar out o' the gate — and my lord said yes. Oh, my lady, save me!"

"If it's possible — but you know Lord William will do nothing for my asking."

"If you'd speak for me — keep me with you — if you'd get Lord Adam to ask it — m' lord won't refuse him nowt he asks. Please, m' lady! I'd serve you faithful — I can sew and wash and cook — but not that smutty beast! I'll chuck mesen ower t' cliff-end afore I'll lay wi' him!" She was wailing like a child in the dialect of the peasantry, all her painfully-learned French cast from her. Julitta stiffened. Avice read the revulsion in her face, uttered a lamentable howl and buried her face in her gown.

"Get up, get up, you shameless girl!" Lady Matilda

clucked. "You'll do as your lord bids you. Obedience — Lord Adam!"

He was standing by the stairhead. Avice cast one wild look at him over her shoulder and clutched Julitta's legs, gulping sobs. He frowned at her, his mouth twisting in distaste, and Julitta stiffly did her what justice she might.

"She was Ivar's sweetheart. My uncle would give her to a man she hates."

"Fellow-feeling? Is there naught in her but salt water?"

"Ask him — oh, ask him!"

She had to swallow twice before she could force the words between her teeth. "My lord, I ask a boon."

"This misery?"

"She is in great distress."

"You'll need a decent girl to attend you; the castle wenches are strumpets every one. Only keep her from dripping under my feet."

"I thank you," she began, illogically resenting his acquiescence.

"Ask and it shall be given unto you," he said. "A bridegroom's ardor, burning undamped." He took her hand in the grip she was coming to know, and she forced it to stay passive. The oaf was grinning; there could be no trace of delicate feeling in all his carcass. She looked up indignantly, and he stooped his head to drop a kiss on her cheek. The women behind cooed and giggled, Julitta's face flamed, and he drew her down the stair and the length of the hall to the dais, the perfect semblance of a bashful bride.

Before the high chair that was now hers he turned her to face them all, guests and household officers, soldiers, serving men and wenches, and released her hands. One of the men passed him something that gleamed and clinked. "My lady," he announced formally, "as morning-gift I lay all I possess in your hands." He placed in them a bunch of keys on a silver chain.

She bit her lip and looked down at them, trying to utter some equally formal acknowledgment. Courtly gesture and words were all a maid's dreams might spin for her, all she had hoped someday to receive, and they came in mockery from the wrong man. But she had to collect herself; he was beckoning forward man after man to present to her.

"Sir Bertram FitzAlain, seneschal of Brentborough."

This was he who had passed the keys, massive and gray, his bones stark under withering flesh. The brown eyes peering under heavy brows were friendly, and so was the rough voice that declared him at her service. Until he fumbled at her extended hand it was hard to realize that he was nearly blind.

"Sir Brien de Tornay." He was smallish, past forty, glumly dispirited.

"Sir Giles FitzGodfrey." He was older, blear-visaged, his belly sagging through his belt's grip. Relics of old Lord Maurice's rule, and no assets to the household, she judged them, as they mumbled over her hand and furtively surveyed her.

"My guest and comrade, Sir Reynald de Carsey, you have met before," her husband's voice said, an undertone of rueful humor to its formality.

Sir Reynald smiled into her angry eyes and said insolently, "You should remember it with more pleasure, my lady, since it has been your rare good fortune."

"I remember in what fitting state we left you, Sir Reynald," she retorted, looking straight at the sot they had left that night wallowing in his vomit. The sneer vanished as though smacked off his face.

"God's Head!" her uncle's voice growled from her other side, jolting her with remembered menace. "You've not curbed that tongue yet? There's a devil in the wench needs exorcising, Lord Adam."

Red Adam's hand closed on Julitta's, and he moved between them. "I am content with my wife beyond my deserts, Lord William."

He snorted. "Take your belt and beat a seemly meekness into her at the start is my advice."

"If that's your method of procuring domestic concord, I marvel your wife has never seasoned your pottage with henbane," Red Adam replied dispassionately.

Lord William's wits, impaired by his overnight celebration's lingering effects, were slow to recognize menace. "What — oh, aye, you jest. I've no intention of quarreling with you, lad —"

"A pity, for I have every intention of quarreling with you, my lord." He was white as milk, and his hand quivered on Julitta's.

"God's Blood, we are kinsmen now!"

"Kinsmen? If you were thirty years younger and half a yard less around your belly, I'd challenge you to combat for the way you've used my lady."

"You misbegotten whelp!" Lord William surged forward, his face engorged. Julitta, her hand fast gripped, stiffened herself from recoil. Then Gilbert dived forward.

"My lords! Father— peace, peace, I pray you!" He flapped his hands like a woman shooing hens from her kitchen. "It is unseemly —"

"Never fear, he'll strike none but a woman." Red Adam's glance flicked from face to face. "I uttered a challenge, Lord William. Which of your sons will take up the gage, and vindicate your conduct towards their cousin?" Gilbert recoiled, and Gautier gaped in consternation. "More than they can stomach?"

Gilbert drew the shreds of his dignity about him. "We w-will withdraw from under your roof, Lord Adam, b-before more is said we shall all regret."

"Who bade you speak for me, you whey-blooded mouse?" snarled his sire. "Regret? This daft whelp will be the one to regret, when the power is in our hands and we remember our enemies!"

"'If,' not 'when,' should be your word. I'm not daft enough to join your feckless treason with young Henry."

"Treason? He is our Young King, crowned and anointed, asserting his rightful claims."

"With rare incompetence and peculiar allies." Red Adam grinned at the unhappy brothers. "It's an interesting life following the tourneys, but if you have to take to it when your sire has Chivingham escheated for treason, I doubt you'll fancy it."

By the sick anger in the face of Gilbert, who had worn out his youth and was rapidly withering into middle age waiting to sit in his father's chair, he had prodded his sorest dread. Lord William turned on his son a glare that wilted him to the limpness of boiled cabbage, jerked his head at his wife and daughter standing by the dais's steps, snarled all round the company, and stalked out, his family trailing after him. Reynald de Carsey laughed softly in the hush.

Julitta fetched what felt like her first breath since the quarrel's eruption. The company roused from petrifaction, stealing sidelong glances, nudging ribs and muttering in ears. Such a breach of decorum enlivened few bridals, and already another Brentborough scandal had leaped its wall and was winging over the North Parts. Red Adam drew her forward. "Entertain our guests, my lady, while I do your kinsmen a host's parting courtesy," he bade her, and followed Lord William. She caught at composure, undutifully cheered to have seen her uncle routed and been spared Gilbert and Bertille as mentors. She moved towards Ranulf of Hostby, the eldest guest, and initiated a discussion on the damage done the harvest by the past week's weather.

Everard FitzJordan supported her as a gentleman's duty, but Gerald of Flackness regarded her with a kind of sour surprise, as though her relief at his loss were an affront, and pointedly gazed into an empty ale-horn. Julitta signalled to a servant to fill it, and kept the talk limping along by sheer persistence, conscious of Reynald's malevolent grin behind her and the scorched sensation mounting to her cheekbones. Then someone mentioned the lack of news from Leicester, and at once they were off.

It all came pouring forth in a yeasty froth; rancor at King Henry's encroachments on noble privileges in these past nineteen years; at his new-made upstarts who usurped the places and profits of their betters; at royal extortion, protection of Jewish usury, and laws that set at naught a nobleman's right to settle his disputes sword in hand. There was talk of the Holy Martyr of Canterbury, numbered now among the Saints. The world had ceased waiting with held breath for Heaven's judgment to crash upon the King, but if God's justice were tardy, there were men eager to avenge His servant. Julitta, listening, could comprehend their anxieties. They were all but committed to rebellion, but its lack of progress had filled them with doubt and dread. She wanted to cry out that the enterprise was folly and doomed, but that was no part of the courtesy she owed guests in her hall.

She turned impatiently to the nearest window and glanced out at the sky. Sir Everard joined her. "This is heavy talk for a bridal morning, my lady" he observed. "I wish you well, and am thankful to see you reconciled to your marriage."

"I thank you, my lord."

"It's no light task laid on you. Brentborough has been too long under a curse. Now that he is wedded, Lord Adam must break it; entertain, visit, join in his neighbors' pleasures." He smiled. "I might be your father, so let that excuse my presuming."

"I account it kindness," she answered honestly, even though she recognized the direction of this laborious approach.

"In these times friends and kinsmen need each other. A pity Lord Adam forced this breach with your uncle, and between us we must repair it. If I try to persuade Lord William, you must endeavor to soften your husband's heart while —"

"While a bridegroom's ardor renders it malleable."

"Felicitously expressed," said Red Adam's amused voice in her ear, and his arm slipped round her shoulders and drew her to his side. Her pulse raced. "It is malleable as a lump of butter, my delight, so what are you to persuade me to?"

"Amity with my uncle."

He grinned. "That amity will be best assured if we never come within arm's reach."

She repressed a giggle. "My lord, your wish is my law."

"I reckoned in that matter it would be." His hand tightened a little, and he looked, suddenly grim, into the older man's face. "I am the King's man, and you'll not entangle me in this plot against him. If you've the sense of a tadpole under your hair you'll climb free of this coil before it throttles you."

"You insult me!" Everard exclaimed, his mild face darkening.

"Flatter you! No rebellion yet has unseated the man on the throne. Even that fool King Stephen kept it under his backside to his life's end, for all his foes could do."

"The Young King has his rights —"

"That daft whelp's not man enough to achieve aught."

"God's Blood!" Gerald bellowed. "That's treason, and you'll answer for it!"

"Whenever you choose to challenge me," Red Adam responded, regarding him with wounding tolerance. "Stop frothing like a brew-tub and *think*, man. You've seen him at court; he's favored you with a gracious word, he's comely and pleasing. But I've followed the tourneys with him. Hell's Teeth, it's only William the Marshal's prowess pays his debts." He was addressing them all now, wholly earnest.

"He's rightful King!" Sir Ranulf asserted.

"In his father's lifetime? He's a vain lad puffed up with flattery, and the French King's collar about his neck."

"Yet the rebels are doing none so ill, and they have great force among them," Everard said soberly. "There's King Louis in Normandy, all Brittany up —" He checked suddenly, looking foolish; everyone knew that Red Adam had spent the spring and early summer campaigning with King Henry's forces in Normandy, and had returned to Brentborough by way of the siege of Leicester.

"If they could but combine together we might need to worry," Red Adam commented.

"Leicester is still untaken," Gerald pointed out.

"And what do its defenders achieve but the enmity of their neighbors whose lands they ravage, while they wait for the Earl to return? The last heard of him, he'd skipped to Flanders. What sort of mercenaries d'you reckon he'll recruit there, with naught to pay them but promises of English loot?"

A small snort of appreciation was forced from Julitta, who was probably better acquainted with mercenaries than any other of his hearers. They murmured sullenly. Red Adam's gaze moved contemptuously from face to face.

"Oh yes, you'll sit fast until your rumps grow roots, and blather about the homage you've done to both King Henry and his son. You know what the King's wrath is, and you know the whelp has promised to reward those who win him England with his opponents' lands, so you'll take up no weapon until you're sure of joining the victors. But I've sworn one fealty and I'll hold to that and to Brentborough, not squat on my tail bones waiting for the dice to fall. Hell's Teeth, I'd sooner follow the tourneys!"

"You may yet reckon yourself lucky if you can," grated Gerald.

Red Adam raked the troubled faces with a stare few cared to meet. "Why, do you also find my hospitality discomforts your innards!"

Everard smiled a small, grim smile. "Some of it is not easy of digestion, Lord Adam. We are loath to disrupt your marriage feast —"

"But in these days a prudent man sees to his own," old Ranulf blurted.

"I'd best send forth for guests into the highways and byways," Adam retorted irreverently. "I'll not press you, nor yet blame you, but I'd advise you to consider where prudence truly lies."

"God's Death, you're magnanimous!" jeered Gerald. "Or timid."

"Oh, I've a deal to lose — as you have. Including a cordial relationship with my neighbors."

"Did you become a tourney champion with your tongue?" snorted Gerald. "You prate like a priest."

"I have not forgotten you are guests under my roof, if you have."

"We'll not linger there!" He stalked down the hall without more ado, and his companions exchanged uneasy glances.

"It would be best, Lord Adam, if we took our leave," Sir Ranulf declared.

"We wish you and your lady a long and prosperous life together, and many children to crown it," said Sir Everard, descending the dais steps. "Indeed the breach grieves me, and I earnestly hope you'll reconsider —"

"Let be. I've sworn allegiance to one King and I hold by him." He shook his head at Julitta as she started to join them. Sir Everard's voice floated back as they went down the hall.

"— overdue at my home, and my wife is with child and easily alarmed —"

"Fussy as a big-bellied woman himself," jibed Reynald de Carsey, downing the last of his breakfast ale and looking about him for a servant to refill his horn. Seeing none, he pitched the vessel on to the sidetable with its stand of plate, bringing several dishes clanging down, grinned offensively at Julitta's anger, and slouched out after his pot comrade.

Julitta hastened to check the plate for damage and set the unimpressive collection to rights. As she stepped back she noticed a curious object on a bracket above the table, a very curious object indeed; skull-shaped, crested and dingy green. Peering at it from all angles, she made out, under dust and cobwebs, an ancient helmet of corroded bronze, with one side crushed in.

"It's Roman," her husband's voice said in her ear. "Old Bertram told me. When the ruins on the headland were demolished for stone to build the keep, they found two skeletons still joined in a death-grapple under them, and one was wearing that. Old Maurice set great store by it; called it the Luck of Brentborough."

"His taste in luck pieces matched his luck," she commented, repressing a shiver as she peered up at the relic and wondered that he had not left the skull inside it. "Are your servants willing to sleep under it, and does a Roman ghost stand guard over your plate?"

"I've not heard of such a sentry, but I do know that never another stone was lifted from that ruin, nor will any venture near it by day or night." He reached for her hand, and Reynald de Carsey, loitering by the door, sniggered.

Julitta held back. "My lord —"

"Get into your riding dress, and throw that hideous gown of your cousin's to the kitchen wenches! Oh, it's obvious — she's half a head shorter and buxom; for all their cobbling you look six months gone." He impelled her towards the

59

stair, speechless between anger and agreement. "Where's that wench? Attend your lady, ninny!"

"M- my lord? At once, my lord — my lady!" Avice put her nose over the gallery rail, quailing and twittering. Reynald lounged further into the hall to scrutinize her, and she flinched from sight. Julitta stalked past both men and up the stair, wishing the pair of them collared with millstones and sunk in fifty fathoms.

4

Red Adam too had put off scarlet when she joined him in the bailey, and was sober in dark blue tunic and chausses as shabby as her own homespun. His finery had been a shorter and heavier man's lending, though on a masculine figure its deficiencies of fit had been less obvious than her own gown's. He looked taller, trimmer, his hair a fiercer red above the bandage. He was addressing his pot comrade, and she caught the tail end: "— some pretence of decency!"

"You're not pretending a fondness for the wench? Take your belt to her; she needs it." Reynald scowled at Julitta as she descended the stair, and tramped away to the stables.

Odo and the redhaired groom brought out their horses. Her mare squealed at the unfamiliar hands, and he cursed her. The fellow was unmistakably a Lorismond, a stock which bred embarrassingly true; doubtless a by-blow of old Maurice's. A welt's end showed on his neck, and she was sharply reminded of another man less justly beaten because of her. She turned on Red Adam.

"What of my man Ivar?"

"I've set inquiries forward." She stared, but for once he was not mocking. "He's been wrongly used, and I was responsible."

61

"What do you know of responsibility?"

"I'm learning." He joined his hands and stooped to mount her. As she arranged her skirts a pack of mismatched hounds surged baying from the kennels, and the mare reared up snorting and danced sideways. Red Adam leaped to seize her bridle and hauled her to a stand.

"What was your uncle doing to set you on this brute? Trying to break your neck?"

Julitta firmly reined her in. Folie was the most edgy-tempered beast in her uncle's stables, which was precisely why he had assigned her to his niece and left her as his wedding gift. "It wouldn't grieve him, but I'll acquit him of the intent."

"She's no fit mount for a girl."

"I can handle her." He looked up at her keenly, and she cursed her unruly tongue. In her wanderings she had straddled everything from a knight's destrier to a woodcutter's donkey, but her husband knew nothing of her discreditable past and she would prefer that he never learned. He did not challenge her; the household knights and the huntsmen were assembled, and they rode out behind a tumult of dogs.

The weather had cleared, and while the fine days lasted they scrambled about hills and woods after wolves and foxes, without much profit; hawked over moors and stubble, and visited outlying farms to assess the harvest now in the barns. Julitta, who had been kept rigorously at her needle under her uncle's rule, rejoiced in air and exercise, but whenever she returned to a castle still governed by Constance, who made no pretence of consulting her lady, she itched to assume her rights. But Red Adam insisted that she should stay beside him, provoking Reynald to jibe that he dared not trust her out of his sight. In public they maintained courtesy according to their bond; in private she nursed her rancor.

As August wore out, the rain clouds blew back, and on a gray morning Julitta emerged to find only Folie and Red Adam's bay waiting in the bailey. "Ride with me," he commanded, and led her, not to the gate but between the castle's outbuildings on to the headland.

Wind tore at their clothes and hair, sword-sharp from the sea, and her eyes watered and her cheeks stung from the force of it. Among the rough grass were almost-silted trenches, and fragments of wall foundations made square-cornered patterns where the horses trod delicately; the Roman ruins whose stones had helped build the castle. Then the turf broke before them, the headland lurched down in dizzy jags and pitches to a tumult of rocks and spray far below, and they looked over gray sea that glinted now and again as sunlight stabbed through the clouds. Endlessly the waves crept in, gathered crests, and shattered against the cliff in a smother of spray that the wind tossed cold and salty into their faces.

Red Adam watched in a rapt silence, until Folie shook her head with a snort and a jingle of bit chains. He started, and took up his reins. "I come here often," he told her. "Here one stands in awe, facing God's majesty."

Such reflections deprived her of any power to answer. He turned from the verge. "Stay back from the edge," he warned. "The cliff falls. And that's odd. I'd believed rock everlasting, and water soft and unstable. Yet it's the water beats down the cliffs, and grinds the rocks to powder. 'Here shall thy proud waves be stayed' — but the stone crumbles." He paused for her to join him, and swung his mount to ride between her and the edge. He shrugged and grinned, the grin she yearned to clout to the other side of his face. "It's a wife's duty to listen to her husband. You're likely to find it onerous."

"I'd begun to suspect it," she replied sourly.

"Not given to hasty judgment," he commented. A gull, riding the updraft, uttered a derisive squawk, so apposite that she had to stifle a giggle. Red Adam lifted a hand in acknowledgment, and the bird swung away. They followed the headland's curve until they looked down on the river-mouth, the wooden bridge, and the fisher-village of Arnisby straggling inside the curve of the opposite headland. Smoke drifted from the curingracks and salt-boilings, and from the cottages' roof-vents. Four boats were drawn up on the shingle, bare at ebb tide, and figures moved about them.

Under the hill's edge the wind cut less keenly, and he reined in.

"What's the truth of this old scandal about Lord Maurice?" he asked abruptly.

"Anyone at Brentborough could tell you better than I."

Anger reddened his cheekbones. "I'd reckoned on an honest answer from you if not others! I've had naught but lies and evasions from his people, and how could I ask it of the peasants, even if I had English enough? Why did he roost the year through like a molting shag on this rock, and let his estates go to ruin while his neighbors shunned him?"

"He murdered his wife."

He stared a long moment, and then said, "Tell me."

"But it was all long ago, in King Henry's early days, when the castle was still building — before I was born. Who's to say what the truth was, after near twenty years' gossip?" He waited, and she picked out what honest fact she knew. "He was a lecher, filling these parts with redhaired bastards from his youth. He was not young then; he was past sixty when he died last October. She was his second wife, and my uncle would call her ill-schooled. She upbraided him for his rutting with trulls and peasants. And she was carrying the first child he'd begotten in lawful wedlock, and near her time.

"Whatever happened, it was on this very headland. There are parts cannot be overlooked, even from the keep roof —"

"This path, for one," he agreed, and glancing about, she saw that it was so. "And the sentinel watches landward; this way there's only sea and sky."

"He'd ride out, none doubting his purpose. One day in jealous rage she followed him. That's why folk claimed she surprised him with a woman, and in his anger he was the death of her. Lord Maurice declared that her horse bolted with her and fell into the sea. There were hoofprints, and the rock broken away, and the horse dead below. But no trace did they find of the poor lady, God rest her, with the child in her belly that should have been heir to Brentborough."

64

He looked at the dim path below the ridge that cut off their view of the keep, and the fall on their left. "It could have been true."

"No more has ever been *known*. Folk have guessed eighteen years. But it was a gentle palfrey, fit for a big-bellied woman to ride."

"If nothing were ever found, she must be dead."

"And if he were guiltless, why did he never clear himself with her kin? He never entered a church nor went to bed sober thereafter, and flinched whenever a skirt rustled at his back. Truly she haunted him, and all believed he had killed her and the unborn babe."

"Surely if he did he'd have confessed it on his deathbed?"

She shook her head and crossed herself. "He damned himself. Though he ailed many months, death surprised him at the last."

"He served his Purgatory on earth, I reckon," Red Adam commented, likewise crossing himself. He folded his hands on the pommel and watched the waves, his hair whipping up from his face. "He sent for me. It's in my mind that he wished to entrust his secret, whatever it was, to his heir, for he desired me most urgently to come to his side before he died. I was too late. I'm sorrier now than I was then, if his soul depended on it. And I am deep in his debt for the pains he took to secure the inheritance to a stranger."

"A stranger?"

"We never met. He was my father's second cousin. I'm the youngest son of a younger son, and never dreamed of standing near the succession. I did not even know my brother Aymar was dead. . . . Did you ever see Lord Maurice?"

"Often. He'd a kinswoman in Saint Hilda's nunnery, and visited her every month."

"Visited a *nunnery* — every month?" he exclaimed, between derision and incredulity, and then his mouth softened. "If he found comfort so, why not?" he murmured, more to himself than to her.

"Why not?" she echoed. "She is silly and kind." She remembered too vividly the old man stalking along passages

65

gaped at by scandalized nuns, his white hair still streaked red, his drink-raddled flesh strained over craggy bones, seeking in his loneliness comfort from a woman's twitterings. She glanced at her husband. He had Lord Maurice's cheekbones, brow and nose, and like him would never lay on flesh, but grow gaunt with age. But the reckless humor of his mouth was his own, and his eyes' thoughtfulness.

Abruptly he moved on. The way had diminished to a yard-wide ribbon of grass twisting along the slope, a one-time track no longer trodden. It dipped towards the ravine that almost separated the headland from the ridge beyond. The castle overlooked the ridge, which sloped on the one side to Brentborough village and on the other to the River Brent's estuary. Its outer wall ran along the ravine's crest until it faced the river, and no missile could reach it across that gulf. Julitta glimpsed its terminal buttress above and beyond them as their horses sidled past the crag that marked the steepening descent. Here she was surprised to find nothing within her vision but sea, cliff and sky; the headland's curve cut off even sight of the fishing village. Then she was compelled to give all her attention to her mount's footing; the way was a narrow ledge above the drop to the churning sea, and an unwelcome thought lodged in her mind of the wife who had perhaps gone from this very path to her death. She glanced at the bright head guiding her down, and wondered whether Red Adam were tempted to rid himself likewise of an encumbering wife.

"That's the worst of it!" he called back encouragingly, and a few yards further down the green ribbon widened and he moved faster. His mount's shoes had bitten into the sodden turf. No other hooves had printed this track at least throughout the harvest season, nor had men's feet worn down the thin grass.

They were in the ravine now, here wide and shallow-sloping, its further ridge hiding from them the track between the castle and Arnisby. A stream quarreled with the boulders below them, and a carrion crow lurched from a rock with a squawk and flapped away. A little further, and Red Adam turned right into a small gully and followed it upward. A trickle of clear water twisted and dropped and pooled along it, and the stones of its bed were stained rusty red, like a streak of blood in a gash. Superstitious peasants might have crossed themselves, but Julitta regarded it indifferently. Pockets of ironstone were common in these hills, and the springs that rose through them always carried the stain and flavor of rusty iron. In some parts their water was drunk as a remedy for certain ailments, but not here.

"The dead men's blood still running," Red Adam observed, grinning over his shoulder. "You'd not get a peasant near it after dark, nor in daylight for that matter. I reckon no one has ventured up here since I came in January."

"Is this way accessible from the other side?" Julitta asked, nodding back at the ravine.

"An active man could scramble across, yes. There's at least one place where it can be done unseen; I tried it."

"It's a weakness in the defences?"

"No one could bring in an army that way, but it's a weakness, and I don't like it," he admitted readily. "When I can afford it, if I still rule Brentborough, I'll take a wall down the hillside to the sea, and build a jetty at its foot so that boats can moor there."

"That would make it impregnable. But what do you mean, if you still rule?"

"After this rebellion has been put down, King Henry, if I know him, will take all castles of importance into his own hands."

"But that would be injustice, to dispossess so loyal a vassal!" she exclaimed, momentarily forgetting for whom she invoked justice.

"And Leicester's case has proved, my dear, that the most loyal of vassals may at any hour be succeeded by a far from loyal heir."

"I am not your dear!" she snapped childishly, recalled with a jolt to her state of feud with him.

"The sole object of my unrequited devotion," he declared, gazing at her with so idiotic an air of yearning that she bit at the inside of her lip to steady it. He was trying to tease her into laughing, and she felt obscurely that succumbing would be her first step in capitulation.

"Your true vocation is that of court jester!"

"That's exactly how a tourney knight earns his winter quarters, entertaining some great lord's household — though it has its hazards."

"Husbands?"

"Yes, I'd reckon them foremost."

They turned to the right about a sharp outcrop, and the gully opened into a hollow that looked as though an age ago a giant's spoon had scooped it from the hillside like a lump of butter. The iron spring welled from under the rock into a basin of rusty-red stone which might have been wrought by men's hands, it was so regular in shape, and trickled over its lip to start the stream. Ruined walls, jaggedly broken, lifted out of the grass tussocks and tufted reeds.

Red Adam dismounted, tossed his reins over his mount's head, and put up his hands to lift her from her saddle. Taken by surprise, she could not evade his courtesy, and his hands gripped her by the waist as she slipped down. Her heart thumped sharply and her body quivered in his hold. He set her on her feet and loosed her, smiling crookedly. The horses snuffled at the water, blew in disgust at the taint of iron, and turned from it to crop without enthusiasm at the poor grass. Red Adam caught Julitta's hand and drew her to a gap that had once been a doorway.

The wind could not pursue them inside, and a burst of sunshine suddenly filled the roofless shell with warmth and light. Centuries of rain and wind and frost had crumbled the stones and the mortar and mossed them with orange and white lichens, had hung them with ivy, permitted stonecrop and toadflax and harebells to root in the crevices, and cushioned over the wreckage on the floor with hummocks of fine turf. Only the walls themselves, between knee and shoulder height, showed recent breakages, scarcely weathered, where they had been part-demolished for the stone. A tumble of raw debris at the foot of the furthest demonstrated the work's abandoning with strange eloquence. As Julitta looked, a weasel popped out of a cranny, poised on his hind legs to turn his snake-head this way and that, and flicked from sight again.

"That's where the skeletons were found, and the helmet," said Red Adam, nodding at an excavation under the wall. The tug on her hand was needless; she peered eagerly into the shallow hole, slightly silted, and saw only ends of square-cut stone and fragments of curved red tile, mixed with black and gray soil like the ashes of dead fires. "It's all tiles from the roof and rubble from the walls, under the grass," he told her, and picked up a shard of tile. "The place was fired; see, even the broken edge is blackened, and there's the ash. The bones were lying in the angle of the wall; I suppose when the roof fell the beams wedged above the dead men and protected them, for they were neither burned nor crushed. I persuaded Sweyn the oldest sergeant to tell me of it, but he shied like a balky horse from showing me." He flipped the bit of tile from him, so that it rebounded from the wall and fell back into the hole with a tiny clatter, and his face lighted with enjoyment as he went on.

"One morning when the workmen entered they found a new hole, and a helmed skull perched over it grinning at them. They flung down their tools with one accord and fled, screeching of dead men rising from their disquieted graves. By the time they'd drunk the alehouse dry they were yammering of skeleton hands reaching for them out of the earth and teeth gnashing at their necks, and I doubt not found them between the blankets with them when they fell into bed."

"But — but where were their wits that they did not realize —"

"Peasants have only two thoughts about old ruins; one's ghosts and the other's treasure. Lord Maurice and the priest kicked half a dozen guards here, and found a spade and a doused tallow dip. The priest sprinkled holy water and exorcisms about, and Lord Maurice belted the guards into digging out the bones, with the helmed skull tucked under his arm and grins matching. Very eloquent Sweyn was, sweating just to remember it; he'd been one of the diggers. My kinsman wanted to set up helm and skull together in his hall; he'd a witty humor, though his taste in trophies was a trifle grisly. But the priest held to it there'd been Christians in Roman times, and one of them was Roman — by that time they'd uncovered the second skeleton — and christened bones would lie quieter in a consecrated graveyard. Old Maurice had no mind to surrender his skull, and by reason of the diggers' haste, by the time he was convinced there was no sorting Christian bones from heathen. So they bundled all the fragments into a sack and so into hallowed earth.

"Of course, a day or two later the other story trickled out. They'd come to dig for treasure in the night, two of them to hearten each other, poor fools, and melted to their entrails for fear of dead Romans. Then the spade strikes metal, and one knave scrabbles with his hands to grub it out while the other slavers down his neck and holds the taper. And just as he lifts up the helmet and sees the skull grinning within it, there's a shriek that never came from mortal throat and out of the dark some presence swoops upon them with silent wings and the light blinks out. Incontinently they cast all from them and never stop to take breath until they're in their own beds with the blankets over their heads, palsied witless." Her eyebrows had lifted skeptically, and he shook his head. "No, that's the exact tale as it was told me. True, Sweyn forgot to mention how owls favor ruins. There's a nest in that hole by the corner."

She smiled despite herself, and then recollected her rancor and tried to conceal her lapse by gazing about her. She was not a fanciful girl, and Red Adam's tale of helmed skulls and ghostly wings had given her no more than a momentary thrill. The men who had killed each other, long ago when these blackened fragments had been a roof flaming over them, were shadows out of a remote age. That was not the cause of the unease that prickled the hairs on her nape. Her senses sharpened; the yelp of a gull wheeling overhead, and the flicker of its shadow in a glint of sunlight, made her start. Yet there was nothing to perturb anyone of sense, in this empty ruin set in the hollow of the hill. It was incredible that the raucous castle stood not a half-mile above this secret place.

"What's amiss? Has my tale of skulls and ghosts scared you?"

"That? Oh, no!" She hesitated, but he did not mock her. She blurted out, "This place — it's a lovers' trysting place."

"Perfect for the purpose."

"And Lord Maurice set up the helm and called it Brentborough's Luck."

Red Adam needed no laborious explanations. "Likely enough he forced the luck too hard, since it was on this headland his lady vanished."

"He'd not bring a peasant here unless he haled her by the hair," Julitta pointed out, and shivered. The sun had gone, but it was the adding of hint and suspicion into a total that tingled down her spine.

"I'd as soon lay a wench on a tombstone, myself," candidly commented her husband, and his arm came about her shoulders and urged her towards the doorway. She flinched, and stiffened against the contact, but no resolve could stay her heart from thumping and her blood from quickening.

The last gleam of sun blinked out, and as they traversed the hillside path, stooping their heads into the rising gale, heavy drops came spattering and chased them back to the castle, where they arrived half-soaked.

Red Adam lifted her from the saddle at the foot of the keep steps, hustled her up them, and shouted for Avice as they emerged into the hall. The windward fireplace was gushing smoke like Hell's hearths newly fueled, the rain came hissing down the chimney vent, and every window along that wall admitted a deluge, while the hangings flapped and the rushes blew along the floor and drifted against the dais step. No one had attempted to remedy these matters, though half a dozen serving men were engaged about the other fire in a game of knucklebones. They did not stir while Red Adam stalked towards them, and only recognized menace when his foot thudded against the nearest rump. Tart words sent them scuttling, and Julitta moved to the heat and wrung what water she could from her hair and clothes. Her husband surveyed her critically.

"See whether there's aught in the bower to contrive you new clothes," he ordered, "and be done with your kinsfolk's lendings. There's a gaggle of idle strumpets to set stitching — and where's that misery, your wench?" A squeak turned him about to scowl at Avice. "Don't goggle, drizzle! Help your lady out of those wet garments!"

Avice squeaked again, her hand up to her mouth, and as he strode to the door she cringed away from him.

"Mary Mother, girl, do you expect my lord to devour you?"

"He — he frightens me — so angry."

"He'll do you no harm, silly child."

Sitting on her bed in her smock while Avice rubbed her hair dry with a musty-smelling towel yellowed along its folds with long lying, she wondered again what was amiss with her. The girl had been timid enough, harried by Lady Matilda, but never so wretchedly terrified. Again she tried to hearten her.

"You've no need to fear my lord. Don't cringe from him, and he will like you better."

"God forbid, my lady! I'm — it's that I'm afeared —"

Julitta jerked back from the towel and thrust it down to stare into her twitching face. Her mouth squared into a wail. "The — the other girls ha' telled me — as how m'lord — as he'll tumble me for his sport — and gi' me to that friend o' hisn that's randy-drunk every night — so's I'll be a whore like them — and what'll become o' me then!"

"Neither of them will debauch my servant," Julitta declared grimly.

"But you don't know — m'lady, they tells me —" She broke off, reddening, on the verge of recounting Red Adam's lapses to his new-wedded lady, and then seized the towel and scrubbed at Julitta's hair.

"All that is past," Julitta declared, with a certainty that afterward made her marvel. "My dress, now." She resumed the scarlet for lack of any alternative and reckoned obedience to her husband's command marched agreeably with her own desire.

The bower, which should have hummed with work, was empty but for a middle-aged woman in a corner, spinning as she rocked a cradle with her foot. She jumped up nervously, hushed a howl from the cradle's occupant, and named herself as Hodierne, widow of Brentborough's marshal, and entirely at her lady's service. Her deference and anxiety to please embarrassed Julitta, though she recognized that a widow past thirty, dowerless and burdened with a posthumous child, must live in dread of being cast adrift. She had existed too long on sufferance herself to fail in sympathy; she admired the baby, listened to the tale of the marshal's excellences, and invited Hodierne's aid in checking the bower's resources.

They opened boxes and chests and dragged out linen, winter bedding, clothing and material, exposing neglect and deficiencies. There was scarcely any work in hand; no new hangings, bedding or napery. Even the New Year's gift of clothing for all the servants, part of their wages, was as yet unstarted. The cloth merchants had not ventured north through the rebellious Midlands, and the season's woolclip remained unsold, so they would be lucky to receive anything. Sewing thread, embroidery materials, needles and pins were all wanting. The work set up on a loom showed by dust, broken warp-threads and displaced shed-sticks that it had not been touched for months. There was no sign even of the carding and spinning that should have occupied all disengaged hands in a respectable bower. Julitta tightened her lips over these proofs of demoralization and pursued her investigations.

Hodierne avoided the last chest, in the corner beside the big bed, and her face lengthened with alarm when Julitta moved to it, found it locked and began sorting through the keys at her girdle.

"M-my lady, all inside that — is reserved to Lady Constance's sole use."

"It was," Julitta answered as she found the key and the

73

lock clicked back. She regarded folded cloth with pleasure. Though Hodierne flushed, a certain satisfaction in her expression suggested that she might not object to Constance's discomfiture. She helped lay out the stuff across the bed.

Julitta was mildly disappointed. The seneschal's wife had the blonde woman's depressing preference for blue, and as woad was one of the cheapest dyes, she had in the past worn more than enough of it. But there was a dark green, and a well-dyed black betraying none of the natural black wool's rustiness; a little embroidery and they would look well enough. A deep blue mantle lined with a lighter shade would also please her.

Avice and Hodierne held the material against her, folded it and marked off the lengths. She crunched the shears through it. She could not remember when she had had clothes new-made for herself, not contrived from another's discards, and she forgot to resent obedience to Red Adam's orders. They measured and cut and pinned, rooted out needles and thread, and were surprised in the preliminary seam-stitching by the dinner horn.

From foul the weather had deteriorated to atrocious. All the seaward windows were shuttered against a gale, and the fire allowed to dwindle to embers hissing as the wet ran in. Drafts swooped and whistled, rain percolated round shutters and pooled in window splays, and the remaining fire belched smoke and ashes. The dishes brought in from the outside kitchen were greasily congealed and slopped with chill water. Julitta, having listened dutifully to an exhaustive discussion of what royal and rebel forces should do, detached her attention when the argument began to repeat itself and considered the reforms essential to civilized existence at Brentborough. An interview with the head cook came near the list's top. All depended, of course, on the measure of authority Red Adam would allow her.

The cloths were removed and the tables taken down. Folk gazed gloomily out, and agreed that it was unfit for man or beast to poke a nose beyond doors. Julitta contemplated for the first time the problem of how to occupy housebound knights, every chatelaine's winter nightmare. Fortunately they found their own entertainment; the four of them pulled stools to a corner of the dais and settled down with a wine-jug to swap lies of old campaigns.

Red Adam leaned a while in a window, absently whistling, and then jerked his head at Odo and made for the stairs, giving orders to a couple of scullions as he passed to set up a table. When he came back, his arms heaped with parchments and Odo bearing tally sticks enough to roast a hog, men started up and gaped at each other. Dust billowed as he cast the rolls on the bench. Odo set down his load, spread a cloth painted in chessboard checks, laid out counters, a corroded inkhorn and a fistful of draggled quills, and stationed himself by his master's elbow.

Sir Brien cleared his throat with a rasp that rang in the hush, reddened and mumbled, "If—if you're wishing to check the estate accounts, my lord—"

"What else?"

"The village priest kept them, my lord. He can be sent for—to explain—"

"Why, I'll put no man to such misery." He unrolled a yard of discolored parchment. "I'll make what sense I can of them myself." He ran his glance down the columns and chose a quill, drew his knife and deftly trimmed its point. Dismay stirred in the room, suggesting uneasy consciences arousing. Sir Bertram picked up his stool and moved to the table.

"I can aid you with the tallies, Lord Adam, but it's past my sight to read." He nodded acceptance. Lady Constance came in, regarded them blandly, and sat down with her embroidery, ready to assist her husband with the figures. Julitta retired to continue sewing, wondering what investigation of Brentborough's accounts might reveal. She was now certain of what she had already suspected. Red Adam had at one time been destined for the Church and educated in the cloister.

5

By supper-time the rain had blown over, though the gale still screeched round the battlements and boomed in the chimneys. An untalented and unpracticed quartet of viol, lute, harp and recorder caterwauled to entertain them, while Red Adam's body-servant and a couple of fumble-fisted scullions clumped about the dais and breathed gustily down their necks. Lady Hodierne effaced herself, and Lady Constance devoted herself equally to consuming the more succulent delicacies and charming Sir Reynald.

Julitta distastefully surveyed her domain. She knew what housekeeping entailed; poor as the nunnery was, it had been meticulously swept and scoured, and her uncle's lady was a notorious martinet who spent her days harrying servitors. Though some effort had been made to furbish it for the marriage with a layer of fresh rushes and a perfunctory whisk about with brooms, the hall looked and smelled like an annex to the kennels. It could be a noble apartment, but near twenty years with no mistress, an apathetic lord and unsupervised servants had debased it to squalor. There had been no sweetening done last spring nor yet the spring before; the plaster had known no limewash since first it was laid on, the hangings had been gnawed by mice and moths, and the new rushes overlaid but did not hide the matted remains of several years' strewing. They were hopping with fleas also; every mistress of a household must wage incessant war on the vermin, but here they had been conceded victory.

Red Adam played the solicitous husband, giving her the choicer morsels from their platter, cutting up her roast pigeon to save her from soiling her fingers, and assailing her silence with such scandalously entertaining tales of a knight-errant's life following the tourneys that no resolution could sustain it. A splutter of laughter, and she was lost. He had the whole company yelling delight, the servants loitering behind him to snigger, and even the minstrels hushed until the ewers and towels came around for the last time, the platters and trenchers were cleared, and all relaxed over the final cups of wine. Julitta sipped from the silver cup she shared with her lord. It had been refilled only once during the meal, and he was as sober as she was. And when she set it down, he drank formally to her and to his companions and signed to the servants to take down the tables.

The scullions and wenches clattered utensils out to the kitchen. Odo supervised a more respectful treatment of the silver. The musicians twanged through a tune or two, and then, receiving no encouragement, joined a group of off-duty guards casting dice. Sir Giles and Sir Brien murmured something about stable inspection and withdrew. A chessboard appeared between the seneschal and his wife. Everyone was sober.

Reynald de Carsey raised an aggrieved voice and an empty cup. "God's life, Adam, are we on siege rations?"

Red Adam motioned to Odo, who poured impassively. "The only restriction is your capacity, Reynald," he assured him, but his lips tightened.

"But it's cursed in- inhospick'ble to leave a friend to drink alone," he complained, a small difficulty with polysyllables proclaiming that he had been less austere. "What's amiss, Adam? Over a week you've stayed dull-sober."

"And I intend to remain so."

78

Reynald turned a disparaging stare on Julitta, who had seen too much of drunkenness to be alarmed. "God's Blood, doing penance forever? You've wedded her, and that's amends enough."

"Amends I cannot make again. Reynald—"

"A couple of hours' daylight left. Let's ride out, you and I, and see what sport we can stir up, and find us each a new wench to lay." He drained his cup and held it out to Odo for refilling.

"I've forsworn such sports since I wedded."

"Wedded! Daft you were, to thrust your head into that doleful noose without a clipped penny profit! Same tongue yapping at board, same tricks between the sheets and those the ones you've taught her, same silly face—"

"Guard your tongue! You may swill your skin full and take a kitchen slut to bed, or there's the tavern in Arnisby and a couple of public women if you'd ride out. And the drawbridge will not be lowered between sunset and dawn."

Reynald subsided, muttering indistinctly of kitchen sluts and public women he had tried too often. Julitta judged him not truly drunk, just sufficiently moistened to have loosened the superficial layer of courtesy disguising his basic ugliness. Red Adam glanced at her apologetically, smiled to see her unperturbed and let the matter rest. He spoke over his shoulder to Odo, who went out, and leaned to watch the chess players.

Lacking other occupation, Julitta did likewise. The seneschal played a slow, sound game, but his wife's moves were careless, her thoughts obviously elsewhere. It was no more to her than another duty to be scamped. When the serving women came back she rose in the middle of the game, announcing that she must see all put to rights in the bower. It was for Julitta as mistress to order the bower, and the malice in Constance's eye challenged her, but she mentally notched up another tally and answered, "You have my leave, Lady Constance." Had she been a worthy chatelaine Julitta would thankfully have learned from her, but Brentborough's state proclaimed her neglect.

79

Sir Bertram sat fondling a holly-wood pawn and gazing vaguely after his wife: On impulse Julitta rose and took the empty stool. "May I match you, Sir Bertram?"

He peered under brows shaggy as thatched eaves, and she wondered how much he could see of her; merely a scarlet blur, or could he distinguish her irregular features? He smiled. "A kindness, my lady. Your move."

She was out of practice, but her father had trained her into a tolerable antagonist, and one of the convent's lay boarders had devoted as much of Julitta's time as she could command to her passion for the game. At her first move to save a castaway match the seneschal straightened his spine, laid aside the pawn and considered her play.

Reynald de Carsey raised complaint again. "Here's a dismal roost. Naught to entertain a man but an alehouse full of stinking fishermen and a brace of thick-bottomed trollops."

"I've no remedy to reduce their bottoms," Red Adam retorted.

"You don't intend to squat on this cliff all year through like your kinsman? You've cosier quarters in the south; that estate of yours near Bristol would suit me."

"Bordeaux wine and sailors' brothels?"

"Turning dainty? What's a man to do, winter evenings, but drink and fornicate? No fun here. Why did your old cousin skulk here?"

"He had sufficient reason."

"He was mad. When do we move south?"

"The rebels must answer that. You nag like an aggrieved woman, Reynald."

Sir Bertram turned his dim gaze a long moment on his lord. "So he knows?" he murmured. "You told him?"

"He asked me."

"It should be buried with my lord. I gave orders none here was to speak of it, and there is yet weight to my word."

"It was his undoubted right."

He moved a knight. Red Adam watched, a preoccupied frown between his brows, but he could not have heard their talk. As the knight came down, Odo approached his master

80

and muttered in his ear. Red Adam excused himself and went out. The peering eyes lifted to challenge the girl.

"It should have been buried," he repeated, and her casual pity changed to respect for a power still formidable, however fettered. "He was no murderer."

"But they never found trace of her again."

"He'd never have killed her. Not with his heir in her belly. All his hope was set on that. Put it from your mind and his. She went over the cliff into the sea."

"Were you here?"

"If I had been I'd have rooted out that lie with every tongue that spoke it. He was my lord, my true friend and my lady's in our sorest need. When all men turned against me he succored me, gave me an honorable place in his household. And I was gone on pilgrimage to Jerusalem when *he* had need, and all condemned him."

"You are loyal."

"I do him justice," he growled. "Folk snigger over the count of his bastards, yes. But I left my lady, my dear wife, in his charge. And when his wife vanished, to prevent any taint of slander from touching her, he conveyed Constance to a nunnery near Bristol, to bide there until I returned. He kept faith by me, and so do I by his memory."

"You do well," she murmured, impressed against her will, yet seeing again the sinner crumbling under his burden of guilt. No one who had seen Maurice de Lorismond in his last haunted years could have believed him innocent.

Sir Bertram sighed and pushed at a pawn as though it were a discomforting thought. "He dealt truly with me. Constance bore our son there, and he died. I never saw him, and we had no other. But that was for my sins and mine alone... Your move, my lady."

She murmured some condolence and pored over the board, shifting a pawn of her own at random. A blue blur loomed on the edge of her vision, and she looked round at Constance, softened by her tragedy. She saw a woman who had borne one son among strangers, and seen him die; whose husband had become a half-blind hulk hunched over a chessboard, who had wasted beauty and youth in this bleak hold, bound to Maurice by one act of magnanimity. Regret for their enmity stirred in her, and was stilled by a malevolent glance.

"A gracious charity you do, my lady," she murmured sweetly, and billowed away to her embroidery.

"Gracious indeed," growled Sir Bertram, frowning at the wound's prick.

"My pleasure," Julitta disclaimed sharply. Constance had learned of her appropriations from the locked chest, and there could be nothing but war between them now.

Some servants returned with the plate and arranged it on the sideboard, under the helmet within which her imagination conjured a sleepless skull. A pretty girl in a good blue dress, far gone with child, brushed against Reynald de Carsey, glooming into his empty cup. He turned on her and demanded wine. She fetched the jug and poured for him, remaining by his elbow. Julitta caught her eye and signaled to her to return the jug to the serving table. However tolerant Red Adam might be of swinish misconduct, no servant in her hall should abet it.

The girl not only ignored the sign, but touched the knight's shoulder to direct his attention to Julitta. He absently patted her bottom, said thickly, "Not with that belly between us, sweetheart," and tipped back head and cup. As he lowered them, his gaze followed hers. He scowled at Julitta. "Fill again, lass."

She smirked at Julitta and obeyed.

"Get to your own place, bower or kitchen!" Julitta snapped, and resentment flared. Her gown proclaimed her of the bower; the kitchen wenches were the servants' trulls, common to all the household. She opened her mouth to retort, and Constance swept between them.

"Yes, come to the bower, Thyra, you foolish child. You must consider only your baby's welfare." She smiled maternally over her shoulder at Julitta as she turned the girl towards the stair. "Forgive the silly girl's jealousy, my lady. It is your husband's child she carries."

Julitta caught her breath as if she had been struck, but

commanded her wits and tongue to demand contemptuously, "How can she possibly know that?" Resolute to betray no feeling, she stared at the black and white shapes that blurred over the board. Steadying her hand with an effort she made some move. Her heart thumped at her breastbone, and her anger astonished her. It should mean nothing to her. If a tithe of gossip were true, she might expect a crop of by-blows from the seed her husband recklessly sowed. Yet emotions very old and savage choked her with their force.

"Check, my lady."

She had not seen the move; her eyes had been blinded. She hesitated. Behind her Sir Reynald heaved himself up to find his own wine, lurched sideways and thumped down on the bench where the musicians had laid their instruments. He picked up the recorder and juicily tootled a few notes. They shaped into a sequence, and then into the tune of "I kissed a girl in Paris city," a soldiers' ditty bawled in camp and tavern and brothel but never tolerated in any civilized hall. Rage scorched up her throat and face as she leaned over the game, ignoring the implicit insult that he could not know she understood. Sir Bertram turned on his stool, urgently motioning him to silence, but the fellow's brains must have been pickled to the hairroots, for he threw back his head and yowled it to the rafters.

> "I kissed a girl in Paris city,
> Before I rode away,
> She was a choice and gamesome kitty,
> Plump little—"

With a jangle of snapped strings and rending wood the lute burst upon his skull, and he sat blinking, collared with the instrument's belly and bleeding from several scratches. Julitta, white-faced and breathing herkily, let go the lute's neck and backed a pace. He lurched up, clawing at the wreckage and snarling threats.

"Most musically appropriate," declared Red Adam's voice. He thrust his friend one-handed upon his bench. "Reckon yourself fortunate, Reynald. She reformed *my* way of life with a stool." He broke away shards of wood. "Best conform courteously to my lady's requirements."

"Require—it's a belt she requires!"

Julitta waited on her lord's reactions with righteous anger stiffening her spine. Sir Bertram had come to her side. Beyond him Constance lifted horrified eyes. Knights, soldiers, minstrels and servants goggled all about.

"You're doubly fortunate, Reynald, that she reached you first," Red Adam added gently, "for I'd have been less inspired." He ripped the last fragment from his friend's neck and turned to his wife. Braced for his wrath, she was disconcerted to recognize approval in his face. "Oblige me by retiring, my lady," he requested, and she could escape with honor.

She sat on the bed's edge, listening to the gale's violence, and stared at the candleflame leaping and guttering as drafts swooped round the rattling shutter. She wondered just how much harm she had done herself. It depended on the regard Red Adam had for his friend. She knew what her uncle's reaction would have been, and she was entirely at her husband's mercy. No man could expect her to accept that drunken lout's insults, and Red Adam had at least upheld her in public, a forbearance she had not looked for.

Remembering another aspect of his character, she shivered and scrambled out of her clothes and into the bed, where she assured herself that she was a fool to let it trouble her. She had known what he was before he constrained her to marry him, what every Lorismond had been, and it would be cause for marvel if Thyra proved the only one bearing the fruit of last January's indiscretions. Yet the fury still curdled in her belly. It was fury for the girl's insolence; she could not be jealous of Red Adam's favors. Constance's barbed shaft would not easily pull out.

The door opened, fluttering the candleflame, and her husband came in. He barred the door and stood over her, his face harsh in that erratic light. She braced herself.

"I apologize for Reynald," he said abruptly. "He'll not offend that way again, if I have to ration his wine."

"What set him against me so, except that I saw him in his beastliness?" she asked, relaxing.

He shrugged. "That's reason enough for him. He resents my marrying unprofitably, against his advice, and turning sober. Also he reckons that a wife should tolerate whatever her husband chooses to put upon her, including his friends' abuse. It's an interesting view of marriage, but not for a man with a vixen to conciliate."

"Do you expect a vixen to tolerate his conduct, my lord?"

He smiled ruefully and perched on the bed's edge by her feet. "I can't be rid of him as easily as I was of Stephen and Piers."

"Who—you mean your fellow raptors of Monday night?"

"Old friends from the tourney circuit. After being restrained from battering down your door, and informed that marriage meant an end to wine and wenches at my charges, one word led to another, and they departed at first light next morning."

"You will not lack friends on those terms when you backslide."

"My intentions at the moment are excellent, but the flesh is exceedingly weak," he conceded amicably. "Yet you opened my skull to thought with your stool, and high time. There's more to lordship than wine and wenches, though Reynald will not agree."

"Not so long as they are freely available."

He shifted his buttocks from the box-bed's edge, nearer her feet. "True. But it's hard to deny him. He saved my life."

"How?"

"Cried warning of a knife at my back in a dark alley. Then I had Lord Maurice's summons, and promised Reynald fair provision as seneschal over some estate of mine."

A promise he now regretted, Julitta recognized, but must fulfil. She recognized also, in surprise, how great a compliment he paid her discretion and good sense by this confidence, and shut her teeth on condemnation of his rashness.

"There's more to lordship than wine and wenches," he

repeated soberly. "Between campaigns I've been bounding about England like a flea. I've dismissed a seneschal and two bailiffs; another got my scent and beat me over the Welsh border with the estate strongbox. We found him with his throat slit, but not, to my sorrow, the strongbox."

"A sore grief!"

"Sore indeed, so many hands dipped into my coffers and I scratching every penny together to pay a hard relief."

"So that was why, this afternoon—"

"I was serving fair warning that I can read and cast accounts. Oh, there's been mismanagement and muddle, but here under my kinsman's own eye little peculation. Sir Bertram's honest. But to give Reynald such a charge, no. I dare not trust him with authority outside my sight."

"And he has set his heart on your estate by Bristol?"

"You miss nothing. As long as the threat from Flanders hangs in the wind, and the rebels hold out in Leicester, I've reason to keep him by me. Bear with him as you can; he's only fit company for a like-minded lecherous sot." He lifted one eyebrow, a trick of his that the candlelight exaggerated to weirdness.

"Then restrain him from ravishing my maid-servant."

Both eyebrows lifted. "That ninny? Hell's Teeth, what's the harm if he does?"

"Harm—that lout forcing a helpless maid?" she protested indignantly, sitting up in her smock heedless of the covers sliding to her waist.

"Do her good," he declared callously. "She'll have something real to wail about."

"You monster!"

"All the bitch is any use for."

"Yes, the only use you'd have for a servant girl would be to make a whore of her!" she blazed, memory of the fair girl weighted with his sin stinging her to indiscretion. "Like that wench Thyra who is carrying your child!"

"Thyra? Oh, the towhead. She claims it's mine?"

"You deny it?"

"It could be," he admitted shamelessly. "Though it's as likely to be Reynald's, or any man's. It needn't grieve you. It was before we wedded, and done with."

"Now you have a maiden to debauch for your sport instead?"

"There's only one maiden for me now," he replied, and reached a hand to her. She recoiled, flung back the covers and twisted off the bed. She was at the door, tugging at the bar, when he seized her.

"Where are you going?"

"Do you reckon I'll stay in the same room with you?"

"You'll not run from it in your smock to make a public jest of our dispute."

He wrenched her away from the door. She dragged back and struck at his face, and he caught her wrist, hauled her to him and embraced her, pinning her arms. She kicked at his shins, but bare toes made no impression; he swung her from her feet. She writhed desperately, and they collided with the bed and fell across it. A triumphant kiss flattened her lips against her teeth, and for an appalling instant her body flamed response to the male strength of his. Then he loosed her, rolled to his feet and stood breathing jerkily.

"Mother of God!" he whispered. "I came near forcing you—after I promised—Julitta, I'm sorry!"

She twisted over, snatched the dagger from under her pillow, and snarled, "Keep off!"

"You'll not need it. I won't touch you. In God's Name, Julitta, don't be afraid of me."

"Afraid? Merciful Savior, I loathe you!"

"That's evident," he said wryly. Rain drummed on the shutter, and water dripped near it. He moved to thrust at the boarding, and she gulped and scrubbed her smock sleeve across her eyes. He spoke over his shoulder. "But you don't much like any man, do you?"

"No!"

He turned and leaned on the bed-foot, the crooked smile twisting his mouth again. The candle alternately lighted his face to a harsh mask and softened it into shadow. "Was your father the same breed as his brother?" he asked disconcertingly.

Agreement started to her lips, and then she caught back betrayal. "He was my father. He loved me." And that was truth; in his way he had loved her, that morose man with no patience in him, burdened with a motherless girl he could not provide for.

"I'm sure of it. And then your uncle, that faceful of teeth he'd have given you to, the Ladies' Delight, and now Reynald — and me. I reckon you've reason." He straightened, and came round the bed. "I understand what I must contend against. And I know now it's blood in your veins and not buttermilk." He lifted the bar and went out.

The door shut. The wind shrieked and worried at the keep. Julitta twisted over, buried her face in the pillow and wept.

6

The gale's wrath was dying in random gusts that tore at garments and set the horses snorting and sidling. It hunted gray clouds over the sky and drove them across the sun's-face; shadows and sunshine raced over the headland, and the sodden grass dulled and glittered alternately. Julitta, sullen-faced, followed Red Adam over the slippery turf. "You'll ride with me," he had announced, taking her hand in a grip there was no denying. Nudges, whispers and stares had already informed her that all Brentborough knew of last night's quarrel; ears must have been flapping close to their chamber door. Her husband's company was more tolerable than facing mockery and gloating alone.

"You'll ride with me every morning," he told her over his shoulder.

"Why?"

"Your chance to curse me to your heart's easing with no witnesses to tattle," he suggested cheerfully, and by that permission paralyzed her tongue. He reigned his mount back to close in beside her, and smiled into her resentful face. "I shan't beat you, so you can put by defiance."

He had read too clearly her dread of violence and her

refusal to be cowed by it. "I'll prove you first," she said bitterly.

"I've a sympathy for you," he said unexpectedly, "because as a boy I too was thrust remediless into a hateful life. But maids of your station never have any choice in where they wed. You know how your uncle would have bestowed you, and without conceit, I've used you better than Tusky Gerald would."

"You are intolerably magnanimous," she retorted, "and I'd have hated him worse than you."

His face alight with mirth, he reached to close a hand on hers. "My truthful lass, you rejoice me. Next, I'll aim to raise myself above your dear uncle in your esteem. A difficult goal, I'll own—"

She bit at her lip, but too late; it twitched into a smile. "You've achieved it," she retorted, trying to retrieve the lapse. "Just."

"That's encouragement!" He grinned, and caught her hand to his lips before she knew what he was about. His jesting stabbed through the mail of resentment that protected her misery from assault. She jerked away, her hand closing into a fist, and he lifted his mount into a canter, slowed to negotiate the ruins among the tussocks, and walked out towards the dizzy brink.

Cold salt, uphurled from the turmoil below, tingled on her skin. A sword of sunlight cleft the clouds and struck its rage to white splendor. The green waves marched in, shattered water glittered with rainbows, rock fangs darkly glistened through, and the wind snatched at her clothes, lifted her hair and beat the breath back between her teeth. Gulls swung shrieking round and over, riding the updrafts, and Red Adam yelled exultantly through the clamor. The wind tossed the words to Julitta, verses from the twenty-ninth Psalm.

"It is the Lord, that commandeth the waters: it is the glorious God, that maketh the thunder. It is the Lord, that ruleth the sea!"

The horses tossed their heads and rolled white-rimmed

eyeballs. Julitta, tightening control with hands and voice on her undependable palfrey, glanced aside at the wild creature joyously misusing Holy Writ, his hair straining stiffly back from his face. Full sunlight dazzled her; the clouds were shredding into tatters and the wide sea's leaden green was brightening to blue.

"Hell's Teeth!" Red Adam leaned forward, shading his eyes with one hand. "There's a ship!"

She followed his pointing arm. Northeast, out upon that dazzle, she was driving in fast. Under a rag of close-reefed sail, she dipped and lurched crabwise, fighting southward with wind and sea on her larboard quarter thrusting her at the cliffs. The waves clutched at her, hurling spray across her poop, but she shook free every time, fighting buoyant as a gull over their crests. Julitta, tensely watching her borne closer and closer, guessed how those aboard must look with dread on the waiting cliffs and repeated an *Ave* under her breath for them.

"If they've fought through last night's storm they've earned safe harborage," her husband commented, and started his mount along the cliff to watch more easily. She followed, her fingers gripping the reins in futile sympathy.

The ship was close enough inshore for clear view: longer and narrower than the squat Channel cogs she knew, part-decked fore and aft with a tarpaulin over her well. She could see the helmsman braced to the tiller's kick, lashed with spray by every wave crest as it rose in menace and then slid under the keel, tiny figures hauling on the sheets to win as much southing as they could from the straining sail, the lookout crouching against the stempost carved to the likeness of a bird, a huddle of dark shapes under the break of the poop. Regular gouts of water indicated frantic bailing along her lee side. They walked their horses along the headland's curve, watching the struggle they could do nothing to aid.

"If they can only win round the point," Julitta whispered. Red Adam said nothing, and his face showed only an indifferent interest. She demanded savagely, "Do you care nothing?"

91

He did not heed her, nor show that he had heard. An eddy of wind, recoiling from the cliff's face, caught the ship. She lurched and staggered, the next wave drove green water across her poop, and then she lifted again and steadied to her course. For a heart's beat Julitta thought the rocks would have her, and then she shrieked with triumph; the ship had clawed past the point and could run for the harbor in the estuary.

"They've done it! Praise God! They're safe!"

"Dear God!" Red Adam's voice ripped through her delight. "It's high tide! The reef—they'll run full on it!"

He was wrenching at his cloak brooch. As the ship, clearing the headland, swung to her new course that would hurl her onto the rocks that thrust from the lower, southern headland, he rose in the stirrups with a piercing yell and swung his cloak overhead in a sweep that startled his horse into plunging. The wind whipped away his shout so that it was unlikely any aboard heard it, but his signal was seen; an arm gestured, and pale spots of upturned faces acknowledged it. He swirled the cloak widely, and the wind spread it into wings; then with imperative arm and nodding head he signed to them to take the inside passage under the cliff where they stood. The steersman flung up an answering arm, and the wind bore his shout, hoarser and deeper than a gull's cry, to their ears. The ship ran shuddering through the smother of foam at the river's mouth, and under the cliff's lee, where she lost the wind. Men scurried. A complicated maneuvre, and four pairs of oars were out. Like a many-legged pond creature she crawled up the safe channel for the shelving beach where the fishing boats lay above the tide-line.

"Praise God!" Red Adam ejaculated, swung his mount about on his haunches and touched spurs to his sides. Julitta scuttled after him across the headland, cantered between the castle outbuildings scattering scullions, brats, pigs and poultry, over the drawbridge and down the Arnisby track. Mud spattered. The carrier, leading his string of half a dozen packhorses across the long wooden bridge, recoiled in alarm, but they reined aside to let him pass, and Red Adam dismissed the apology he attempted with a wave of his hand. More soberly they cantered along the straggling street to the huddle of fishers' cottages at its end, by the pebbly strand where most of the populace was watching the stranger work in, with a communal disgruntled expression which swiveled towards their lord.

"Devil melt them, why are they all scowling as though I'd kicked their teeth in?" demanded Red Adam.

"You've cheated them. Wrecks are rich pickings," Julitta murmured.

"Hell's Teeth, are they ravens to pick dead men's bones?" he exclaimed righteously, and then added, even more righteously, "Yes, and wreck rights are lord's rights."

"If he gets up first," Julitta agreed, chuckling despite herself.

"I'd have to rise early, I see," he said grimly, thrusting through the resentful throng to the shingle as the vessel grounded on crunching pebbles and the seamen swung overboard to heave her higher up the beach on the crest of the tide. The steersman, relinquishing his post at the tiller, threw up an arm and shouted a greeting in rough French, recognizing his benefactor and deceived by his shabby attire.

"Ho, friend Fire-in-the-thatch! Our thanks for your signal!"

In the shocked hush a child's voice squeaked, "But that is my lord himself!"

The steersman, over the side, checked thigh-deep for the space of a long breath, his cheekbones and nose coloring dull red. Then he waded to them through the shallows.

Red Adam, rechristened for his lifetime, grinned cheerfully, dismounted and went plunging and sliding down the shingle to meet him at the water's edge. "I'm Adam de Lorismond. You're very welcome to Arnisby, and to Brentborough Castle."

"Erling Thorvard's son of Trondheim," the seaman responded, still flushed. "My lord, I intended—"

"I'm aptly served; make no more of it." Red Adam was

a tall man, but he had to tilt his head back to grin at the seaman, who overtopped him by a hand's breadth and would have made two of him in girth.

A stiff smile parted the sailor's salt-soaked whiskers. He bowed. "Yet it was ill said. But for your warning I'd have lost my ship."

"Enough! You're free of what harbor facilities we have." His gesture took in the strip of shingle, the fishing boats, the racks of drying stockfish and the salt-boiling cauldrons slung over sulky fires. "Any damage?"

"A few seams started. My thanks, Lord Adam. We'll heave her over." He spoke French fluently, but with an accent much like North-country English. "We were bound for Yarmouth from Flanders, but we were storm-driven north as far as Scotland. I've passengers aboard, and a hard voyage they've had of it."

"My guests, as you are. Get them ashore." He looked round for Julitta, already picking her way to his side. "Wife, let me present Master Erling Thorvard's son. Master Erling, my lady."

Erling bowed over her hand with dignity. She took an instant liking to him. His hair and beard, tangled with seawater, were so fair that they scarcely betrayed any gray, and his eyes, bloodshot from the long battle, were very blue and alive in his leather-brown face. "It is an honor," he said in his stiff French.

"You must call on us for all your needs, Master Erling," she endorsed her husband's hospitality.

The seamen had by now lowered mast and sail, propped the ship with timber balks so that she would stay upright when the tide withdrew, and were helping over the side a woebegone company, green-faced and tottering. Julitta, who had pricked her ears at mention of Flanders and Yarmouth, now assimilated their significance; those men who were not too far gone to forget all but the reality of land were clutching the unmistakable shapes of cased arbalests.

One man, clad in what had been emerald green, now soaked to the hue of over-boiled cabbage, his visage a paler reflection of its color, wobbled through the surf on the arm of a blond young giant, and squelched wide-legged and reeling over the wrack of weed and shells and driftwood the ebb tide was stranding on the shingle. Half-dead from sea-sickness and exposure, he yet shook free of the supporting grip while the lad stared at Julitta, braced himself on the insecure footing and lifted his head to confront his host. His jaw sagged open, and he gaped like something flapping in a net.

"Hell's Teeth! It's Baldwin Dogsmeat!"

"Red Adam!" His mouth snapped shut, a faint insolence tilted the corners of his hard mouth. "A long way from the tourneys, Adam."

"I've inherited," Red Adam answered, with an upward jerk of the head that included harbor, village and the castle looming on the promontory beyond.

The man swayed, steadied himself, and broadened the insolent smile."Pleasant to hear of an old comrade's good fortune."

"You're welcome to partake of it, Baldwin," Red Adam answered with unruffled humor. "Bring your scoundrels up to the castle as soon as their legs will make it, and I'll feed and house them—for old times' sake." He nodded in dismissal, and Baldwin's hard mouth tightened. Red Adam would present the shipman to his lady, but not a mercenary captain. His gaze flickered to Julitta, standing beside her husband, and for the second time recognition gleamed. He grinned like a shark.

"Here's old acquaintance well-met again! You'll not recall me, but you're Gautier de Montrigord's daughter. I encountered you in Toulouse when you were a little maid—a matter of five years past it'll be."

"That is so," Julitta replied sedately, conscious of her husband's sharp scrutiny. She was not surprised; the world of landless knights and mercenary soldiers was a small one, a world of abrupt partings and unexpected meetings. The shark's grin was already turned on Red Adam, taunting him with knowledge of his wife's unacceptable antecedents.

The sailor lifted a fist, wrath mounting in his face. Julitta caught his eye and slightly shook her head; he smiled sheepishly, blushed, and gazed at her with a look she had seen often enough, but never directed at herself: frank admiration and something more, that won a smile from her. A keener regret pierced her; she was married to Red Adam, whose esteem would sink to nothing now he knew how her childhood had been passed.

The mercenary captain suddenly turned, distracting all eyes seaward. Julitta exclaimed under her breath; the passenger being assisted over the ship's side was a woman, and as she steadied herself thigh-deep in the water a seaman passed to her a small child. She held him against her breast and stalked ashore, apparently unimpeded by dragging skirts, sucking waves and pebbles rolling beneath her feet, still less by any bodily distress. No power on earth, Julitta thought confusedly, would dare impede her.

"Your latest woman?" Red Adam asked Baldwin Dogsmeat, respect in his voice.

"My wife." Baldwin corrected him with pride he had right to feel, and floundered to meet her.

She was taller than her stocky husband by three fingers' width, her vigorous flesh laid over broad bones. Her hair was that indeterminate brown to which fairness is apt to decline, her skin was weathered to the semblance of leather and lined about eyes and mouth, and if she had not passed forty years, at least thirty-five of hard living lay behind her. But her eyes, gray under level brows, lighted her face, and the sharply-defined cheekbones and jaw gave it a distinction more memorable than beauty.

Julitta stepped forward impulsively, looking from her to the drooping child. "You're cold and wet and weary. Come up to the castle and remedy all."

"You're gracious, lady." She spoke as to an equal, and her voice proved her gently bred.

Her low-born husband jumped in feet-first where Red Adam had not permitted him to set a toe. "My lady, my wife Adela."

96

"Julitta," Red Adam interposed smoothly, "we'd do well to ride ahead and make ready for our guests. Hot water, dry clothing and food are their needs."

Julitta looked at the little boy's shadowed face and closed eyes as he lay against his mother's breast. "Let me take him." she said, holding out her arms.

The woman held him closer and shook her head. "I thank you, but he'll go to no stranger."

The mercenary set his arm about her shoulders. "You're gracious, my lady, We'll follow as soon as our gear's ashore, and thank you."

Red Adam nodded, took Julitta's arm and turned her towards the horses, which half a dozen fisherlads were competing to hold. He checked to smile at the sea captain. "Grant me your company at dinner this day, Master Erling," he invited, and it was a command rather than a request.

"At your service, Lord Adam," he accepted, smiling drily. "With news from Flanders—and Scotland."

"Like as the hart desireth the waterbrooks," Red Adam declared, "so longeth my soul after news—from Flanders, Scotland, Leicester or anywhere. Keep it for me, friend." They regarded each other with perfect understanding.

They picked their way slowly along the foreshore, avoiding puddles, garbage and foraging pigs and dogs, while the fisherfolk converged on the stranger to compensate themselves for lost wreck-pickings by a little more or less honest trafficking. Julitta, bitterly contemplating Baldwin Dogsmeat's betrayal, waited for her husband to denounce her, and then supposed drearily that he was magnanimous to wait until no listeners were in earshot. He maintained his silence even when they had passed the last hovel, until she ranged belligerently alongside him.

His face lighted with amusement. "I've been most shamelessly deceived in you," he reproached her.

"You know now I am no convent-bred innocent," she burst out in defiance.

"I'd already found cause to suspect it."

"Cause? she repeated, disconcerted. "What cause?"

He grinned. "For one, it's an odd convent would teach you to carry a dagger inside your sleeve, where you've kept mine since you won it. I've one with a smaller haft you'll find handier. For another, your drastic way with Reynald."

"Then — then you don't *mind*?" she whispered incredulously.

"Why should it matter? It's no shame that you accompanied your father."

"In castle and camp and army's tail—among routiers and ribalds and whores—and it doesn't *matter*?"

"I respect you the more, lass. And I'm glad to be enlightened on a puzzle that had me wondering; how you knew precisely at which word to silence Reynald."

Julitta felt her face burn. His mingling of jest and earnest was beyond all her experience of men. "Yes, I'd heard it before," she admitted dourly.

They had reached the newer part of Arnisby that lay by the bridge. That structure, built before King Henry's accession by Lord Maurice's predecessor in a fit of exasperation at the perilous fords it had supplanted, had gathered to its head a growing settlement. The coastal road had diverged to use it. Country folk came to barter their produce for fish and salt. A colony of seven weavers plied a thriving craft, absorbing a fair proportion of the local woolclip and the output of every distaff for five miles about. Fulling, shearing and dyeing engaged another three households. Two smiths, a carpenter, a wainwright and a baker found trade enough to occupy them. To the opposite shore, on the narrow level beyond the bridge, a tanner's noisome premises and limepits had been consigned. A carrier with an increasing string of packhorses made the village his headquarters, driving his regular rounds of the hill hamlets, York and the Pennine dales beyond on a traffic whose staples were salt, stockfish and wool. A hospice and tavern accommodated transients and residents, as after their different fashion did the brace of enterprising wenches who shared a nearby hovel. One of them, taking the air at her door, waved an impudent greeting to Red Adam as he passed.

"Should do brisk business with old Dogsmeat's routiers this night and I'd best double the curfew patrol."

"Why that name?"

"It's from the siege of Chastelbrûlé in Toulouse. Lord Berengar had a pack of hounds he cherished and fed as his own children. When it came to quarter-rations Baldwin rashly proposed dining on dog, and Berengar swore that before he'd slay his hounds to feed a mercenary he'd slay the mercenary to feed his hounds."

She chuckled involuntarily. "A proper appreciation of values!"

He grinned. "If you weren't accustomed to such animals, I'd warn you to keep your distance from him and his whore."

"She *is* a whore?"

"I'd not knowingly slander her, but certainly the child's not his; when I encountered him, a year last spring, he had another woman to warm his bed." They passed a group of gossiping housewives coming from the well with buckets, greeted them and clattered on to the bridge. "It's my guess — and no more than a guess, from tavern and campfire talk — that she's Adeliza Dagger-hand."

"She's gently bred."

"And there's many a gently-bred strumpet in an army's tail, as we both know."

"My mother for one," she agreed savagely.

Surprisingly, his face burned. "Julitta, I'd no intention —Devil fry my reckless tongue—"

"It's true. She's such a one as Adeliza Dagger-hand, if she's still living—I pray she's not."

"Yes, death's an easier grief than being abandoned."

"Oh, she never cared for me. My brother was all her life. He was two years older than I, always ailing. I suppose the life was too hard for him, and there were two younger boys who died. But I was hardy as a young goat, and my father preferred me and despised Henry for a cossetted weakling. And they quarreled! Holy Mother, I don't remember any peace between them." Once started, she could not check herself, and not until later marveled that she had betrayed to

Red Adam all that she had hidden and brooded over so many years. "Never any peace, never comfort or love; nothing but hate, and Henry and I between them, and no love there either. God rest him; I suppose it was sickliness made him spiteful.

"One of my father's men gave me a rabbit, a pet rabbit warm and soft to hold, and Henry wanted it. When I refused him he tore it from me and threw it to the dogs. My father beat him, and my mother was furious; she reckoned it was his right, and a sister's duty to give up whatever he chose to demand. And within three days he sickened, and was dead before the week was out. My mother blamed us. She had borne with my father only for Henry's sake; when he died she would stay no longer. We never heard of her again, never knew whether she were alive or dead — and — and — the fear's always in me — any worn-out whore starving in the gutter might be my mother."

"Do you remember her, Julitta?"

"It's eleven years and more, and I was a child. Now and again there's a memory. She was fair, I think, and tall, with a high color and a scalding tongue that put men in awe of her. But remember her—no."

"How did you come to the nunnery?"

"My father could not dower me, and his fortunes fared worse as he grew older." She could not recount the morose temper, the self-pity, the drunken bouts and the cheap strumpets that ousted him from every employment he obtained and ruined him. "I was a burden that grew heavier, and he feared for me. You know what happens in the end to any girl in an army's tail. So he brought me back to England, to his brother, but they'd quarreled over his marrying my mother and he'd have none of me. But the old Abbess was of my mother's kinfolk, and she took me in. My father went back to France and died the next year. I remained near four years, until the Abbess died too."

"And the she-weasel cast you upon your uncle's charity," he finished. They topped the rise beyond the bridge, and stirred the horses into a canter across the level ground. The

100

watchman's horn blared, and as they crossed the drawbridge four men of the guard scrambled into station two by two at the gate and brought up their spears in slovenly salute.

Scarcely were they out of the saddle when they were surrounded by a vociferous crowd, and a dozen voices clamored at their lord in accusation and counterattack. Red Adam took one step forward and slashed the back of his hand across the nearest and loudest mouth. The noisy one staggered back into his supporters, the throng fell silent, and he glanced about him with the white wrath Julitta had seen before.

"Hell's Teeth, am I to be beset in this unseemly fashion as soon as I set foot in my own bailey?"

The fellow he had smitten, a greasy lout with a straw-hued thatch, wiped blood from a split lip and glared at Odo, aflame with righteous wrath, while the skirmishers behind tried to dissolve into the pool of spectators. A curt "Stand!" halted them, a gesture brought the crowd to order, and the bailey, its ruffled mud glinting under the sun, was suddenly a court of justice, and the lanky lad an austere judge. Julitta attended alertly.

Odo, inquisitively looking into the kitchen, had surprised a scullion in the very act of making water into the cooking-fire, to the peril of meats on spit and in pot, and had incontinently tried to kick his backside through his teeth. To this chastisement the lout in office, the head cook, took exception with a meat cleaver. Odo had rammed him in the belly with a bread peel, and partisans and idlers had fallen on in a joyful scrimmage.

Under Red Adam's cold stare the cook made no attempt to defend the indefensible, though Julitta privately reckoned that any nasty malpractice might be expected in a kitchen of his. He took his stand on the principle of lawful authority; it was for him alone to discipline any scullion under his rule, not some prying hound who had no business to set his foot over the kitchen threshold. "And him seeking what he could thieve most like! He'd no right!"

"You stand on your rights, do you?"

"He'd no call to put his nose inside my kitchen—m' lord."

"If you've rights, you've duties, and tolerating such filthiness isn't among them. Hell's Teeth, is my table to be served with food so sauced? Stand out, the swine who did it."

A mat-headed oaf was thrust forth by his fellows and scowled about, shifting from one bare foot to the other and absently scratching himself. A rank stink heralded him, and Red Adam took one sniff.

"Since filth's your nature you may go to it. Set him forking dung from the stables and cleaning the kennels; there's need enough, with good horses risking hoof-rot fetlock deep in dung." The redhaired groom hurriedly retreated from the front rank of the witnesses. "You'll not enter the kitchen again. Out of my sight!" He swung on the head cook. "You've yowled about lawful authority. If you'd keep it, set your kitchen in decent order and discipline your scullions — yes, and scour them clean also! Or there's a dung fork for *your* hands!"

The man departed with what dignity was left him. Red Adam turned to Odo and removed the smirk from his face. "As for you, the next time righteous wrath assails you, restrain yourself from brawling and bring it to me." He regarded the spectators distastefully and demanded, "Is it Christmas Day that you all keep holiday?"

An empty bailey presented itself. He tucked Julitta's hand under his arm and made for the keep. "The marvel is we're not all poisoned."

"Master," Odo said plaintively, "you could take my head—"

"What use have I for it, unless we run out of mangonel missiles in a siege?" Red Adam demanded, with the exasperated affection he kept for his tame bear. "It's what's inside it I wish you'd stir up."

"But you'd never have let pass such mucky doings."

"I'd most likely have booted him through the rafters," admitted his lord. He looked down into Julitta's interested face, and grinned most unjudicially. "Lord, I'd have given a month's rents to see the set-to! A bread peel this time! He once routed a tavernful of roisterers with a broom, but

102

I was under all their feet and missed the best of it." She chuckled, and he sighed. "And now I must find time to reform this den of a kitchen, if that lout's not to make middens of our bellies."

"No, my lord," she declared. "Your lady orders your household."

He looked doubtfully at her. "That's truly your wish? Constance is an idle slut, but I'd not be a tyrant to you, Julitta, and I feared to lay so heavy a burden on you, young and untried."

"It's every woman's desire to govern her own establishment," Julitta corrected him, her heart leaping, "and by Our Blessed Lady, here's need beyond words."

"Best borrow Odo and a broom. And now we must stir ourselves to provide for our guests before they are through the gate."

7

The company, to Julitta's merciless eye, wore the aspect of a flock of hens in a rainstorm; even with due allowance for seasickness and exhaustion, whoever hired them would find these third-rate cutthroats a dear bargain. Baldwin's acquisitive gaze flicked over the hall, lingered briefly on the paltry display of plate on the sidetable, and surveyed his host and hostess jauntily as the formal greetings were exchanged.

"I've to felicitate you on your bridal, I hear," he commented, his leer proclaiming he had been regaled with the scandal. "A triumph of virtue, eh, Adam?"

"I might retaliate in the same terms, but you are my guest. Sweyn!" The garrison's senior sergeant stepped forward. "Take these fellows, find them dry clothes and fill them with ale. Odo will see to your comfort, Baldwin. Mistress Adela, the women will take you to the bower." He caught the wondering stare of the little boy, an elf of three or four with his mother's eyes, and smiled at him. "Hey, my bold sailor! Hot milk and a warm bed for you, and when you wake, will it please you to inspect my castle?" He held out his hand, but the child gazed without comprehension and made no answer.

105

"He does not understand you," his mother said flatly. "He is deaf and dumb."

Shock held them all rigid for a moment. "That is great grief," Red Adam said gently. She looked not at him but at Julitta, who murmured whatever confused words of sympathy came to her and led the procession to the bower. Water steamed and clothes were laid out. An officious girl tried to take the child, and he clung to his mother in panic, the terror in his eyes stabbing to Julitta's vitals. He must be paralyzed with fear, she reflected, after the storm-driven voyage and the abrupt entry into this strange place.

"Let be!" Adela ordered sharply. "So many strangers frighten him." Over the draggled head buried against her breast her face turned to Julitta in command rather than appeal, and the girl nodded.

"Bring that empty cradle and lay bedding in it," she ordered. "Gertrude, fetch soap and towels. Eadgyth, Arlette, wait to take these wet clothes to the laundry. I fear they are beyond saving, Mistress Adela—"

"That's a slight matter," the woman replied, deftly peeling the garments from her son's body, "since most of this past week I've reckoned our lives in that case." She popped him into the large bowl of water and set about him with soap and washclout.

"Have you all you require?"

"You've been most competently gracious," she said, glancing up with a grin that had little mirth in it, "and even Red Adam must deplore his wife's attendance on a routier's whore and her bastard, my lady."

Julitta caught her breath. "You are none the less our guest," she declared. She had stayed to supervise the women because Constance had ostentatiously withdrawn the hem of her garments from contact with a camp strumpet, however improbably she might claim to be a wife, and the wenches followed her lead as though she were still mistress.

"On charitable sufferance." She lifted the child from the bowl. Julitta's flush scorched up face and neck. The girl Gertrude drew back as from a leper, and she turned ferociously on her.

106

"Hand those towels! Don't dare pretend to be dainty when all here know you for a trollop yourself!" She added coldly to Adela, "I oversee the service because otherwise it would disgrace a bawdyhouse, and I'll have some decorum in my household."

Adela hoisted her child to her knee and swaddled him in a towel. She grinned again. She had magnificent teeth. "If you set about it so forcefully, Lady Julitta, it will be decorous as a nunnery. And now, with your leave, we'll dispense with your trollops and I'll cope for myself." She carried the child, already asleep, to the cradle and laid him down. As she covered him Julitta saw the tenderness in her gaze and forgave her high-handed dealing with Brentborough hospitality. A jerk of her head dismissed the servants to impart their toothsome scandal to the rest of the household, and the two looked at each other across the cradle. In the far corner Hodierne sewed silently, her own cradle creaking faintly under her foot's rhythmic pressure.

"We will meet again at dinner, if you are then sufficiently rested," Julitta said, and withdrew.

On the stair she admonished her unruly speculations and fixed her mind on her duties. In the hall she found Lady Constance surrounded by serving women all gabbling together, and was pleasurably surprised that they fell silent at sight of her and made motions of dispersal.

"Lady Constance, it is more than time that I inspected the household," she announced formally.

"It shall be my privilege to conduct you, my lady," the fair woman answered, mounted the dais and held back the tattered hanging that covered the door to the privy stair. Julitta clattered through the keys at her girdle, but before she could discover the right one, the door was swinging open for her without a creak. It had not been locked.

Her mouth tightened, but she said nothing. That was a grave breach of housekeeping, an incitement to pilfering, and under some circumstances an imperiling of the whole castle, and Constance knew it as well as she did and was blandly awaiting her disapproval. She motioned to the woman to lead the way, conscious of a strong reluctance to have her at her back on a dark stairway. She hesitated, looking oddly at Julitta, and then started down. Julitta circled after her, two floors down the dim spiral to the undercroft's odorous gloom, with only the scuffle of their shoes and the whisper of their gowns to sound in the stairwell, until a squeak and a giggle above told that at least two of the girls had chosen to follow.

At the stair-foot a lantern hung on a bracket, its feeble glimmer showing a bunch of rush-dips and half a dozen unlit torches handy on a ledge. Constance opened the lantern, kindled a dip and then a torch, and beckoned Eadgyth to light the way.

Squat pillars supported the low ceiling. Barrels, bales and bundles were stacked between them and against the walls, leaving narrow alleys for their passage. Squeaks and scuttering, a glint of tiny eyes in the torchlight, a whisk of tails, betrayed rats. The well-housing, carried up to the floor above, loomed like a greater column. A bundle of arrows had broken, scattering shafts across the path. She stooped to gather them together, and noted that they had been lying for some time, for most were damaged by treading feet. The cool dry air was heavy with commingled scents. Predominant was the pungency of wool in grease, warring with the yeasty fragrance of ale, the sharper odor of wine, and the aromas of hides, cheese, tallow and honey, but her nose also detected undertones of mice, musty meal, weevily grain and ill-cured meat that cried alarm to her mind. Matters went badly with the major stores that were held from one year's end to the next.

"We must have the rat-catcher down here with his ferrets," was all she said, as they turned between two tiers of barrels and heard the vermin scurry.

"He shall be commanded for tomorrow, my lady," Constance agreed.

Julitta was noting where and how everything was disposed so that another day she could dispense with guidance. The arrangements were intelligent, the food and drink and stores in constant demand nearest the stairs, but the slovenliness and neglect that pervaded Brentborough had prevailed over the original order. For two or three years no one had troubled over the household, and it was as though a decent housewife had suddenly degenerated into a slattern. Still she said nothing to the woman responsible, but gravely inspected the smith's stack of bar-iron and a heap of rusty horseshoes in the furthest corner, and returned to the stairs. She halted at the rank of wine-casks to sound them, moved by a suspicion that proved accurate. Only two remained untapped. A smile was on her mouth as she signed to Eadgyth to extinguish the torch. The end of Reynald de Carsey's wine-swilling was speedily overtaking him.

The still-room, in one of the wall-chambers off the hall gallery, was dusty and forlorn, its locked wall-cupboards all but empty of the spices, sugar, dried fruits and almonds, the preserves and syrups, the drugs and purges and remedies that should have ranked there. "Is no one in the household skilled in physic, Lady Constance?" she inquired.

"No one, since Sir Brien's wife died last winter, my lady."

So they would go into the winter with little to help or comfort the sick; it was already too late in the year for Julitta to procure most of the herbs and simples needed. Still she was silent, which should have been a warning to the seneschal's wife. Instead it misled her into contempt.

Julitta was hardly surprised to find few sick in the hovel in the bailey that served as hospital; a groom with a broken leg, a child with fever and a skin rash, and an elderly man wheezing and coughing in a huddle of foul straw and blankets. The girl in charge was willing but ignorant, set to that distasteful duty because she was unfit for other labor. One look at her in a fair light told Julitta that she was far gone in a decline, though she protested desperately that she had naught but a cough and all men knew that a summer cold was hardest to be rid of. She would scarcely last the winter, and Julitta was inwardly furious that the medicines which might have eased her would not be available. Those sick who could drag themselves about their affairs were, she learned, mostly afflicted with fluxes and bellyaches, a sure indictment of water supplies or kitchen practice.

The dairy was a slut's rancid domain. The brewhouse was

in reasonable order, but that did not surprise her; idleness and ale-swilling had demoralized Brentborough, and a strict limitation of brewing and consumption must be one of her first reforms. The bakery too was not ill-run, though the baker complained of insufficient firing for his ovens. The laundry was a dusty chaos, no drop of water in it and the fire a scatter of cold ashes. Julitta's wrath mounted. Whatever deficiencies were uncovered, Constance remained shameless.

The garden under the northern wall's shelter was well-tended, its grass scythed, fruit trees and bushes staked and trained, beds weeded, hives throbbing with well-doing. The gardener was soon expounding plans for improvement to match Julitta's.

"And we must have an ample planting of medicinal herbs."

"Aye, m' lady. And if so be as you'd come by seeds or cuttings in southern parts, I'd try 'em in sheltered corners."

"Lady Julitta will have more important considerations on her journeyings, Wilfric," Constance chided his presumption.

"But will find time for lesser matters none the less," Julitta finished, as he stammered apologies. "And you must have a stout lad to help dig." He escorted her to the gate, snatching a fistful of marigolds as they went and twisting them into a chaplet which he presented on one knee.

Embarrassed and delighted by the pretty compliment that no man had ever paid her before, she settled the flowers on her head and smiled at Wilfric with a silly sparkle of tears in her eyes. One person in this inimical household was her supporter. It heartened her as she turned towards the kitchen, wearing the marigolds as triumphantly as a tourney queen her crown.

In the bailey Red Adam was putting his destrier through his paces, cursing the redhaired groom for some sin of omission, and supervising the endeavors of Sir Brien and Sir Giles to turn as unpromising an assemblage of herring-gutted, sheep-witted, duck-footed, cow-fisted mothers' lapses as ever shambled out of a guardroom into a troop a lord might bear to have behind him. At sight of her he clouted the groom, raised an arm in greeting, and sent his chestnut stallion thundering down on the spearmen muddling through their drill. His scathing denunciation followed her. She was not the only person in Brentborough attempting to remedy the neglect of years.

Julitta had left the kitchen until last so that the head cook should have no excuse to deem himself persecuted; he had had three hours' warning to amend his domain's state. A tightening in her entrails stiffened her as she approached the flimsy wooden shed.

Stench and uproar smacked her to a standstill on its threshold, and she peered into a very lifelike semblance of Hell. The acrid stink of burning flesh billowed about her, while shrieks of torment and yells of brutal mirth assaulted her ears. Then her eyes adjusted themselves to the gloom; a roast was scorching on a halted spit while the cook belabored the spit-boy's hinder end with his huge wooden spoon and his acolytes applauded. The lad, head down between the cook's legs, suddenly twisted his head and sank his teeth behind the man's knee. Squalling sharply, he jerked away. The boy wrenched free and bolted, swerved round Julitta and sheltered behind her skirts.

The cook almost rammed her before he realized who stood in his way, and lowered his avenging spoon. He shifted from foot to foot, truculently scowling, while the smoke of burning mutton swirled nauseously about them.

"While you gawp the roast burns!" Julitta reminded him, and he bellowed at an assistant. The spit turned, and when suffocation no longer menaced her she stepped inside.

Nothing in her experience matched the kitchen's state, and she had witnessed what passed for cookery in an army's tail and had entered a routiers' den immediately behind its captors. The fires glared on filthy half-naked louts; on tables and chopping blocks black with blood and grease; on unscoured utensils, and on a floor that was a welter of meal, fat, blood, spittle and dung. An acrid reek proclaimed that Odo's culprit had but conformed to custom, and now that the burned roast's stink had dissipated some of its pungency, a heavier stench assailed her.

The cook blocked her passage. She recalled his name. "Stand aside, Godric. I will inspect this midden."

He failed to budge. "There's not time!" His bruised lips did not altogether account for his thickened utterance, but a gust of ale-laden breath explained it when next he opened his mouth. "There's nobbut an hour to dinner, and all to ready—m' lady."

"Indeed it would be wiser to return later, since we entertain guests," said Constance.

Julitta ignored her. "Out of my way and to work!" she snapped, and Godric recoiled from her venom. Lifting her skirts clear of the floor, she marched past him, and Red Adam's oath exploded from her. "Hell's Teeth! You'll cleanse this den before you cook another meal in it!"

"Cooking's allus mucky work," Godric argued, and appealed over her head to her predecessor. "Lady Constance, you'll bear me out. There's no keeping a kitchen clean."

"True, I know. Godric works well. A certain liberty—"

"*Liberty!*"

"Nay now, m' lady, there's nowt amiss wi' t' dinner. Lord Maurice never interfered—"

"Nor would Lord Adam neither!" The girl Thyra pushed belligerently out of the shadows to stand beside the cook. "He'd not come finding fault wi' t' dinner still on t' spit—"

Beyond noting that the two had plainly dipped from one barrel, Julitta paid her no heed, but thrust between her and the table. She had traced the worst stink to its origin, a heap of heads, hooves and entrails in a corner, humming with blowflies and aquiver with maggots.

"Holy Mother, I wonder the whole household's not dead of the flux!"

"Nobbut the killings from Saturday, m' lady," Godric growled.

"That foul offal should have been thrown to the dogs and swine three days ago."

"We've been that pressed—"

112

"Clear it! Though the only way to purify this lair would be to burn it down."

"I doubt Lord Adam granted you authority for such drastic measures, my lady," Constance declared sweetly.

That was incitement enough for Godric. "I'll take orders from none but m' lord hisself," he asserted, and the girl behind him sniggered.

Julitta did not deign to dispute with him. "Mend your manners and set this den to rights," she commanded, turning to the door. Encountering the girl's smirk, she checked. "If you loiter here, stay to do kitchen labor!"

"You'll not let me visit wi' me own brother—m' lady?"

Julitta glanced from her to Godric, who grinned and nodded.

"Aye, he's me brother, own uncle to Lord Adam's son!" She laid her hands on her belly, so great for one but seven months gone that Julitta wondered whether she carried twins. "And m' lord for sure won't have his son born in t' kitchen, m' lady!"

"Kennel where you choose, but outside my bower!" Julitta blazed, and stalked from the kitchen in white fury. The girls flinched away, but Constance billowed serenely after her. Beyond earshot of the kitchen Julitta whirled.

"Countermanding my orders was an insolence you'll rue!"

She smiled in purest malice. "Go whine to Lord Adam, my lady, but he was regretting his charity before he learned he'd wedded a whore's daughter bred up in an army's tail."

Comprehension came. The whole household, knowing that she had quarreled with Red Adam last night, had instantly concluded that, though he had publicly condoned her assault on Reynald de Carsey, in private he had upheld his friend, and therefore her status was negligible and her authority safe to flout. The realization chilled her rage but did not extinguish it.

"I am Lord Adam's wife and mistress here, and you'd best acknowledge it."

Constance's face, its beauty faintly blurred in the merci-

113

less daylight, convulsed with despair and malevolence. "Acknowledge you—*you* to supplant me! A surly wench wedded in penance, and not grace enough to be thankful or to ask advice! And you've nothing—not a penny dower, no beauty, no birth, no breeding! And you stand and bid me—Mother of God, where is justice?"

"Lady Constance, calm yourself!"

"Calm—when I see—Mary Mother, I had beauty and dower and birth and love, and you *order*—you, raw from the convent! What do you know of life and how it cheats you? Yes, beauty cheats you, and love cheats you, and all life, and at the last death itself cheats you! And now my last right is snatched from me by a brat without even courtesy to take counsel—"

"One look about Brentborough proclaims its worth," Julitta replied bleakly as the woman halted in mid-spate, consternation checking the spite and fury. She had offended beyond pardon, and she knew it. Yet in that moment the untouched girl understood her bitterness, even pitied her thwarted years, though her malice and selfishness forfeited sympathy. Lovely women expected life to grant them more than womankind's common fortune, and age's onset was their tragedy.

Under her considering gaze Constance turned crimson, then white, and then swung about and almost ran for the keep steps, her kerchief fluttering agitation and her buttocks jolting with the first gracelessness Julitta had seen in her. A few more years, and fat would swallow her beauty. She was still watching the blue back retreating when the horn blared from the gate to announce visitors.

Red Adam came loping across the grass, his hair on end, mud spattering his tunic and smeared across one cheek. She moved to meet him beyond earshot of the whispering girls, still frowning.

"Hey, never look so forbidding, sweet! You remind me of a schoolmaster waiting with the birch, and it doesn't match the pretty flowers."

She flushed and snatched at the forgotten garland, but

his hand caught hers and rescued it. He set it straight on her head. "My lord, it is not fitting!" she protested.

"Fitting? You're yet my bride, and rightly crowned with flowers." He touched the petals delicately, and smiled down at her. "Nothing could become you more."

"But—"

He gripped her hand and turned her towards the gate. "I am rightly shamed," he said plaintively, "when I reckon up all the garlands I've twined for idle dalliance, and leave it to a gardener to adorn my own lady." She laughed outright, and he pulled her closer. "Has no one ever told you that you're a very pretty girl when you smile, Julitta? Come and smile on our guests with me."

8

Red Adam, totally disregarding any opinions but his own, set Erling Thorvard's son at his right hand. Reynald, displaced by a mere merchant, glowered into trencher and winecup. Baldwin Dogsmeat, a mercenary captain of dubious origin and no knight, conceded in courtesy the lowest place at the high table, comported himself with an assurance that set his betters' digestions at war with their meat. His wife's deportment testified to gentle breeding, however far she had fallen from it.

During the first course the conversation naturally ran on the hazards of voyaging, most folk contributing some gruesome recollection. The servants were going round with ewers, basins and towels for washing hands when Baldwin concluded his preference for being buried in one piece in a Christian churchyard rather than in the maws of a legion of fishes.

"Instead of a concourse of worms?" Red Adam grinned.

"And you living on fish from these seas all through Lent! And when Death's hands were feeling at my neck, I did wonder whether seafaring came near the sin of suicide." He shook his head at the company's laughter. "I wished very earnestly I'd stayed in Flanders with the Earl of Leicester."

"He's still there?" Red Adam asked, and faces all along the board sobered to attention.

"He was when we sailed, a fortnight ago. Waiting for a south wind, and it blowing north, east and west since July."

"What sort of force has he?"

Baldwin snorted professional contempt. "A Godforsaken rabble of guttersweepings and raw recruits. Out-of-work weavers for the most part."

"And between sickness and desertion, less than half he first assembled," Erling put in.

"What do you expect, when he's paying with promises and at his wits' end to supply them?" Baldwin grunted. "What's this little bird, boy? Not pigeon? Grouse, eh? New to me, but I'll try it."

Nothing destroyed an army more surely than waiting, Julitta knew; scanty food as the countryside was eaten up; fouled earth and water disseminating disease; boredom, gambling, whoring leading to criminal acts and retaliation by an increasingly hostile populace, and the steady attrition by death and desertion. If the winds remained foul a few weeks more, Leicester's Flemish reinforcements would disintegrate about him.

"The Count of Flanders withdrew support when his brother Matthew was killed," said Erling, "and Leicester's money and credit are spent."

"So I reckoned a man of enterprise might profit by reaching England ahead of that rabble," Baldwin declared, suspending his assault on the grouse. "Master Erling thought it might be done roundabout—"

"Make out northing towards Denmark, pick up an easterly and run before it," Erling explained.

Baldwin's teeth stripped the flesh from a legbone, and he stabbed it emphatically at Erling as he chewed. "True enough," he pronounced through the grouse, "but I didn't bargain for going round by Scotland, near drowned and battered silly, not to mention puking my guts out all the way. Oh yes, we're in England. A hundred miles and more too far north, and the King's Justiciar in the way."

118

Red Adam nodded, and looked from his own grouse to Erling. "So you made landfall in Scotland?"

"North side of Forth mouth, and across to Leith." A grim smile stirred his whiskers. "I've fine stuffs I thought to trade in Edinburgh, but the King and his knights are on the border."

A similar smile twitched Red Adam's lips. "Maybe across it by now."

"From the talk of Leith, likely enough."

Baldwin licked his lips like a fox scouting the poultry run. "It might advantage any lord in these doubtful times to increase his forces, Lord Adam. Would you consider hiring my company?"

"I couldn't afford you," Red Adam said frankly. Baldwin's face hardened in unbelief. "I've just paid a heavy relief, and the honor impoverished by near twenty years' neglect. Your best course, Baldwin, is to return to Flanders—and put no faith in Leicester's promises."

"Pitch myself back upon the North Sea when I've barely set foot on solid ground?" yelped Baldwin. "My belly heaves at thought of it."

"If I could afford to pay you, I couldn't afford to hire you, Baldwin. Mercenaries, and those who employ them, have been well hated in England by King and people since the days of King Stephen. You're neck-deep in murky water. Get out while you can."

"Go back like a whipped dog to kennel? No, by God's Head! Your neighbors may be less delicately minded—" His wife touched his elbow, and he subsided before uttering unpardonable offence and plied his knife upon the grouse's ruins. A moment later Julitta saw him lay it down to give his wife's hand a reassuring squeeze.

Erling said calmly in the embarrassed hush, "I suppose, Lord Adam, that you've not sold your woolclip this year?"

"The merchants have not ventured north this season, Master Erling."

"And in Flanders the looms stand idle, and the price of wool higher than I've known it. Would it ease your problems if I bore it there and drove the bargain?"

119

"I'd be your debtor. Your fee, Master Erling?"

"One-fourth of the price."

"Agreed. You're modest."

"Crafty, Lord Adam. I hope for a long and profitable association between us."

Reynald emerged abruptly from his cup. "God's Head, thash insult, Adam. Unknightly—buy and shell."

"This isn't the tourney circuit. Be quiet."

"You've another asset that could profit you in the future, Lord Adam. You've the only fair harbor between Humber and Tees, and a growing town. If you built a pier and wharf you'd attract coasting trade and foreign merchants, and gain by harbor dues and more commerce. A market also—"

"Turn huckster?" Reynald sneered. "True knight takesh profit at sword'sh point."

"I have often wondered," Erling stated equably, "why the knightly sort should reckon it more honorable to cut a neighbor's throat and steal his goods, rather than buy and sell to their mutual benefit."

Most of his knightly hearers choked on their food. Reynald's fogged intelligence visibly groped for comprehension. By the time he lurched up, mouthing outrage, Red Adam had signaled, and Odo and Sir Brien took him by either arm. Odo set his cup brimming with unmixed Gascony, Sir Brien put it to his lips, and tilted it while he gulped. Even his head was not proof against such a draught; he subsided on to his stool and laid his brow on the table.

"I apologize for him, Master Erling," Red Adam said curtly.

"If you share his sentiments, consider, Lord Adam. It's not the knightly kind produce a country's wealth. It's the men who grow and the men who make, and those who buy and sell."

"Oh, I reckon I'll turn huckster. I stand in need of profit. Your advice may not be entirely disinterested, but it makes sense."

"That is why."

They grinned at each other. The second course was

removed, and the servants went round again with water and towels.

"If you've fine cloth for sale we'll be pleased to view it," Red Adam said. "I don't doubt, my lady, that we need it?"

A little startled at being consulted, Julitta summoned her wits. "Greatly, my lord, since the New Year liveries are all to make. The local weave will suffice for the servants, but for the knights we must have better."

"That's for you to order."

"Also we have but two untapped wine-barrels between Sir Reynald and sobriety."

"Can you remedy that, Master Erling?"

"Not this side of Flanders, Lord Adam. Passengers this trip. I'll consult with your lady for the next."

"Order it between you." He formally offered Julitta the cup for the last drink, and when she returned it, deliberately set his lips to the place hers had touched and drank to her. Then, while men and women stared and nudged, he gave the empty cup to Odo and signaled for the cloth to be withdrawn. He leaned back, apparently oblivious of surmising faces and his wife's flush. "Speaking of orders puts me in mind, my lady. How did your foray into the kitchen go?"

"It will go better next time, my lord, if you resolve one small difficulty," Julitta said, her cheeks cooling as she realized that his lover's gesture made amends for last night's quarrel.

"Yes?"

"Am I truly Lady of Brentborough, or in tutelage to your seneschal's wife?"

"You are undisputed lady of all I possess." He stood up, and the company rose, buzzing with consternation. "Sir Brien, be pleased to give teeth to my lady's bidding."

Sir Brien came to life like a somnolent terrier at mention of rats, grinning at Constance's chagrin. Sir Bertram turned to her in bewilderment, and she murmured angrily in his ear. A diversion was provided by Reynald; hoisted to his feet by two servingmen, he vomited copiously, so that all hurriedly vacated the dais.

121

Julitta, marveling at her husband's endorsement of her authority, stalked towards the kitchen, and behind her Brien hummed a little tune between his teeth. Warning had of course flown before them, but time for acting on it had been lacking. Godric was sitting on a chopping-block, a leather mug in one hand and his spoon of office in the other, brandishing both in vague menace and mumbling curses, while his scullions scrambled about beyond reach, achieving such chaos that Julitta knew just how his underlings liked him. He surged up like a hog from its wallow, glared at his lady, belched, muttered indistinguishably and collapsed back on to the block with a thump that made his teeth clack.

Brien jerked a thumb. Two spearmen dispossessed him of mug and spoon, wrenched his arms behind him and heaved him up bellowing. The thumb jerked again. They propelled him through the doorway, kicking his hinder end when he resisted, and across the bailey to the stocks. His sister, equally drunk, reeled after them, screeching and beating ineffectively at the men's backs until the other women hustled her inside the keep. Julitta turned to purging the kitchen, while its tyrant, sobered by a pailful of water, his backside in a puddle, sat festooned with the riper entrails in token of his offence and pelted by urchins with mud and dung.

Half the wooden utensils were pitched incontinently into the fire. The rest were sand-scoured and scalded, metal burnished, the walls swept down. Scullions shoveled up the nauseating offal into baskets and bore it to the smouldering refuse-pit behind the stables. As they neared the bottom of the pile one fellow, swinging his basket awkwardly, spilled a mess of fowls' heads, guts and fat and kicked it into the fire. Flame spat and smoke gushed. Brien started forward swearing, and the man blundered at the fire, flapping so that the smoke swirled about them. By the time Julitta had cleared her eyes and throat the fellow was shambling out bleating abjectly, and in the furthest corner another was unostentatiously hanging a carcass of mutton to a hook in the rafter.

Julitta exchanged pregnant looks with Brien. Both knew

that the mutton had been concealed under the offal, but its removal had been so contrived that accusation would be futile. The knight in fact had his lips parted to make one, but her tiny headshake checked him. She sent men scuttling for water, for scouring sand and rushes, for rakes and spades to scrape the floor, while her wits marshaled facts and made deductions. Kitchen workers, with the unrestricted pickings of every meal, had no need to pilfer food. Members of the household, their bellies filled twice a day at a generous table, would have small use for a whole mutton carcass that no single family could eat. It had been hidden for discreet removal from the castle, and in Arnisby was one establishment whose owner could not only dispose of stolen mutton but also pay in coined silver for it. By the furtive glances all about her, every servant knew of the peculation.

Odo's bulk darkened the doorway. He bowed clumsily. "May it please you, m' lady, Lord Adam bade me tell you the merchant Erling awaits you in the bower with his stuffs."

Red Adam waited with the merchant, conversing so seriously that they did not notice her entrance. All appearance of gaiety had been abandoned; the frown puckering his brows made of him a worried boy. Then Odo coughed, and his face lighted as though the sight of her was his fairest pleasure. He took her hand. Erling bowed, and conjured from the air a small bundle which he presented benignly.

"In token of my thanks," he rumbled in his heavily-accented French.

"You are most gracious, Master Erling," she began formally, lifted the loose cloth wrapping and gulped at her first sight of the sables of Norway; a score at least, silken, supple and shining like jet. *"Oh!* For—for *me?"*

"It's a royal gift," said Red Adam quietly.

The merchant smiled. "But for you it would be washing in the tide with all my merchandise, and like as not our bodies too." The smile broadened to a grin. "Moreover, I am reckoning your lady will need a new gown to do them honor." He gestured to the stack of canvas-swathed bales by the great bed.

123

Odo coughed again, and contorted his whiskers in a grimace, jerking an urgent thumb at his master lest his subtle intimation that he was required elsewhere be missed. Red Adam grinned, "You'll not need me," he observed, and left them to it.

Under the furthest window Avice and Hodierne stitched at Julitta's green gown, and Adela mended a small tunic. The two cradles rocked at their feet. Quietly, in consideration of their occupants, Erling and the two seamen he had brought unpacked the bales, stitched up in layers of tarred sailcloth, and spread out the cloths on the bed.

She had made her calculations, and as she had said at dinner, the coarse local weave in the natural grays and browns of the wool, or dyed with madder and bilberry and hawthorn bark, would do well enough for the scullions and grooms, and even for the waiting women. Linen also was to be had in Arnisby; one or two farmers usually sowed a little, troublesome as its preparation was, since there were craftsmen to work it at hand, but as the chief demand was for sailcloth it was usually harvested late for the strongest fibers, and the best of it was harsh stuff only fit for tablecloths and hangings.

A little apprehensively, for she had no idea how the silver stood in Red Adam's strongbox, she selected Flemish broadcloths; crimson, blue and green for the knights and ladies; heavy black, brown and gray for mantles; a little of the costly scarlet for trimmings, and then fine linen for smocks and shirts. Erling pointed out their merits, recommended this or that for each purpose, and left the choice to her; he was crafty in his trade. He measured and cut and folded, and the pile mounted.

"For Lord Adam's own use?" he asked as she checked at last, and lifted a corner of scarlet.

"Holy Mother, no!" she exclaimed, wincing from the memory of her marriage day and her husband ablaze in red. All the costliest colors, scarlet and crimson and purple, appropriate to his rank, were incompatible with his flaming head. Erling chuckled and pointed out the sky blue, much dearer than the common woad, but that reminded her of Constance. She chose instead a tawny brown and a stripe woven in two shades of green. He would need a cloak too, but she was almost at the end of Erling's resources and had to settle on a holly-leaf green with more of the tawny to line it. At least he was no peacock to complain of her choice. Erling beckoned the seamen forward to pack and restitch the diminished bales, while he lifted the last four smaller bolts to the bed and deftly whipped out the stitches.

"After business, pleasure. For your own consideration, my lady." He unwound the canvas swaddlings as tenderly as a young mother unwraps her firstborn. "This, and this, are from the workshops of Firenze in Italy, where they weave the finest wool in Christendom."

Julitta fingered them, rose and violet, marveling at the craftsmanship that spun and wove and dyed so flawlessly. She battled against temptation. The rose was not for her, but she considered the violet's combination with her sables, and how her skill might enhance it if she dared afford silk and gold for embroidery.

"This is silk from Byzantium."

It shimmered like water, the deepest blue-green of a peacock's neck, and she exclaimed and caressed it. Then Erling swept clear a space on the bed to display the last. "Silk of Damascus, my lady, to do justice to your furs." Reverently he folded back the canvas, and she could only stare.

Silk the color of a sun-flushed apricot was woven with golden yellow and flame in a pattern of formal flowers. With the black furs it would marry to a perfection a queen might envy. She had no beauty, but this would enhance her hair's bright brown and flatter her fair skin. Nothing could become her more than this loveliness, and she gazed, rapt with desire.

Of course it could not be. Silk such as this was a queen's extravagance. Even her uncle's wife, who had ruled her household near forty years, had never dared purchase aught but the cheapest cendal, and had been rated like a thief for it at that. She touched the shining surface as one relinquishing a dream that flies with starlight, and shook her head.

125

"My lady, for you it is perfection. And this once you may surely count on your lord's indulgence, new-married as you are."

She looked blankly at him; he must know that hers was not that sort of marriage. "No, Master Erling."

He folded the silks, and then gestured to the woolen cloth of Firenze. This was temptation indeed, for it lay within the limits of possibility. She remembered Red Adam's candid admission that between muddle, embezzlement and a tenant-in-chief's relief he was sorely impoverished. She looked at the cloth piled on the bed, recalled that she had two new gowns and a mantle in the making, more than she had ever had at once in all her life, and put temptation from her. "No, Master Erling."

He parted his lips to expostulate, and then took up the huge curved needle and waxed thread to stitch up the bales.

Red Adam clashed aside the curtain and strode in. He had just been very angry; he was breathing fast and his eyes sparkled dangerously. Julitta thanked the Saints that prudence had ruled her; the thought of having her purchases repudiated by a furious husband made her blench. She waited warily, her experience of masculine wrath being that the handiest scapegoat served for its venting.

"Completed your business, I see," he said, civilly enough. "What have you bought, my lady?"

Nervously she indicated the pile and began to account for each item.

"That's no matter," he interrupted. "For yourself, to do justice to your new furs?"

She stared. Erling came to her rescue. "My lady has chosen nothing for herself, Lord Adam."

"That's gracious, to let your husband have the choosing. Unpack your goods again, Master Erling." He caught her wrist in an ungentle hold to draw her out of earshot. "What's amiss? Do you detest me too hardly to accept anything from my hands?"

"No, not that," she gasped.

He glanced about, hauled her behind a mass of drawn-back

126

curtain that partitioned the bower at night, caught her shoulders and shook her so that her head snapped on her spine. "You'll not shame me or your station!" he snarled in her ear. "*Why* would you not buy?" He shook her again, and she snarled back at him.

"The cost—you said you could not afford—"

"My poor sweet girl! Forgive me. I forgot you'd known only mean men." He closed his arms about her, pulling her close; she set her hands against his chest to hold him off, and felt within his ribs his heart's thudding. Her breath quickened, her own heart thumped. "Listen, Julitta. You are my wife. You spend as you will, unquestioned. If I can't afford a mercenary company, I can yet clothe my lady. Understood?" She gulped and nodded, his face swimming in a blur of tears. He kissed her lightly on the brow, surprising her before she could duck. "Come, no tears! What took your fancy?"

She scrubbed her eyes childishly on her sleeve. "The—the violet wool, my lord," she told him in a small voice. He put his arm about her and marched her back to Erling, under the interested scrutiny of the two seamen and the women sewing in the far window, and held her to his side while the merchant laid out his stuff again.

"The violet wool, yes, but not for black furs; you're new-wedded, not widowed. What else?" He surveyed the blue silk with the knowledgeable air of a man at home in princes' courts amid their splendid ladies. "Fair indeed, but it needs ermine, not marten." But when the apricot silk blazed across the bed he caught up its end and flung it across Julitta's shoulder.

"That's perfection," he said, tossed the priceless stuff aside, gathered her under his arm again, and nodded to the merchant. "Both silks, and the violet wool, Master Erling."

Julitta squeaked like an agitated mouse. "B-but my lord—the cost—"

He grinned. "Will the woolclip cover it, Master Erling?"

"At present prices, likely enough, my lord."

"B-but all *three*—"

"My pleasure, so don't dispute it," he murmured in her

ear, and she subsided, her wits in chaos at his extravagance. It behoved her to speak her thanks, but no words would come, and neither her husband nor Erling seemed to find anything lacking in her silence. She gathered her senses at last to purchase needles, thread and silks for embroidery, Red Adam insisting on a couple of skeins of gold for the violet gown, lest any mistake it for a widow's.

"Now for the woolclip," he said briskly, as the last item joined the pile. "Coming, lady wife?"

"I—these must be—be bestowed behind locks, my lord," she excused herself, imagining Brentborough's undisciplined strumpets clawing at the cloths.

"Join us when you can." He sauntered out with Erling and the two seamen, who bore greatly diminished burdens. Hodierne left her cradle and came to help and to murmur awe over the silks. While she and Avice laid away the common stuffs, Julitta tenderly gathered up her own and bore them to the chest that had been Constance's. On her knees beside it she smoothed the apricot silk and blinked away a rush of silly tears that had a two-fold source; the irony that her unloved husband should be the first man to lavish generosity upon her, and memory of the hurt in his eyes and voice as he laid hands on her. The welts on her shoulders still smarted where his fingers had gripped, but that was no matter. Red Adam was vulnerable, not armored in villainy.

"What a surly whelp you are!" a harsh voice spoke in her ear. She leaped to confront Adela.

"What—"

"Your husband gowns you like a queen, and has no word of thanks for it. Are you soured to the core?"

Julitta was too astounded to do more than gape in bewilderment. "But—I was not—" she stammered like a chided child before the force that was in Adela's gaze.

"Don't whine that you were constrained to wed him; every maid of your station is constrained, and you could have fared a deal worse. He's kind and gay and generous. Lord of Hell, if he'd been a cross-grained brute like the husband thrust on me, you'd have reason for sour looks."

"You?" she asked involuntarily.

"Oh, I was wedded in youth. But the only free woman in this world's the whore with a dagger in her hand."

"I'd die first!"

"Easily said. It's not so bad a life if you keep a sharp blade handy." So she was Adeliza Dagger-hand, no doubt of it. "But if that's not for you, you must bear with your yoke-mate a lifetime, and by God's Death, you sulky brat, you'll fare a deal better if you show a pleasant face."

"That is between my lord and me alone."

The woman snorted. "If you've wit you'll heed me. You're luckier than most, but one man is much the same as another. You've yet to learn it, but the core of a woman's life is the sons she bears." And she glanced aside, with fierce yearning, at the cradle where her deaf-mute child slept.

Julitta's hands folded on her slight belly. "If God wills it I shall bear children—"

"Children? It's the son bears the name and carries the blood. What's a daughter but a she-thing that goes to another's house? Her sons are a woman's life, and her husband matters little enough so that he gives her them."

"I should hate to think," said Red Adam's voice, amused yet sharp edged, "that my wife valued me solely for my prowess at stud."

Adeliza Dagger-hand turned and challenged him. "Do you not desire sons, Lord Adam?"

"Very greatly, but I have observed that God disposes such matters at His will, not man's. " He uttered the pious sentiment lightly, yet Julitta recognized his sincerity.

She snorted again. "So you will not be enraged if the first brat your wife bears should be a girl?"

He smiled at Julitta. "I should name her Annora, and love her with all my heart."

"Annora?" Adela repeated, disconcerted.

"I had once a little sister who was very dear to me." He put his arm about Julitta's shoulders. "You take a gracious interest in my wife's affairs, Mistress Adela, but I assure you it is needless."

129

That courteous rebuke achieved the distinction of silencing Adela; she stared at the cool lad with jaw ajar, and then a flush mounted to her brow, her mouth snapped shut and she stalked back to the cradle. Julitta, suppressing an urge to giggle, locked the chest and inquired demurely, "You required me, my lord?"

"You have the key to the undercroft." His gaze followed the mercenary's woman with odd intensity, and a slight frown gathered his brows. "Timely returned—don't heed her effrontery, Julitta."

"I can heed nothing except your—your generosity," she began awkwardly, and he shook his head, smiling, and seized her hand.

"My pleasure. Come, Master Erling awaits us."

Out in the bailey they stood beside Erling while the bales were loaded on a cart, and the blond lad, presented as Erling's son Hakon, notched up the tally on a hazel rod and gazed on Julitta. One bale lay open for inspection, and the merchant twisted a lock of wool in his horny fingers.

"It'll fetch its price, with half the looms in Flanders idle, but it's not first quality, Lord Adam. Coarse and hairy, and your hill sheep are miscolored beasts. It dyes ill, and is only fit for peasants. It's the fine white fleeces from the south fetch the good silver in Flanders."

Red Adam frowned at the gray and brown masses bulging from the bale. "I doubt the southern breeds would thrive in our hills, Master Erling."

"Might be worth your while to try bringing in a couple of rams to tup your best ewes, Lord Adam. If they breed true for fleeces, maybe you'd have to coddle them more through the winter, but it would double, triple the value of your woolclip."

"There's rough graze without limit on the fells," Red Adam said thoughtfully, "and wild hay for the cutting. Shepherds are cheap enough too. War to wage on wolves and foxes. Yes, I'll try it."

"Moreover, there's a market in Flanders for stockfish and salt herring could profit your fishermen and you, Lord Adam."

"You're most anxious to see me profit," he remarked, grinning.

"So that I profit with you, my lord."

"It's a deal less chancy than meddling with rebellion, and we'll look to our mutual benefit."

"My ship is old, and so am I," said Erling. "I've a new one building for my lad Hakon here." He clouted his son lightly. "Dreaming of her, lad? If you've missed the tally, Lord Adam will doubtless hang us both for thieving outlanders! Aye, he can sail next spring on far ventures; my gray hairs will be better suited to small traffic and safe gains between here and Flanders." Julitta glanced up at him, reckoning his gray hairs too scanty to warrant such consideration, and his eyelid flickered in the smallest of winks. Red Adam cocked a quizzical eyebrow, and nodded to the waiting seaman to lash up the open bale. It was heaved on to the cart, and Hakon cut the last notch with a flourish, deftly split his rod from end to end, and presented the halves to Red Adam and Erling.

The cart lurched towards the gate, and they strolled behind it. Julitta made known her requirements for wine, and inquired as to her chances of procuring such drugs as opium, camphor, cardamoms, aloes and rhubarb. Red Adam put in a word for pepper and spices, and she, emboldened, suggested foreign delicacies like dried fruits, sugar and olive oil, so that by the time they reached the gate and parted with expressions of esteem, Erling could have small doubt of their association's profits.

With a word of excuse Red Adam left her and made for the stables, while she stalked zestfully back to the kitchen. As she reached its door she glanced past the corner, and observed that Godric had company in the stocks. The red-headed groom shared his discomfiture and his puddle, his feet ridiculously upturned, and the girl Thyra was leaning on the upright post, her face tear-blubbered and her hair starggling from its plaits. Red Adam's reactions to slovenliness and disobedience matched her own.

On her way up to her chamber to wash and change her

131

gown before supper, she checked on the hall landing. Adeliza Dagger-hand's voice came hard and clear through the curtain: "... break my marriage vows for a cur?"

"Marriage! God's Death!" snarled Reynald de Carsey. "You're a penny whore with a bastard whelp, and no marriage alters that."

"My price was never as cheap as a penny, and I could always afford not to lie with swine."

"God's Blood, when a gentleman condescends to favor you —"

Julitta peeped circumspectly round the curtain in time to see Adeliza spit in his face. "Lay hand on me again," she said coolly, "and I'll spill your guts across the floor." She started for the door, leaving him sleeving his eye and gobbling curses, and Julitta caught up her skirts and fled noiselessly to her own chamber, hoping that neither might know that she had witnessed the dispute.

She shed her riding dress, washed hands and face and assumed the detested scarlet, her frown quelling Avice's whines to silence. The problem of Reynald de Carsey gravely perturbed her. If no woman in the castle were to be safe from his drunken advances there would be disaster. Adeliza Dagger-hand could very efficiently protect the remnants of her virtue, but she reflected uncharitably that it was a pity she had not strewn his entrails over the rushes and removed an incubus. There was only one person she could consult, and she grimaced into the silver mirror at the thought that she would welcome an hour alone with her husband.

The thought sent her memory spinning back to the accusation that had stabbed her that afternoon, and with a queer qualm at her midriff she wondered if she did indeed appear sour and surly, if she had inherited the unlovely temper of the Montrigords that had ruined her father and made her uncle detested by all who knew him. Her resentment was righteous, the Saints knew, but the idea that folk might thereby reckon her as detestable as her uncle made her scowl into the mirror.

"I — have I displeased y-you, my lady?" whispered Avice, halting the comb.

"I was not thinking of you, silly girl."

"And — and you'll let me stay up here, m' lady, out o' th' way, and sew for you? To be safe from *him*? You — you knows I sets good stitches, m' lady, and none o' t'other wenches wants to do it."

"Mary Mother, girl, don't whine! What harm can come to you when you're attending on me?"

"So's he don't see me, m' lady, and — and lay for me —"

But Julitta too was weary of her apprehensions' ceaseless drip. "He'll not drag you from my side, so find a little courage! And don't weep into my hair!" She caught the comb from her hand and briskly completed the task, heedless of Avice's sniffles. She was beginning to share her husband's contempt for the girl, and it came to her suddenly that, though she had a deal to say about her own miseries and fears, Avice had yet to utter a word of concern for Ivar's fate.

9

When Julitta reached the hall she found Red Adam conversing with Sir Brien and Sir Giles, while Reynald sulked at his elbow. She looked at him with foreboding; his company was a particular hazard at mealtimes, when household and guests assembled. He was in truculent humor, replying to her civil greeting with a surly grunt, and as Adela and Baldwin approached the dais he growled, "A brave sight, a whore and her pimp at a lord's high table."

"Curb your tongue!" Red Adam snapped, too late.

"The lady's my wife," said Baldwin, his face deadly.

"Wife? If she wedded, it was but to give her bastard a name."

Baldwin mounted the two shallow steps. "How else should I have won her?" he demanded, with a pride that invested his squat figure with majesty. "And I'll challenge the man who misnames her to the death."

"My peace holds within my walls, and while you're both my guests you'll maintain it," Red Adam said flatly. He gestured to the avid audience to take their places, and murmured quickly in Odo's ear. The asking of God's grace, the bustle of seating and service, provided some cover for the ugly incident, but Julitta's apprehension mounted.

135

Reynald was restored to his place at his host's right hand, and divided his resentment between his one-time comrade and the mercenary pair. His appetite and temper were both impaired by his dinner-time indulgences, but not his capacity for wine, and his offensiveness grew sourer with every cupful. Red Adam, very white about the mouth, recounted tales of the tourney circuit, crumbled the edge of his trencher and scarcely swallowed a morsel. Julitta prompted and abetted him as best she could, with an angry sympathy for his mortification that should have surprised her. Twice he overrode the mumbled beginnings of some squalid reminiscence aimed at Adela's hurt, and Odo replenished Reynald's cup until at last his chin dropped on to his chest and he slumped over his trencher, soused to the eyeballs.

A faint stir and sigh told how the whole company relaxed, as though all had been holding breath. Red Adam, his story unfinished, lay back in his chair and ran a hand that was not quite steady through his hair. He looked directly at Adela, his urbane mask discarded.

"I'll apologize for him" he said.

"Have done, my lord. No blame to you."

He grinned wryly. Julitta silently shoved the winecup to his hand. Reynald subsided forward on to the table with a blubbery snore, Odo whisking the gravy-soaked trencher-bread from under his face by a bare inch. Wary murmurs of conversation strengthened as his slumber showed profound. Up in the gallery overhead the quartet of instrumentalists seized on the comparative silence to afflict them with disharmony; their new lute was even more tuneless than the one Julitta had broken over Reynald's head. Red Adam gulped a mouthful of wine, distastefully rejected the congealed mess on his trencher, glanced along the table and nodded to Odo to remove the first course.

The second went more comfortably, talk rising along the board. Julitta, recognizing duty, took hold on the first chance and steered it into discussion of horses and hunting, that never-exhausted topic. She was absurdly pleased when her husband touched her hand in thanks; his approval should

136

mean nothing to her. When the talk flagged the minstrels renewed their assault, and when the dishes were removed and the cloth withdrawn Red Adam's tolerance snapped. "Hell's Teeth, stop that caterwauling!" he shouted.

Baldwin chuckled. "I marvel that you, of all men, should have borne with them so long!"

"Yes, you've had dolorous entertainment this evening. We'll amend that. Odo, my own lute!"

All hushed as his head leaned to the lute and the strings sang to his tuning. It was seldom that a tenant-in-chief entertained his guests as a *trouvère*, especially in the north where civilization's graces barely penetrated. He turned to Julitta and spoke so that all might hear.

"My lady, I sing for you. What will please you?"

Her pulse fluttered. She knew what would best please all there, and steadied her voice. "A story, my lord."

"Being myself enchanted, I sing of enchantment."

He recited and sang a weird tale, new to her, of how the wizard Merlin, infatuated in his dotage with the witch Vivien, disclosed to her the spell there was no undoing, and was by her bound forever in a hollow oak in the forest of Broceliande. Dusk deepened in the hall, the fires sank, and the servitors spellbound on their benches never stirred to kindle lights. His voice softened almost to a whisper on the last lines.

> "Between the boughs the sunset crimsons die,
> Black bats flicker in the pallid sky,
>   The wild swans' wings beat back towards their mere,
> Through the gray twilight mousing owlets call,
> The white hart halts and lifts his antlers tall,
>   None else in the enchanted wood may hear
> Lost Merlin groaning, never to be free,
> Till Doomsday's trumpets tear the land and sea . . . . ."

A long moment's silence paid tribute to the spell he had cast himself, and then applause crashed. Someone called for light, and servants scurried with tapers. He sat half-smiling, reddening to their approval as probably he had never done

137

in other men's halls, and Julitta, knowing what was required of her, rose to make him a formal curtsey. Then, as the noise subsided, a surly voice demanded more robust entertainment.

"Here'sh dish — dismal stuff! Lesh have shojer song — chorush —"

Odo advanced with the wine-jug. Red Adam frowned, strummed at random a moment and then swung into a dance-tune. Reynald lurched up, ignoring his refilled cup.

"Shing kish a girl in Parishity — or willing wench come to me —" With some difficulty, as though the cup presented itself in duplicate, he brought it to his mouth and gulped. Wine dribbled down his chin and slopped upon the table. He slumped down, heaved his bottom more securely on to his stool and glared blearily at Julitta. "Show wha' woman for — lay 'em an' leave 'em."

"Use courtesy to my lady!"

He shook his head over the wine. "Good comrade onesh," he mourned. "Besh man empty cup or shwive wench — gone now. Turned dull-sober—turned 'gainst ol' frien'sh—grudge li'l wine — married proud wench —" Two tears coursed down his cheeks and dripped into his cup. "Ol' comrade — ol' daysh all forgot — all gone —"

"You're maudlin," Red Adam pronounced in disgust. "Drink yourself speechless and have done."

"Who comesh first — ol' comrade — new wife? An' we'll have proper shong — shojer shong —" He lunged for the lute lying across Red Adam's knees. His fingers clutched discord from the strings, and he began to bawl, "Willing wench — come to me —" Red Adam fended him off, tossed the lute to Julitta, and twisted out of his chair, striking up the fist wavering for his face just in time; drunk or sober, that insult could only be expunged with blood. Odo and Brien seized him from behind and mastered him. He heaved against them, and then the wine clubbed him senseless and he slid to the rushes.

"Take him to his bed!" Red Adam snapped, and Odo stolidly hoisted him over his shoulder. "Hell's Teeth, are we never to digest our meat in peace for him?"

138

"He drinks to forget the comrade who has forsaken him, my lord," Constance said sweetly.

He ignored that insolence, and gave the winecup into Julitta's hands. Receiving it again, he bowed to her before all there. "To my dear and honored lady!" As he had done at dinner, he set his lips to the place hers had touched and drank to her. Blood scorched to her brow, but she could yet command her body to salute him in a deep curtsey. Gravely, disregarding the hum of comment, she paced from the hall and fled to her chamber's privacy.

Her brain in turmoil, she dismissed Avice and got herself to bed. It was outside her craziest dream that any man should show her so much honor. She peered into her mirror. Her gray eyes under thick dark brows stared back; a plain girl with too wide a mouth, too sharp a chin, and hair in disarray from hasty undressing. He had wedded her because his conscience demanded it; she was not desirable. Maybe it was his conscience, remorse, even pity that had pricked him to that day's splendid extravagances, the gestures of a lover.

He came at last, barred the door, took her by the shoulders and kissed her squarely on the mouth. "Now God be praised, we're the same breed of wolves, you and I!"

She lifted a hand to rub her lips, and let it drop. "You mean —?"

He sat at her feet. "That I thank the Saints I'm not saddled with a convent-bred ninny. No, you don't need your dagger. I'll cultivate patience, since that's the virtue will best serve me."

"A useful one to start with!" she agreed waspishly, covering her senses' reaction to his touch.

He leaned back, drew up a knee and linked his hands about it. "I've to apologize again for Reynald. It's hard to credit, but he was a good comrade when he followed the tourneys. Now God knows what I'm to do with him."

She hitched herself up against the pillows. "He's from Normandy," she observed. "It's beer and cider they drink there. A man can swill ale until his back teeth are awash, and it will only make him barrel-bellied and dull-witted. But

139

when he moves south and does likewise with wine —"

"It corrodes his bowels and his brain together," he finished. "Yes, we've both seen it." His voice softened a little on the last words, as though he guessed her father had taught her that truth. "It's easy for a landless man and a mercenary to go that way," he added thoughtfully. "When he grows older and hopes and ambitions turn sour in him, when the younger men surpass him and he looks to dying in a ditch, and brothel and tavern are all his fellowship — yes, Julitta, it's easy to find comfort in a wine-jug."

"He's gone past comfort. He's turned beast."

"And for that I'm greatly at fault. This past year he's swilled his fill at my charges — Hell's Teeth, I've swilled and wenched and roistered as swinishly! Sottish too, I saw no fault." He frowned at his laced fingers. "Then I saw myself in your eyes, and was sickened. I stay sober."

"Because you regret —"

"Regret? Best night's work of my life when I slung you over my shoulder and carried you home!" He swung from the bed and began to unlace his tunic. "Apart from all else, with whom but you in this bleak eyrie can I converse?"

She considered that in startled silence as he peeled his tunic over his head and tossed it across the perch. Then he knelt to rummage in the chest, and came to her. "Fulfilling my promise." He held out a sheathed dagger, flat and slender. He drew the six inches of steel to show her, and gave the ivory haft into her hand. The sheath had a buckled strap to fit a forearm. "Until the times mend, my girl, never go abroad without it."

Julitta tendered him his own weapon. "Indeed, my lord, I am grateful —"

"I won it from a cutpurse at dice," he told her, grinning over his shoulder. He hauled out his pallet, and put out the candle.

She wriggled down in the bed. "You have been very gracious to me this day, my lord —"

"Don't underrate your value, vixen."

He was still now, rolled up in his cloak. She settled for

140

sleep. Then his voice came quietly out of the dark. "Julitta, I ride to York at first light."

"The Scots are over the border?"

"From what Erling says it's almost sure. I must consult the Sheriff. I'll take Reynald with me; a forty-mile ride will shake up his spleen admirably. Benefit fat Giles too. You found Brien serviceable to your orders?"

"Yes, my lord."

"I'll leave him with you. While I am gone, my lady, you'll command Brentborough."

10

Red Adam's parting kiss still tingled on Julitta's lips; he played the part of a devoted lover more vigorously than there was need. Yet she warmed to him; his public delegation of authority to her had been absolute. Only one person had temerity to contest it; Reynald de Carsey, stale-drunk and scarcely able to heave himself astride, rocked beside him, his expostulations at not being granted the command instead of a whey-faced ninny floating back through the grey glimmer of dawn until they faded into the wind. She stood by the gate until the company had vanished behind the ridge, and then nodded to the guards to close it and hoist the drawbridge. She drew a deep breath, lifted her chin, and zestfully set about earning a reputation as the hardest-driving mistress in the North.

There was very nearly a mutiny when the servants realized that immediate repayment of several years' deficit of labor was required of them, but they looked from her to Sir Brien, tapping a riding whip against his boot, and then to the spearmen, and resentfully chose to preserve their skins. With shovels and rakes and pitchforks they swept up decayed rushes from bower, hall, chambers and guardroom, choking the narrow stairs and stirring up the filth of years as well

143

as a multitude of fleas. A bonfire in the bailey consumed the refuse and its vermin, gusting malodorous smoke at every shift of wind. Most of the tattered, moth-ravaged hangings were tossed into the blaze. Women armed with brooms assailed walls, ceilings and floors; weighty furniture was heaved aside; the piles of ash were cleared from the hearths, and the castle cats grew bored with pouncing on evicted mice and stalked tails aloft from the turmoil.

Julitta, her old gown caught up above her ankles and her hair bundled away in a kerchief, hounded laggards from task to task. As soon as the dust had settled she had the floors thrice broomed over with scalding lye, compounded of wood-ash boiled with urine,* to kill the fleas and their eggs in the crevices of the boards. Fleabane and elder leaves were scattered over the damp wood. The village women and children, promised their bellyfuls of bread and beef and ale, had been deployed since daybreak along the river cutting rushes. In the laundry, the carpenter was patching leaky tubs, which were then filled and refilled with water to swell tight their warped seams. Every horse was out of the stables, even the destriers picketed at grass on the headland, while swearing grooms scraped floors, scoured walls and posts and mangers, and swept the last locks of aged hay from rat-ridden lofts. Sir Brien only left off snarling at their heels to have every weapon, piece of armor and strap of equipment out of guard-room and armory, inspected, burnished and sorted for repairs, and the smithy clanged through the rest of the day. Julitta, hurrying up and down stairs and from one end of the bailey to the other, thanked the Saints for him as she harried servitors who leaned on their brooms to complain of ill-usage whenever she turned her back.

She was thankful also for Hodierne, quietly setting the bower to rights while Constance sulked, bereft of sycophantic wenches. If ever she was rid of Constance she would appoint

---

*Decomposed urine was the usual source of ammonia for domestic and industrial cleansing until the nineteenth century and chemical factories. Fullers' workshops in towns even provided large jars outside their doors for the contributions of passers-by.

Hodierne in charge of the women. She knew gratitude also to Adela, who descended upon her husband's mercenaries to speed their hosts' labors, her tongue a sharper spur than the sternest captain's.

Next morning she purged laundry, dairy, bakery and brewhouse. A new kitchen she was determined to have, and at first chance a new cook. She summoned the Arnisby carpenter, and by the time he appeared she had had Godric's lair knocked apart, the main timbers salvaged and the rest fired. The frame was up on a new site by nightfall.

Every cauldron was devoted to soap-making. Wood-ash was sieved into them, boiled up with water, strained and reboiled with melted tallow. The tallow supplies were scanty, and as the shortage could not be due to any inordinate consumption of soap and it was too early for candle-making, her suspicions turned inevitably towards Godric. She could guess his market; the tanner's two sons drove a thriving by-trade as chandlers and soap-boilers with the inferior tallow from the lime-vats.

Julitta turned from the cauldrons to the fumes of lime-slaking and a tremendous mixing of whitewash. The servants manhandled ladders, trestles and planks up and down spiral stairs. Buckets clattered and brushes slapped. The plaster was sound enough, and if one layer of whitewash did not cover the grime a second would.

Sir Bertram moved about, peering unhappily as she compelled cleanliness and order from chaos. Julitta found time to be sorry for him, forced to depend on incompetent assistance for his duties' performance and betrayed by it. Every omission she rectified indicted his governance. His first friendliness had soured; his wife was always at his elbow muttering of slights, and now he shunned Julitta.

Baldwin Dogsmeat offered his sixteen men to augment her garrison without charge, for as long as Red Adam should be absent. It would suit him to have his men housed and fed while he sought an engagement. The troop was less of a menace within Brentborough wall than without, ranging loose to plunder the peasants or employed by rebels. Adela was worth a dozen Hodiernes as an overseer, though she set the women simmering with resentment. Her elf-child roamed like a small ghost, and folk who would have cuffed a normal brat from under their feet tried to coax him to them. He would go to no one but his mother, and drifted erratically as a tassel of thistledown past the noisy business of living. Julitta wondered with pity what future God would provide for him.

Erling and Hakon came to make their farewells, surveying her work with approving grins. "A valiant labor," Erling pronounced, "and your lord will know how to value you for it."

"Not he!" muttered Hakon. His sire ignored his indiscretion.

"Wine, spices, the drugs you listed, and if the winds serve I'll put into a south coast haven for a well-fleeced ram. No more, my lady? We are at your service."

"All the news of Flanders?"

"That of course, my lady. God be with you!"

She gave them her hand. Hakon's grasp was no formality, nor his lips' pressure on her knuckles. "Always and wholly at your service, Lady Julitta," he murmured fervently, and trod after his sire to the gate.

A fortnight ago life could have offered her nothing fairer than Hakon's devotion; she would thankfully have matched with him and built content, borne his children and loved him for his simple kindness. Now she was bound to Red Adam, and Hakon would wed a girl of his own north and remember her as a dream. She was no legendary beauty to inspire an undying passion at first encounter. Her chief feeling was surprised gratitude ,that he admired her at all.

The kitchen walls had the wattle set in, and the workmen were troweling plaster over the withies. Cookery was going forward over open fires, whose flaring kept Godric active as a flea.

"You've sweated a summer's tallow off their ribs, my lady," said Brien's voice in her ear. "Aye, and proved that Constance an idle slut."

146

"Here's venom, Sir Brien."

"She used my poor wife most spitefully, Lady Julitta."

"Reason enough." She looked round on the confusion, and burst out, "But why? She was undisputed chatelaine! Why turn slut?"

"Lord Maurice would sanction nothing that disturbed his peace, but within his limits she ruled well enough, until his death-sickness took hold of him two years ago."

"But she was still mistress, until his heir should bring home a bride."

"It's my belief," he said, lowering his voice though none could have heard him through the turmoil, "that she hoped he'd wed her."

"But she has a husband!"

"Did you not know, my lady, that Sir Bertram lives on the grave's edge? He suffers cramps in his breast that seize on his heart's beating, and thrice in four years he has received the last rites."

"A grievous pity," she said, and crossed herself, shocked and sorry. More to herself than to the knight, she murmured, "Odd, that Lord Maurice inspired so much loyalty."

He smiled bleakly. "It was not altogether loyalty, my lady. We are all fugitives from vengeance."

"Fugitives?"

"How else could he have officered his garrison? You've a right to know. Bertram killed his half-brother for insulting his wife; he made pilgrimage to Jerusalem in penance. Giles cuckolded the wrong man. Nicholas the Marshal, God rest him, got a troop butchered in an ambush on the Welsh Marshes, and his lord's son was among them. And I carried off my lord's bastard daughter when he'd promised her elsewhere, and never regretted it." He watched the plasterers, and then shrugged. "I reckon Lord Maurice felt a fellowship with wanted men, for he too dared not put his neck in reach of his wife's kinsmen."

"There can be no doubt she died?"

"My lady, I've been here sixteen years, and heard it chewed over all that time. This is sure: alive or dead she never passed

147

the gates, and alive or dead none set eyes on her again."

"But *he* knew," Julitta murmured. A suspicion rooted itself in her mind. Then she roused herself. "Holy Mother, here I stand gossiping!" she cried, and fled up the keep stairs.

A squad of well-bribed heroes emptied the garderobe pits and dumped their reeking tubs at the furthest end of the garden. Dung carts trundled the manure heaps out to the fields. The kitchen was finished, and Godric, pungently admonished as to the standards he was to maintain, moved in. Drunkenness would in future be hard to attain, for Julitta had restricted the ale-brewing. That was her most unpopular measure, and probably prompted the rock that narrowly missed her head as she walked past the stables that evening. The attacker escaped in the dusk and uproar, and Julitta overnight devised the most fiendish atrocity of all.

In the chilly dawn the men-at-arms rounded up all the grooms and scullions, marched them down to the river and made them strip and scour a lifetime's grime from their carcasses, shear off hair and beards and assume clean clothing. The troopers found it a jest less hilarious when they were ordered in themselves, but no one was actually drowned and there was no mutiny. By midday every man had been scrubbed and shorn beyond recognition, and the laundry billowed with steam for three days as the women set about a monument of washing.

With such demands the well was down to noisome sludge, and after testing it with a lighted candle two volunteers climbed down to dredge out mud, bones, the remnants of several buckets and a decomposed cat. The carpenter hurriedly constructed a cover, and Julitta's comments on fluxes would ensure its conscientious use for all of a fortnight.

In eight frenzied days the task was accomplished. All the linen and soiled garments had been washed, and now the tubs were filled for the women to bathe and wash their hair before settling to a mountain of mending. Julitta, filled with the satisfaction of achievement, wondered what her husband would say. She missed him. She would not have con-

148

fessed it except in her own mind, but she missed his stirrings in the darkness, his company at table, his pungent speech; all other men were savorless as unsalted bread. In fact, he had seduced her into liking him.

In the morning she ordered a horse saddled and rode to Arnisby. Alain, the redhaired groom, offered to escort her. Washed and shaven he was a personable fellow, anxious to remedy his error of their first encounter. He worked a little too hard at it, but she was amused rather than displeased; she could not yet accept her consequence.

The weavers entertained her with ale and honeycakes in a long room dominated by three looms, and lighted by windows whose shutters were paneled with oiled linen to admit daylight whatever the weather. Her hosts' faces brightened at her orders for woolens and linen. She listened sympathetically to hints about the benefit of a market and even a town charter but said nothing that might commit her husband, and departed in an atmosphere of goodwill.

Goodwill was less apparent among the fisherfolk. Wulfstan, the chief of their community, a barrel-shaped veteran whose raiment stank vehemently of his calling, seated her with a kind of surly courtesy on an upturned skiff at the shingle's head, and yelled to a woman to bring ale and bannocks. Both were impregnated with fish, but she swallowed heroically, and asked after the prospects for Friday. Other men drifted over, were presented as Wulfstan's three sons and two sons-in-law, and settled in a half-circle before her. Her proposal of a profitable bargain in stockfish and salted herring for the winter thawed some of the stiffness out of them, but they were plainly cherishing their grudge.

She grinned up into Wulfstan's blue slits of eyes and said, "Wreck rights are lord's rights, Master Wulfstan."

His whiskers twitched. "We'd not cheat Lord Adam, m' lady."

"But you'd expect your pickings from the carcass?"

Teeth glinted yellow through the thicket. "Summat for t' trouble o' picking up. Took no thought, didn't Lord Adam."

149

"Do you imagine he'd have let them wreck?"

"There'll no luck come of it," offered a son-in-law. "'Tis ill done to cheat t' sea."

"A man as you saves from drowning'll allus do you a mischance," said the other gloomily. "Drown you in t' end. T' sea'll have its meat."

They all grunted agreement. The sea was a harsh divinity, and their ancestors had propitiated her with the blood of sacrifice. "Don't let a priest hear you say so," Julitta drily advised. "And Master Erling's goodwill will be worth more in honest trade than goods washed out on the tide."

They looked at one another, a secret certainty in their faces, and the youngest blurted, "What washes out t' tide brings back."

Her gaze challenged Wulfstan, who scowled at his loose-mouthed son and nodded. "Aye, m' lady. Owt as goes out on t' ebb, comes in on t' next flood into Lykewake Bay." He jerked his head at the southern headland that recurved beyond the low point into a wide bay.

She stiffened. The lykewake was the corpse-watch between death and burial. "The dead return there?"

"Aye. Any as drowns in these waters, t' tide brings back."

She thrust aside her enlightenment to say severely, "You are a tribe of corpse-picking ravens."

They took it as a compliment, and grinned. There was an uneasy stir and another exchange of glances. Sons and sons-in-law nodded to Wulfstan, who cleared his throat, pursed his lips, recollected in whose presence he stood and swallowed instead of spitting. "Is it true as Lord Adam'll build a sea wall and make all on us pay harbor dues?"

Julitta knew peasants' minds, that their grinding toil filled with envy, suspicion and avarice. Only a lord commanded money and materials for any major project of public benefit, but once he charged a fee to recover his outlay it became an intolerable imposition to be evaded by an stratagem. Every lord who built a mill knew that, rather than pay for their corn's grinding, his serfs would set their women to back-breaking hours every day at the quern. Someone ill-disposed to her husband had made the worst of casual talk at his table.

"It's no more than a thought," she told them. "Would a safe harbor harm you?"

"What was good enough for my gran'feyther'll do me," Wulfstan growled.

"Your grandsire fished inshore with lines from a coble," Julitta retorted, "and ate his catch and little enough else. Will your grandsons be content with a shingle strip? Trade with outlanders like Erling would mean you could sell more fish." Seeing that she had set thought creaking inside their skulls, she stood up and shook sand and fish scales from her skirts. "Discuss it with Lord Adam when he returns."

Wulfstan, his brow furrowed, escorted her to her horse. Alain was flirting with a bare-legged girl, but he roused at once to meet her and swing her into the saddle. She gathered the reins, and the old man put out a hand to detain her for a moment.

"M' lady, are t' Scots ower t' border?"

"It's very likely."

His lips lifted from his teeth. "I'll be edging up me owd wolf spear. We've not forgot t' last time. I was a lad wi' me beard just sprouted, but I blooded steel when t' holy Archbishop Thurstan raised t' Standards in the invasion of 'thirty-eight. Aye, blooded proper; we seen what them Galloway men done." He checked, breathing hard; then he jerked her a bow. "God go wi' you, m' lady."

Alain looked sharply from him to his mistress, but she urged her mount towards the bridge. She was riding a placid gelding the grooms reckoned a suitable lady's horse, without vice or any turn of speed in him. She turned off the castle track and ambled into Brentborough village. The geese, hens and pigs had been turned into the stubble, and the autumn ploughing had started in the fallow. Flails' thwacking resounded from barn doors; the smith's hammer was clanging; the carpenter and a team of villagers were erecting a new cottage at the far end of the street; women in garden patches bobbed curtseys, and a cluster of children peeling

151

rushes ducked shaggy polls. She rode straight to the alehouse, where she owed a debt.

Gunhild surged from her door. "God save and bless you, m' lady! Heartily glad I am to name you lady in truth. Come taste my last brewing, if you'll do me t' honor."

There were no men within doors, tippling away working daylight; no one but the same shriveled woman on the same bench, cuddling what looked like the same piggin and regarding them with eyes pugnacious as a robin's.

"And don't you think as you'll shoo me out like I was a stray hen, *Mistress* Gunhild," she snapped. "Ho, mighty lofty we be now m' lady sets foot inside, but an alehouse it is an' here I sits an' sups me ale as I've paid for."

"That's no talk to set afore m' lady, you cantankerous besom! Don't you heed her, Lady Julitta; crazed in t' wits she's gotten, an' muzzy wi' t' ale."

"Take more nor your washy brewing to touch *my* wits!" the crone retorted. "Me as helped me mother to birth you, and a nasty squalling brat you was too!" She up-ended the piggin for a swig that would have won a veteran man-at-arms his peers' respect, emerged for air and wiped her sleeve across her mouth. "Since there's nowt better to be had, fill up and stop grouching, Mistress Lofty-nose."

Julitta caught her wicked eye, which gave her a portentous wink and slewed round to Gunhild. She burst out laughing, sat down and accepted the ale-horn. A grin chased the scowl from Gunhild's face; she whisked at the impeccable hearth and poked up the logs, and they were all smiling in amity.

"I owe you thanks," Julitta said, "for your defence of me that night."

"Defence, m' lady? This is an honest house an' I'm no bawd. What else should I ha' done?"

"It cost you indignity and damage none the less."

"All done wi', m' lady. Lord Adam hisself made t' damage good, t' next morning."

"Lord Adam did?" Her incredulity gave tongue before she could halt it.

"Oh, there's no vice in t' lad," said Gunhild, with the

152

large tolerance of one who has been over-compensated for loss. "He's nowt but a randy young stallion a-feeling his oats. Reckon as he'll settle steady to t' harness now he's wed."

"Cold-sober to bed each night an' his wife's bed at that!" contributed the old woman, grinning with three snaggle teeth. "Young Fire-in-the-thatch! Eh, but it's early days still."

"Mind your tongue, Hallgerd! Remember m' lady's wed to him."

"Oh aye, she's wed." Julitta felt the blood burn up to her hair; those shrewd eyes had discerned at once, she knew, that Lord Adam's bride was virgin still.

"Praise God for it!" said Gunhild with simple fervor. "When I knowed he'd carried you off, m' lady, down I goes weeping on my prayer-bones amidst all t' ruin and prays to t' Virgin to guard you."

"Aye, he's man enough to make amends for his sins wi'out whining o' t' cost. Sobered him rarely, I reckons."

"And what's past's done with," Gunhild continued the antiphon of advice from veterans to neophyte. Rank was ignored; they were three women joined together in the Eve-old conspiracy against the male half of mankind. "Just you set to turn that den o' whores into a seemly household t' way you're framing, and no carping on what's best forgot."

Julitta opened her lips on bitter comment, and swallowed it unuttered. Hallgerd grinned again, retired briefly behind the piggin, and read her mind.

"Don't fret you about that silly trollop Thyra, m' lady. T' brat'll be born afore t' month's out, wi' all its finger and toe nails, and likely it'll be redheaded — like t' last 'un."

"The last one?"

"Two she's had and lost. T' last was red — Alain t' groom's."

"*Alain's* —"

"Wolves breed true, and Lorismonds ye'll know by t' head-mark."

"Wolves!" Gunhild snorted. "Yon's no wolf. Nowt but a randy tup wi' no mind above his belt."

Such relief had shaken Julitta that she scarcely heard their

153

opinions of Alain's morals and intelligence; they mattered not at all to her. The child was not Red Adam's; the claim had been made in spite and folly, by Constance and not Thyra, she remembered, and the girl was plainly near her time. It was illogical to be so thankful; her husband had frankly admitted his commerce with the girl, months before their wedding, but she praised Heaven for so much mercy.

The three yellow teeth gleamed again. "Happen she reckoned folks couldn't count up to nine?" Hallgerd suggested.

"She don't reckon nowt," snorted Gunhild. "'Twasn't *her* thought o' that one. Watch thissen, m' lady; t' fair 'un's a mortal ugly foe, and you've shown her up proper for a shiftless slut and took her place besides."

Julitta nodded. "I'm grateful to you both," she said, setting down the empty horn. "And I'd ask your aid on another matter. Do you know what happened to my groom Ivar after he fled?"

The two exchanged pregnant glances. "Took service wi' Humphrey o' Crossthwaite, m' lady," Gunhild said shortly.

"Oh!" She might have expected it; hatred to hatred for a common vengeance. Yet a shock of disappointment assailed her. She looked bleakly into the fire, and then with a small sigh rose to make her farewells.

"M' lady, is it true t' Scots're out?" Gunhild asked urgently as Wulfstan had done.

"It's very likely," she answered again, guessing at the rumors flying, talk repeated from the castle table, speculation about Red Adam's sudden journey to York, all slashed scarlet with old folk's memories of King David's invasion thirty-five years past. Hallgerd must have been woman-grown in those times; she would have lain down and risen up in deathly fear when the Picts of Galloway were making the name of Scot accursed to unborn generations. Her withered face was grim as Julitta turned to her.

"Fire-in-the-thatch'd best look to his walls; t' rats're in 'em," she said cryptically, and again the peasant women looked at each other. Hallgerd nodded slightly. Gunhild hesitated, and then spoke in a rush.

154

"M' lady, there's talk as how Lord Maurice's true son's come to claim his rights. His rightful son out o' his wedded lady, and Lord o' Brentborough by birth."

Amazed beyond speech, Julitta stared into the troubled face. "But — but that's not possible!" she exclaimed at last.

"I'd ha' said that mesen, m' lady; vanished outa sight she did, and never a trace of her from that day. Never passed t' gate, nor seen on t' roads, nor yet washed up in Lykewake Bay."

"Yet yon's t' tale," Hallgerd corroborated. "Nowt but a whisper and no telling where from, but there's mischief in it. And wi' rebels a-plot and t' Scots ower t' Border, I reckon young Fire-in-the thatch's owed a warning. I've knowed worse masters in me time."

"Whatever's behind the tale, I'm grateful, and I'll thank you on my husband's behalf too," Julitta answered, her wits buzzing with conjecture. "Rats in the walls? I'll turn ferret! God be with you both!"

One glimpse of her face brought Alain at an alarmed run from his conversation with two girls on their way to the well with yokes and buckets, but she merely nodded acknowledgment of his apologies and took the slope at an easy walk. It was quite incredible that Lord Maurice's lady — what was her name? Beatrice? Bertha? No, Bertrade, that was it — should have fled undetected, lived unsuccored by kindred or friends, borne her child in secrecy. A woman distraught, heavy with child and near her travail; a lady unused to hardship, who had never traveled but by horse or litter; a lady of spirit and temper, insistent on her rights, carrying her lord's lawful heir; such a one would stand fast, secure in her expectations and status. It was the seduced and deserted girl who fled to cover her shame, or was thrust by outraged kinsmen into the shelter of some convent. All Julitta's robust common sense rose up to reject the conception. If some claimant had appeared, he was an impostor. And remembering Lord Maurice's reputation, the easy guess was most likely the right one.

Thought of sheltering convents set some memory nagging at her brain, until she chanced to glance over her shoulder and sight of Alain's red head recalled it; a memory of the more tedious hours of her tedious years in the nunnery, sitting with Lord Maurice's elderly cousin, sewing or playing decorous chess, surrounded by her little dogs and listening to an endless trickle of gossip, enlivened only by pungent comment from her old serving woman. She had paid little heed to reminiscences of thirty cloistered years, but some facts lodged in her mind; something to do with Lord Maurice's kindness in helping her to move to this nunnery in North Parts from one near the Lorismond holding by Bristol, after an officious Bishop had bidden her be rid of her little dogs or depart. Some mention of a redhaired baby had stayed with her, but more than that she could not recall.

"Alain!"

"My lady?"

"I shall require Folie this afternoon; I must visit the convent."

"Aye, my lady. May I escort you?"

"If you wish."

Sir Brien helped her from the saddle. She had an engagement with him that drove all else from the uppermost layers of her mind, though her new problem was an uneasy pressure on her consciousness. The undercroft had been roughly set to rights during Brentborough's upheaval, but today she intended a thorough investigation of all within it. With rebellion plotting among the neighbors, Scots over the Border and a doubtfully loyal household, she did not propose to take a gang of servants below to publish abroad any deficiencies. She locked the stair door behind herself, Brien and his body-servant, a middle-aged Englishman warranted close-mouthed, and they went at the task by the light of torches.

The rats no longer obtruded on ear and eye, after the rat-catcher had carried out a sackful of carcasses at the end of a half-day with ferrets and terrier, but their ravages were everywhere apparent. Gnawed sacks, riddled through and through in their ranked piles, spilled their fouled contents. The great grain bins, mounted on small staddlestones to baffle them, had escaped, but as lid after lid was lifted and the musty smells of mealworms and weevilly corn arose, Julitta reckoned that small benefit. Plainly the bins had not been cleaned out for years; each new supply had been tipped in upon the tainted remnants left inside, and infected in its turn. The Englishman silently scooped up a fistful of wheat and held it to the light, crawling with repellent life.

"We'll have the lot out; it's fit for nothing but fowls' meat," Julitta decided after the briefest of hesitations. Fortunately the harvest was still in the barns, unthreshed. "The bins scoured out with vinegar and well smoked. Yes, and we'll have the bread grain parched in the ovens after the baking's done, since the season's been a wet one." For damp corn was speedily infested with weevils and mealworms, besides being liable to mould and sprouting.

There were eel-worms and ropy slime in the vinegar, so that most of it was only fit for cleansing, and the casks must be recharred. The stockfish was rat-ravaged. "Siege rations," said Brien apologetically, kicking a broken remnant aside. When fresh fish was available no one would willingly eat it, but in winter there might be weeks of storm. The butter and cheese, of that summer's milk, were scanty in quantity but sound. The honey was good. The stock of candles and rush-dips was naturally low, but must wait on the Martinmas butchering for renewal since so much tallow had been expended on soap-boiling. Brien growled over damaged arrows, warped bow-staves and rusty metal, but on the whole the imperishable articles had suffered small harm. They continued their circuit, poked their heads into a couple of cells occasionally used for confining the criminal or the belligerently drunk, and turned back towards the stair.

Before the ranked tiers of salt-meat barrels Julitta halted, her nose twitching. It had been assailed by a number of unsavory odors, but here was another, alarming as a bugle blast; a whiff of tainted meat. The Englishman snuffed like a questing hound, and Brien's nostrils flared. In the torchlight they eyed each other with misgiving.

"Hold the light nearer, Alfwin; there's mischief here."

The full casks were ranged in three tiers against the wall,

one before the other. The front row was depleted by three-quarters, the other two were almost complete. Julitta noted dust layers and veiling cobwebs, and an incredible suspicion could not be dismissed.

"Hand me the torch, Alfwin. We'll have that cask out." She indicated one of the rearmost standing alone. The two men silently laid hold on it, tipped it on edge and trundled it from its bed, scared spiders and woodlice scuttling. Silently they wedged it on its side and removed the bung. The stench of decayed mutton gushed out. Still in silence, they beat back the bung and replaced the cask.

"Two years!" hissed Brien. "Two years that sluttish bitch has let the cooks take the last-come meat!"

The incredible suspicion was reality. This went beyond neglect; it was an appalling, criminal shiftlessness, ignoring the first rule of food management. Each autumn the new-killed meat, salted for storage, had been stacked in front of the old instead of behind it, and the unsupervised cooks had started to use it immediately instead of finishing first the previous season's salting. The Scots were over the Border, rebellion abroad, a siege more than possible, and Brentborough Castle's salt meat was mostly rotten.

"By God's Head, it's a hanging matter!" swore Brien. "Give the word, Lady Julitta, and we'll have that lout Godric swinging before dinner's served! And that shiftless bitch should hang beside him." He started for the stair, and Julitta extended the torch in a flaring barrier that halted him.

"*No!*" she declared forcefully. "This must not go beyond the three of us." They stared at her, the torchlight dancing on their faces and reflecting from their eyes. "We must not let a whisper of it go abroad among our enemies."

Brien nodded soberly. "True, my lady. It'll gall me sorely, for if ever a man deserved hanging — but you're right."

"It galls me also," she agreed frankly. "And we know he's a thief too, but we'll have to wait for an accounting."

"A thief?"

"The mutton carcass under the offal, remember? Peddled to the inn, I'll wager my head."

158

Brien thumbed his chin, his scowl suddenly lightening. "Now there's a hope. If he's taken in the act — my lady, there'll be a watch on him a mouse couldn't evade."

He looked so like a terrier bristling at a rathole that Julitta grinned. "When the cat's away —" she said. "I have business at the convent this day. Good hunting, Sir Brien!"

She mentioned her intent at dinner, and did not correct Baldwin Dogsmeat when he impudently guessed aloud that it was always a pleasure to visit old friends. Sly grins the length of the table told how most folk interpreted her errand. The Abbess's charity was justly famed, and all knew that to receive the girl she had rejected, as patroness of the convent and the greatest lady in the district, would cause her the most exquisite chagrin. Julitta serenely dealt with spiced pork and frumenty; they might believe she sought that ignoble satisfaction so long as they did not guess at her true motive.

When the company dispersed after dinner Sir Bertram stood alone at the dais's edge, gazing vaguely out of a window. Something forlorn in his aspect suddenly put her in mind of blinded Samson grinding among the slaves. In compunction she realized how she had practically ignored him in the hectic days since Red Adam gave her command of Brentborough. She moved to his side, and he turned at the rustle of her feet in the new rushes, his face still vaguely questioning until she spoke.

"There's been little time for diversion since my lord departed, Sir Bertram, for which I'm sorry. Will you favor me with a match after supper?"

His sagging face hardened, and again she glimpsed what he had once been. "No, my lady." She gasped at the rebuff, and he added sternly, "I may not, after your discourtesy towards my dear lady."

"If you mean that I have exposed her neglect of duty," Julitta snapped, "whose was the neglect?" Then she closed her lips, disdaining to justify herself at Constance's expense, or to complain that the initial discourtesy had been hers. The woman was his wife. If he did not know her for a malicious

159

slut he was purblind in mind as in body. She stalked to the stair, reflecting uneasily on her suspicions. The seneschal had given his loyalty twice only, to his lady and his lord, and if she proved right a fearful and undesired vengeance was in her hands. Not for the first time she wished that she might lay the whole problem before her husband.

Sulky wenches had to be herded back to the bower and set under Hodierne's charge, informed in plain words that the Christmas livery of new clothing for every other member of the household must be completed before their own stuff would feel the shears. That spurred them. But Thyra, dawdling heavily after them, stared at Julitta with dull-witted insolence. "I've no call to set hands to scullions' gear, wi' m' lord's son in me belly."

"You fool, you should be sewing swaddling bands for the groom's brat." Julitta leveled a finger at her waist. "You're nine months gone, not seven, and you'll need them before the week's out."

The girl gaped stupidly, fright in her face, and pressed both hands to her burden in the age-old gesture of a woman who feels the babe kick in her womb. She lurched after her companions, her silly lie exposed naked, and Julitta frowned after her. The girl looked ill; her pretty face was puffy and her high color faded to a greenish pallor. A prescient instinct told her that the birth was imminent, and it would go hard.

Adela spoke grimly in her ear. "You'll have no order in your household, my lady, until you're rid of that Constance, inciting those trollops to insolence."

"That I know," Julitta answered as grimly. "And I'd give much to accomplish it." Resentment at the interference stirred in her; the problem was obvious.

Adela hitched the elf-child higher on her hip, her hard mouth twisting into a smile. "Oh, I'm meddlesome, but believe me, I wish you well."

Julitta flushed. The woman was, after all, of an age to be her mother. "It's her husband would have to go, and he's served Brentborough loyally for many years."

"He's blind and besotted. Guard against him; the man's a dreamer, and dreamers are dangerous."

"Dangerous?"

"They see things as they would have them, not as they are." She hesitated, and added, "His loyalty's neither to you nor Lord Adam."

"Mistress Adela," Julitta challenged her, "you hint at treachery. Have you knowledge?"

"None," the routier's woman answered. Julitta had scarcely to raise her eyes to meet the straight gaze; they were almost of a height. "If I'd facts you should have them. But it's not love she's forever whispering in his ear, and her eye on you all the time. Be wary." She moved away, striding arrogantly as a man. Julitta frowned after her. Then she mounted to the bower to check the work, commended Avice and Hodierne who were finishing her green gown, paid her third visit of the day to the kitchen and her second to the hospital. The elderly man with lung sickness, against all expectation, was recovering, and the girl attendant was looking worse. An excited throng brought to her a small boy who had fallen out of an appletree, and she set his collarbone and bound him up before an audience which decided that, young as she was, Lady Julitta knew her chirurgery.

She came more than an hour late to the stables, to find Folie fretting under the saddle. She sidled and stamped, and Alain leaped to her head. Julitta reined her to a sober walk, away from the distracting scents and sounds of the stallions in the stables, and once through the gate held her to a canter.

Alain closed up behind on his dun gelding. "M' lady, did you know as Sir Bertram and his lady rode out right after dinner, wi' Roger and Oswald for escort?"

"No word where?"

"No, m' lady, but they took this road."

11

The valley road, once they passed Brentborough village and its fields, angled northwest along the river and plunged into dense woods. It kept to the north bank, sometimes following the river's twists and sometimes swinging away, but seldom beyond sound of the water wrangling with the boulders of its bed. It was a turbulent river, subject to fierce spates when rain fell in the hills, and before the bridge was built at Arnisby its fords had yearly claimed their toll of lives.

High clouds, shredded like thistledown, glided across the sky, and the sun blazed undimmed among them. A breeze from the sea stirred the leaves, crisping already for autumn. Shade and sunshine patterned the track; birds called alarm as they advanced; dragonflies flashed in and out of the shadows; flies buzzed about them and clustered round the horses' eyes and nostrils so that they blew and tossed their heads in irritation. Squirrels flicked chittering away as they passed, and once a pursuing marten poised on a bough to stare arrogantly at them before bounding higher. Far away a stag roared; the rutting season was approaching.

Julitta's anxieties slackened their hold as she gave herself to enjoyment of the fair day and escape from her duties; even thought of her distasteful errand ceased to press. She

163

found herself humming as she rode, and checked with amused consternation as she realized it was the tune of Red Adam's song about the harlot. They overtook the carrier and his string of packhorses, starting on his round of upland hamlets and isolated farmsteads with salt and fish and woven cloth. Julitta halted to warn him also of the Scots, and soberly he promised to bear the warning with him. They left him standing in the track, plainly debating whether a wise man would return to Arnisby and let his profits go.

The track forked, one branch angling left down to a chancy ford and then over the fells to Crossthwaite. It was little used, and Alain checked his horse and pointed to hoofprints plain in the floury dust.

"M' lady, here's where Sir Bertram went. I'd know that big gray's prints anywhere; throws out wi' his off hind."

"Crossthwaite!" Julitta said aloud, gazing between the trees with narrowed eyes. Bertram and Constance were at liberty to ride where they would, but when they chose to visit the Ladies' Delight without a word to any it set her wondering. Reckoning it along with the rumors she had heard this day, she was frankly uneasy. These were no times for the Brentborough seneschal to consort with even undeclared rebels.

"There's Hartleap Farm and Ravensghyll afore you gets to Crossthwaite, m' lady," Alain ventured. "Happen they've affairs—"

"With Sir Humphrey," Julitta said, and set her palfrey moving again. The pleasure had gone from her ride, the castle's troubles returned to vex her. The golden day, the valley's beauty, the river's vigor, were forgotten; now she noticed the pestering flies, the dust that sifted through her clothing and gritted on her skin, the sweat sticking her fingers to the reins and her clothes to her body. Alain, more sensitive to her mood than she would have expected, fell silent.

They entered a clearing snagged with pale stumps and scarred with black patches, old charcoal burners' pitsteads. Higher up the hillside a faint ring of axes and a thin plume of pale blue smoke revealed this season's work site. The track dipped to the riverside again, and by a shallow strewn with boulders they halted briefly to let the horses drink. Then they climbed to a wide terrace some twenty feet above flood level, and entered a more extensive clearing. In the middle of it crouched a tumbledown hovel of wattle and daub, erected by the woodcutters who had lived here a year or so until they had cut all the trees convenient to the river and floated down their timber to Brentborough. A man stood in the track, waiting for them.

Julitta exclaimed and started forward, her palfrey whickering in recognition. "Ivar!"

He came to Folie's head as he had been used to, dour and unsmiling, but a warmth of pleasure softened his brown face. "Lady Julitta!"

"Oh, but I am glad to see you! Is all well with you, Ivar? I was grieved to have brought such trouble on you—"

"Aye, m' lady, all's well, and t' better for seeing you. D'ye reckon I'd forget as you married that devil to save me?"

"He's no devil, Ivar. He never intended you harm. But I must hear—we must talk—"

"There's t' owd house yonder, m' lady, if you'd trouble to dismount and set out o' t' sun?"

"Of course." She signaled to Alain, regarding Ivar suspiciously, and turned her palfrey towards the abandoned hovel. Part of its roof had fallen in, and the thatch sagged over rotting rafters, but enough remained to provide shelter. A horse whinnied greeting from behind it, and Folie shied and answered.

"Don't your lord reckon enough to you to find you a fitter mount than this fool beast, m' lady?" Ivar demanded disparagingly.

She flushed. "There's been no chance—" she began, recognized in his flinty face the hatred that no defence of Red Adam would abate, and checked in dismay; she would never persuade him to take service in Brentborough as she had hoped. Biting her lip, she reined in before the crazy hut, and Alain swung down and was at her stirrup, with a challenging glance over his shoulder at Ivar, to help her down.

165

"It's no fit place for you, m' lady!" he declared, reaching for the bridle that Ivar held.

Privately she agreed, but she had already accepted Ivar's suggestion. She shrugged and approached the gaping doorway, expecting Ivar to relinquish the reins and follow her, but he did not move. Then something large advanced in the shadow, and Humphrey of Crossthwaite ducked his head under the lintel and smiled triumphantly.

"Well met, Lady Julitta!"

She wasted no time on words, but leaped for her mount. She snatched at the pommel from the off side, and Folie reared and squealed. A strong arm tore her away and sent her reeling back towards the hovel; her heel caught in her gown and she sat backwards with a jarring thump. Alain uttered one yell and hurled himself at Ivar, and the frantic mare lashed out at both with her forehooves, broke free, and danced beyond reach, while the two men rolled together in the grass. Alain bounded to his feet and leaped at Humphrey of Crossthwaite, who struck at him savagely with the loaded stock of his riding whip.

Alain went down, rolled over, heaved himself to hands and knees and stared dumbly at the sword blade whose point pricked under his chin. Julitta, scrambling up, saw his face whiten, but he looked to her, contusion rising on his brow, and croaked, "M' lady!"

"Take your horse, knave, and ride home with a whole windpipe!" Humphrey brutally commanded, jabbing so that a red trickle started down the groom's throat.

He looked again to Julitta, repeating, "My lady!"

"Your lady is mine, you may tell Red Adam. Be gone!"

Alain sullenly picked himself up, hesitated, looked from Julitta to the sword, and tramped to his placidly grazing horse. He smeared a streak of blood across his brow, scowled white-faced at the fair knight, and rode from the clearing without looking back. Ivar had run to Folie's head and now brought her up, sidling and dancing, the uneasy whites of her eyes gleaming.

166

Julitta turned on him. "So for revenge on my husband you procure my ravishing, you vile Judas?"

He gaped at her. "No—"

A hard hand closed on her right arm. "Ravishing, fair Julitta? That's no word for our sweet loving," Humphrey protested.

She regarded him with cold loathing. "I am not your whore."

He grinned and drew her towards the hovel's doorless entrance. "You are my sweet friend and have been from the first, Julitta." He pulled her under the roof's shadow and seized her. His mouth bruised her lips against her teeth, and she set them fast, stood stone-still in his hateful embrace and endured, so that he lifted his head, held her at arms' length by the shoulders and said cajolingly, "Are you frozen to ice, Julitta? This is no time to be coy."

His arms closed on her again, and her belly quailed so that she thought she would vomit where she stood, but the little knife was in her sleeve and she knew she had the mastery. "I am no man's whore!" she declared.

"Sweet Julitta, with me you'll find true delight. Here's our vengeance, cuckolding Red Adam, and I'll teach you the love you have desired since first we met." He swung her round and pulled her towards the heap of bracken forethoughtfully piled against the wall that leaked daylight around the rotten withies, from which the chinking clay had cracked and fallen.

"Take your hands from me!" she flared. The words of the harridan who had instructed her in the use of edged steel sounded in her ears. *"Never threaten a man, don't let him know you've a blade until it's under his ribs, and never strike but to kill."* At the last resort she would do just that, but only if she could save her honor in no other way. She did not want a man's blood on her hands, not even that of the Ladies' Delight, and she had not grown up in an army's tail without learning a trick or two.

"You little tease!" he exclaimed, still grinning, still

armored in his vanity. "Must a man marry you to enjoy your favors, puss? I'll make you Lady of Crossthwaite yet, but we're wasting our joyous hour, Julitta." He closed his hold, and she shifted her feet slightly to be sure her skirts would not impede her legs.

Hooves clattered outside, a young voice called, "My lord!" and he checked. His hold slackened, and she jerked free. A tall shadow ducked under the ragged thatch, blocking the entrance, and the voice said eagerly, "It's sure, Lord Humphrey—" and halted.

A lanky boy he was, stamped with the Lorismond seal; red head, bony nose, prominent cheekbones and wide mouth. He could have been Red Adam's younger brother, or, even more surely, old Maurice's son, for he had the blue eyes the old lecher had passed on to his bastards. This was the boy who claimed to be his rightful son, and whoever his dam had been no one would have denied his sire.

He gaped blankly at Julitta, glanced past her at the eloquent heap of bracken and back to the man and girl. His eyes rounded like a startled child's, and bright blood burned up his throat to his hair. "I—did not—" he stammered in confusion, backing a little.

Humphrey grinned, but his voice was edged with annoyance. "You're untimely come, Lord Geoffrey—"

"Most timely, indeed," Julitta said firmly, and tried to pass him. A hard hand snatched her back.

"The lady—the lady seems unwilling—" the lad stammered, staring uncertainly from one to the other.

"She's feigning coy to heat my ardor," snapped Humphrey brutally. "What do you know of women, you fledgling monk? Leave us to it, instead of bleating—"

A screech startled them all, and she wrenched free. Round the building, yowling like a scalded cat and swinging a knotty branch for a makeshift club, came Alain. He hauled his stocky dun to a turf-tearing halt, bowling aside the red lad. Humphrey yelled and snatched at his swordhilt; Alain lunged over the dun's neck, ramming the club into his belly. All the wind gushed out of him in an anguished grunt, and he

168

went down writhing. The doorway was blocked; Alain backed his horse and smashed with all his force at the rotten wall. Clay flew wide, the withies burst apart, two more blows broke out half the hut's side and set the whole structure reeling, and Julitta dived through the gap, out under the noses of three scared horses and an open-mouthed Ivar.

Alain crowded his dun against Folie and dropped his own reins to grab hers close to the bit and force her to stand. Ivar rolled frantically from under the hooves, and the club menaced him. A bellow of wrath and pain from within the hut spurred Julitta; she flung herself astride, her skirts flying, caught the reins and hauled savagely to bring the terrified mare's head down. Alain grinned, loosed his hold and wrenched the dun round on his haunches.

"Stop them!" Humphrey, gray-faced and bent double, had staggered to the gap and was yelling at Ivar. "Hold her, fool!"

Ivar scrambled up. "Run, m' lady!" he yelled, as Julitta kicked her heels into Folie's barrel and slackened the reins so that she fled as if winged. She glanced over her shoulder, and saw Ivar snatch free the tethers, bounce into his own saddle, deal Humphrey's chestnut a cut with the reins that sent him thundering up the slope into the woods, and follow him at a run. Humphrey lurched mouthing through the gap after him, and as he reeled against the shattered wall the hovel shuddered, the wall collapsed outwards, and the thatch subsided upon his head and bore him to the earth. Her last glimpse was of the redhaired boy, gaping helplessly; then she reserved her attention for Folie's footing.

They had regained the Crossthwaite turnoff before Julitta checked the mare and drew her firmly to a walk, though she seemed eager to gallop all the way back to Brentborough. She snorted and sidled, tossing her head and rolling white-rimmed eyes, and Alain, pulling his own sweating dun a little behind, spoke censoriously.

"She's no mount for a girl to handle, m' lady."

"She runs as if the devil had his pitchfork at her rump, and today that's served well," Julitta replied. She turned in the saddle. "So have you, and I thank you with all my heart."

169

He shook his head, reddening. "God's Death, m' lady, if I went back to Lord Adam wi'out you I'd be lucky to get hung!"

"Lord Adam, with me, is deeply in your debt."

He flushed a darker red, but his bold gaze met hers unabashed. "Happen you'll not hold it against me no more, m' lady, that I was once too free wi' my tongue?"

"I'll forgive you. You're an idle scoundrel and you'd rather escort a lady than fork dung—"

"Show me t'man 'd rather fork dung than escort a lady!"

She laughed, suddenly understanding the wenches who strewed his way. "Speaking of tongues, keep yours behind your teeth. If word of this attempt escapes, Lord Adam will tear it from your jaws."

He looked sharply at her. "Aye, m' lady. A mort o' scandal—it won't be me fouls your name."

For a good quarter-mile no more was said. Julitta's ears strained for movement in the woods; she hoped that Ivar would emerge from them to join her. Disappointment filled her as she realized that he would not come. Her service had cost him dearly. Once more he was a masterless man and a fugitive, and Humphrey was a vindictive man who would hunt him down to hang him for a horsethief. There was no way by which she could reach him, nothing she could do to help him.

"M' lady, how'd yon whoreson hound know to meet you back there without some Judas passed t' word?"

"How, indeed? It will be enlightening if anyone betrays knowledge of that meeting."

"If—oh, aye, m' lady." However seldom he bothered to exercise it, the Lorismond intelligence lived in him. "I'll keep me lugs lifting," he offered. "T' traitor 'd look right well on a rope's end." Marveling, she realized that this idle rogue was, for no reason she could guess at, her man. "M' lady, that boy—?"

"Another son of your father's, surely. But out of which mother?"

"And why kept secret? He never hid none o' them he got on serving girls."

170

"No," She looked at him with some respect. Another thought came to her; he must be six or seven and twenty. "Do you remember his lady who was lost?"

"Aye, m' lady. But t' rightful heir 'd never be hid. He can't be hers!"

"She was killed." Everything she learned made her more sure of that.

"He never murdered her, m' lady! Never! Don't you believe that."

"She cannot be alive."

"Lady Julitta, he never lifted hand to a woman in his life. Never so much as clouted me mother, God rest her, and a sillier gowk—No. Soft wi' 'em. Couldn't pass by a sightly lass. Soft as pig's grease. That's the sort has his way wi' 'em. He never killed her."

She believed him. Against all reason, all evidence, she believed he spoke the exact truth. Murder had been done, and Lord Maurice had known it. "Who did?" she asked, and in silence they stared at each other.

12

Julitta and Alain crossed the drawbridge almost on the heels of another party, and drew rein among a throng of idlers gathering to an ominous spectacle. She picked out the participants from her elevation; Sir Brien, retribution on horseback; Godric half-drunk and blustering between two archers, his arms bound; the innkeeper grey-faced with fear, his wrists corded to a soldier's saddle, and a grimy woodcutter jellied with dread similarly secured. His donkey, flicking long ears at the crowd, suddenly loosed a nerve-jarring bray, and Julitta saw in the wicker panniers on his back damning evidence, a forequarter of pork and a great piece of beef flank. She thrust Folie through the jostling spectators, compelling her to obedience though she jibbed and sidled. The woodcutter, in panic at thought of a noose about his windpipe, screeched his own innocence.

"I never knowed nowt, m' lady! I never knowed they was thieving! I only taken t' stuff as they bid me! Oh m' lady, me good lady, 'tweren't no blame o' mine!"

Godric spat in his face. "Whoreson liar! Had thi share, tha did!"

The crowd gabbled, swaying back and forth, and Alain

came up alongside on his steady dun as they pressed close, to force them back from Folie when she tried to plunge.

"Silence!" Julitta cried, and to her secret surprise was instantly obeyed. "Back!" The throng retreated, leaving Sir Brien, his men and the conspirators in the center of their ring. "Sir Brien?"

He saluted her. "My lady, my men and I kept watch on Godric as you bade us. When the woodcutter brought faggots for the ovens Godric placed flesh from the kitchen in the empty panniers, under stale bread and broken meats. Roger and Eric will bear witness to that. We followed the woodcutter from the castle and took him at the inn, in the act of handing over the flesh to Herbert the innkeeper. There are five of us to testify to that."

"A lie!" snarled Godric, his brow greasy with the sweat of fear. "I give him nowt but kitchen leavings, that I've full right to bestow."

"Kitchen leavings?" repeated Julitta, and signed to one of the soldiers to lift the pork and beef from the ass's panniers and hold them for all to see. A gasp went up from the crowd, and she turned sternly on the woodcutter.

He waited for no question. "I did as he bid me — I took t' flesh to Herbert at t' inn — but I swear to you by Our Lady I never knowed 'twas thieving, noble lady." He would have plumped down on his knees but the tether prevented him, and at his distressful wail in her ears Folie danced sideways with upflung head. Julitta reined her in sharply, and Alain swung from his saddle and moved to take her bridle at need.

"Hidden under kitchen leavings? You knew." Her rejection struck him speechless. She turned grimly on the innkeeper, who was of harder stuff.

"I bought what was offered me," he said sullenly. "There's no crime in that, m' lady."

"To buy in open market, no." Julitta demolished that specious defence. "To receive in secret what's sent in secret, that's conspiring all three of you to rob your lord." The crowd was hushed as though she were a judge pronouncing sen-

174

tence, and with an odd shock she realized that indeed that function was hers, delegated by her husband with all else. Lifting her gaze from the three criminals, she saw the nods of agreement, Brien's approval, dismayed alarm among the scullions, the men-at-arms' respect. At one side the girl Thyra drew breath with a croaking sob and stared up with wild eyes, and Constance set an arm about her.

Julitta squared her shoulders. The responsibility of life or death was a chilling weight. She surveyed the three; the woodcutter despicably craven, the innkeeper maintaining his hardihood, Godric invincibly surly. He had committed his depredations unchallenged until he reckoned them hallowed by usage into his customary right; there was no repentance in him. Her hesitation was a barely perceptible pause before decision.

"You robbed Lord Adam. You shall go before him for judgment. Bestow them in the cells."

The guards moved briskly, a pair to each prisoner. Sir Brien dismounted to supervise. Grooms led away the horses. Julitta remained in the saddle, above the bustle, listening with unmoved face to Godric's curses. Comment and speculation buzzed through the crowd. One voice wondered audibly whether Lord Adam would swing them from his gallows or content himself by lopping their right hands, and the woodcutter sagged whimpering between his guards.

"*No!*" shrieked Thyra, breaking from Constance's hold and plunging clumsily at Julitta. "You shall not — bitch — devil — it's all spite — because he's my brother — jealous because Lord Adam favored me!" A man grabbed her and recoiled with a yelp, blood leaping; red-streaked steel gleamed in her grip. Julitta reined Folie aside; the mare squealed and flung up her head. The crazed wench stabbed, reaching high over the saddle bow to gut her, and she struck hand and knife aside. The point scored Folie's rump, and Julitta straddled a fury. A kick sent the girl spinning; then the palfrey was rearing up with forehooves flailing, shrieking outrage. Men scattered. Julitta clung grimly. Alain's face and upflung arms were at her thigh; his open mouth yelled something she did not hear; the crupper jarred her spine as Folie bucked, twisted, bucked, reared again. Hands gripped girdle and knee and dragged, hauling her from the saddle as Folie towered back and up; then the bright arches of steel drove down to shatter her. Bone crunched, warm wetness spattered her face, the earth jarred her side and a heavy weight flattened her.

A clamor of voices filled her ears. The inert body across her own jolted and lifted away; an arm passed under her shoulders and heaved her up, while a distracted voice exclaimed, "My lady! My lady!" in her ear. Someone was screaming steadily and witlessly. She gulped for breath, found a man's shoulder behind her head, put up her hand to her face and brought it away stickily red. The shock cleared her senses. She blinked up into Brien's horrified face, past his head to two appalled soldiers staring at something beside her. She twisted to her knees beside Alain, sprawled with upturned face, his hair soaking scarlet and his eyes gazing blankly at the sun.

She stiffened. The blood had almost ceased to run, was blackening into clots as she looked, and through it she could see the crescent-shaped wound crushed into his left temple and the brain spilling through it. She reached out a shaking hand and closed his eyes. "Lord, have mercy!" she whispered aloud. Then Sir Brien's arm was about her again, and his anxious voice in her ears.

"My lady, my lady, you're not hurt? Dear God, that mad bitch — she didn't —"

Julitta shook her head and climbed unsteadily to her feet. She was trembling in every muscle, and her knees were unstable under her, so that she was thankful for the knight's arm and leaned dizzily on his strength. "Alain —"

"Poor gallant fellow — but he saved you — you'd have been trampled but he shielded you — killed instantly —"

She stood shaking, gazing down at his body. Violent death she had seen many times, but this man had given his life for hers, had gone from her in that instant's unhesitant valor as she had just learned to value him — gone before God's judgment with all his sins upon him. But the Lord Christ had spoken words she recalled about those who laid down life for love or duty; she trusted God to deal mercifully with Alain for that sacrifice.

"Send for the priest," she commanded, recovering control of her voice. "And his kin — what kin had he? There must be Masses said for his soul. And this night he shall lie before the altar."

Someone spread a blanket on the trampled earth. Two archers lifted the dead man on to it, and one knelt and with rough piety straightened his limbs and folded his hands, before they covered him and carried him away. Others had caught and brought back the struggling mare, wild with the scent of blood in her nostrils; Brien's angry gesture dismissed her to the stables. The forgotten prisoners were hustled away.

Only then did Julitta give heed to the mindless screams that had not ceased since first she had become aware of them. She freed herself from Brien's hold and turned to Thyra. The girl was crouched on the ground, her hands on her belly and her head thrown back, howling like a bereaved dog. Constance hovered over her, holding her by the shoulders and trying to coax her into quiet. The donkey pattered forward and brayed again. Julitta felt a crazed giggle rising in her, and as she fought it the nightmare steadied to reality.

Brien slapped the girl's face, halting her in mid-howl. "Murderess! You've killed your child's father!"

She blinked at him and lifted a hand to the print of his fingers on her cheek. Her gaze sought Julitta, and malevolence made it human. "Bitch! I'd ha' gutted you but for him!" Then intense surprise wiped all else from her face; she gripped her belly and wailed on another note.

"Her travail's on her!" cried Constance.

Brien backed, looking helplessly to Julitta. Justice must relinquish Thyra until her labor had been accomplished. Adela moved from the crowd to stand over her, and Julitta was relieved; here was competence. She drew a long breath and spoke firmly.

"Take her in, to the chamber next to mine. And someone in Heaven's name rid us of that ass's voice!"

177

The chamber, next to the stair, was cluttered with the seneschal's accounts, but they made room amid chests and tally sticks to lay a straw pallet on the floor and the girl on that. Lack of space gave good reason for excluding all but Adela and Constance, and since the sight of her incited Thyra to snarls or whimpers, Julitta left her tending to them and watched from the doorway. Constance would have been rid of her.

"It's not seemly for a girl who's never borne a child to witness a delivery."

"I am mistress of this household and my duty is here." Julitta could have added that she had played midwife more than once, in camp and castle.

Folie's kick, though it had caught Thyra only a glancing blow on the flank, had accelerated labor. A third bearing should go easily, but this was going very hard. The girl threshed and writhed, exhausting her strength to no purpose, and beside herself with fear of her body's travail and fear of hanging.

Julitta was summoned away to speak with the priest, a peasant huddling his spiritual authority about him like a cloak. He agreed to Alain's lying that night before the altar with watchers and candles, to Masses for his soul's repose, to the arrangements she proposed for his burial. "And when all's dealt with, come back, Father Simon. There'll be a child to baptize, maybe in haste, and the mother's in a grievous state."

It had worsened even during her brief absence; Thyra was moaning, her knees drawn up to her belly, and at sight of Julitta she screamed and passed into a convulsion. Constance had been trying to give her wine, but it had dribbled over her chin and cheeks in red streaks. Adela rose from her knees and joined Julitta on the gallery.

"The waters have broken, and she's passing blood," she murmured. "She's beyond our skill. I reckon the babe's cross-lodged, and we can't budge it."

"There's a wise woman in the village. I'll summon her," Julitta answered, looking at the girl with appalled pity. A

178

cross-birth was perhaps the most dreaded mischance of childbed, and usually meant death for mother and child. She dispatched one of the girls, and stood outside the door. Unconsciously she laid a hand on her own unburdened belly, and thought of the time when this travail would be hers. She crossed herself and prayed.

Thyra clung wailing to Constance, who somehow persuaded her to drink wine and lie still. The blood came in a steady seeping they could not check, and Julitta, conning over her little knowledge, suspected that Folie's kick had done worse hurt than she had guessed.

Wooden shoes clattered on the gallery, and Hallgerd stood at Julitta's elbow, breathing ale fumes. "'Save you, m' lady." She regarded the prostrate girl with more exasperation than sympathy. "Now you'd reckon a wench as allus makes a hard do o' birthing 'd show a mite o' caution in her coupling, wouldn't you?"

"You're drunk!" Constance snapped. "Find some respect for your betters. She's brought to bed untimely —"

"Respect where it's earned, and not so drunk as I can't tell seven months from nine." Hallgerd joined battle. She dropped to her knees more spryly than a young nun to her orisons. "I've been a midwife forty-odd years, so don't tell me it's Lord Adam's brat."

"You're insolent!"

"Aye. I'm insolent, and you're a liar. What now?"

"Take yourself out of this hold!"

"Thought as this birthing was too much for you? 'Twasn't you summoned me, and 'tisn't for you to dismiss me. You're not t' mistress now."

Julitta herself had hesitated to say as much so bluntly, and Constance choked. Thyra moaned and reached to her. Hallgerd, having established beyond doubt who commanded, turned to the girl. Ale had not impaired her competence. Her knotty fingers explored the gravid belly, her concentration so absolute that all expression was wiped from her face. She sat back on her heels, and nodded. "Aye, t' brat's crosslodged." Her hands kneaded and manipulated, and Thyra

179

cried out. "Too far along to turn it." She reached for the oil flask, tipped a generous palmful and anointed her hands and wrists. Presently she straightened and wiped blood from her fingers. "T' passage not far enough open," she reported, frowning at the strained rag. She shrugged, took up the winejug and poured. She raised the cup to salute Julitta. "Mary Mother save you, m' lady. Not often wine comes my way."

"I don't grudge it so long as you remain competent."

"Never nowt else," she asserted, and Julitta believed her.

The afternoon wore on. Adela slipped away, murmuring that she must look to her little Charles. Julitta had not known his name until then. No one called by name a child who could neither hear nor answer. She herself remained to preserve the decencies between Constance and Hallgerd, for enmity rose between them as the wine sank in the jug and the midwife's tongue grew saltier. After an hour or so she oiled her hands and probed again.

"Times you can reach t' child's legs and bring it forth," she explained over her shoulder, but a foreboding in her face told Julitta the chance was desperate. There was no doubting her dedication. Thyra was quieter, staring at their faces.

"Not time yet. Give her more wine." She watched Constance raise the girl's head, watched Thyra lie back exhausted, her sweat-darkened hair strewn across the straw pillow, caught Julitta's eye and stood up. They withdrew on to the gallery.

"T' afterbirth's come away first. That kick. I can't reach t' bairn; passage blocked. It's God's will she won't hang." She crossed herself.

"The child?" Julitta asked, mechanically repeating the gesture.

"Can't be born. More blood; she'll go on a rush of it. Send for t' priest, m' lady."

He was talking to Brien in the hall, and started for the stair at her signal. Julitta went back into the chamber that reaked of sweat, blood and wine. Thyra stared from her to Hallgerd and said starkly, "I'm going to die."

"God have mercy on you," Julitta said. "Here is Father Simon to shrive you."

180

"My baby? What o' my baby?"

"I shall see to its rearing. I promise you."

Her face twisted. "Godric — you'll hang me brother! Spite —"

Julitta, a dull ache in her breast for the wretched creature's torment, said gently, "I'll procure your brother what mercy I can from Lord Adam. That also I promise."

"Spite — me own lady said you was jealous — nowt but spite —"

"What cause had I? The child's not my lord's. Your brother's a thief. There's plain truth."

"Alain's baby — leastways I think so. Oh!"

The cry was for the entrance of the priest, bearing the pyx. The three women sank to their knees in reverence. Then they rose and filed out that he might hear Thyra's confession. Leaving the other two at the stairhead, Julitta ran down to tell Brien to have Godric out of the cell and sobered so that he might bid his sister farewell. Returning more slowly, pondering her promise to rear the baby that could not be born, she was checked at the stair's foot by Constance's venomous voice.

"Drunken hag, and you know nothing of your trade!"

"Enough to know as when't' husband's gone afore Lady Day a wife's wise to bear t' brat by Christmas," Hallgerd retorted.

"You slanderous liar, I'll have you in the stocks!"

"I've eyes to see." She chuckled maliciously. "When it's too late for t' pennyroyal, time for t' seven grains o' black-spurred rye.* Aye, and in a dry season they're mortal hard to come by. So what's to be done by a wench as doesn't know her simples but to bear t' brat?"

Julitta, who did know her simples, stood locked in comprehension. A cry of fury mingled with the smack of a blow. A yelp, a thump, and a succession of slithering noises heralded Hallgerd's descent, bouncing round the newel and rebounding from the wall with her feet tangled in her skirts. Julitta lunged and caught her as she toppled the last half-dozen

*Ergot, the poison of rye fungus, has been known from ancient times as a powerful abortifacient.

181

priest had gone back to his window to pray; she waited until he rose from his knees and they went down together.

Sir Bertram came to her, peering in the ruddy sunset-light so that she wondered whether, like the blind man in Holy Writ, he saw men as trees walking. "Both dead, my lady?" he asked heavily. The priest's movements, and the cessation of all sound from the birth room, had made that an easy deduction. At her affirmation he bowed his head with his customary dignity. "God rest them. My lady, there's a woman awaiting you. The innkeeper's wife."

The woman came forward. She had been weeping, but she stood hardily before her lady as her husband had done. She understood that confession and restitution, besides conferring spiritual benefit, soften the rancor of the wronged. She admitted the whole conspiracy, attributing its origin to Godric, and thrust a weighty bag into Julitta's hands.

"It's all here, m' lady — every penny we have! You'll turn him loose, m' lady?" She dropped to her knees, tears starting. "What's to become o' me bairns an' me — five I've borne, and three living, and another on t' way — what's to come if you hangs me man? Ha' mercy, gracious lady!" She clawed at Julitta's gown, blotched with Alain's and Thyra's blood, and the girl jerked away.

"I cannot — it's not for me —" she stammered. Power of life and death she had never dreamed of wielding, and three had died already for this thievery. Then she glimpsed calculation in the frantic eyes, watchful for the appeal's effect, and hardened against the woman who consigned Godric and the woodcutter to the gibbet without a word of extenuation. "This must wait on Lord Adam's judgment," she said firmly.

"But — but then he'll hang!" she blurted, lurching to her feet.

"I will ask his mercy," Julitta promised. The woman crumpled.

"He'll hang — he'll hang for sure — and what'll become o' me and t' bairns?" she muttered, and stumbled towards the stair, blind with weeping. Sir Bertram signed to a soldier, who steered her out. Julitta clenched her hands so that her nails dug into her palms, and ground her teeth together to keep her tongue from granting her prayer. Justice was not so served, and authority must serve justice though her own harshness hurt her heart.

"You're a she-wolf for vindictiveness," Constance declared in her ear. "You'll hang three to be revenged on Godric, because he upheld me."

"Did you license him to be a thief?"

She turned into her husband's arms. "Hear how I am used — after all my years — and my poor Thyra butchered by the drab she brought in!" She buried her face in his shoulder and sobbed.

He patted her, and over her kerchief frowned at Julitta. "Indeed, my lady, you are of an age to be her daughter, and you use my wife with gross discourtesy."

"Discourtesy? Am I to tolerate her inciting the servants to defiance because she'll not accept me as mistress?" Julitta blazed. Constance had achieved an unmendable breach between them.

13

Julitta locked the door of the undercroft, where she had spent a dusty morning supervising the grain bins' cleansing, and looked down the hall at the preparations for dinner. The servants found a new alacrity with trestles and tableboards, a scullion hurriedly kicked up a couple of boys wrestling in the rushes, and a couple whispering in a corner broke apart and scrambled to find separate tasks in a spreading hush of guilt. She stood a moment in bleak appreciation of these manifestations, and then started for her chamber to wash and freshen herself.

The watchman's horn blared, startling every head up, and then a clatter of feet on the stair heralded the roof sentinel.

"Company approaching the gate, m' lady!"

"Not Lord Adam?"

"Nay, m' lady. I'd not sound the alarm for m' lord. Looks like your uncle o' Chivingham in t' lead."

"Hell's Teeth!" she said. The fellow grinned. "And how many?"

"Six more. I thought to recognize t' lords o' Digglewick and Crossthwaite."

Her first impulse was to refuse entry to any, her second

187

to exclude the Ladies' Delight, but sense and courtesy restrained her; one would be an offence against kinship, the other would rouse the very scandal she wished to avoid. And in her husband's absence she was Brentborough, its honor hers. "Pass the word for Sir Brien, and tell the cook we entertain noble guests," she commanded, and fled to her chamber calling for Avice and warm water.

She met her uncle's unconvincing smile, Humphrey's smirk and Sir Everard's courtesy with equal civility, and set them at table in order of seniority, so that her uncle sat beside her and Sir Everard by Red Adam's empty chair. Throughout the first course she maintained decorous conversation, kept a watchful eye on the service, and ignored every smile or meaning glance that Humphrey sent her with a composure that at last pierced the hide of his vanity, so that he attended sulkily to his trencher. Inwardly Julitta marveled at herself. A few weeks ago she had flinched from her uncle's frown, fluttered in silly infatuation at Humphrey's slightest smile. Now she had only contempt for both.

The course was removed. The serving lads went round with ewers, basins and towels. Sir Everard commended her on the changes she had wrought in so short a space. "We'd heard of drastic measures," he added with his diffident smile.

"Drastic measures," she agreed with a smile, "and a deal of whitewash."

"It's the sound training she had in my wife's household," Lord William declared. "I hope you bear that in mind, girl."

"Every day I remember your charity," Julitta declared with perfect truth.

"It's brought you to high rank and rule over great estates, and it's right that you should show gratitude," he continued. "I'd expected to hear before now that you had reconciled your husband to me. After all, I am now his uncle by marriage, and this foolish quarrel—"

"He has little time left him for deciding," Lord William declared harshly. "Any day Leicester will land with reinforcements. He may be in Norfolk even now, and soon all England will be the Young King's."

188

"He has little time left for deciding," Lord William declared harshly. "Any day Leicester will land with reinforcements. He may be in Norfolk even now, and soon all England will be the Young King's."

"I doubt a rabble of unemployed weavers will achieve so much," Julitta answered grimly, "or that many will see Flanders again."

His head reared up. Everard spoke quickly. "Your husband's been misinformed. The Earl has a strong force, and only contrary winds have so far prevented his landing to seize England. You must realize it's urgent Lord Adam should join our rightful King."

"If he waits until England's ours he'll forfeit all he has," William declared forcefully. "It's your duty, I tell you, niece, to bring him to his senses."

"You waste your wind," said Humphrey. "He's the Old King's man, and you'll not budge him."

"God's Head, am I to stand by and see my niece and her husband driven back to following the tourneys?"

"You're magnanimous, after he ordered you out of this very hall."

"Let be, let be, since Lord William is prepared to forgive it." Everard hurried to make peace. "There is nothing nearer to his desire than reconciliation. You must persuade Lord Adam to it, my lady."

It was by now clear to Julitta that her uncle and Everard did most earnestly desire reconciliation and Red Adam's alliance in rebellion, and Humphrey emphatically did not. "Be sure I shall faithfully repeat your arguments to my lord," she said sedately, and nodded to the servers to bring round the second course.

"I marvel," Humphrey said sourly, "that you'll so tamely swallow his insults."

"God's Death, he insulted you also, and here you sit swallowing his meat! Nor did we ask your company—"

"My lords, no good will come—"

A sudden bustle at the stairhead checked the rising voices, and Red Adam himself threw back the leather curtain with

189

a clatter of rings on the rod, and strode impetuously up the hall. Julitta half rose in her chair, her face alight with welcome.

"My lord!"

He grinned at her through a mask of dust streaked to mud by sweat. It matted his hair and dulled his blue riding gear to dim gray as he came closer she saw his eyes-rimmed and bloodshot by its irritation and fatigue. "God save you, my lady!" he saluted her, took the dais steps in one stride, and swung round the table to grasp her extended hands and kiss her on the mouth. Then he turned, still holding her hands, and surveyed his uninvited guests with one sardonic eyebrow lifting. "A pleasure I'd not looked for," he observed with edged politeness; Julitta knew him well enough now to recognize intense anger hard-held.

"We are here on your behalf—" Everard began.

"To command your allegiance to your rightful King—" Lord William took up the tale.

Red Adam's grin was a mirthless snarl. "Your rightful King, my lords, has sold the North Parts to the Scots!"

They gaped in plain unbelief. "No!" Everard whispered.

Lord William lurched to his feet. "That's not true!"

"Your feckless whelp has acknowledged King William's claims to Cumberland and Northumberland in exchange for his aid."

"He could not! He could never—it's a lie put about by his enemies," Everard desperately protested.

"Hell's Teeth! Are you besotted blind? The Justiciar and the Constable are in York. They made truce with the Leicester rebels. The Scots are over the Border; they've overrun Northumberland; you know better than we do whether Hugh de Puiset, Bishop of Durham, is of your party, but if he hasn't raised Durham to fight them off they'll be over the Tees next. Will you blather of plots when the Galloway devils are beating your doors in?"

"It's a good tale," Humphrey sneered, "to keep us sitting fast at home when our King needs us."

"You haven't a daughter to be raped or a wife to be ripped up," Red Adam retorted brutally. The two men had gasped

190

and glanced in quick alarm at each other. He drew a long breath and spoke more temperately. "In God's Name, heed me! Send out the warning and look to your defences, or we'll have the invasion of thirty-eight over again!"

They looked resentfully at him, reluctant to credit his story. Lord William, still standing, pushed back his stool. "We waste our time," he said heavily. "Maybe you will regret not heeding us, when the Young King rules. Come, friends. We are not welcome here."

"Finish your dinner, unless your appetite's clean departed," Red Adam jibed. "I don't drive my guests from my table midway through their meal."

Lord William glared at him. "Only concern for your welfare, nephew, brought me here, and small gratitude you show. Next time you will beg our charity." He shook his head mournfully over Julitta. "Farewell, niece. You have failed in your duty, and will regret it!"

"If I can reconcile—" Sir Everard began ineffectually.

"Enough!" growled Humphrey, though he seemed pleased at the outcome as he smiled at Julitta behind Red Adam's back; satisfied as a cat at an unguarded cream bowl, and unresentful of yesterday's discomfiture. In courtesy she and her husband accompanied their guests to the stair, and for all her wariness Humphrey contrived to possess himself of her hand and bent ostentatiously over it, murmuring just too audibly, "Until our next meeting, fair lady, when I promise amends for the last."

She flushed to her hair. Red Adam cocked an inquiring eyebrow as the clatter of departure ceased in the stairwell. "And what did that cryptic farewell signify, sweet wife?"

"Why, you are a day too late, Lord Adam," Constance said smoothly from behind him. "Yesterday your sweet wife met him secretly in the woods."

He whirled, and as she recoiled he caught her by the shoulders. "You filthy viper, you *dare* slander your mistress?"

Fury turned her white and red, and she spat malice. "Ask her why she said she would visit the convent and never went! Ask her—"

191

"Hold that foul tongue or I'll rip it from your jaws! You'll not make me believe the least ill of my lady!" Sir Bertram was blundering forward, and he thrust her into her husband's arms. "Remove her from my sight! Before God, I'll have you out of my household, Lady Serpent!"

The half-blind giant folded protective arms about her, and Julitta caught the glint of triumph in her face as she hid it against his shoulder.

"If God would but grant me my eyes to avenge your wrongs—"

"You're blind indeed!" Red Adam snapped. "She defamed her lady, and the wrong's not hers!"

"It's truth! Ask her!" cried Constance.

Julitta stood frozen with dread and anger, defenceless against any lie; her one witness, Alain, was dead. Avid faces gaped at her as she stood accused of whoredom before all the household. Scalded by shame and injustice, she lifted her face to her husband's.

"My—my lord—"

His arm came about her rigid waist. "You are my chaste wife, and you don't stoop to answer such filthy ravings," he declared. "Take that reptile out!" His fierce gaze turned on the audience. "Hell's Teeth, is this supposed to be a seemly dinner?" Men and women cowered on the benches, not daring to look up from their trenchers. He drew Julitta back to the dais through a grisly hush. Her heart hammered in her breast as she took her seat, and her breath came with difficulty. She kept her wits to nod to the servers, who brought on and set forth the second course with anxious care.

Red Adam struck a cloud of gritty dust from his tunic, and the boy came scuttling with water. "I'm not fit to sit at a decent table," he said, "but rather than delay further I'll pray you pardon my state." She murmured acknowledgment, knowing the reckoning was but postponed, and tried to eat. Nor did he find much appetite. Half way through the course Reynald, Giles, Odo and the men of Red Adam's outdistanced escort came clattering in, saddle-sore and empty. It seemed an eternity before she and her husband could leave the hall to seek privacy.

"Walk with me, my lady," he said, gripped her hand beyond withdrawing and led her briskly between the buildings, out on to the windy headland. He uttered no other word until they reached his favorite outlook over the sea. His silence was that of bitter anger, the more terrifying for its restraint, and she stumbled after him among the stones, afraid as she had never been for all her uncle's blaring wrath. He stared out over the gray-green waste all alive under the sun, and drew and loosed one hard breath. Then he turned abruptly and grasped her shoulders. She flinched, and surprise widened his eyes.

"Julitta, you're not afraid of me?"

"My lord, truly—truly it was not by my design—"

"My dear, there's no need to assure me. It's not you I'm angry with."

He believed her. He dismissed all insinuations with a perfect trust in her integrity. She gulped on a sob, tears flooding her eyes. He tipped up her face and kissed her on the cheek like a child. "Never be afraid of me, Julitta," he bade her, and she realized afresh that she could hurt him.

He drew her to a hollow in the lee of a rocky outcrop, with a lichened slab for a seat, and curled up on the turf at her feet, hugging his knees. "How I kept my hands from throttling that female viper I don't know," he commented. "Tell me what happened."

She started on the story. "She must have been the one who betrayed me. How else did he know I'd ride that way?" she interrupted herself.

"Oswald," he said cryptically.

"Yes, he was her escort."

"He's the one runs her dubious errands. She'd have sent him ahead to give Humphrey time to intercept you. I'll take him into a corner with my riding whip and hear all he knows. Go on." His face hardened, but all he said at the end was, "The Ladies' Delight doesn't know how lucky he is to have his guts still safe in his belly."

"What will you do to him?"

"I'd like to challenge him and carve his liver out, but since that would involve you in worse scandal I'll have to

193

pretend ignorance. *He* won't boast that a groom and a girl bested him. I wonder, though, that he had the impudence to show his nose in Brentborough today."

"He's at odds with my uncle. None of them trust each other. And he was against your joining the rebels, while my uncle and Sir Everard were urging it."

"I suspect that his intentions are matrimonial."

"But how—oh!"

"When you were a dowerless maid you were only fit to be his leman, but he'd condescend to marry my widow—reminding you of his condescension every day, and thrice on Fridays."

"That means—"

"I reckon the next move in this plot is my murder, and the production of this boy as rightful heir in my place. Brentborough controls the coast road and the moors; the rebels can't move south or on York and leave it at their backs. The Ladies' Delight is a foresighted man. If the Old King wins, when the dust of battle settles he hopes to emerge wedded to my widow and professing loyalty."

"And he imagines I'm besotted enough to fall into his arms!"

"He's a vain man. At the least your dower-rights would give him one-third of all my estates. As I'm the last legitimate Lorismond he'd have a claim to the whole."

"I'd put my knife under his ribs first!"

"You'd do well. There's neither mercy nor honor in him. Even your uncle has some trace of feeling in his carcass, if he strives still to convert me to his cause rather than slay me."

"You are in danger, and enemies in our own household."

He grinned. "Lady Viper and that drunken lout in the kitchen conspiring to poison the pottage?"

"He'll afflict our bellies no longer," she declared, and finished yesterday's story with the account of Alain's valor and Thyra's end.

"I thank God for him," Red Adam said, with such earnestness that she flushed and stared out over the sunlit sea. "If I'd lost you—"

He reached up and caught her hand. She felt her flush burn hotter, and spoke hurriedly to hide it. "Alain told me of old Lord Maurice and his wife. He—he said that he was too soft with women ever to strike one—that he did not kill his lady."

"That old tale haunts you too?" He was silent a long moment, plucking at the coarse grass with his free hand. "He knew she was dead. He sent for me."

"Yes. He'd not have done that—no. But he was soft with women."

"Feckless," he amended wryly. "It's in the breed—witness that valiant knave Alain. So was I. My father too. He was a landless knight, forever wandering from war to war Fecklessness runs in the Lorismond blood. It's ruin to them, unless they marry advisedly." He smiled up at her, his hold tightening on her fingers. "My mother was a merchant's daughter; maybe she explains my taste for Erling's unknightly practices." He plucked again at the dry seed heads. "She held my father to sense. She and Annora were heart and core of our family. Annora died of hunger and the bloody flux in the siege of Laverne castle; my mother two days after we were relieved, in untimely childbed of a stillborn girl."

He gazed out to sea, and abruptly released her hand to link his own about his knees. She gazed in appalled sympathy on his dust-matted hair. "She was scarcely buried when he conceived a crack-brained scheme to amend his fortunes by going on Crusade and marrying some heiress of Outremer. He'd one encumbrance: I'd survived. So he bore me to the nearest monastery and offered me as an oblate to be bred up a monk. Aymar and Adrien were already provided for, squires to a lord in Poitou; he could sail with a clear conscience." He held his voice level, but she sensed the outrage of abandonment to that desolate boy.

"I could not abide it. I was eleven years old, raw from that free life. You know it too; you also were thrust into

195

that cage. Rules, supervision, the endless spying and tale-bearing, no liberty, and dear God, the boredom—the creaking bell-ridden hour by hour routine from year's end to year's end! And the novice-master had the weightiest arm I've ever encountered.

"I ran away seven times in four years, and each time I was dragged back, as soon as my stripes healed I'd be planning the next try. The last time, a knight guesting in the monastery on his way Outremer had pity on it and offered to relieve it of me. By then I reckon the Abbot suspected I'd disrupt any cloister, and the novice-master admitted I'd a devil he couldn't thrash out of me, so they consigned me to his charge and I sailed off to the Holy Land with a witless notion of finding my father again."

"Did you?" she asked at last, as he stayed silent.

"He was dead. He'd died within three months of reaching it." He sighed and wriggled down to stretch full-length at her feet, his hands clasped under his head. "Oh, it wasn't entirely wasted. I can read and write Latin, so I can occupy my old age inditing scandalous chronicles—"

"If you achieve old age."

"Vixen! And I can misuse Holy Writ, and also cast accounts, which makes me a hard man for an embezzling steward to cheat." A wheeling gull swung down to inspect them, uttered a raucous squawk and soared away on an updraft. He grinned at it. "Mention of stewards puts me in mind. You've done marvels, lass. What's been the state of stewardship here?"

"Criminal," she answered briefly, and told him of the meat store. He took it calmly, as though he had expected no better.

"I'm not afraid of a siege," he explained. "Only disciplined mercenaries can sit down to a siege; knights and raiders like the Scots won't dig. Moreover, this countryside can't support siege warfare; the besiegers would be starved out first. It's surprise we must guard against. I've promised Richard de Luci, the Justiciar, to lend him thirty men, and he expects me to lead them in person. He's scraped up what force he could, but he had to leave a watch on Leicester, and his raw levies need stiffening. There's no trusting that shifty knave the Bishop of Durham, and still no sure news from over the Tees, but we reckon he's let them pass. You'll be captain of Brentborough again, Julitta. Simple enough; keep the drawbridge hoisted and all rebels and Scots outside."

The prospect daunted her, but she knew her duty. "I'll endeavour to justify your trust, my lord."

"Valiant vixen! At the first chance I'll rid you of that serpent Constance. You report well of Brien; he shall be seneschal."

"Sir Bertram—he has served long—"

"He's too blind to perform his duties, and he's given his wits into his wife's keeping. He goes. I've a small estate down in Sussex; he'll manage that harmlessly. Hell's Teeth, I'd have that creature out this day but for the consideration I owe him! I can guess what battles you've had."

Julitta grinned. "I won every skirmish." She did not relate the tale of her grievances; in her experience nothing interested men less than a recounting of women's paltry disputes.

"You take a deal of defeating, obviously," he said lazily, shifted a little on the turf and shut his eyes against the sun's glare. Julitta, her story done, sat looking out over the sea, down the swoop of the cliff's side to the foaming turmoil at its foot. A contented silence fell about them, compounded of many harmonious sounds: the roaring of the waves, the wind's thin song in the grass, the gulls' crying, the shrill exulting of a lark twinkling high above them, the chirp of grasshoppers and a faint popping of gorsepods. The sun was warm, reminding her of days under hotter skies than England's. She sat and dreamed until it occurred to her that Red Adam's voice was unnaturally stilled.

He was asleep. He looked, with his dirty face and tangled hair, like an overgrown urchin—like that boy who had lost the heart and core of his life, his mother and little sister, and been abandoned like a stray pup by his father to a hateful existence. She understood his revolt, his embracing the disorderly life of the tourney circuit, his reckless wenching and

197

drinking with like-minded profligates; what no contemplation could fathom was his sudden access of sobriety at his
enforced marriage.

She leaned back against the rock, soaking contentedly in
the sun. For days she had been driving resentful servants
and herself to perform prodigies of labor, bearing responsibility for all Brentborough; yesterday had been overpiled with
horror; after a haunted night had come the morning's burials
and her uncle's advent. Now gloom fell away. It had no place
in this warmth and peace, with her husband asleep at her
feet. She could study his face; the harshly-defined bones of
brow and cheek and jaw, his beak of nose and slightly project-
ing ears, the red stubble pricking through the dust and the
fair skin that even high summer had but lightly tanned. With
his mocking eyes closed and wide mouth relaxed, he looked
vulnerable as now she knew him to be, not the monster she
had once reckoned him. She found herself flushing unaccount-
ably, and turned her attention elsewhere.

She peered under shading hands at the blinding sky to
find the lark, a palpitating star hung high aloft. She watched
the gulls sailing in their endless spirals or riding the breakers
below. A long-tailed mouse ran out upon the turf near Red
Adam's foot, misled by their stillness, and sat up to groom
his coat and whiskers, his eyes and quivering nose constantly
alert for the least stir. Julitta smiled, and sat unmoving until
the tiny beast had finished preening and flicked away into
the tussocks. Then a blue-gray missile hurled past her and
down among the sailing gulls. One exploded in a burst of
feathers and blood, and with one fierce scream raptor and
prey plummeted towards the sea, checked, leveled and beat
away for the cliff beyond Arnisby.

Red Adam was up on one elbow, blinking against the
dazzle, his right hand on dagger haft. He glanced inquiringly
at Julitta.

"A peregrine!" she cried, and pointed. He followed the
speeding arrowhead, dark against the bright water, with the
carcass dangling from its talons, out of sight. Then he sat
up and clasped his knees.

198

"Flagrant discourtesy, to fall asleep in a lady's presence. Why didn't you kick me in the ribs, vixen?"

"I was enjoying the novelty," she answered demurely. "In my lord's company, and he not uttering a word."

She had never heard him laugh aloud before, this chuckle of delight. He jested for others, but his grin had little mirth about it; occasionally he had smiled at her with kindness, and now this rare laughter joined a frail bond between them. He scrambled up and reached both hands to pull her to her feet.

"Oh vixen, vixen, I adore you!"

She saw his intention in his mirthful face, and drew back sharply. He checked at once.

"No, you're not ready yet. The dog-wolf must woo and wait until his lady yields freely." He slipped his arm almost absently about her waist and faced out over the sea.

"I . . . it's not . . . I must seem surly and ungrateful . . ."

"Don't put gratitude between us! In your own good time, Julitta. Moreover, I've observed that the surest way to your tender heart is to be hurt or sick or wretched, and I don't qualify." He smiled down, and turned back towards the castle while she digested that. He gave a jaw-cracking yawn, and then seemed to notice his own state, for he dropped his arm and beat at his filthy tunic. "Hell's Teeth, I'm too foul to be handling a lady!"

"A bath will amend that."

"It's digging out I'll need, after forty miles on these roads. We were benighted at a lonely farmstead, where the fleas rejoiced in us. They'd not heard of the Scots until we gave warning. If those fools had listened to me we could have set watchers and beacons five leagues out on the hills. Hugh de Puiset must have let them pass. If he'd raised Durham he'd be howling to York for reinforcements. He hasn't learned yet there's more to being Bishop of Durham than building a vast cathedral to his glory!"

He strode into the castle precincts shouting for Odo, and disappeared into the laundry, where a cauldron of water was

199

now always simmering over a low fire. Half an hour later Julitta was summoned from the bower. A court was convened in the hall, and the household assembling. Her husband was already in his great chair, sleek-headed as an otter and trimly shaven. As she joined him he leaned to murmur in her ear, "Oswald's run."

"What do you wager he's at Crossthwaite?"

"Not a clipped penny; you'd win."

The errand-runner mattered little; Constance's treachery was known if unproven, and in her spite she had over-reached herself. She would go as soon as Red Adam could arrange it. Yet when Julitta looked at her, standing beside her husband, she did not seem downcast. Indeed, her face was secretly satisfied, so that uneasiness prickled along Julitta's spine.

The household knights stood on either side of the high chairs. The sergeants had marshaled the guards below the dais. Father Simon, there to administer the ordeal or to shrive condemned sinners, set out ink-horn and manor rolls at the side table and unhandily trimmed a quill. Servants and a sprinkling of peasants were gathered together to see what kind of justice Lord Adam dispensed.

The prisoners stumbled in, blinking at the daylight. The better part of twenty-four hours in which to think on the noose had worn threadbare even Godric's truculence, and the woodcutter seemed a walking corpse. They had no possible defence, and they knew it. Brien's indictment was a formality. Red Adam, contemplating them stone-faced, was curt.

"You confess?"

Godric licked dry lips, glanced from him to the waiting soldiers, and jerked his head. "Aye, me lord." The innkeeper echoed him. The woodcutter, beyond speech, writhed colorless lips.

"You're hanging-ripe, all three. But three lives have already been paid for this sin, and my dear lady has asked mercy for you. I refuse her nothing. Sweyn! A hundred lashes for Godric the thief. Fifty each for his accomplices. Then cast them forth."

"Turned squeamish?" Reynald sneered as the hall

200

emptied. He shot at Julitta a glance of sour dislike. "If you'd heed *my* advice inst—"

Red Adam thrust erect, and he recoiled, his utterance chopped off in mid-syllable. For a moment he stood slack-jawed; then he scowled impartially at them both and slouched out to watch the entertainment in the bailey. Red Adam drew audible breath. "One of these days I'll tear his lewd tongue out!" he growled, and stalked after him to supervise the punishment he had ordered. Julitta saw that whatever substitute for friendship had once linked her husband to Reynald was irrevocably sundered. They had come to detest each other, and Reynald blamed her for it.

A flogging was an entertainment Julitta preferred to miss. She hastened to the bower with Avice, and tried to close her ears to the sounds rising from the bailey. The green gown was finished, the black well advanced. She worked until the women came chattering back, dwelling with relish on the spectacle's horrid details. They would despise her for squeamishness if she forbade the discussion, so she set them to work and left them to it.

On the landing she was almost overthrown by her husband, bounding up three steps at a time. He caught her arms. "Here you are! Your pardon, lady!" He drew her round the corner to the window splay where yesterday the priest had knelt, and gently pushed her on to the stone seat. He leaned over with one foot resting on it.

"You'll command again tomorrow, lady captain. I'll leave you Sweyn and the four oldest spearmen; they're dependable. A dozen archers, and Sir Brien of course. It's a scanty garrison, but if the Scots appear the peasants will take refuge here, and those that haven't bows can at least throw rocks at their heads."

"I warned Arnisby and Brentborough yesterday."

"If your uncle and his friends weren't too addled to heed me—a bloody lesson they may find it, and too many innocents with them. Chivingham might be held by a stout defence, but Digglewick and Crossthwaite haven't even walls to keep them out." He pushed erect and ran his hand through his hair; he looked tired and harassed. "We'll be gone at first light, and in York by nightfall if the horseflesh holds out. It's in a wretched state, and if you can trace that groom of yours, drag him in by the hair. We need him." He jerked his head at Avice, shrinking against the wall. "Here, girl! Run down to the stables and send Odo to me."

She cringed into the plaster. "Oh no, m' lord . . . please m' lord, not me . . . oh m' lady . . . "

"What ails you now? Do as you're bidden!" snapped Julitta.

"That ugly beast . . . he'll ravish me . . . oh, please . . ."

"If he stays for that when I've summoned him I'll have his ears. Go!" he ordered, and she took one white glance at his face and fled wailing. "Your Ivar can count one gain out of his troubles; she's no use to any man."

"She's a timid creature," Julitta agreed temperately. "She'd reason to dread wedding Cuthbert; he's a brute and his first wife was happy to die. And the sluts here fill her with tales of rape until she's scared of the sight of a man."

"She's coddled her fears until there's nothing else in her. As soon as you can procure a decent maid-servant I'll be rid of her."

She looked up curiously. "I'd not thought so poor a thing worthy of your loathing."

He grimaced. "I've always loathed those pale things that scuttle from the light when you lift a flat stone. Irrational, I know."

And all the stronger for that, Julitta realized. His antipathy had been plain from the first, though he might not have voiced it had his temper not been frayed by strain.

"Have I angered you, Julitta?"

"No, my lord," she answered honestly. "She was to have married Ivar, but she's never uttered a word of concern for him. It's only herself she whines for, and I'm sick of it."

"So much damp I wonder you're not covered with blue mold!"

A shaggy head poked round the corner. "You wanted me, Lord Adam?"

"Salute your lady, you unmannered lout! You'll pardon me, sweet wife?" He turned to Odo. "All's ready in the stables?"

"Ready as it'll every be, Lord Adam."

"Then furbish up my good hauberk and see my sword's well edged. A spare lance, and the open helmet."

"Now, Master Adam, the closed pot's a deal safer—"

"Apart from being stifled in a hot engagement, one sideways swipe and the thing turns and blinds you. I'll see what's about me."

"None the less, I'll take the closed pot—"

Their voices faded in the stairwell. Julitta firmly collected her sniveling maid-servant and marched down to the kitchen, where Godric's successor came near steaming under his mistress's eye in his anxiety to reach her exacting standards.

When the household was assembling for supper Baldwin Dogsmeat and his wife approached their host to thank him for his hospitality. "I trust we've been of service to your lady in your absence, but we've burdened your graciousness long enough, Adam, knowing your views on mercenaries," he finished, with that shaft of malice to point his courtesy.

"I hope you'll find my uncle-in-law as gracious," Red Adam answered drily.

He blinked, disconcerted. Adela grinned at him. "Well informed, Lord Adam?"

"You've met no one else who could afford you," he explained. "And if he's promised you the plundering of Brentborough, I warn you, your share won't buy a week's drinking for your company." Baldwin's gaze involuntarily sought the display of plate on the sideboard, and swiveled back to his host's smile of grim amusement. "And if you go hunting with that pack, you'll need sharp teeth to tear a mouthful from your comrades' jaws."

His warning had bitten sharply into Baldwin's own doubts about the venture; Julitta glimpsed the uncertainty in his face before his shark's grin covered it. He shrugged jauntily. "You'll not deter me, Lord Adam. Even a mercenary must live."

"More's the pity," his host agreed mordantly, and moved away for a word with Brien and Giles.

Adela said quietly to Julitta, "Indeed, it's past time we went."

"I have been truly glad of your helpfulness."

"You've been most gracious, as my husband said, to welcome me into your household, when you knew I was a whore and my son's not his."

"That's your concern, not mine."

"Oh, I'm not repentant," she said coolly. "I married for my son's sake. Baldwin's an honest enough scoundrel, and he knows Charles is all my life."

"It's a grievous pity," Julitta murmured.

"God's judgment on my sins, the priests say," she answered harshly. "Four sons I've borne and lost, and only this one left me." The fierce face was maternal as Julitta had only seen it when she looked on her elf-child. Then it hardened again. "I grow maudlin. Yet believe I wish you well, and whatever I can do to further your happiness is yours to command." Her clear eyes gazed levelly into Julitta's, she bent her knee and was moving to her place at the table's end when the girl's attention was jerked from her by a growl of intense wrath two paces from her side.

"You are dismissing me fron Brentborough!" Sir Bertram confronted Red Adam, towering as he had done in his mighty prime.

"I'm offering you an honorable retirement to easier duties, after your hard years here.'"

"You imply I'm incapable—"

"Imply!" Reynald jeered. "You purblind dotard, there's hoof-rot in the stables, the cook thieving—"

"Be quiet, Reynald! Sir Bertram, you must admit your handicap, and that you've had to trust too much to worthless underlings. My lady—"

"Aye, there's the heart of it! It's to satisfy that wench you've wedded, because she resents my gracious lady's help and counsel." His voice rose to a lion's roar, and his huge hands lifted in threat.

"Hell's Teeth, are we disputing who's mistress of this household?" Red Adam's own tinder-dry wrath had kindled. "Your wife's a slatternly chatelaine, and you've closed your nose to it, whatever the state of your eyesight."

One knotted fist drew back and then dropped. Sir Bertram reeled, a spasm of pain screwing his face, and stood drawing careful breath. Red Adam, poised to dodge the blow, started forward with extended hands, his wrath turned to compunction, but the older man's glare checked him in mid-stride.

"I have lived too long," he said desolately. "My own true lord would not have used me so."

Constance was there as he turned away, her arm about him, and he labored towards the stair, leaning on her solid shoulder. For all the solicitude of her hands, the look on her face was one of satisfaction. Red Adam watched them go, biting his under lip. As the curtain fell behind them he shrugged slightly and moved towards his high chair.

"If you're planning to make me seneschal in his room," stated Reynald aggressively, "I've no wish for it. That place of yours near Bristol will suit me best."

"No."

"What d'you mean?"

"That I'll have no drunken incompetent mismanaging my wealthiest estate, nor yet this one."

"God's Head, is your word worthless? You promised me—"

"Neither. You may have the manor in Devon, or that by Chester, and drink and wench at my charges. There's my word fulfilled."

"God's Death, here's piety! The wildest devil ever emptied a jug or tumbled a whore, and now your blood's bewitched to whey! With all the choicest wines and strumpets in York for your pleasure, not once would you go sporting with me of a night like a comrade."

"Why, you did double duty by both," Red Adam said evenly. Reynald, sober enough to recognize peril, sat down grumbling under his breath, but by now folk were so accustomed to his boorishness that, as long as he did not interrupt the conversation, none heeded him. The talk ran on the Scots. The memory of their last incursion was still raw in the North Parts, and stories of atrocities provided enlightenment for the incomers; priests gelded, pregnant women ripped up, babies spitted on spears, naked girls roped in droves and driven away to shameful slavery. It was not conducive to good appetite, and Julitta was glad when the company dispersed.

Red Adam went down to the guardroom to make the final arrangements for the morrow. Reynald, for once moderately sober, engaged with Giles in a game of dice. Julitta made a brief round of her household, but forebore to enter the bower, where Sir Bertram lay in the great bed that should be Lord Adam's and hers, had they not preferred the wall chamber's privacy. Conscious of a long day behind her, she mounted to it now as the last sunrays slanted to fill the western windows. Her hands were sticky with unguents from the hospital. "Fetch water and towels, girl," she commanded Avice at the landing. Her hand was on her door when a squeal on the stair swung her swiftly about. A rush of stumbling feet, and Avice hurtled out shrieking with every breath, and flung herself at Julitta.

"Save me, m' lady! Oh Mary Mother, save me! Don't let him—no! No!"

Reynald lumbered grinning through the doorway, and she fell to her knees, scrabbled round behind Julitta and clung wailing to her skirts. Julitta slapped her smartly.

"On your feet, you silly wench, and be quiet! He'll not touch you."

"God's Blood, lady whore's get, you're lofty now you're wedded!" Reynald sneered. "You'll do as Adam bids you, and he'll not refuse his comrade a serving wench." He lurched forward, and Avice shrieked again and cowered between Julitta and the heavy door, without wit to dive within and bar it.

"You drunken lout!" Julitta wrenched free to confront him. "There's a household of strumpets for your use; my serving maid's not for your ravishing."

206

Her contempt scalded his self-esteem. His face suffused almost purple, he snarled at her. Feet pelted up the stair, and Red Adam projected himself on to the gallery.

"Hell's Teeth! Whose throat's being cut?" Avice uttered a thin cry and crouched against the door. He looked down at her in utter disgust. "Stop squealing like a pig with the knife at its neck, you drizzling ninny! It's time you learned what a man is."

"You've refused me my due rights, Adam," Reynald stated thickly. "You'll not deny me this serving wench tonight—or are you keeping her for yourself?"

"For myself? I've no use for the misery."

Reynald took that for consent, and grinned at Julitta in brutal satisfaction. Avice squealed and scrambled up. Julitta thrust her towards her chamber, but she backed away along the gallery, mouth and eyes witlessly agape. Julitta set herself in Reynald's path, staring past him with all her earliest aversion into her husband's shocked face.

"She is my serving maid under my protection."

"You heard Adam. Give her up as he bids you!"

"You make me a bawd to provide a brothel for your friend's pleasure?" Julitta demanded savagely of her husband, her right hand at her sleeve. Appalled comprehension filled his face.

"Reynald, no! My wife's honor is mine! *No!*"

Reynald was already launched. He grabbed Julitta by the arm and spun her back into the doorway. Red Adam hurtled past her and sprang on him as he clawed for the screaming girl. They grappled, reeling against the wall. Reynald, his forearm under Red Adam's chin, tried to crack his skull against the stone. The younger man twisted lithely, back-heeled him and flung him off. He shot backward, arms upflung and whirling, and crashed against the gallery rail. With a splintering screech the rotten wood gave way. For a heart's beat he hung poised on the edge, a yell of alarm bursting from him. Red Adam lunged, making a grab at his tunic skirts, but the falling weight was too much for him. The two toppled together to crash among the stacked trestles, boards and benches below.

207

14

Reynald breathed, but he was a dead man. Just behind his left ear the skull was dented in by contact with a bench end; the right side of his face was drawn awry, his right arm and leg twitching, and blood already dribbled from his ears and nose. No chirurgeon on earth could do anything for him. Julitta crossed herself, murmured, "God have mercy on his soul," and rose from her knees. Red Adam, hunched on the bench. lifted his head from his hands, looked into her face and bowed it again. She considered him closely. Blood had been streaked across his brow and was trickling down the back of his left hand, and he breathed with a care that told her enough.

"Ribs?" she demanded curtly, and without waiting for an answer nodded to Odo. He and Brien helped him out of tunic and shirt and stretched him on the bench, where he stared gray-faced at the rafters. Purpling bruises stained all down the right side of his chest; it had not been the fall, but the stacked furniture that had done the mischief. Neither her eyes nor gently-exploring hand could discern any distortion of his ribs. She acidly dissuaded Brien from prodding to learn whether they were broken, cracked or merely bruised;

it made no difference to her treatment, which was to bind him tightly with half a dozen swaddling bands. The blood came from his hand; the nails of the first two fingers had been ripped back from the quick by his desperate grab at Reynald's tunic.

Still wordless, he twisted up and swung his feet to the floor. Again he bowed his head into his hands, and she laid her hand lightly on his bare shoulder. He had the skim-milk skin that commonly afflects his unfortunate coloring, so that she felt the scars before she saw the white network of them over his back, and remembered the novice-master with the weightiest arm he had ever encountered. Weighty indeed; she wondered at the stupidity that reckoned by such usage to inculcate in a wild boy any vocation for the cloister.

At her bidding four men carefully lifted Reynald on a tableboard and carried him to the nearest wall-chamber. She followed. There was nothing to be done for his body, but she was mistress of this household and the duty of vigil by his deathbed was hers. She knelt again, repeating formal prayers. It came to her with a shock of candor that her only regret for this drunkard's end was that her husband had been its instrument.

He came after her, dressed again and moving stiffly, to stand over his victim. For a little space he watched the congested face, its flaccid left side sharply contrasted with the distorted right, his own face drained of all color but the blotched freckles.

"As God is my witness," he said painfully, "I intended him no hurt."

"Your hand testifies to it," she said, nodding at his broken nails still oozing red. He spread his fingers and stared as though he had not known their state, bemused with shock. Presently he knelt at the improvised bier's foot, his lips moving soundlessly.

Father Simon bustled in. He regarded Red Adam's plain distress with an odd mixture of condemnation and sympathy, shook his head and administered Extreme Unction. As a conscientious priest he announced that he would wait until the end, for the unlikely chance that some return of consciousness might enable the dying sinner to repent and be absolved. They waited. Odo, unbidden, had stationed himself outside the door-curtain to repel the morbidly curious.

Julitta narrowly eyed her husband. He should be in bed easing his damaged ribs, but she knew better than to suggest it. She still resented the way he had used Avice, but compassion warred in her with anger. His own reckless tongue was responsible for Reynald's death; by apparently granting him leave for rape and rescinding it with his next breath he had provoked the quarrel, and he knew it. This penance he had set himself. Julitta recognized that Red Adam had brought away from his monastery an unappeasable conscience. He kept his vigil through the night alone, as though unaware of Father Simon's censorious gaze and Julitta's own irritated concern.

Reynald died just before dawn, without regaining his senses. When the last breath had rattled to silence in his throat, Red Adam shivered and covered his face with his hands. Then he lurched to lifeless feet and reeled against the wall. Odo was within the curtain on the instant, his arm clamped under his master's shoulders to hold him erect. For a long moment he leaned on his servant, looking down on the dead man. "Lord, have mercy on his soul," he said quietly. He limped out, and the priest and Julitta gazed eloquently at each other.

Twilight was murky gray in the window-slots when she emerged and saw her husband, engaged in consultation with Sir Brien. In the raw dawn it was Sir Brien who led the troop across the drawbridge in his lord's stead, and took the track for Arnisby and York. Certainly Red Adam was in no state to ride forty rough miles, but that he should concede as much astonished his wife. She would have expected him rather to insist on achieving it if he had to be tied in the saddle. When the men had departed he withdrew to his own chamber with Father Simon.

Julitta found Avice huddled in a corner of the bower, half demented with terror, her face swollen almost beyond recognition from a night's weeping. She shook her without sympathy. The silly creature invited violence.

"Get up! You've nothing to fear now. Wash your face and get to work."

"Oh m' lady, I'm feared! I'm mortal feared!"

"Sir Reynald's dead. Pray for his soul's rest and stop blubbering."

"But Lord Adam killed him for me. Now he'll take me. Oh Mother o' God, what's to become o' me?"

"Lord Adam would not touch you with the butt of his lance shaft."

"But they all says — they tells me —"

"Must you believe every folly they pour into your ears? Out and get to work!"

That would be the scandal that went abroad, murder done in a sordid dispute over a serving woman, and Red Adam had no defence against it. She herself had been the only witness who could testify that Reynald's death was sheer accident, and few would choose to believe her. She strode away fuming, and made her anger serve her on her rounds, so that the mere whisper of her approach spurred diligence. She came to the death chamber, and stepped inside to see that the dead man had been shrouded and disposed in decency, and to pray. Red Adam stood keeping vigil at his feet, his hands clasped on the hilt of his drawn sword and his face almost as gray as the rigid one on the bier. His shadowed eyes lifted briefly to her face, but he neither moved nor spoke, and she forbore to utter her opinion.

Lifting the curtain, she almost collided with Odo, gloomily propped against the archway. His face lighted a little as their gaze met in mutual exasperation, and he stepped after her. "My lady, can *you* not budge him?" he muttered. "He'll not heed what I say; he'll keep the deathwatch until he drops."

She stared, momentarily astonished; she had never thought of the influence she could exert over a man who had proved he desired to please her. She pondered a moment under Odo's anxious gaze, an obscure distaste suddenly hardening to conviction that it would be wrong, a lessening of them both.

212

"I'll not come between him and his conscience."

"My lady, he'll heed *you*. No rest he's had all night, nor bite nor sup this day —"

"It's the expiation he has set himself, and I'll not diminish him."

"What sort of wife're you to comfort a man?" he demanded, and trod growling back to the curtain. She throttled her own temper, the more convinced that Red Adam, though he might have yielded to an appeal from her, did not desire comforting but upholding in his resolve. She herself was not blameless; her own edged tongue had done its share in precipitating that final quarrel. As soon as she had bidden farewell to Baldwin Dogsmeat and Adela, she returned to kneel by Reynald's bier and share his vigil, mildly grateful to the convent that had taught her the appropriate Penitential Psalms to repeat. Red Adam, she was sure, was repeating them too. Occasionally he glanced at her, but there was no readable emotion in his drained and weary face.

He held out until most of the afternoon was spent, and then Odo half-carried him up the stairs, berating him all the way, and helped him into the bed where Julitta had slept alone, fending off her assistance. She ran down to mix a posset of eggs, milk and hot spiced wine and bore it to him. Odo set an arm under his shoulders, but he thrust up on one elbow, reached out his other hand for the cup and silenced his tame bear's expostulations with candid ingratitude.

"Hell's Teeth, you cluck like a nursemaid over a wet-bottomed brat! And I'll not be fed like one." He gulped, coughed, spilled the liquid down his bare chest and swore fervently. She took back the cup, signaled to Odo to get out, and mopped him dry with his discarded shirt. He regarded her warily. "And if you're going to reprove me likewise —"

"Not I. If you reckon your carcass beaten out of iron, you'll learn your error without my telling."

"Vixen!" He sipped more cautiously at the posset, and watched her over the cup. "Odo's a fool," he said abruptly. "You have been light in great darkness this day, Julitta."

She flushed, and could find no words to answer him. He drank off the posset and lay back, frowning abstractedly

213

at the rafters. She sat on the bed's edge and waited, hoping that he might fall asleep; he was utterly spent.

"That girl must go," he announced harshly. "I'll not tolerate her another day in my household."

"Avice? But —"

"She's been a man's death, and never showed herself to say a prayer for his soul's rest. If I know her, she's done naught but wail and weep over her own senseless fears."

"That's true."

"And I'll not have it said I killed my comrade and dishonored my wife to debauch her serving maid. She goes."

That was the tale men would believe none the less, and both knew it. The murderous Lorismond blood, folk would say, and remember Lord Maurice's vanished wife. "I cannot return her to my uncle to be forced into Cuthbert's bed," she said practically, "nor can I cast her adrift in a world of men. She sews well. Doubtless the convent could make use of her." Avice was her own servant, but she would not dispute his very real aversion.

"Deal as generously as you see fit, but she goes tomorrow, willing or not."

"She'll be thankful beyond words," Julitta replied incautiously.

He jerked up. "Does that gutless ninny actually imagine... I'd sooner lay a wet fish!"

Such virtue made her giggle, and he smiled reluctantly and subsided again on the pillow. He pulled the covers over his shoulders against the breeze from the window, and she rose to close the shutter. When she turned back he was asleep. She stood a long moment in the dimness, listening to his even breathing, and then sought out Avice.

The girl plumped on her knees, fresh tears dripping from her chin, and clutched at Julitta's gown in an ecstacy of thankfulness. "Oh, my lady, Mary Mother reward you for your goodness! I'll be safe there. M' lord can't ravish me... I'll not be made a whore... "

"You insult my lord," snapped Julitta. "The thought was his. He has no desire to take a — a wet fish to his bed.

Stop blubbering! You must have an inexhaustible well within you."

And as she stalked indignantly away she knew that the girl, once safely behind the nunnery walls, would boast for the rest of her life how Red Adam had slain his comrade for her. She too would be happily rid of this creature. She had lived without a serving maid for seventeen years, and could do so a few months longer.

At nightfall she slipped into her chamber without attendance or candle, and stood inside the door listening to Red Adam's quiet breathing. She felt her way round the bed and bent for the straw pallet. It scraped faintly on the floor, and he stirred in the dark.

"Come to bed, vixen," he said softly.

She stood irresolute, thankful for the darkness that hid her blush. "I — I meant this night —"

"If you don't join me I'll return to that penitential lying." He moved more purposefully.

"No, you must not!"

"No risk to you," he added wryly, "for I'm not fit to give you pleasure or do myself credit. Come to bed, Julitta."

Under his words' lightness she sensed an appeal that ended her reluctance. She scrambled out of her clothes and between the sheets, warmed by his body, a nd lay tense beside him, waiting for she knew not what. But he remained motionless, and she relaxed, and with belated solicitude inquired, "Do your ribs pain you, my lord?"

"No. Your bandages are the worst of it; itchy as Pharaoh's plague of lice."

"They are apt to be." She matched his dryness.

For a long time he was silent, but Julitta, aware of every breath he drew, knew that he was not asleep. Abruptly his voice came from the dark, "I never before killed a Christian soul."

"Without intent," she said swiftly.

"He's no less dead. In his sins, with no time to repent."

"We cannot know that," she answered, uncomfortably stirred. "My lord, do you not believe that Almighty God,

215

who is our Father and knows all men's hearts, must judge more mercifully than mankind?"

"I wish I could. At the monastery they'd a most fearsome Last Judgment painted in the church, with Hell-mouth all dragon teeth and fire and tormenting fiends. I've dreamed of it again, with Reynald screeching —"

Impulsively she reached across the few inches of impassable gulf between them and found his arm, whose slack flesh stiffened into corded sinew at her touch. Her hand slid down to his, which closed sharply on it. "You're over-watched and sorely troubled, my lord. Say a prayer for his soul's rest, and then sleep."

"Sensible Julitta," he murmured, faint amusement in his voice. He repeated under his breath words that she knew well enough to say with him, translating them from the Latin in her mind. "Suffer us not, at our last hour, for any pains of death, to fall from thee." Presently he slept again, still loosely clasping her hand. She did not withdraw it, and only when she slept herself did their fingers unclose and fall apart.

15

Under no circumstances could the Abbess be cordial, but she received her guests with civility, and even found an acid graciousness in response to Red Adam's courtesy. She accepted his warning of Scots over the Border composedly, and was scathing about a Prince who bedded with such vermin and fools who conspired with him, but her manner intimated that no Scot would dare thrust his nose inside her sacred precincts, and to all his urging of precautions she returned only cool thanks. She had very little to say to Julitta, beyond admonishing her to give thanks that Almighty God had raised her to such high estate. Her tone conveyed that she reckoned Him grievously misguided. Julitta sensibly said no more than courtesy demanded and left it to her husband to cajole this wasp of a woman.

The Abbess stiffened when he presented Avice, but his words and Julitta's silence somehow implied that she had cast out a potential rival in jealous fury and he was the one anxious to bestow her safely. He warranted her virtuous and diligent, and the Abbess conceded that a sewing maid might be of use to her community and he certainly could not permit a helpless maid to be cast adrift. The discreet presentation of a chinking bag ratified the agreement, and she smiled thinly at Julitta's resentment. That was unfeigned; the bag contained all too high a proportion of Brentborough's resources in coined silver.

A bell tinkled, an elderly nun appeared, and Avice was whisked away without a backward look or a word of gratitude. Julitta wondered grimly whether she would be as happy after a few days of this notorious martinet's governance. Red Adam expressed his obligation. In the bleak parlor, under the northern window, he looked gaunt and drained, his resemblance to Lord Maurice more marked than usual. Then the Abbess formally blessed and dismissed them, and the door thudded at their heels.

Red Adam wriggled his shoulders and released his breath. "Is she wholly compounded of vinegar and venom?" he murmured irreverently. "I'm properly humbled that you once would have returned to her rule rather than marry me."

A weight lifted from Julitta, and she laughed at him over her shoulder. "A desperate choice," she mocked, leading him swiftly along familiar passages towards the boarders' parlor, and rejoiced in the flash of his teeth as he strode after her.

Uproar greeted their entry into the parlor, and a wave of small dogs surged about their ankles. Skirts they knew offered no pleasurable sensation to testing teeth, but they snapped and snarled about Red Adam's spurred riding boots, and scrabbled yelping at his shabby hose. Suppressing his natural impulse to kick them the parlor's length, he stood fast amidst the onslaught, while their mistress fluted ineffectually from her armed chair deep in cushions.

"Sweetings, sweetings, you must not! Come back to your own lady — come back, wicked doglings!"

Up rose her aged serving woman from behind the chessboard, and trod into the yapping pack. They scuttled before her, voicing indignation, and subsided about their mistress's chair and in her gown's folds, ears pricked and nostrils quivering. Restraining giggles, Julitta took her husband's hand and led him to the chair.

"Pardon my silling darlings; they have not seen a man in months," said the high voice.

218

"Lady Cecily, this is my husband, Lord Adam de Loris-mond."

The plump old face, softly wrinkled like a hand long immersed in water, beamed at them. She lifted a hand from the pair of pups slumbering in her lap and held it out. Her dark gown was liberally furred with dog hairs, and the parlor stank like a kennel. Red Adam bowed, smiling, and raised her pudgy fingers to his lips. "God save you, Lady Cecily."

She appraised him candidly. "A Lorismond surely. You've a great look of my kinsman Maurice, God rest him. You must be the baby we saw born in Saint Osburga's nunnery near Bristol?"

He shook his head. "I was born by a roadside in Provence."

"You're sure?" she asked foolishly. "He was such a beautiful redhaired baby. Maurice brought the mother to the nunnery for succor. A kinsman's widow she was. So very young to be widowed, so golden and pretty."

"Too old," observed the serving woman behind her chair. "It'll be but eighteen years come Easter. Year afore we come her."

"I'm two-and-twenty," Red Adam told her, "and my father outlived my mother."

"But I don't understand. Maurice told me, that visit before he died, he'd sent for his heir. His last legitimate kinsman, he said, and I was sure that must have been our baby. Emma here was midwife, and I washed and swaddled him — a fine strong child, and without doubt a Lorismond. There's no mistaking the hair, is there? Maybe he died; so many babies do. I bore three myself, but they all died before they were out of swaddling bands." She looked down at the sleeping puppies, and stroked their soft bodies; then her oddly innocent eyes lifted to survey Red Adam again. "I'm Maurice's father's cousin's widow, you know. I never did find out whose widow Constance was; she was too grieved to talk of it."

The servant's skeptical snort rang like a worhorse's. "Not her! Heartless little strumpet, and no widow at all, I'll wager!"

"Shame, Emma! That's prejudice and scandal-mongering. I've reckoned the kin over and over. My husband's brother was childless, and his sister a nun. Such an ugly girl, but

219

then, red hair and freckles are very unbecoming to a female. But there was another cousin, and I did hear he had two sons, Aymar and Arnulf. I supposed she'd been married to one of them."

Again Red Adam shook his head. "Aymar died unmarried. Arnulf was my father."

"She was Maurice's leman," Emma declared, "and the boy his bastard. I've told you often enough."

"Maurice would not lie to me —"

"He couldn't tell the Reverend Mother one tale and you another," Emma pointed out. "You're too trustful, m' lady."

Julitta dared not look at her husband. "What happened to the baby?" she asked.

"I never learned. Maurice came and fetched them both away that summer, before little Geoffrey was two months old. He told me he'd found a husband for Constance. Was it all lies?" She looked up at Red Adam, easy tears brimming in her eyes, her voice plaintive and bewildered. "You mean she wasn't . . . she was . . . oh, I'd never have believed Maurice could have deceived me so!"

"It's a way men have," Red Adam said, wryly gentle. He took the agitated hands. "She was another man's wife, and Lorismond brats are known by the headmark. Forgive him and let be; it's eighteen years past, and he's dead."

"Old sins cast long shadows," Emma croaked, and gave him a peculiar look. Julitta wondered how much she knew, and whether talk of a strange Lorismond boy at Crossthwaite had penetrated to the convent kitchens. Servants and serfs knew everything about their betters, and news flew on the wind.

"All those lies!" Lady Cecily mourned, tears dripping from her chins and spotting her dingy gown. "But it was his weakness; all Lorismonds are fools over women. I dare say you're one too, and I should be sorry for Julitta here, but they are always *kind* to their wives even when they're most unfaithful, so I suppose she'll forgive you. Though Julitta — a dear girl, and so clever with her needle and skilled with simples — but she *is* rather inflexible, so don't be *flagrant* about it, like

Maurice, will you? He'd seduce Bertrade's serving maids, and the girls give themselves such airs a wife's bound to resent it. And it makes for such an *unsettled* household."

"That's excellent counsel," said Red Adam with admirable composure. Julitta avoided his eyes.

Lady Cecily shook her head mournfully. "Do heed it, dear boy. It's the family failing. Poor Maurice couldn't resist a pretty girl, and look what befell — at least, no one knows what befell, but he rued it to the day he died. Besides, it's so *uncomfortable* — unless you're married to a jellyfish, and dear Julitta isn't that. I mean, marriage is for a lifetime, and I don't know whether it's worse if she forgives you or doesn't when you have to live with it, so for your own sake as well as hers, dear boy, do be *discreet* —"

"If I can't be faithful," he finished gravely.

"Lorismonds never are. And *blatant* too. So a timely word, I thought, as you're new married — people are so *uncharitable*, and there's talk of that wench you brought, and Julitta's a girl of such hardy spirit —"

"Such a vixen, you mean. I shan't dare transgress."

Julitta, ruffling in ready protectiveness, subsided. His amusement was kindly. Having accepted Lady Cecily's admonitions meekly, he seated himself behind the chessboard at her first hint that she would welcome a fresh opponent, and never stirred when a puppy lifted a leg against his boot. She watched the play. Lady Cecily's father, she had often been told, had bred her up to it. Her game was unexpectedly shrewd, Red Adam's erratically brilliant. She would like to match with him herself, she thought, following the battle. He paid the old woman the compliment of winning, and they smiled at each other over the pieces.

His stool scraped on the flagstones. "I regret your revenge must be postponed, Lady Cecily, until our next encounter," he said, towering above renewed yelps and scrabblings. "We'd best begone if we're to return in daylight." He hesitated, his face hardening. "I've warned the Abbess, but I fear she reckons me unduly alarming. The Scots are over the Border, and they are no respecters of nunneries."

"Dear boy, I'm old enought to remember 'thirty-eight."

"Be ready to run." He looked at Emma. "Prepare your bundles; food, warm clothing, money and jewels. If I prove unduly alarming, I'll thank God."

"Good lad," Emma grimly commended.

They both reduced him to the status of a ten-year-old urchin, but he accepted it in amiable deference to their years. He knelt with Julitta to receive the old lady's blessing; she kissed them both, and bestowed on her a silver brooch, whispering in her ear, "Not *too* inflexible, dear girl."

At the gate, where their bored escort hurriedly broke off dicing and scrambled for the horses, he surveyed the head-high wall of unmortared stone that enclosed the nunnery buildings. It would hardly impede a scrambling brat, let alone a loot-crazed Galloway wolf. Behind the enclosure trees scattered and failed as the ground climbed to bare fells dyed by flowering heather; before them the open fields dropped away to the narrowing valley where dark woods closed in menace. In the saddle, he turned again, searching the purple tops as though he thought to see Scots bursting from the sky and streaming over the slopes.

Peasants were straggling home from the fields to the huddle of huts near the gate. Red Adam beckoned one to his stirrup and in halting, careful English repeated his warning. He was understood. The man's face of alarm, his urgent thanks, his hasty summoning of neighbors showed that indeed 'thirty-eight was not forgotten in the North. Red Adam frowned again at the gate, and then impatiently urged his horse into a canter.

"At least they're warned," he said grimly. "Not that there's much use in warning the she-weasel of what she doesn't wish to heed. But that good old woman —"

"She's silly, but so kind."

"Simple, but not silly. She spoke rare sense. Witness our King's example. He insulted his high-couraged Queen with his low-born paramours, and she's bred up his sons against him."

They approached the woods, and he signaled to the six-

222

archer escort following two by two. Four took station fifty yards ahead, Odo and the other two dropped back a similar distance. "Any suspicious sight or sound, yell and spur straight through," he ordered. "That's the last thing ambushers expect." He checked his sword's oiled movement in its scabbard. Julitta glanced into his face and surreptitiously touched her knife's hilt. His mouth twisted wryly, and then he frowned.

"We should have stayed behind walls," he admitted. "I'm a fool. I could have borne with that dripping misery a little longer."

"You expect —?"

"I've the scent of trouble in my nostrils. Unchancy times to ride abroad. But at least the warning's gone forth."

Yet the dusty miles spun back beneath their horses' hooves, and the woods were quiet. Birds and beasts, alerted by the advance guards' passage, were hushed and hidden, and only the chuckle of hurrying water and the dry leaves' whisper accompanied the clatter of iron shoes. Rainclouds were blowing up behind them, darkening the evening as they swallowed the sinking sun. At the derelict cottage where the Ladies' Delight had waylaid Julitta they halted briefly to breathe the horses before the long climb out of the valley, and swung down to ease their legs.

"It's just reached my addled wits," said Red Adam, "that you're an uncommonly forbearing vixen. Here I've bereft you of your one honest serving maid, and you've not torn my ears off."

"An oversight. Would it have availed me?"

"No. But in truth I've brought you to a wretched household. You should have a dozen demoiselles of good family to attend you, not a handful of insolent strumpets. Though how I'm ever to provide them the Devil knows."

"They will come, she said serenely. "No careful parent would place his child in Lord Maurice's charge to be debauched, but when your peers know that ours is a decent household we shall have demoiselles of good breeding, and pages and squires too, to train up."

"Hell's Teeth, can you imagine a peer of mine sending a maiden daughter to be trained up in *my* household?"

"Not easily, but if your access of virtue should last long enough —"

He laughed outright, and she warmed with pleasure. "I've a horrid foreboding, wife, that you'll reform me into the virtuous head of that seemly household."

"Consider its advantages. At least you'd not need guard against affronted husbands."

"I'll be far too frightened of my vixen wife," he agreed, his face alight with mirth. He glanced up at the sky behind her, and beckoned Odo to bring up the horses. The tame bear's face was creased with bewilderment as he looked from one to the other, unable to match his own opinion of Julitta to his master's frank delight in her. Red Adam swung her up with a grimace for his bruises; his ribs had proved intact, but gaudily sore. Odo scowled and fell in behind.

They passed unchallenged through the woods, and came through spitting rain into Brentborough village as the dusk shut down. Dim candleshine illumined the church windows. Red Adam glanced aside at the three raw graves in a row, and crossed himself, his lips moving. Then he looked rather oddly at Julitta, his face shadowed.

"I'd come to loathe him, but he'd been nearly a year beside me."

"You miss him."

"Yes. A foolish matter; he was the only person left to call me by name."

The words fell bleakly, and in vivid insight Julitta saw him exposed naked; not the wild young lord, arrogant in his honors, but the harried lad encompassed by enemies and burdened by responsibilities to which he had never been bred — and unlike her, he did not find them exhilarating.

"My wife might," Red Adam suggested, "if it pleased her."

Startled, she stared mistrustfully. He offered an uncommon privilege, and in her softened humor she might have agreed to his appeal, had she not recognized that acceptance entailed

224

capitulation. He smiled at her, and she read sureness in that smile. The hatred of her enforced marriage day had worn away little by little as she lived with him, but a small remaining core of resentment hardened at his confidence; she was not to be cozened so easily.

"My lord, it would not be seemly," she answered woodenly.

"And you're not truly my wife." Her refusal had smitten the smile from his mouth. "Julitta, a bargain. If ever you do call me by name, I shall know that you *are* my wife."

She considered it a moment. "Agreed."

The horses quickened their pace up the last incline, eager for their warm stables and well-filled mangers. A head moved against the gray sky in a crenel above the gateway, a helmet glinting. An order rasped. The drawbridge's planks, hoisted in their faces, stirred and groaned, descending with ponderous precision a yard from the hooves of Red Adam's mount, so that he trod it without breaking stop. They clattered across, beneath the portcullis's teeth and into the arch's black tunnel, the rearguard crowding close. The portcullis clashed down unbidden behind the last horse's tail. Red Adam, swinging from his saddle as he reached the bailey, turned a startled face.

"Who — *ah!*"

Four men, standing unseen, flattened against the inner wall, pounced forward. A single cry of surprise was jarred out of him as he went down under their onslaught, and was answered by a bellow. Julitta's palfrey reared up whinnying with terror at the scrimmage under his nose, and as she fought to control him, men sprang from every shadow. Odo charged roaring from the gateway, his right hand pointed with a stripe of light, straight for the first person he encountered. Julitta's screech mingled with Red Adam's breathless yell, "No, Odo!" The impact sent both rolling, a voice she knew squalled rage and pain, others flung themselves upon the pair. Someone caught the palfrey's head and brutally mastered him, squealing and plunging; other horses were neighing frantically. She loosed the reins, and then arms wrenched her headlong

225

from the saddle and pinned her fast. She stood still in their hold, a familiar laugh triumphant in her ears.

Red Adam, his wrists lashed behind his back, his sword-belt, spurs and weapons in his captors' hands, his face and tunic patched with mud, was hauled erect. Odo was less easily subdued; twice he heaved up like a baited bear hurling off the dogs, before they clubbed him half-senseless with spearbutts and bound him fast. Others assisted Lord William of Chivingham to unsteady feet. He was nursing one hand in the other, dark-dripping, and swearing savagely. The pity was, Julitta thought bleakly, that his hauberk had saved his belly.

She looked about her. Her cousins Gilbert and Gautier were supporting their father, Gerald of Flackness stood swinging Red Adam's swordbelt, and beyond them she recognized the redhaired boy's shocked face.

"He drew steel on his lord!" Humphrey of Crossthwaite proclaimed, his breath warm in her hair. "Hang him!"

"God's Death, he all but murdered me!" snarled Lord William, cherishing his gashed hand.

"He defended his master — you're no lord of his!" Red Adam exclaimed sharply.

"God's Head, you'll learn who rules inside these walls!" Humphrey checked, and as an afterthought recited, "I have taken possession of Brentborough on behalf of its rightful lord Geoffrey, son of Maurice de Lorismond, in the name of our true King Henry, third of that name."

"Two thieving whelps!" Red Adam snapped, contemptuously glancing at his kinsman. Gerald of Flackness swung about and clouted him across the face, right and left, while his guards held him braced to the blows. His nose began to bleed. The redhaired boy exclaimed in protest. Odo lurched erect, straining against the ropes and tugging his foes this way and that.

"Take the knave out and string him up!" Lord William ordered.

"Ah, no!" the boy cried. "I am Lord of Brentborough — I can pardon him."

"That you can't, you puling monk! You're not of age, and in my wardship. He hangs."

"But my lord ... unjust... he was loyal to his master!"

"What's loyalty to do with it? He's a churl who let noble blood."

"What do you know of loyalty," Julitta raged, "when every servant in your household will skip for joy at your burial?"

His bloody hand slapped against her cheek, beating her head back against Humphrey's chin. Her eyes watered, but she snarled back at him. Humphrey chuckled, tightened his hold that gripped her arms to her sides, and shifted a hand to fondle her breast.

"Enough, enough!" Geoffrey entreated. "This is evil you do — to abuse prisoners and hang a brave churl for faithfulness."

"In God's Name!" Red Adam protested passionately. "Your spite's for me, not my poor fool! Isn't my life enough? I beg you — on my knees if it please you — spare him."

An uneasy stir among the guards endorsed his appeal. Odo, standing still now among them, said wonderingly, "Lord Adam!"

"Think what you do!" Geoffrey charged them. "Whose man will defend his master at such a price?"

"He hangs," Lord William pronounced. "Without this example, what's to keep other knives from our backs?"

"In the Name of Christ, " Red Adam pleaded, wrenching against the hands that held him. Another blow in the face snapped his head back, and only their grip kept him on his feet.

"Take him out!" Lord William ordered, and the portcullis creaked up.

"A priest — your own soul's at peril if you murder him unshriven," the boy croaked, sick with horror.

A jerked hand, and a man went running for Father Simon. The whole company moved out into the drizzling twilight, Julitta and Red Adam forced along with them, to the foot of the gallows beside the track to the village. The priest came, ventured objection, and was grimly bidden to do his office

227

and leave justice to his betters. He was not of the stuff that makes martyrs. Julitta stood in paralyzing nightmare as the business was concluded.

Odo died with the stolid hardihood she expected of him, with a brief, "God aid you, dear m' lord," as the noose was adjusted. It was Red Adam who broke.

"*Odo!*" As the swinging body threshed and twisted, his cry tore through the priest's drone and strangled to a sob. Tears of grief and helpless fury streaked through the mud and blood. "God damn you all to Hell's fire, you murdering recreants! Now kill me too and make an end, or I'll avenge him!"

Geoffrey, shuddering with shock, lifted his stricken face from the hands that had covered his eyes against Odo's death throes, and pushed between Red Adam and the rest. "No, no! There's no question... no intent..." He blenched from his distraught glare, stammered a little and then propounded his idiotically untenable idea of reason. "K-kinsman, if — if you will only peaceably acknowledge the — the righteousness of my accession, I swear no harm will be done you."

"A man lays a righteous cause before the King, addle-wit! He doesn't ally it with treason."

Gerald of Flackness thrust the lad aside and drove his fist thrice into Red Adam's face, beating him to his knees. "Raked from the midden, was I?" he growled, and took to kicking him in the belly. He crowed raspingly for breath, and Julitta winced herself, straining against the hold on her arms.

"Be warned, sweet friend," Humphrey's amused voice murmured in her ear. "An edged tongue provokes resentments, and Gerald cherishes his grievances."

"Stop him!"

"Why, haven't you a grievance or two yourself it's a pleasure to see avenged?" He squeezed her breast again and chuckled. The boy was screeching, clutching at Gerald's tunic. The disgusted guards had let Red Adam fall on his face as a measure of protection; the soldiers were muttering resentment, the huddle of peasants gathered to the noise whispered

228

in dismay at this exemplary start to their new lord's rule. Gerald threw off the frantic lad and yelled at the men to hold up his victim again; Julitta looked with loathing on the brute who might have wedded her, and prayed desperately to God and the Lord Jesus and His Mother to aid her husband, and give her strength to take the way her enemy had suggested.

It was Lord William who barked, "Have done, Gerald!"

"I've not finished with the whoreson knave —"

"He's a Lorismond and a knight, not one of your serfs. Also he's my kinsman by marriage —"

"Have you not forgotten that?" Julitta demanded icily.

"He had his chance, and this was his own choice. In with you!"

Red Adam was already struggling to his knees, no easy achievement with his hands fast behind him. Crouched in the grass, he breathed in retching sobs through a mask of mud and blood. The soldiers helped him up and steadied him until he could straighten himself and lift his head. He looked once round the ring of faces in the thickening darkness, once at Odo's body turning slightly on the rope, and then fixed his desperate gaze on Julitta.

"My fault — sorry" he croaked.

Her inwards churning with pity and rage and fear, she stared coldly at him, her resolution stiffened by pride in the man who made her that apology out of his own anguish. "Your folly indeed," she answered harshly, and felt his flinching in her own flesh.

Humphrey of Crossthwaite laughed aloud. "Have *you* forgotten he's your husband?" he jibed.

"By no choice of mine!" she retorted, her wits suddenly alive. His hold eased in surprise, and she jabbed an elbow backward. "Nor am I your whore!"

He hooted. "My sweet Julitta! Marriage or nothing, eh? Still laughing, he loosed her and caught her hand to lead her in behind Lord William, leaving the guards to bring Red Adam after them. She grimly restrained herself from looking back, but she was aware in all her body of his stumbling progress through the rain that now slashed before the wind, striking through her garments to shrinking skin. She heard the soldiers' muttered encouragements; they respected courage if little else, and she knew when some measure of recovery steadied him and their help was not needed.

William of Chivingham, self-appointed master of Brentborough, took command in the hall with all the arrogance Julitta expected of him. The scared servants and disarmed, depleted garrison were menaced by a score of men-at-arms who herded them against the walls; on the dais half-blind Bertram towered upright, his wife at his side, and Giles sat weaponless and three parts drunk on a bench, glowering at his own feet. William gestured to Red Adam's chair.

"Take your rightful place, Lord Geoffrey."

"I *am* true Lord of Brentborough," the boy announced with pride, and his head flamed against the high back as, a few hours ago, Red Adam's had done. Bertram turned on him a smile of thankful joy that lighted his brooding face. Lord William planted himself in Julitta's seat, and as Humphrey drew her on to the dais she heard behind her the collective moan of indignant pity as Red Adam was marched in.

He walked erect between his guards. Rain had sluiced most of the mud from his face, but his nose was still bleeding, dripping scarlet over mouth and chin and down his tunic; as he came nearer she saw, with a sick shock, that it was broken askew.

Giles glanced despondently up and started to his feet, all at once stark sober. "Lord Adam!" His face flamed. "Lord Adam, before God I'd no hand in opening the gate to the swine who mishandled you so."

"I know the purblind Judas," Adam answered flatly, lifting his hazel stare to his seneschal's face.

Bertram flushed, but stiffly justified himself. "I opened the gate to my own lord's lawful son, and you forfeited my loyalty when you dismissed me from Brentborough."

Geoffrey leaned forward, "I *am* true lord of Brentborough — Lord Maurice's own son," he asserted. Red Adam started to speak, choked slightly and spat a mouthful of blood upon the rushes. "I've only claimed what's my own," the boy protested shrilly as his gaze, glittering with involuntary tears, transfixed him. "I *am* his lawful son, who else?"

"You're his bastard out of his seneschal's wife," Red Adam told him brutally, jerking his head at Constance.

Half a dozen voices cried out in anger and surprise and denial, but Bertram's roar overbore all others. "A lie — a foul lie!" He lurched towards the dais's edge, while Constance's white horror proclaimed her guilt to all who looked on her. "Take back that lie —"

Red Adam raised his voice, distorted by his blood-blocked nose and battered mouth, so that all might hear. "Judge whether I lie! A very fair girl named Constance was delivered of a redhaired boy who was christened Geoffrey in Saint Osburga's nunnery near Bristol at Eastertide of 'fifty-six. I have spoken with the midwife who delivered her and the woman who swaddled the child, and they will bear witness to it at need."

In the silence Bertram raised huge fists to crush him, his face engorged with blood and his lips strained back from snarling teeth. Then he tottered, half-turned, reached groping hands towards his wife and said thickly, "Constance —" His mouth squared into an agonized grin, a line of froth gathered along his lips, and he toppled full-length down the steps and rolled at Red Adam's feet.

Every man on the dais scrambled to him. Julitta, standing alone, gazed over their bent backs at her husband, and he looked steadily back at her. She dared not betray the slightest pity or fondness; the loathing she felt for his enemies must be turned on him, and she prayed that he might understand. But there had been too much treachery. His eyes closed an instant in agony before he stared down at the men busy over his seneschal's body.

Lord William straightened. "Lady Constance," he pronounced heavily, "I regret your husband is dead."

"It's two years too late," she answered indifferently, and shocked everyone speechless. She came forward, glanced

231

down at the dead man and mechanically crossed herself. Geoffrey, gray beneath the freckles, challenged her.

"It's not true? He's lying — he's lying, isn't he? You're not my mother? Swear to me it's a lie!"

She had no answer to that appeal. Lord William caught him by the shoulder. "Of course he's lying! It's his claim to Brentborough!" he assured him. "Come, sit you down in your rightful place. Hamon! Richard! Bear Sir Bertram out and bestow him decently, and someone fetch the priest."

Four men had hard work of it to shift the great body to the side-chamber where two nights before Red Adam had kept the death watch over Reynald. Humphrey trod back to Julitta's side, plainly shaken, and muttered in her ear, "What do you know of these witnesses of his, Julitta?"

"He's told me nothing," she answered, which was precisely true. She thought of the two old women and the drystone wall a child might climb, and shivered slightly. He gripped her hand. His own was sweating.

"There's this usurper to deal with," Lord William prompted the boy. The three older conspirators regarded one another with grim agreement, and Julitta knew that after his disclosure they dared not leave Red Adam alive.

"Make an end," Gerald of Flackness advocated bluntly.

"He's my kinsman — and he inherited in good faith," Geoffrey objected.

"You waste your pity," Lord William growled. "He's a ravisher and murderer that killed his comrade fighting over a serving wench."

The boy winced. Red Adam spat out another mouthful of blood, and he shuddered. "He's still my cousin. There'll be no more hurt done him. He can be safely kept —"

"He must not remain here, where he ruled and may find help," Lord William pronounced, glancing at Humphrey.

"I'll hold him securely at Crossthwaite," that man promptly offered.

"In — in honorable captivity?" Geoffrey asked anxiously. "Later — when my succession is assured — he can be freed, perhaps provision made — but he's not to be harmed!"

232

"Trust me," Humphrey said smoothly, and signaled some-one in the body of the hall. "We'll ride at once."

"He's best out of here," Lord William agreed.

"You poor witless whelp!" Red Adam said in vast con-tempt, and his mouth twisted in a ghastly parody of his grin.

"There's our cousin," Gilbert hesitantly reminded them.

"I go with my husband," Julitta said, and deliberately turned and smiled up at Humphrey. He gave a great shout of triumphant laughter, caught her to his side and kissed her, and with his arm about her led her from the hall. She pressed the comforting hardness of her dagger against her body and yielded shamelessly before her husband's face.

Down in the bailey the torches hissed and spluttered as the rain lashed them, and their flames flattened sideways in gusts of wind. A wild night, a murderer's night, Julitta thought, standing tensely beside Humphrey as grooms dragged reluctant horses out from their stables. Her hands clenched until her nails bit her palms, and she was praying over and over, the same desperate prayer for the chance she needed. Red Adam would not reach Crossthwaite alive, and this night she was the only friend he had free and armed to help him.

She called the nearest groom. "Roger! Saddle me Folie! Brunel is going lame!"

"Folie, m' lady? But — yes, m' lady." He scuttled into the stable.

Folie belonged to the church as a deodand, having caused a man's death, but Father Simon had flatly refused to receive her. She came forth squealing and tossing her head at the torches, a diversion in glossy brown hide. Humphrey started forward as she reared. "Hold the brute steady!" he yelled; he too sounded nervous and irritable, but a man did not steel himself to do murder every night of his life. At last the guards brought out Red Adam, raising his bloody face to the rain and the wind that blew his hair back like the torch flames. Julitta lifted her hand and stalked towards him, thrusting past the startled guards.

"In remembrance of our marriage night, Adam de Loris-

233

mond!" she cried for all to hear, and her left hand slapped viciously, once and twice, against his cheek. There was no pretence; she dared not pretend, and felt blood start sticky on her tingling palm. Between their bodies, unseen by any, her right hand slid the little dagger up his left sleeve, and his fingers closed convulsively on the haft. She stepped back, praising God for His mercy.

"Vixen!" he grunted, and she needed no more.

"God's Death, vixen's the word for you!" Humphrey exclaimed, hooting laughter. He caught her to him and she went unresisting, though her belly heaved with revulsion. "If you ever do that to me I'll take my belt to you," he promised.

She pushed him off, and somehow achieved a challenging smile. "And before God, you'd rue it!" she retorted, and jerked free. No yearning meekness could hold his attention, nor did she think herself capable of feigning it; this night she was all virago. She strode to her horse, and Humphrey followed grinning, leaving his men to hoist the prisoner into his saddle and lash his ankles under his mount's belly.

He rode by her stirrup, swearing at the gusts that clawed his cloak. They took, as she had expected, the coast road; it was nearly a league further by that way, but this was no night for the river track and swollen ford. The rain scudded over, and thin moonlight reached between the clouds; a few stars blinked through the gaps.

"Urgh!" Humphrey growled, huddling his cloak about his ears. "The Foul Fiend's own weather! But before midnight we'll be merry between my sheets, sweet Julitta."

"I am not your whore," she told him, feeling much like a talking jackdaw that had learned but one phrase.

"Marriage or nothing, you virtuous wench?"

"I go with my husband."

"Content you; when we reach Crossthwaite you'll have another husband. You were mine from the first, my Julitta."

He chuckled, and she marveled at the fatuous vanity that reckoned her enchanted forever by his face and smile. She had much ado not to snatch back her hand when he reached

234

for it, and jabbed Folie with her heel so that she sidled snorting aside.

The troop's hooves drummed hollow on the bridge. Curfew had darkened the village, and no one moved in Arnisby Street, though probably eyes enough were peering round doors and through windows to see who rode so late. But where the headland curved round the shingle-beach torches flared, streaking the shallows with gold and scarlet. Shouts came thinly across the water, and the thump of heavy oars. Her heart lifted as she saw the black hull creeping in on the full tide, dwarfing the fishing boats. Erling was back. She and her husband had one dependable friend in Arnisby.

The cavalcade climbed the slope beyond the bridge at a walk to spare the horses. Torn shreds of cloud parted to let the moon's light shine out as they reached the top. The ground sloped away to a ragged edge, and beyond was nothing but sky and sea.

Humphrey drew rein and looked about him. "Here's as fit a place as any," he announced.

"For what?" she demanded sharply, her heart slamming.

"Widowing you, Julitta. An essential preliminary to our marriage." The troop closed in and halted likewise. A horse blew noisily, and another champed its bit with a musical jingle of metal. She looked quickly to find her husband, wondering whether he had yet been able to free his arms. Folie might provide some diversion; she had chosen her with that intent. She gathered the reins. Humphrey moved off the track a few paces, towards the drop, and glanced back over his shoulder. The moonlight caught a faint glint of eyes and teeth. "It would look amiss if his corpse had its throat cut, Julitta. But if he tries to escape, and his horse bolts over the cliff, that's a regrettable accident. Hubert, tie his reins to the saddle and drive the brute over!"

"Drive it —" a startled voice protested.

"You heard!"

"Yes, m' lord."

Julitta tightened her thighs. Folie sidled. The moon dimmed.

235

"Hey, hold up!" Among the dark mass of horsemen a head sank forward. "Prisoner's swooning, m' lord!"

Humphrey laughed. "Red Adam mislikes the jump? No matter —"

Julitta, knowing better, drove her heels fiercely into Folie's sides and hauled on the bit. Up she came, squealing and flailing, swung round on her haunches and snapped vicious teeth at Humphrey's wrist as he grabbed at her. He yelled. Another yell answered from the troop as the captive swung upright, snatched the reins from Hubert's hand as he reached to tie them, slashed at an impeding body and hurtled at Humphrey.

"He's loose! He's got a knife!"

"This way, Adam!" Julitta shrieked, wrenching Folie aside.

Instead he drove straight at his enemy, clawing for his swordhilt. The dagger winked. They crashed together, grappling, and Humphrey yowled. The impact sent his horse reeling backward, the two men locked fast.

"Ride, Julitta! York — Brien!"

Folie danced aside from the mêlée. The kicking, squealing beasts plunged away, the men on their backs wrestling savagely. The dear fool, risking his barely-seized freedom for hers, as if she would ride without him! The moon was darkening, fresh rain spitting, and only helmet and mail distinguished one man from the other. One horse broke sideways from under its rider, and charged neighing into the troop, turning it into a turmoil. Both men toppled, and rolled threshing down the slope. Humphrey squalled. They broke apart, lunged upright against the vast glimmer of the sea, and Julitta screeched.

"Adam! *Adam! The cliff!*"

The wild-haired shape leaped heedlessly. A sucking, grinding sound, the rain-sodden earth shuddering from the weight, and then with a roar the cliff-edge fell away. Both men were gone. The moon went out.

16

The dark filled with clamor; men shouting, horses neighing, and far below the landslip's diminishing rumble. Dim figures cautiously approached the cliff. Julitta, dread clutching her inwards, wrenched Folie to a stand and strained to see or hear. Then Humphrey's voice came shakily from the void, and her senses reeled.

"Throw me your belt, Hubert—no nearer—God's Death, you'll take me with you if you go over! Devil burn him, he's ruined my sword-arm!"

"He's gone, M' lord!"

A scrabbling, grunts of effort, careful movement, an oath or two, were followed by a triumphant, "Got you, m' lord!" Julitta numbly looped the reins about her saddle bow, kicked her feet from the stirrups, slashed Folie with the loose ends and slid from the saddle as she reared up squealing. She flung herself down under a gorse bush and lay flat, pulling her cloak over her head. As Folie's forehooves touched earth she shrieked resentment and bolted.

Humphrey, staggering back to the track amidst his men's helping hands, halted and howled. "The girl! She's run!" The truth hit him. "God's Head, she's tricked me! After her—catch the lying trollop—"

In spattering rain and blinding dark they struggled with frightened horses and scrambled astride. Humphrey snarled at Hubert. "Lend a hand to tie this arm up—I'm bleeding like a stuck hog! Take a look, one of you, for that red devil—here's the moon again—"

"We'll need daylight, m' lord. But it'll have carried him straight down into the sea. Savior Christ, no man could live—"

"After the girl, then! She deceived me, the jade—"

Hooves jarred past her head, and their clatter faded down the slope. Julitta scarcely waited. As the clouds blew from the moon's face she was leaning at the broken edge, peering and listening, her lips moving in prayer. Stones and earth might go plunging senselessly into the sea, but not a man with hands and feet to save himself, not her young leopard. And if God had seen fit to spare that murderer Humphrey, could He destroy her gallant fool who had gone over the cliff for her?

"*Sancta Maria, Mater Dei, ora pro nobis peccatoribus, nunc et in hora mortis nostrae,*" Julitta said aloud, hitched up her skirts to her knees and tightened her belt to hold them, and slid cautiously down the crumbling earth and rubble, over the cliff's edge. Loose stones went rattling into the dark, but she set her teeth and went on.

The drop was not sheer, but a broken slope offering hand and foot holds in plenty. After the first heart-stopping movements, pressing close to the rocks with all four limbs extended, she found she could progress easily enough, if she kept her mind from the depth below. Once she called softly, "Adam!" and then bit her lips at the fear he would never again hear her use his name. Then she pushed that dread from her and bade herself think. He would automatically have tried to fling himself aside from the fall, so she clung to a jutting rock and peered left and right through the deceptive shadows. The moon, swept clean of cloud, shone on stone faces and tufts of tenacious plants that rooted in their crevices. Down the slope, to her left, on the edge of the fall's dark scar, a white bar winked at her. With a choked sob she scrambled and slid to the little dagger that had saved him once already.

He sprawled face down against the outcrop that had held

him from the drop, a spreading stain under his head. He did not answer when she called his name, but he moaned faintly when she moved him, gripping his shoulder to turn his face up. Had he been conscious she would have kissed or clouted him in wild relief, but now she set her arm under his shoulders and rolled him as gently as she could on to his back, his head in her lap. She had not known she was crying until her tears splashed into his upturned face, blackened with blood and bruises.

He stirred, and mumbled indistinguishably. "Adam!" she cried joyfully, her tears dripping faster, and he blinked open one puffy eyelid and peered up at her. "God be praised, you're not dead!

The other eye opened, and he shifted his head more purposefully. "Wha'—Julitta?" He tried to rise on one elbow, and subsided with a grunt, screwing his eyes shut.

She smeared her tears away with a sleeve and cautiously felt along his arms, and then over his ribs. His legs lay naturally, with no visible distortion. A broken leg would be as fatal as a broken neck, but it seemed that the cracked head was the worst of it. Blood was warm on her thigh, soaked through her gown, but the flow was slackening. Scalp wounds always bled alarmingly.

She looked up at the cliff edge above, calculating grimly. Folie would probably never check her running until she reached Chivingham's familiar gates, and with her start there was a good chance that Humphrey would pursue her there before discovering she was riderless. Then he would know where to search for her, and return slavering for vengeance on them both. They could never get over the hill, through Arnisby and along the shore without betrayal; the dogs roaming on guard through the night would give the alarm. Nor could they escape over the moors or through the woods; at first light horsemen and hounds would be on their trail. Her belly lurched as she looked down the fall. It would be much harder than climbing up, she did not even know whether Adam could move at all, but she accepted that being shattered on the rocks was preferable to recapture.

She gripped her husband's shoulders. "Adam! Adam!

239

Rouse up! We must move." He groaned, and she shook him pitilessly.

"Le'—lemme be—don'—"

"Adam! For your life—rouse up!" She slapped him, and he blinked up reproachfully, mumbling her name. She set both arms about him and heaved him from her knees, and some of her urgency pierced to his wits. He caught at the rock and dragged himself up to sit against it. She seized his arm. "We must go down. This way—lean on me—" She braced him with all her strength, and clumsily he twisted to hands and knees and crept at her bidding along the rock.

Afterwards Julitta marveled that she ever accomplished it. The climb would not have been easy in daylight, unencumbered; now she had to guide and support a dazed and injured man who was never more than half-conscious; a tall man, and heavy. Their salvation was his obedience, as though he surrendered all his will to hers. When clouds covered the moon she waited, holding him in her arms and huddling her cloak about them both against the drumming rain. Sometimes she left him and went ahead to pick the way. Once they slithered and bounced and scraped at a terrifying rush down a kind of rain-washed gully, and fetched up battered and breathless against an outcrop where they lay panting a long time. She had to use Adam ruthlessly to drag him away, whimpering herself in pity and misery.

She concentrated on steering him from hold to hold. She had no time to think of danger, no time to pray. She could only work down step by step, guiding his hands and feet. Her soft shoes split, her hands and knees were skinned and cut, her nails broken. Every time they had to wait out a rain squall it was harder to move. Below them, louder and nearer, the sea roared among the rocks, and they groaned together against the surges. The moon was high in the south; presently it would swing westward behind the cliff, leaving them blind in his shadow, but Adam could make no better speed. She marveled that he could move at all.

Again they cowered in the lee of a rock against cold rain, and she shielded him as best she could with her sodden

240

cloak, propping his dizzy head with her shoulder. He mumbled something she could not catch.

"Hush!" she whispered, and laid a hand over his mouth as the wind carried other sounds to her ears. High and far off, hooves struck on rock and men shouted; too high for words to reach her, but they rang angrily and she knew their portent. Some part of Adam's brain responded yet to danger; his mumbling ceased, his head came up to listen. She stared up the height, but she was too close to the cliff's face to see anything. The rain blew out to sea and the moon returned; the shouts passed back and forth a little while as men searched and called to each other, and then abandoned the futile exercise. Hoofbeats died away.

"The Ladies' Delight?" Adam asked rationally. "After us?"

"They'll not follow us before daylight. Come, Adam!" She caught his hand. "We must get down."

The last thirty feet were the worst of the climb. The cliff-face was wet with spray, below tide-line the rocks were hung with treacherous weed and crusted with limpets and barnacles that tore unwary flesh, and the boulders and scree at the bottom were a menace to stumbling feet. Somehow they won down, and at last trod soft sand, water seething about their ankles. The tide was coming in. Julitta had traversed northward during the climb whenever she could; fifty yards across a little cove lay the point, and over that the harbor and Erling's long ship. She pulled Adam's arm over her shoulders and set her face towards it. She could count on Erling. As she looked, something moved against the sky, blotting out the stars. She steered Adam to the nearest rock-face, propped him against it and drew the dagger.

"Who—leave me, Julitta! Hide yourself!" he whispered, rousing again to danger.

Someone was scrambling down the slope, someone agile and sure-footed, to risk such a pace in the dark. A low voice hailed them, in good French with a Norse accent.

"Lady Julitta—and my lord with you?"

He splashed through the shallow waves, black against the black headland; she could discern only his legs in the yeasty

241

water, the loom of him in the night. She stepped out, lifting an arm in signal, and he churned towards her. "It's help!" she gasped, her voice cracking with relief. Adam sighed and quietly began to slide down the rock.

The man thrust past her, caught him before he could souse into the sea and heaved him up in his arms, making naught of his weight. Julitta looked up at his towering height, at his pale head, and knew him for Hakon. A sob of thankfulness choked in her throat, and tears blinded her.

"If he had died," said Hakon slowly, "I would have borne you away to my own land and cherished you for all time. Even now, if you will it . . . " A jerk of his head at the creaming waves finished his sentence.

"He is my husband," she answered simply.

"Since you brought him down the cliff that is proof enough. I am at your service, my lady."

"My—my lord's service is mine, Hakon," she whispered, her voice shaking. He nodded over Adam's senseless body. There was no more to be said.

He stalked through the deepening water, and she trotted to keep up. The scramble over the point was nothing after that grueling climb, and the paling gray over the sea spurred her. Presently he spoke, in an undertone that would not carry five paces. "My father saw you moving on the cliff in the moonlight, hours ago. No chance of finding you until dawn. That fair hound came back raging with his arm bound up, and had everyone out of house and ship, searching the town."

"He'll be back at first light," Julitta said grimly. Daybreak would reveal traces of her climb in the fall's moist earth, prints of foot, hand and knee; would show where Adam had lain and the signs that she had helped him away. Her trickery was an affront beyond pardon to Humphrey's vanity, the most vital part of him, and knowledge that folk were sniggering would drive him to monstrous vengeance.

Erling waited by the bulk of his ship, stranded high-prowed on the crunching shingle. He growled concern and lifted Adam from his son's hold. Adam groaned and muttered, shifting his head against Erling's shoulder.

"A cracked head's the worst of it," Julitta said quickly, reassuring herself as much as the seaman. "They beat him too. Will you—can you help us away—before daylight—before they search again?" Panic fluttered against her ribs; the veriest landsman must recognize that the ship could not be refloated until the tide returned, and it was now not half-full.

"The skiff?" Hakon suggested, nodding at the small boat dancing at the end of a painter from the ship's stern.

"They'd slaughter the rest of us and burn the old *Greylag* for vengeance," his father grunted. "Cunning alone will serve." His crew had drifted together, and he issued a few low-toned instructions in his own tongue. "We're making repairs," he told Julitta. "Caulking spewed, and a mastblock splitting. And the sail would be the better of new reef points."

She could not imagine how such matters might help, but the men moved purposefully. Erling knelt on the shingle, holding Adam across his knees, and felt him over for broken bones as Julitta had done. Hakon brought ale and bread, which she accepted thankfully. When she tilted the horn to Adam's lips he gulped automatically, opened his eyes and croaked, "Julitta—"

"Here with you, Adam. Drink this."

He gulped again, lifted his head from Erling's shoulder and put up his hands to hold it on. "Hell's Teeth!" he muttered, gingerly exploring his blood-clotted hair, and a giggle of near hysterical relief escaped her to hear his familiar oath again. The horn tipped, and as ale trickled over her fingers she forced control on herself and offered it again. He put a sticky hand over hers and drank more temperately. He looked about in the murky dusk that lightened with every moment, his senses back in his skull.

"I remember—fighting the Ladies' Delight—and the cliff fell," he said slowly. "No more. How... "

"Your lady brought you down the cliff," Erling told him.

"My own vixen," he murmured, his hand tightening over hers on the horn. As he lifted it to drink again, his lips secretly touched her fingers. He finished the ale, shook his head at the bread, and sat up to survey their position.

243

Two seamen were scooping out a trough in the shingle to larboard of the ship, hidden by her from the cottages, bridge and castle; a shallow grave that Julitta regarded a moment in puzzlement, until she caught one man's measuring eye on Adam's legs and comprehension came. One spread a cloak in it, and then Erling helped Adam to lie full length, face down, and she joined him in the trench. The sail's salt-caked, board-solid canvas was hauled out and spread flat. A little judicious shifting and packing of pebbles, and then it was dragged over them, shutting down weightily as a coffin lid. Erling chuckled. "Not a sign," he declared, and his feet creaked away.

Even mitigated by a fur-lined cloak, the shingle made villainously uncomfortable lying. Adam was shivering, and she pressed closer to warm him, her knowledge of medicine setting another worry to nag at the back of her mind. He stirred, and the thick voice that she would hardly have recognized croaked, "My light in black darkness, Julitta."

Erling creaked back and reported, "Daylight near on us. We can get to work." He squatted cross-legged on the shingle close to their heads, heaved up the sail and started some operation on its upper surface, a regular plucking and twitching. Air and a measure of light came past his legs. Presently the crackle of a driftwood fire reached their ears, and after a while the reek of heating pitch tingled in Julitta's nose. "We caulk her seams with pitched cowhair rammed tight," Erling explained, as a steady hammering began. The light strengthened. Easy talk and occasional laughter indicated that the seamen had nothing on mind or conscience. Then a man raised a raucous voice in song about a King Harald who for a vow never washed nor cut nor combed his hair for seven years. The Norse was like enough to the northern English for Julitta to understand it except at speed. Very close at hand a sheep unexpectedly bleated protest. "They've come forth from the castle," Erling said, and shifted something beside him that chinked on the pebbles. Julitta peered and saw the head of a formidable axe lying handily by his knee. Her heart jolted.

244

"They are riding out to the cliff-top," Hakon's voice announced, quite close. The hammering went on. The songster hummed tunelessly. The drum of hooves on the bridge sounded clearly. "Some of them are coming down this way," Hakon said, and then, a little later, "They've gone out to the point. Two of them are sitting their horses on watch; the others have climbed down on the other side."

"Small use that will be," Julitta said. "The tide was in when we reached the bay."

"They've reached the cliff-top now. I can see five men climbing down."

"He'll be a man or two short before an hour's out if he sets them to that," Erling prophesied.

"Four hours to high water," murmured Hakon, shifting restlessly on the betraying shingle.

"Nothing you do will hasten it. Sit you down and stitch reef-points," his father placidly bade him.

Now and again they informed Adam and Julitta of the search's progress. Sometimes shouts came to them through the shrieking of the gulls. The distant rumble of another rockfall ended the climbing, and, considerably later, eight men carrying two others in stretched cloaks crossed the bridge and tramped up to the castle.

The pebbles grew harder and knobbier with every passing moment. The risen sun beat upon the sail. Julitta's clothes, from clammily chill, grew sticky with heat and clung itching to her flesh, and every muscle in her body ached separately with the strain of long lying in one position. Adam lay rigid beside her; she could guess at his misery of mind and body, and the only comfort she could offer was to lay her hand over his.

"They're coming down to search the houses again," said Hakon. "Seven—eight—there's eleven of them. Nine of us."

"Don't be daft," Erling squashed his aspirations. "Go on stitching."

The searchers were working their way down from the bridge, house by house, turning their occupants out of doors. Hakon suddenly began to laugh. "There's an old woman just

245

chased two of the knaves out of a cottage with a broom," he said. "A scrawny little beldame, but you can hear her screeching—"

"Hallgerd the midwife," Julitta declared, as the shrill voice drifted to her, and smiled despite herself. "Afraid of nothing."

The search worked nearer. The sun grew hotter. Julitta became aware of a faint purring that vibrated through the pebbles beneath her; the sea was returning. Gradually it increased to a grinding growl as the tide sucked through the shingle, stone gritting on stone until the ridge was astir under her. The sheep bleated again, the singer gave them a few more lines of King Harald coming to his own shearing with his vow accomplished, and then a clop of hooves, a jingle of harness, and a voice she knew well snapped orders.

"Hubert, down to the right, Ranulf, pull in that little boat and see if our pair are hiding in it. You whoresons, out of the ship and down by your stinking tar-pot!"

Erling clambered unhurriedly to his feet. "And what's your wish, my lord?" he inquired with ironic courtesy.

"We're searching your ship, huckster."

"You searched her last night."

"And we know our pair went down the cliff in the night, and since you are Red Adam's partners in greasy chaffering I'll go through your dirty tub again."

"Down the cliff in the night? Nay, then, if they're not dead on the rocks, you'll have to wait for the tide to bring them back. A grievous end—a grievous end for the gallant lad and lass."

Someone had floundered down the shingle; as Erling's mournful voice ceased he shouted, "The boat's empty!"

"Back up here then! Save your moaning, you old trickster; we're searching every foul cranny of it!"

"Search all you've a mind to," Erling responded.

Julitta tried to suspend her breathing, all her faculties concentrated in her ears. Adam stiffened beside her in the dark, and she touched the haft of her dagger that would not save them this time. Clumping feet reverberated against the *Greylag's* planking, and the clatter of a wantonly destructive search rampaged the length of her. The sheep bleated indig-

246

nantly, and was answered by a shout of laughter. "Mutton on the hoof he's carrying!"

"That's a breeding ram Lord Adam ordered to improve his flock!" Erling protested.

"God's Head, Red Adam's lord no longer, and his tup's mutton for our dinner!" jeered Humphrey, and the bleat rose to an agonized yell and broke. "Take it to the horses, Martin. Break me open this trapdoor, Jehan, and we'll see what's hiding behind it."

"It opens—" Erling began, but an axe's crash overbore him.

"Barrels, m' lord."

"Trundle them out. See who's behind them—poke them out."

"No one, m' lord. Nowt but barrels—salt fish and oatmeal by the smell—and these three looks like they holds wine."

"More of Red Adam's ordering? Roll them out; we'll drink them for him."

"They're not paid for—you've no right—"

"God's Head, you whoreson huckster, d'you expect *me* to chaffer with you? It's a light enough tribute you're paying for upholding Red Adam. Heave them out, you fellows! Briskly now! Any sign of our quarry?"

"None, m' lord. We've ransacked her through."

Feet crunched the pebbles, coming nearer; his voice when next he spoke was so close that he must be standing by the ship's stempost. "Hell's devils, where else could they have found aid? Jehan, Richard, Henry, seize me the tall towhead!" The rattle of spurned shingle, grunted oaths and hard breathing reached Julitta. The hated voice went on, harshly mocking. "Your son, huckster? Prick your point at his belly, Hubert; just at his navel. Now, old man, tell us where to find Red Adam and his strumpet wife, or Hubert's spear goes through to your son's backbone, and you may watch him squirm for an hour or two after."

Adam braced elbows to the pebbles to thrust up, but Erling moved faster, taking two steps forward that set one foot on his shoulders and crushed him flat. "By Thor's Hammer, you rabid wolf," he blared, "you've searched my ship, you've

247

looted my cargo, and now you'll butcher my son? You know they're not here!"

"Towhead, answer for yourself before the spear goes in! Red Adam and the wench—where are they?"

"By the White Christ," Hakon defied him, "if they *were* here I'd tell you nothing!" He ended on a sharply indrawn breath, and Adam squirmed helplessly. The canvas pinned Julitta rigid with horror, but she recognized that Hakon's life could not be sacrificed for Adam's, and tried to find purchase to rise. Instantly a foot on her back drove her painfully into the pebbles, and while she lay winded, the sail jerked thrice as Erling plunged across it. His voice spoke, deadly quiet, through startled silence.

"Give the word, butcher, and your head lies in two halves! Your helmet's no protection against this."

"You madman—"

"Drop that spear! Loose him! Back aboard, Hakon—all of you! Bring that tarpot! Anyone who blocks your way, give him a snoutful of boiling tar!"

Humphrey managed an unconvincing laugh. "Let be!" he ordered, on a note of chagrin. "A test, no more. That threat was bound to fetch the truth out of you."

"A test? Aye, so my axe blade tested you! Keep yourself and your men out of its reach until the tide's in. We'll be out of here in an hour, and you'll not see me or any other outland captain bring ship again into this thieves' haven."

"God's Head, you're free-tongued for a clip-penny pedlar! Don't press your luck too hard," Humphrey growled, but the clatter of retreating feet and then the ring of horseshoes told that he had withdrawn. Harness jingled, feet squelched along the miry path and curses dwindled away. Julitta gulped in a breath and her quailing flesh eased away from the imprinted pebbles. Beside her, Adam jerked air painfully into his lungs.

"The Devil roast you, Lady-face, for a thieving coward!" Erling said dispassionately. He tramped across the sail to the ship's side, and Julitta could hear a murmur of conversation in his voice and Hakon's. She reached in the dark to touch her husband's arm.

"Dear God!" Adam whispered, and shuddered violently.

Presently Erling returned, took up the sail again and resumed his task. As the light dived under it, the first thing Julitta saw was the axe blade, and she did not wonder at Humphrey's withdrawal.

"My apologies," Erling said placidly, "for using you so roughly, but I had to hold you down."

"Erling—dear God," Adam croaked, "your own son—and we are nothing to you—"

"Our guests," he answered with flinty finality. "And it was not for your sakes. What man buys his life with his honor and dares call himself a man thereafter?" Other feet moved on the sail. "Hakon, lad, if I'd betrayed Lord Adam to save your life, what would you do?"

"Spit in your face," answered Hakon. "When I carried him here I took up a host's duty, and you upheld my honor as your own. Luckily the knightly kind mislike an axe."

"That kind's only brave with the odds in his favor."

"He's left a couple of men on watch, up on the rocks there—"

"As I've seen. Lord Adam, my lady, you must lie in your hole a little longer. A hard wait it's been, but the only way."

"We're alive," said Adam, in that odd thick voice, "and that seems a miracle."

Yet their purgatory's term was fixed. The tarpot was cold, the caulking mallets silenced; the seamen waited on guard behind the vessel's bulwarks. The waves thrust under the *Greylag's* stern, lapped over and between churning pebbles, fingered coldly to where they lay. The ship stirred. Then the heavy canvas was peeled up and back, and Julitta was dazzled by sunlight long withheld. Too cramped to move unaided, she and Adam were unceremoniously hoisted up, covered from the shore by the sail, and tumbled over the gunwale. They sprawled under the break of the poop, tingling with returning sensation, while the *Greylag* lurched free, the oars were run out with a disciplined thump and rattle, and she swung away from shore, round the reef now awash at nearly full tide, and stood out to sea.

Julitta sat up and twisted round to her husband, and her

249

first sight of his wrecked face in daylight jolted her heart. Hakon stared, swore, and fetched a wooden bowl of water and linen rags. Between them they washed the clotted blood from his hair and face. Both eyes were blackened and swollen to slits, a ring had gashed his right cheek and his lips were cut against his teeth; the front ones were slightly loosened, but she thought they would grow firm again. She closed the gash in his scalp by tying strands of hair across. The worst damage was his broken nose; she straightened it as best she could for the swelling. For the rest of his life Adam would have a kink in it.

She sat back on her heels, blinking tears away. He leaned to scrutinize his reflection in the discolored water. He flinched, and then shrugged. "It was never a face to charm the ladies," he said wryly.

"Now you are virtuously wedded that need not fret you," Julitta retorted, matching jest for jest lest she weep.

A seaman brought more ale, bread and fresh broiled fish. She was ravenous, and food put heart into her. Adam ate too, breaking morsels and chewing carefully, but his hunger was soon defeated and he left the greater part of his portion. The *Greylag* idled a quarter-mile from the castle headland; outside arrow-shot of land a seaman could thumb his nose at his foes' impotence.

Erling beckoned a gray-bearded sailor to take the tiller and joined them under the poop. He scrutinized Adam's face, and nodded. "You were not born to die of a broken neck" he observed. "What do we do now, Lord Adam?"

"'We'?" Adam sharply caught at the word. "Master Erling, you've risked too much already, and this is no quarrel of yours."

"That lady-faced hound made it my quarrel," Erling pronounced, and Hakon murmured assent.

"You've done more than any man could ever require—"

"In my own land," Erling stated, "a merchant who voyages overseas in his own ship is reckoned equal in worth to any landed warrior. He dishonored me. Am I to accept shame from a mailed thief and sail home unrequited?"

"He set a spear at my belly," Hakon added.

"He and his like hold rule in Brentborough now," Adam pointed out.

"Rule? He's not fit to hold dominion over a dunghill! My lord, we are yours to command."

Adam frowned at Brentborough keep, and drew a hand across his eyes and brow in a betraying gesture. A blow hard enough to unsteady his wits through the whole night must have jarred the brain inside his skull, and Julitta knew his head ached so that he could hardly see. "I've Brien and thirty men in York," he said at last, "and there's a way into Brentborough from the ravine."

"Better still, there's a place under the headland where a boat could tie up," Erling amended.

Adam looked up into his grimly-smiling face, his lips parting on expostulation, and then nodded. "Better still," he agreed. "If you'll land me a league or two up the coast, I'll make my way to York. Julitta—"

"I go with you."

He considered it dubiously. "I suppose you'll be safer in York than elsewhere."

"How long will it take you?" Erling asked.

"Two days, perhaps three, on foot."

"For the next ten days, Lord Adam, I'll hang offshore here, to be ready at your need. Seamen climb handily, and they are handy also with edged tools."

"Notably axes? I cannot refuse, and indeed you'll be warmly welcome."

"I'll be sorely disappointed if I don't meet Lady-face," Erling commented, and Hakon grinned. "And there's that profitable association to be safeguarded, remember." He stood up, turned his nose to the southeast breeze, and issued brisk commands. Up went the yard and sail, and the ship pointed her prow north, the sea creaming under her stem and curdling white in the wake she ruled out behind her.

Adam climbed to his feet and leaned against the larboard gunwale, watching Brentborough's keep diminishing to a child's toy, until a headland's shoulder shut it from sight.

251

When he turned away Erling touched his arm. "It'll be yours again, Lord Adam. Now lie down in my cabin for an hour. You'll need all your strength to reach York afoot."

"I swore fealty to the King for it." Adam said bleakly. He lifted his battered face to Erling's. "They hanged Odo for defending me. My seneschal opened the gate, and it's my bastard kinsman sits in my place." He passed a hand again over his brow, and blundered blindly into the cabin. Julitta dived after him, and steered him to the low bed, upon which he almost fell—he who was never clumsy. He rolled on to his back and reached for her hand. She gave it into his clutch, sank down beside him on the bearskin and put her free arm over him, drawing his head to her shoulder. He turned his cheek to her breast, shuddered and was still. Outside she could hear Hakon cursing savagely.

"I doubted you too, Julitta," Adam whispered. "Only for a little space, but I doubted you."

"There was no other way, Adam. It served."

"If it had been so—if I'd gone unsuccored over the cliff—I'd have died thankfully."

"Enough, Adam. Rest now." She smoothed his hair from his brow and kissed him. His arms closed round her in an urgent embrace, he shifted his head slightly and muttered her name. She held him close, in a fury of pity and love for the lad whose world had disintegrated under his feet for the second time in his life. She was all that was left to him now, and he was hers to cherish.

Astonishingly, he slept. She lay with his slack arms about her, his head heavy on her breast, tears sliding down her cheeks for his misery that was hers through him. She remembered, with a pang, his jesting on the headland four days ago: "The surest way to your tender heart is to be hurt or sick or wretched." Wryly she recognized the truth that informed most of Adam's jests; she had not relinquished resentment until she saw him hurt, nor admitted love before it joined with pity and pride at his bearing in humiliation and defeat. Out of all his loss, at least his wife should be a gain to him.

17

An hour past noon Julitta and Adam stood on the strand
of a cove under towering cliffs, bidding farewell to Erling
and Hakon who had set them ashore in the skiff. Erling had
done his utmost for them. Each wore a heavy dagger, and
Adam had a short sword at his belt. Thick cloaks, rolled and
strapped, rode their shoulders. Their ruined shoes had been
replaced by seamen's rawhide brogans, crude ovals of hide
stitched to a heel at one end, punched round with holes and
drawn up by a thong. Slung at Julitta's girdle was a bundle
of ready-cooked food, buttered oatcakes, cheese and fish
enough for two days.

"It's little enough, and I wish it were more," Erling
growled, when she tried to thank him.

"You have our hearts' gratitude," Adam told him reaching
out both hands.

"Nay, my lord." He gripped them warmly. "It's our profitable future I'm providing for, remember. God keep you safe
and bring you to your own again!"

"God be with you," Hakon said, his gaze steady on Julitta's
for a long moment. They pushed off the skiff and swung
aboard. As their oars dipped Adam turned resolutely to the

cliff, and Julitta hitched her gown half-way to her knees, which would have been reckoned unseemly by any peasant wench at field-labor, and followed him up a gully eaten through the rocks by a small stream, offering an easier way up than the rock-face.

The trees straggled and died out in waves of rank bracken that tipped and flattened into tussocks of bent and bilberry; these leveled in turn into wastes laid flat under the sky, somber miles of heather. The rich hues were fading now with summer's end, streaked with bilberry's greenish red and bog's menacing green, spiked here and there with dark rushes. Grouse called upon them, larks shrilled aloft, and at their backs gulls wailed and spiraled; in a notch of the cliffs Julitta glimpsed the sea. Far above, sailing in giant circles, an eagle waited.

Adam turned slowly about, scanning the wide desolation. "Do you know these moors, Julitta?"

She shook her head, "I was never let roam loose, under my uncle's governance."

"Nor do I. We're about two leagues north of Brentborough, and the moors run north and west. I reckoned if we struck so, along the edge —" he gestured a little north of west — "we'd be outside any hunt after us, and tomorrow we could swing southwest until we came on the York road."

It seemed a reasonable proposal. Neither yet knew how unreasonable a terrain the moors presented. They learned. The wide tops lay apparently level, rippling gently under the sun. In fact they were crazily seamed with gullies whose depth varied from several feet to a few inches, the latter offering a peculiar hazard to the limbs, since they were usually masked by vegetation and discovered by falling into them. The close-laced heather grappled their ankles. There were not even animal tracks to follow, for there were no sheep so far from settlements and the deer preferred to keep to the wooded valleys. Bogs waited to entrap the unwary; Adam mired past his knees in one incautious step, and thereafter widely skirted their tufted reeds and inviting green levels.

Another hour found them on the lower slopes, threading

254

along deer trails between the straggling trees; rough going still, but less risky than the high tops. Neither was accustomed to walking, and unused muscles complained at the steep slopes, but they were young and determined. Adam set an easy pace, and trod in somber silence. Julitta respected it. She was there if he desired speech. She knew the successive blows that had hammered him, could guess at his grieving for his tame bear, and was certain he still endured a blinding headache.

After a mile or so they came upon a stream hurrying down from the moors, and halted to drink. Adam knelt and repeatedly dashed water over his face and the contusion under his hair, confirming her diagnosis. He stared bleakly down at his broken reflection a long moment; no youngster could lightly accept permanent disfigurement, and he must have known that his angular features had had a distinction more attractive to women than mere comeliness.

He shook his wet hair out of his eyes and sat back on his heels, caught her anxious gaze and smiled crookedly. "It's no matter," he said. "That is, if — if it doesn't repel you, Julitta?"

"How could it?"

He reached up and drew her to sit beside him, leaning against a rock beside the chuckling stream. After a while she withdrew her hand, hitched round her bundle, took out an oatcake and tore it in two. He ate it cautiously, fragment by fragment, gazing out under the leaves at the bracken rolling up to meet and mingle with the heather.

"Nothing I could say — nothing would have stopped them," he said abruptly. "They were determined on a sacrifice — a warning — and my poor fool served their purpose."

"You were fond of him," she said gently, recalling his exasperated indulgence to Odo.

"The most loyal, willing servant, and the thickest-witted, a man could have. The mischief was, he'd been with me since I was seventeen; he never would admit I was man grown. I suppose he always saw me as the scrawny lad who couldn't fill the mail my lord bequeathed to me."

255

"You found him Outremer?"

"He found me. My dear Lord Hugo died there. He rescued me from the monastery, trained and knighted me, and died at the last of a gangrened wound in a stinking Syrian village. So I resolved to quit that pestilent land, and Odo offered his services on the road back, having lost his master and also had his bellyful. We journeyed back to France and got each other into and out of trouble a dozen times on the way, so that it became a habit. Yes, I was fond of him. And now he swings in the wind, and the crows and gulls tear him." He caught at the rock and wrenched himself erect in one jerk, breathing hard. For a moment he stood with his back to her, gripping the lichened stone with a pressure that whitened his finger tips, then abruptly started along the stream's bank as if goaded by a devil's red-hot pitchfork.

During the next two hours a spur of the hills pushed them southward; they climbed its lower slopes, and over the ridge came on thick woodland, filling the valley with its green-black mass and thrusting up into a shallow dip between the high moors. Julitta regarded it with dismay. To skirt it would take them three or four miles out of their way, and she had learned now to reckon miles afoot differently from miles on horseback. Resignedly she followed Adam along the forest's edge, thanking her Saints and Erling for the comfortable brogans on her ill-used feet.

Within half a mile they came upon a track appearing over the ridge and diving into the woods, and halted, looking dubiously from it to each other. Adam shook his head. "We dare not approach a settlement," he decided.

She summoned up the inadequate knowledge of the district her confinement in the nunnery and in her uncle's household had given her. "I reckon it's Digglewick."

He frowned. "I've never been this way, but it would be my guess too. We'll not linger." He caught her hand and pulled her round a tangle of elder and hawthorn massed with red and black berries. A horseman trampled out from behind it; Everard of Digglewick himself, sword in hand.

"Stand!" he ordered, and then saw Adam's face. His mouth

dropped open, and his sword drooped. "Lord Adam! Who — who used you so vilely?"

"Your comrade of Flackness," Adam answered, slipping forward and to the right.

"*No!* I withdrew — I refused to have part or share —"

"Squeamish, Lord Pilate?" Adam mocked. Julitta edged to the left.

His glance flicked from one to the other, and he actually yielded ground, he the mounted man, weapon in hand, before their menace. Alarm warred with compunction in his indecisive face as he looked on the outcome of his flirtation with treason. "I'd no knowledge — no intent — Lord Adam, I'll make amends. I'll provide you with horses."

Adam, gathered to spring, checked on the instant, catching his breath. "You mean that?"

"Truly, my lord. Horses — food — fresh clothing —" He regarded Adam's tunic, rustily blotched with diluted blood, and grimaced, jarred out of his blindfold complacency by this accounting. "Only come with me." He sheathed his sword in a gesture of amity.

They looked at each other, and Adam nodded. The chance could not be refused; horses would save them one weary day at least. Judging Everard mercilessly, Julitta reckoned him sincere; a weak man, easily overborne by pressure of a stronger will, but well-intentioned, and now honestly revolted by Adam's mistreatment. They fell in beside him, not too near. Everard, inspecting him at closer quarters, shuddered.

"Believe me, Lord Adam, I'd no idea — I insisted no harm should be done you or your lady —"

"No harm to dispossess me for old Maurice's bastard?"

He recoiled, and the horse reared and squealed as the bit wrenched his mouth. "His *bastard? No!*"

"Hell's Teeth, were you daft enough to believe the whelp Maurice's lawful get? His bastard out of the woman Constance, Sir Bertram's wife." And as the man gaped at him in appalled comprehension, he demanded, "Who conceived this crazy plot?"

257

"I — I — the plan was to declare for the Young King — but we had to have Brentborough, and you'd not be persuaded. I don't know who found the boy. William of Chivingham sent his son to bring him — he'd been bred up in some monastery — and Humphrey housed him at Crossthwaite. And we did offer you one last chance," he justified himself almost angrily, "but you rejected it, and Leicester's reinforcements were on the way, and no time to waste, so —"

"So my seneschal was deluded into opening the gates, poor fool, to his wife's bastard," Adam finished in pure disgust. "Aye, and learning it killed him. It was the woman's contriving, and who but that bitch could have provided the boy?"

"You... there's no certainty he's hers..."

"I've proof."

"You've set yourself from the first..."

"I stand by my King."

"An oppressor... a usurper... and he murdered the holy Saint Thomas!"

"I'd rather be oppressed by a murderer," Adam said brutally, "than misruled by a whelp who calls in the Scots."

Adam was being singularly unconciliating, Julitta reflected, glancing up at Everard's resentful face, and then amended that judgment; Adam simply did not know how to be conciliating.

"The Scots... I can't believe it..."

"Believe as you please. It's 'thirty-eight over again."

The unhappy conspirator humped himself in his saddle, staring at the dust, and said no more until the woods thinned and opened, and they glimpsed fields beyond. A herd of ridge-backed swine surged grunting from a patch of bracken, and as Everard swore at them, a man and a dog drove them from the path. Then they encountered a group of children picking blackberries, who scuttled squeaking from the sight of Adam's face, and emerged into a narrow valley where sheep and cattle were foraging in the stubble fields and a plough team was at work in the fallow. A dozen cottages bordered the track, and beyond them the thatched roof of Everard's manor house rose above a decrepit palisade.

"Do you depend on prayer to guard you from the Scots?" Adam demanded, after one comprehensive glance. Everard looked at him with dislike.

"I'll not believe —"

"Until they're beating in your door."

The gate stood open on the cluttered garth. Hens scratching round the dunghill scattered squawking before the horse's hooves, and at the sound a woman came out to the head of the wooden steps that went up to the hall door; a woman in her thirties, with a fretful face prematurely wrinkled and a few wisps of graying hair escaping from beneath her wimple. She exclaimed at sight of strangers and labored down the steps, heavy with child and near her time.

"Who — Adam de Lorismond!"

"And his lady. I've offered them horses."

"Are you mad?" she cried, taking the last steps in haste and lumbering to bar their way to the stable. "Aid our enemies and betray our King and friends? Send them back to Brentborough bound!"

"Our guests —"

"Have you taken thought for me and the son within me, and the vengeance there'll be for your folly?" she screeched at him. Everard blenched; it was plain which of them ruled. "You'll risk all for a murderer and a whore and see me miscarry of the trouble? Give them to justice, and take your proper place among his friends when our King comes to rule."

Faces gaped from doorways and round corners, but she heeded none. Everard's mount sidled nervously as his hands tightened on the reins, and he expostulated without conviction, "Now, wife, I cannot... to be murdered..."

In a kind of frenzy she raised her arms, fists knotted; a heavy ring glittered silver under Julitta's nose. "You fool! Will you risk your son and his inheritance for these?" she shrieked, and clutched at her burden.

"He'll be proud when he learns you turned Judas for his sake!" Julitta blazed, backing away.

Everard hesitated, shamed by the choice he was about to make. Adam leaped. He had jerked his left foot from the stirrup before the older man could move, and a heave under

259

knee and thigh flung him to sprawl across his own dunghill. Adam had vaulted into his saddle as it emptied, caught the reins and wheeled the plunging beast for Julitta. The woman screeched at the servants and tried to block her way, but Julitta spun her off with a stiff-armed thrust and ran. She caught Adam's extended hand, set her foot on his and swung up behind him. The bundle at her belt caught the crupper; she grabbed it with one hand and clung with the other to Adam's belt as he wheeled the horse on its haunches and rammed spurless heels into its ribs. The termagant shrieked to her men to shut the gate; two threw their weight on it, but even as it came ponderously round they were through the gap.

Fading yells followed them. Women, children, poultry and dogs fled the track as he thundered down it. He slithered to a stop in the middle of the street to shout to a face looming beyond a half-door. "Guard yourselves! The Scots are over the border!" They were shattering through spray across the ford before Julitta realized incredulously that she had known that barely-glimpsed face; it was Ivar's. Then they were pounding between the ploughlands, across the waste into the woods. Branches slashed at them. Adam eased the horse to a run in respect for the rutted track.

"Dear God," he said, in a half-throttled voice, "to be a cur like that — and live with it —"

"We've saved two leagues, and won a horse," Julitta replied practically.

"Crows' meat on four legs," Adam grunted, and let the over-burdened brute slacken pace further. When they came to the end of the open woods he halted to listen, but they heard no pursuit. He slipped from the saddle, lifted her into it, and took the stirrup leather to lope alongside, through dense forest untouched by foraging pigs and firewood-cutters. They must conserve the beast's strength, and their combined weights would speedily founder it. Julitta insisted on taking her turn afoot, and they pressed westward, avoiding skylines, while the sun swung round and down until it glared in their faces. The horse suddenly stumbled and began to limp painfully on his near fore.

"Might have expected Everard would ride an unsound beast," Adam pronounced disgustedly, gently exploring the affected shoulder. "An old strain. Take a month at grass to render him serviceable again. He's done."

Julitta hitched up her skirts again and shifted her bundled cloak to ride more easily on her shoulders. They were climbing out of a valley with a brawling stream at the bottom. The sun had gone behind the hill, and already dusk was thickening under the trees. Waves of bracken bowed in the evening wind. Adam looked about him, unconsciously bracing his own tired shoulders, his face hideously blue and purple.

"We'll find a hole to pass the night," he decided, and led the crippled horse back down the hill and along the stream.

Luck was theirs. They shortly found an over-hanging rock-face, and leaning against it a slab thrice as tall as a man. Between them was a dry hollow drifted deep in last year's leaves. A lingering stink and a litter of feathers, bones and scraps of shriveled skin told them a vixen had whelped and reared her cubs in it that spring, but they were past fussing about such tenants and soon kicked it clear. Adam threw saddle and bridle under cover and turned loose the lame beast to graze; with no weight to carry he would most likely hobble home.

Julitta dumped her bundle on a flat stone. "As well we shan't need a fire."

"I don't suppose Everard pursued us." Adam shrugged off his strapped cloak and dropped it beside the food. "He's probably thanking God we won away and sweating for fear your uncle will learn he bungled so." He stretched his arms, and as she turned away closed them about her from behind, holding her to him. His breath was warm in her tangled hair. She stood quite still, but her heart hammered, her pulses leaped, her mind dizzied. "Julitta," he murmured thickly. "The angels that watch over drunken fools guided me to you that night."

261

"Then you don't — don't resent it any more — that you were obliged to marry me?"

"Resent —?" For a heart's beat he stood rigid; then he spun her about and held her by the shoulders. "Julitta, I wanted you as I never wanted anything in all my life!"

She gasped in unbelief, and he shook her slightly. "But — but — *me*?"

"Listen, Julitta! I didn't marry to do penance for my lifetime! When you'd beaten my wits back into my head that night, and I saw you, so scared and so valiant, I knew I'd found you — the one woman — my children's mother — my heart's dear delight —" His voice roughened and broke.

"I — I — I didn't guess — *me*!"

His swollen mouth twisted in a smile. "I've told you before, you undervalue yourself, Julitta. I *had* to constrain you, or I'd have lost you forever. But I love you, my own vixen. Haven't I proved it in my wooing?"

"You never said —" she whispered, too stunned to feel anything but astonishment.

"I feared to," he confessed, pulled her close and kissed her softly on the mouth. Then he loosed her. "I'll not constrain you to anything, Julitta," he promised soberly, and started away up the hill. His sword flashed, gold under the sunset. She watched him scything the rank bracken, standing in a dream. She looked down at the bundle of food, up at the paling sky all streaked with feathery clouds that were just flushing pink. Absently she freed herself of the bundled cloak, wriggling her shoulders to break the grip of her sweaty smock.

Up the hill she could hear Adam's sword steadily slashing. The stream below her chuckled to itself, and its voice reminded her how intolerably heated and grimy she was from the day's dust and sun. She slipped between the trees, following the water until it widened into a pool, not deep enough for swimming, but an admirable bath. She stripped off her filthy garments, stained with blood and mud and seawater, and knelt to souse and pound her linen smock against the stones. She tossed it over a bush to dry. Distastefully she surveyed the wreckage of her new riding dress. The heavy wool would never dry before morning, and she knew well the grappling discomfort of damp clothing on a march. She beat the dust out of it and shook it viciously. Then she knotted up her hair and slid in, gasping at the first shock of cold hill-water and then rejoicing in its embrace. Emerging at last clean and glowing, she dashed the water from her skin with her hands and stood to let the warm air dry her. She was wrestling on her gown when she heard Adam calling her.

"Downstream!" she answered him, tied on her brogans and started back. He was cleaning his sword, unalarmed, and the shelter's entrance was piled with bracken. "I've been bathing," she explained as he smiled at her. "I'd recommend it."

"With reason," he agreed, sheathed his blade and moved away among the trees. She looked over the camp. He had set out a frugal meal and prepared their beds. Two beds, one within the shelter and one at its entrance, deep piles of springy bracken with their cloaks atop. An odd smile quivering on her mouth, she heaped all the fern together under the overhang and laid her cloak across it. The bitter scent of it in her nostrils, she spread Adam's cloak over all. She was his wife. Lying apart in their shared chamber she had wondered shamefully how it would be to know the love of his urgent body. Now, with a half-scared eagerness, she waited to surrender. She did not want him sobered, defeated, bludgeoned into humility; she wanted her arrogant Adam. But the reckless boy, she reckoned sorrowfully, was gone for ever. All she could do was give him this triumph.

He pushed through the bushes, as carelessly attired as she was in unlaced tunic and brogans, and dropped an armful of clothing and weapons with a clatter. She smiled at him, her breath fluttering, and he glanced past her at the bracken bed. His eyes widened.

"Julitta?"

"I am your wife, Adam."

He took her by the shoulders, and she could feel the tremor in his hands. "Julitta, it's not your reluctant body I want. I could have taken that any time I chose. Dear girl —"

263

She lifted her hands to grip his. "Adam —"

"I don't want you out of pity or obligation or duty, Julitta. I want all of you, for love."

She reached up her hands to pull his head down. "All of me is yours, Adam. I love you."

He drew one gasping breath, his face transfigured, then caught her up. She strained to meet him, lifted her unpracticed mouth to his, and the sunset whirled about her. Then he had swung her off her feet and was carrying her to the shelter, helping her from her gown, stripping off his tunic. Naked in the brazen evening, they drew together. He unfastened her hair and shook out the heavy ripples over her shoulders and breasts, running his fingers through it. "My own lovely Julitta!" he murmured, and she went trustfully into his cool, damp embrace. He carried her down beside him on the heap of fern.

18

Julitta stirred slightly, and desisted at a tug on her hair. Completely awake, she realized that it was spread abroad and Adam was lying on it. The weight against her shoulder was his head, and his arm lay warm across her. She smiled up contentedly at the moon flooding the shelter with silver light, remembering his tenderness. To Adam the act of love was a simple pleasure to be shared joyously, and they had mingled love with laughter. She moved a little closer, and with a wordless murmur Adam tightened his clasp. Then he woke.

"Julitta, Julitta," he whispered, his lips moving softly over her breast and up to her throat. She kissed his hair, and nibbled gently at his ear. He chuckled and shifted back to her shoulder. "I never lay with love before," he said wonderingly. "All the bought pleasure is worthless—a regret—"

"Consorting with harlots at least taught you how to pleasure your wife," she said judicially, jarring him from contemplation of his misspent past.

He laughed aloud. "That unseemly observation deserves punishment," he pronounced, and tickled her ribs. Giggling, she tugged at the hair on his nape, bringing his mouth to hers. Mirth and love joined in her; she had never dreamed

One Scot was going down with Adam's sword in his belly; he wrenched it back as the man jolted to earth and whirled under the last man's spear. He struck it up over his shoulder and dived in. The Scot let go and grappled, and they rolled clawing into a bramble patch. She dodged round threshing legs, ran in and stabbed as a yellow shirt and bare buttocks heaved uppermost. A screech, a heaving effort, and red head and white body were atop. Adam's elbow jerked, the Scot squalled and lost his hold, and Adam pulled back to his knees for striking space and rammed in the sword until it rang on rock.

He thrust erect and swung frantically around. She stumbled into his arms and clung crying and shivering to him. He gripped her so that her ribs creaked, and she pressed to his shuddering body, her face burrowing into his shoulder, so pithless that she could not have stood unaided. He was whispering her name over and over, his cheek against her hair. Then one of the horses snorted, and she forced control on herself, lifted her head from its refuge and gripped her husband's arms. "Adam, you're not hurt?"

"You—he didn't—"

"No—no—"

He held her to his thudding heart. "Julitta—my valiant darling— dear God—" Again he buried his face in her hair, and they clung to each other, shaking with shock and horror.

He drew away at last, and their flesh parted with sticky reluctance, glued with the blood she had shed. In sick loathing she ran to the stream and down to the pool. She threw herself into it, and knelt scrubbing at her polluted flesh, remembering against her will the feel of her knife sliding into the Scot, the jerk as the life broke out of his body and left him a dead weight. She told herself savagely that he would have done worse by her, that she had but saved herself, but the memory would haunt her long enough.

Adam had joined her. Silently he scoured himself with a handful of sand; in silence he helped her to wring water from her hair and proffered a checkered cloak for her to dry herself. They recovered shirt and smock and returned to their camp. The ponies were browsing unconcernedly among the bushes. "At least they've given us horses," Julitta observed, and scrambled into her clothes.

Adam went to them. They snorted and sidled at his alien voice and scent, but did not break away, and when she followed he had tethered them securely and was taking a bundle from one of the filthy sheepskins that served as saddles. "Best see what they've looted," he said distastefully, unknotting rawhide thongs. He shook out a mass of gray cloth, a bloody tunic, and forth jumped a bronze-mounted drinking horn, a comb of carved bone, and something small and pale that landed at Julitta's feet. It was a woman's finger wearing a gleaming silver ring. She knew it. She had seen it but yesterday evening.

For a moment she stood frozen, then dropped to her knees, retching emptily. Adam swooped and snatched it up. "Dear God!" he whispered, and his arm came round her.

"Margaret . . . Everard's wife . . ." she choked, and he stiffened. Then he turned her against his shoulder and stroked her hair until she recovered and pushed back. They looked gravely at each other. He touched her hand.

"Julitta, it's at peril of soul we go on."

She nodded. A duty was laid on them. "Murdering rebels I'd not care about, but the country folk—"

"The innocents. Even that termagent—who's more innocent than an unborn babe?"

He tore at the ground with his dagger, laid the finger in the tiny grave and covered the disturbed earth with a stone. He crossed himself. She knelt beside him while he spoke a brief prayer, and then ran to the camp for their belongings, averting her eyes from her victim's hairy nakedness exposed by the yellow shirt. Their refuge's enchantment was shattered, and she found it strange that nothing had changed in the bracken-heaped shelter where they had loved.

The ponies were iron-mouthed unmannerly brutes, accustomed to usage a reasonable man would not deal a balky pack mule, but they proved durable. The sheepskins and clumsy wooden stirrups did not provide comfort, but any

269

kind of horseflesh between their knees was good. The spare horse followed without need of leading, and Adam changed from one to the other. As long as they could they kept to the trees' cover, and when they emerged to climb the ridge Julitta felt a creeping unease between her shoulders. Again and again she turned to look about, but the moors rolled away empty, whale back beyond whale back to the distant blue tops.

Once they halted to breathe the ponies, and to water them sparingly at a small cascade. Discovering hunger, they forced down stale oatcakes, grim chewing even with butter to grease the way. Julitta noticed that Adam had fastened to his sheepskin one of the checkered cloaks. She had not thought him the man to choose such plunder, then realized it was incontrovertible proof of their story.

They drew rein on the ridge beyond Digglewick, looked down on the woods' fleece and over the valley, green under the morning sun. A vagrant wind gusted woodsmoke, harsher and stronger than any household fire, and a more pungent stink also reminiscent of kitchen catastrophe. The underbrush thinned, the woods opened, the fields spread beyond. Both saw the brown huddle in the track, and stopped. Adam slid down.

Gently he turned over the body, and it came woodenly, all of a piece as it had stiffened, from the blotch in the thirsty dust. Blue flies lifted sullenly and settled back. One of the blackberrying urchins, thought Julitta numbly, maybe seven years old. His left arm was gashed to the bone. He had run in terror until he fell, and bled to death in the track.

"Dead all night. Earth-cold, and his smock wet with dew," Adam said hoarsely, and gathered him up. He laid him across his mount's neck, and struck away carrion flies with a muttered oath.

"God have mercy on His innocents," said Julitta, her throat thick with tears.

Adam crossed himself, mounted and held the dead child in the crook of one arm. They followed the dark splashes in the track.

270

The cottages were gray ash and black charcoal; here and there a fringe of smoldering stakes remained of the palisade, and behind it heaps of ruin glowed dully as the wind worried them. Smoke trailed across the ploughland, and with it the stench of burned flesh. But human figures scrabbled in the wreckage to salvage whatever Scots and fire had left, and men formed a rank across the street as they trotted up it.

Bows and spears menaced them until someone called Adam's name, and the men broke to meet them and surround the horses, their faces sullen with shock and grief. One cried out and thrust forward, reaching for the child. Adam dismounted and relinquished his burden into his arms, trying to speak his sympathy. The peasant hugged the stiff corpse to his breast, tears streaking channels down his smoke-grimed cheeks into his beard. The rest closed round him, and then drew him away to a trampled garden where two women and three children lay in a row. Julitta turned her eyes from butchered flesh and the two burned things scarcely identifiable as human. She reached blindly for Adam's hand, and it gripped fiercely.

"Lord Adam!" A man sat propped against an apple tree heavy with ripening fruit, his thigh swathed with bloody clouts; a burly fellow, hair and beard gray-streaked, with a kind of natural authority in his voice and eyes. "We owe it to you," he said in stiff French, "that we are not all dead. Our thanks for the warning."

Adam moved to him, and seeing his weakness went down on one knee at his side. "What happened? When...?"

"Just past sundown. We had driven our beasts into the woods and were all about, not caught within doors or abed."

"How many?"

"Threescore at least."

"Sir Everard and his lady?"

"Dead and gutted and hewed apart," the peasant said brutally, "and the unborn babe spitted on a spear."

"Dear God!" Adam whispered. "I warned him—over and over—"

"If he heeded you, maybe *our* dead would be alive now,"

271

the man declared harshly. He nodded to the row of bodies, his face twisting. "My mother... too old to run ..."

"God rest her," Adam said, and crossed himself.

Behind him there was a scuffle as someone shoved through the crowd. As Adam turned his head, a knife gleamed under his nose. Ivar grinned wolfishly.

"Our reckoning, my lord!"

"Hell's Teeth, is this a time for paltry revenges?"

"Ivar, no!" Julitta cried, checking with poised dagger and pounding heart. Though she avenged him as his blood spurted, she could not prevent Adam's murder.

"My lady, I'll free you o' this ravisher!" Visibly he stiffened his resolution, and a red trickle started down Adam's throat. The crowd groaned, and the wounded peasant made a futile grab at his legs.

"Let it wait until we've done with the Scots, you zany!" Adam exclaimed, his eyes steady on Ivar's. The point jabbed deeper, and for the space of a dozen heartbeats none dared stir. Then Adam put up his hand and pushed the blade aside, took it from a slackened grip and stood up. Ivar stared at him, his chest heaving as though he had run a mile, and the peasants began to growl and edge forward. Adam proffered the knife's haft to its owner. "Cry truce and get astride that ugly dun!" he ordered and turned his back to address the wounded peasant. "We must warn the nunnery and Chivingham. If I live I'll send you help." Ivar was still staring bemused, and he thrust him towards the horses. "Move, man! You're riding with us."

A woman cried, "God reward you for your mercy to my fool brother!"

"Most likely I'll get him killed by the Scots," Adam replied. "God be with you, good folk!"

No one spoke until they were easing their mounts up the incline to the ridge. Then Adam dropped back to ride alongside Ivar.

"In drunken folly I did you wrong," he said steadily. "I acknowledge my fault and am sorry for it."

Ivar roused from bewildered apathy. "I'd forgive that. It's what you done to my lass I'd cut your throat for."

272

"I've not touched her. I'm married."

"What's that to do wi' it? So was old Maurice married."

"You fool, could any man wedded to my lady ever look elsewhere, least of all at your Avice, that wet fish?"

"You murdered t'other ravening hound over her!"

"Defending her. She's virgin still for all I know, and lodged safely in the nunnery."

He caught his breath. "That's truth?"

"My word on it."

Ivar nodded sullenly, and they rode on a little way in silence. Then he said abruptly, "I meant to slit your windpipe—but—a man isn't a sheep. What now?"

"If we both survive, you're head groom of Brentborough. I need one."

"What!"

"Don't I owe it to you to make amends?"

Julitta glanced aside at her husband in a kind of sorrowful surprise. This Adam was half a stranger to her. Ivar was staring as though he found him beyond credit; dumbly he shook his head. Then they reached the wide skyline, drew rein to breathe the horses, and looked about. Ivar uttered a strangled yelp and gestured northward.

The farthest whale back was an anthill swarming with tiny dark figures creeping down into the hollow. Julitta, screwing up her eyes against the glare, could just distinguish the larger insects that were horsemen from those on foot, and make a rough estimate of their numbers. Threescore, maybe four, but more and more were crawling over the crest.

"It's the whole Scots host," Ivar croaked.

"Not quite. Foragers in force," Adam answered, peering under his hand. Again he rammed his heels into his horse's barrel. "Chivingham—that could be held. Not the nunnery. How to get the nuns to safety—"

"There's the old ford," Julitta gasped, clinging to the sheepskin with all the strength of her thighs as the pony pounded down the slope. "If we win time—"

"We must," Adam said curtly.

The Galloway ponies had been hard-used already, but they had strength and valor yet. Adam and Julitta, the heaviest and lightest riders, changed mounts every two or three miles. They chose their grades judiciously, eased the ponies up the long slopes and urged them down, and came at last to the valley's head above the nunnery. A threefold gasp of thankfulness greeted the sight of thatch on roofs and peasants at work. The Galloway brutes were lathered and weary, but they had a gallop left in them.

"The ford's beyond the trees—maybe a mile," Julitta pointed. "And Chivingham over the hill."

"Ivar, bear warning to Chivingham the Scots will be at their gates in two hours or less. We'll bring down the nuns and their folk."

Ivar bore away for the trees. Adam and Julitta pelted down the slope, yelling and waving to the herdboys on the waste and the ploughmen in the stubble, and clattered up the street. At the smithy door he leaped down, snatched the hammer from the smith's hand and beat out a violent alarm on the anvil.

"The Scots! The Scots are on you! Get to Chivingham for your lives!" And as men and women came running and shouting from cottages, barns and threshing floors he threw down the hammer, thrust through the gathering throng repeating his warning, and ran to the nunnery gate. The old porter was already dragging it open, bleating questions; Adam pushed past without checking and ran for the Abbess' lodging.

She was on her feet as they burst into her parlor, icy in dignity. "Lord Adam, if this unseemly intrusion means you seek sanctuary, you cannot find it here. I do not deny it you, but your enemies have searched here twice, not scrupling to invade the church itself—"

"You'll have the Scots invading it before noon," Adam interrupted harshly. "Rouse up your household!"

She glanced once into his eyes, then caught up her handbell. Its imperative tinkle brought her servitor nun in anxious haste. "Sister Scholastica, bid Roger and Anlaf ring the alarm. Assemble everyone in the church—"

"When have *Scots* respected sanctuary? Chivingham's

274

your only chance. Get all your folk out. Bring no more than you can carry—hide your holy relics and treasure—but down to the old ford with all speed."

The daughter and sister of warriors nodded coolly. "See to my people, Lord Adam. I will take order for all here."

She swept her robes from the parlor. The two small bells that decorously clanged for the services now clashed alarm through the valley as the porter and a scared lad hauled on the ropes. Women were hurrying from all sides, servants from the kitchens, veiled sisters, a handful of novices, the boarders and their waiting-women, calling, questioning, clucking alarm. Someone began to wail, and Julitta with familiar exasperation recognized Avice, but before the contagion could spread hysteria through the company a woman in a greasy apron clouted her into sniveling quiet.

Adam drove through all to where his old kinswoman stood beyond the turmoil, ankle-deep in yapping dogs and clasping the two puppies to her breast. She looked anxiously up at him as he reached her side, the dogs leaping round his brogans.

"Oh, but they misused you grievously, dear boy! And you're not safe here, they have searched—"

"It's the Scots, my lady. Hasten!"

"All's readied," Emma said composedly, setting an arm about her mistress; from her free hand swung a neat bundle. "Come, m' lady."

She held back as he took her arm. "My little dogs—"

"Let them run with us!"

"Their legs are too short, dear boy—"

"You can't carry more than the pups, Lady Cecily. They must run." His patience was breaking; he exchanged sharp glances with Emma, who urged her after the throng surging through the gates. She stumbled forward, tears streaking among her wrinkles, the dogs yelping with excitement and scurrying under folk's feet with undisciplined enthusiasm.

They emerged into a disorder in which the dogs' contribution was scarcely noticeable. Men and boys were driving bellowing cattle towards the woods; bristling swine, breaking

275

from their herders, charged squealing in all directions; dogs and children skirmished everywhere; poultry flapped and squawked underfoot; and women with babies and bundles were already starting down the track out of the hamlet. Yet it was a purposeful confusion, and its calm center was the peasant Adam had warned two days ago, who stood at the head of the street ordering all. The Abbess, clasping a silver reliquary to her breast, gathered her robed company outside the gate. One of the servants was leading out her elderly white palfrey, another hauled a donkey that dug in obstinate hooves and brayed.

"Everyone down to the ford!" Adam shouted. "Chivingham's the only chance!"

The porter boosted two novices on to the palfrey's broad back, and handed up a child to sit on its neck.

"Reverend Mother—" one began in protest.

"You are my charge," she answered inflexibly, and signed to the man, who seized the bridle and led the placid beast off. "Come, my daughters!" And they followed two by two as quietly as ever they walked in procession into the choir. Avice broke from the servants as they followed, and ran to claw at Julitta's skirts.

"Save me, m' lady! Take me up wi' you!" M' lady, m' lady, don't leave me to t' Scots!"

"You've legs, use them!" snapped Julitta, thrusting her off. Avice ran at the Galloway pony and tried to scramble on to the sheepskin, mismanaged her skirts, and fell to her knees and stared about her. The donkey-leader was loading his beast with children; she started for it, but the cook seized her by the hair and dragged her away shrieking. Two more ponies, piled with young girls and children, trotted away down the track.

Someone raised a yell and pointed. A tiny dark notch in the skyline high to the north moved over it, followed by another and two more.

"They're coming!"

"Let the cattle go! Leave everything!" Adam yelled, caught Julitta and tossed her unceremoniously on to the Galloway's back.

"Shall we fire t' village, m' lord!" asked the peasant leader. "Sooner'n leave t' Scots to sack it!"

For a heartbeat's space he considered it, measuring the distance to the moor's ridge; then he shook his head. "They'll take time to plunder, and we'll need it." He raised his voice to a carrying call as men and boys came loping back. "Bows and spears, and all out!" He swung up and kicked his pony into a run after the irregular procession hastening down the track, halted to hoist a pregnant woman up before him, and with a squalling baby under his left arm headed the exodus. Julitta took up another great-bellied woman and followed close.

The river was swollen after rainy weeks, and sight of the disused ford, when they reached it through a gap in the wooded ridge, struck dismay into Julitta. The roughly-paved approach was broken away, and the further bank undermined and fallen. The turbid water hid the bottom, but she did not doubt its condition matched the rest, after a generation's neglect. Adam halted on the brink to appraise it, and then urged the Galloway in. A palfrey of breeding would have balked; the stocky brute never hesitated. The woman squealed and wound her arms round Adam's neck as the water splashed, and a wench in the troop behind shouted a jest that drew shrieks of slightly hysterical laughter.

Adam, laughing with them, picked his way cautiously over the ford, his sagacious beast testing every foothold. The water reached the pony's breast, and he leaned into the current's force to keep his footing, but his legs held firm. At the further bank Adam set down the woman and passed the screaming baby to her; then he splashed back to the deepest water and held his horse there.

"Julitta, carry your wench over and then take station beyond me."

She hitched her gown to her knees and pushed her pony in. With a snort and a squeal he soused in, and water wrangled icily against her legs. Its force startled her. The girl clung desperately as they fought across, past Adam who leaned to snatch a kiss as their knees touched, delighting the gathering villagers, to the opposite bank, where she set down the girl and returned to hold her pony between his and the verge. Then the porter coaxed down the old palfrey, less reluctant now the example had been set, and the two ponies completed the living chain on the ford's downstream edge.

The men had overtaken their women and children. At Adam's orders they first carried across their bows, holding them high to keep them from the water, and then stood breast and shoulder-deep across the river to pass children over and help the women, weighted by their gowns, to make the crossing. The water thrust and worried; men braced themselves to withstand it, clung to the horses when foothold failed them, staggered and cursed and floundered. No hill farmer ever learned to swim; without the horses at their backs to buttress them they would not have ventured above the knee to save their lives.

Julitta's duty was to hold her tired mount steady in the current, to lean and grab when the gulping, sodden man at neck or rump lurched, to encourage frightened, dripping creatures handed along the human chain and give them anchorage. Little children, wailing and struggling, went first, and then the mothers; the older youngsters following. On the far bank they gathered up babies and bundles and dripped away towards Chivingham. Terror of the Scots had overcome fear of the river, and the operation was conducted with surprising speed and order. Only the donkey dug in his hooves on the edge and refused to budge; as soon as his load of children was hoisted off he loosed a shattering bray and trotted back, exasperated laughter behind him.

Hooves drummed along the Chivingham road and Ivar topped the slope, pulling his Galloway to a sliding halt at the water's edge. "They're warned, m' lord! What aid can I give?"

"Take my lady's place in the line. Julitta, cross back to the ridge and watch for the Scots!"

It was no easy task to extricate herself from the chain and return to the northern bank, and she thanked God for the pony bred to the harshest usage and roughest country. Adam gripped her lightly by the shoulder as she passed him,

278

his glance an accolade that fired her blood. The Abbess, keeping her household of women together, condemned her bare legs with a censorious glare she scarcely noticed; she smiled at the two old women in the midst of panting lapdogs, and mounted to the highest point of the ridge.

The far skyline was empty now, bare of the scuttling ants that had swarmed over it. She could discern the church tower above the trees, but the village was hidden. Her sweeping survey of the valley found nothing amiss, and at half a league no sound would reach her. Southward she could distinguish the wall and roofs of Chivingham and the straggling line of fugitives hurrying along the track. Below her the crossing continued, regulated by the Abbess and the peasant leader. After the village women and children went the convent servants and boarders, Lady Cecily and Emma cumbered with armfuls of yelping dogs, and then the nuns. Last of all crossed the Abbess, and Julitta grinned to see her soused and gulping, passed from one arm to another while the irreverent water swirled her skirts about her.

A thread of smoke spiraled up, thickening to a column. She shrieked above the splashing and outcries. "Adam! They've fired the village!"

"Are they in sight?"

"Not yet!"

"Watch until they are!"

The last man of the chain set the Abbess on the bank. The wretched nuns, whelmed to the toes in sodden woolen, struggled up the slope. The Abbess wrung water from her robes, clasped the reliquary firmly to her breast, and with impregnable dignity followed them. The human chain was breaking apart. The men stumbled to shore, the palfrey and the two ponies with them; Ivar and Adam joined them for a brief conference, and then her husband came carefully across the ford to her.

His tunic clung like a skin, and his exertions had split one shoulder seam. He shivered as the wind bit, and smiled tight-mouthed at her with that commendation that was more than any other man's praise. He did not touch her, but stared

279

at the haze of smoke thickening beyond the trees and blurring the far fells, and then at the fugitives straggling away from the ford.

"When you see them come between the trees yonder, cross over. I'll keep six archers with me and hold the ford, if they reach it before the nunnery folk are safe in Chivingham."

She gazed at him, chilling with a cold that had nothing to do with wet clothing in the wind. "Adam . . ."

He looked back at the stumbling figures, the women weighted by drenched gowns, old Cecily lumbering among her little dogs, the indomitable Abbess. His disfigured face hardened. "We need half an hour, but I doubt we'll be granted it. What else can I do?"

"Nothing else," she agreed steadfastly. "God hold you in His hand, Adam my dear."

"Julitta, remember always, I love you with all my heart."

She watched him go, his head flaming against the bright water. On the far bank men gathered about him; a few words, and some trotted after the fugitives, while the rest dispersed to ambush among the rocks and alders at the river's brink. She fixed her gaze on the gap between the trees where doom would show, and repeated the *Ave Maria* over and over.

A hoof clicked against stone behind her, and she whirled, her pulse thumping in her throat. A rider emerged from the trees on the track's other side, a tall fair man carrying his right arm slung in a white kerchief. For a moment he gaped incredulously across at her, and then spurred his mount down the slope and up, dragging him back on his haunches along-side her. A brace of men-at-arms followed more cautiously.

"The Scots!" Julitta shouted, as sunlight twinkled distantly on moving metal. She pulled her horse aside, and as Humphrey grabbed at her she screeched, "You fool! The Scots are on us!"

"You little bitch! Oh, you treacherous little bitch!" he raged, and slapped her furiously across her face.

She reeled and caught at her pony's coarse mane to stay astride him, tears of shock and pain blurring her eyes. The Galloway plunged sideways, and recovering, she snatched out her dagger and cried again, "The Scots!"

A yell answered; Adam was storming across the ford, his sword silver-bright amidst the spray, with Ivar half a length behind him. Humphrey grabbed at Julitta; she slashed his wrist, and an arrow whistled past his face. He ducked and swore, looked back at his enemy, at archers rising from ambush and nocking arrows, and recoiled. "You lying whore!" he choked, wheeled about and dashed down the slope as Adam's pony heaved up the bank. Without heeding his challenge he turned his horse into the nunnery track and galloped away, his soldiers at his heels.

She clattered down, her eyes watering and her cheek smarting, into Adam's urgent arms. "The Scots . . . he didn't heed me . . ."

He loosed her and lifted his head to listen. A glance stayed Ivar's curses. The hoofbeats diminished to a drumming felt rather than heard, a pulse throbbing in the head. Then, sudden and sharp, came a far-off cry like a bird's, a clangor and a yelling. Adam caught her bridle.

"God has heard us," he said soberly. "I think we have the rest of our half-hour."

19

Chivingham gate jarred shut behind Adam, and as he swung down into a throng of fugitives, the first Scots loped howling up to the ditch. A voice barked command, arbalest strings answered viciously, and a screech lifted beyond the wall. As Julitta slid down into her husband's arms she saw the rush check, while more and more wild creatures broke from the woods and swarmed across ploughland and waste.

Adam set her on her feet and turned to Gilbert, sweating and fearful in his father's absence, clad in hastily-assumed mail. Cattle, sheep and pigs were milling in the bailey's center and making hideous uproar; women were crying, babies howling, dogs barking. Outside the rough, shoulder-high wall of mortared stone the Scots' yells skirled as they gathered. A handful of men-at-arms held the gate, and flanking it Baldwin Dogsmeat's sixteen crossbowmen were ranged along the wall.

"All men to the walls!" Adam shouted above the tumult. "You've all bows and shafts out of store? Hell's Teeth, get to it — spare strings, bracers and gloves too! Drive those beasts between the barn and stable and pen them with ropes before they run mad! Reverend Mother, Lady Matilda, get

283

the women and children inside the hall. Heat water and prepare bandages; we'll have wounded to tend. Spearmen, stand by in the midst to deal with any who break over! And hurry, hurry!"

Hurry they did, spurred by the yells outside. None disputed his bidding; as the highest-ranking lord he automatically assumed command, and Gilbert was plainly thankful to relinquish it into his competent grip. Gautier regarded him with a surly scowl, but no one ever paid the least heed to Gautier's opinions. Lady Matilda expressed her mind on high-handed insolence that gave her orders in her own hold, but the Abbess impelled her into the hall. Julitta slipped through the throng to acquire archery tackle, and then climbed the outer stair at the hall's end to the solar doorway. From that vantage point she had in range the northern wall with its gate, most of the western wall and the northeast corner, and she would not impede the men defending them.

The Scots veered away towards the village, and on the wall a man loosed a cackle of relieved laughter and flung up his spear. "They've gone! They'll not face us!"

"Hold fast!" Adam shouted. "They'll be back!"

"How d'you know their minds?" Gautier demanded sourly.

"Not their minds, their bellies. They are hungry."

"Hungry?"

"Moorland won't support an army. These are foragers. They'll not turn from plunder while there's life in them."

He climbed the stair beside Julitta, and Gilbert and Gautier crowded after him. They watched the horde ransack cottages and barns, bearing out whatever poor possessions the peasants had had to abandon, pitching sheaves of unthreshed corn into the street, hauling out sacks of grain. More and more loped up from the ford, on foot and astride their rough ponies, yellow shirts and checkered cloaks outlandish in the familiar fields. The later comers grabbed and quarreled with bitter greed; fights swirled and knotted the scurrying throngs. Then, inevitably, thatch flared with a gush of flame scarcely visible in the sunlight, firebrands hurtled, and smoke drifted downwind over the manor, stinging eyes to tears and throats to coughing.

Over the ridge from the ford, at a dead run, came a rider of the knightly sort in helm and hauberk. He burst into the mob barking commands, his lancehead flashing as he brandished it, and by twos and threes and dozens they left their looting and squabbling to gather round him. A prickle of fear ran down Julitta's spine; a low wall, sixteen arbalesters and their peasants who had never seen warfare seemed a pitiful defence against that muster of savages. The knight was marshaling them into some sort of order, and now they broke back to the flaming village in purposeful groups.

"Baldwin!" Adam shouted. "Mark that knight!"

"He's marked," Baldwin answered placidly.

"They'll rush the wall! Wait until they're in point-blank range and don't waste a shaft!" he called to his untried peasants, and then turned on Gilbert and Gautier. "Range your men along the walls — you take the west and you the east — and don't let them break!"

"And you?" Gautier sneered.

"They'll try to burst the gate; that's my post!" He pushed the surly lad half-way down the stair in one jolt. The courtyard's chaos had now been resolved into some semblance of order; peasants and servants were scrambling to the walls with bows and spears, axes, pitchforks and scythe-blades tied to poles. Scots were running from the burning village carrying hurdles and doors for siege-shields; a dozen trotted with a heavy beam between them, emerging from the blaze and smother like fiends from Hell's Mouth. Julitta strung her bow.

"You'll flank them from here as they ram the gate," Adam said in her ear. "Try dropping shots."

She swung round and gripped his arms, gazing into his steady hazel eyes, his grim face that softened as he smiled at her. So she would remember him for all her life, whether that were fifty years or half an hour. "Adam —"

"Dear heart, I must go. If — if the worst befall —"

She nodded as he faltered. "I'll join you cleanly, beloved."

He kissed her on the lips and took the steps in three leaps. She followed his bare head across the enclosure to the gate, a void where her entrails should have been.

The Scottish knight had dismounted to marshal his tangle of saffron shirts; the checkered cloaks had mostly been cast aside. Some swung the heavy pole between them, and he was arranging those bearing improvised siege-shields on either side to cover them from the defenders' arrows. His horde scurried about him, screeching and capering, pressing forward, and all at once broke from his hands singly, in clumps and then swarms, storming headlong for the wall. A few ineffective shafts streaked at them.

"Hold it!" Adam yelled. "Wait to nail his eyeball!"

Baldwin's ribald voice suggested an alternative target, and won a crack of raucous laughter from his troop, waiting as coolly as for target practice, while the Scots, yellow shirts fluttering and naked legs bounding, raced for the ditch. Julitta nocked and drew, chose her man out of the foremost, and placed her first shaft deliberately just under his bristling beard. He leaped high and went down full-length under pounding feet, and she shot coldly and carefully to make every arrow count, closing her mind against their humanity. Scots were not men, but ravening wolves on two legs.

Bows twanged and shafts leaped along the wall. Yellow shirts tumbled and rolled under spurning feet, slackening the assault's impetus a little. Baldwin's men were shooting and reloading in pairs, keeping up a steady execution; Adam's head dodged back and forth by the gate, and the peasant archers, steadying to it, sowed feathered death. Then the Scots were leaping into the ditch and clawing up the scarp; the first heads bobbed along the wall. Down went bows; swinging steel glittered under the rolling smoke and wild clamor filled the garth. Julitta lowered her bow, holding her next shaft nocked but undrawn; she dared not shoot into that confusion. Shaggy heads, round shields and thrusting spears lifted and jerked along the wall, and the defenders jabbed and hacked.

The knight came running with ram and siege-shields and

raged at his wolves' backs; the scrimmage was so thick that he could not bring it against the gate, and all his commands went unheeded. Julitta wasted a couple of shafts against his mail, but at that range her light weapon could not pierce it and she had to stand useless. Two defenders were down, and a Scot swung himself howling astride the wall and over it, heaving up a long-handled axe to cleave Adam's head. Three spearmen waiting by the hall sprinted for him, but Adam had already lunged under the axe's sweep and his sword was through the man's belly. They went down in one tangle, but it was the red head that bounced up again and Julitta drew a gasping breath. Another saffron shirt heaved on to the wall top; Baldwin Dogsmeat hewed down, and it vanished in a spout of scarlet. All at once the attack recoiled and the Scots scurried beyond range. The knight barked at their heels like a sheepdog, and the untried ram was borne back by its crew. A few belated arrows brought down a couple of laggards. Yellow bodies strewed the approaches. Julitta heard Baldwin admonish a peasant who put an arrow into a crawling Scot.

"Don't waste arrows! He'll be there for you to cut his throat when the fight's won."

Adam had the servants frantically barricading the gateway with benches, doors, a spiked harrow and building timber, anything to withstand the ram. He found a moment to wave, and she, assured that he was whole, scuttled down the stair as a serving man hobbled to the hall on a comrade's arm. She was not needed; half a dozen women seized on him with commiserating cries and drew him to the nearest fire. The Abbess sat on the dais with her nuns about her, telling her beads; children had been herded into the furthest corner in the care of the older women, and it seemed that every pot in the manor was bubbling, filling the long room with drifts of steam.

"Boiling water," said Adela's amused voice in her ear. "A bucketful in the snout should discourage even a Scot."

"We need more buckets," snapped Lady Matilda. "You wenches, fetch them from the laundry and dairy while there's quiet!" She had a carving knife thrust under her belt, and Julitta saw without surprise that every woman had armed herself, even if it were with but a roasting-spit or flesh-hook. She regarded Julitta without favor. "I never thought to be obliged to receive you under my roof again, shaming your breeding by flaunting your bare ankles like a strumpet, though what else should I expect of a whore's daughter —"

"You show commendable gratitude," Adela observed drily, "to Lord Adam and his lady."

"And he's a traitor escaped from my lord's justice —"

"Who is saving all here from the Scots."

"Am I to be rated like a kitchen wench in my own hall, where I've ruled these eight-and-thirty years, by an insolent whore out of an army's tail! As if it were not enough to have to accept such a one into my decent household, and any mother of a virgin daughter must feel for me —"

Adela snorted. "She'll be a raped corpse if the Scots burst this door!" she retorted brutally, and caught Julitta's arm. A quick glance at her child, sleeping safely in a corner, and she thrust the girl out. They climbed the stair together. "God's Head, let the fool fume! Is this any moment for her hen's squawking?"

It came to Julitta that Lady Matilda clung to her habit of spiteful complaint as a barrier against horror too vile for contemplation. She soberly checked her bowstring for fraying, untied a sheaf of arrows and stood them against the wall on her right hand. A movement on the opposite side of the garth brought her head round; a brace of sturdy lasses had climbed into the hayloft over the stables and were standing in the wide hay-door with bows ready, above the shifting backs of cattle lowing with distress. Several boys were moving along the stretched ropes that penned them, trying to soothe the beasts. Adam was still ordering his barricades. The Scottish knight had prodded his wolves into some sort of formation around and behind the ram. It started forward at a quickening trot, its bearers covered by the mantlets.

"Wait for the gaps," Baldwin's placid voice commanded, "and bring down the fellows with the ram!"

288

The mantlet-bearers had small notion of keeping rank and holding to one pace, and the nearer they came the wider opened the spaces in their erratic line. Most of the archers had mastered their nervousness, and waited for Adam's "Loose!" Crossbows thrummed, bowstrings twanged, and shafts and square-headed quarrels probed between the shifting shields. Julitta tried a couple of dropping shots, more for the moral effect of steel hailing from the sky than because she expected to do hurt, and the girls in the hayloft copied her. The ram lurched and wavered. Over the din she heard the Scottish knight's yelps as he beat at the mantlet-bearers with his swordblade's flat to close their lines. She was dimly aware that Adela had gone from her side; then she was back, and another bow harped beside her.

The ram was down in a sprawl of naked limbs, saffron shirts and makeshift shields. The Scots broke order and swarmed at the wall again. Combat clanged along it. Julitta lowered her bow, blinked smoke tears from her eyes, and sought out her dear redhead. Adela spoke in her ear, but no word reached her; all her being was concentrated on one anxious desire. The attackers suddenly broke away, and she drew free breath again when Adam hurried back to his barricade. Adela yelled to a lad below to fetch more arrows.

"If they'd sense to keep rank and guard their ram they'd have won in," Adela commented professionally. "A troop of mercenaries —"

Julitta was in no mood for technical discussion. Adam turned briefly from his laboring men to salute her with uplifted hand, and then moved along the wall, with an encouraging slap on shoulder for some and a nod and smile for others, to confer with Baldwin. She prayed earnestly to Our Lord and His Mother and the holy Saints to guard her love who fought unmailed in the thickest of the combat. The Scots were massing again, the indefatigable knight reordering the mantlets about the ram. This time they would have learned to maintain that order. If the gate went down, Adam would die and she would follow him.

"*Ora pro nobis peccatoribus, nunc et in hora mortis —*"

"God's Life, but we've thinned them!" said Adela, reckoning scattered yellow bodies. "There's no more than one try left in them. And if we beat them off, it's your red lad's doing."

"If only they'd heeded him before!" Julitta burst out, turning her tormented face to the older woman's calm one, all her love and fear exposed naked.

Adela grinned sardonically. "You confounded all their plots, my girl. Everyone was sure you were so mad for love of Humphrey of Crossthwaite you'd do whatever he asked."

"Conniving at my husband's murder included? You reckoned me a cringing spaniel as well as a strumpet?"

Her venom made Adela regard her narrowly. "Maybe I unwittingly misled them, but I witnessed your hatred for your husband."

"You discussed my marriage with those traitorous swine?" Julitta flared. "How should it concern you or them?"

"Believe me, I'd no concern but for your happiness. If you reckoned it depended on Humphrey —"

"You meddled to help me to that vain lout? I'd not have had him if every hair of his head hung with rubies!"

Adela shrugged, smiling grimly. "My girl —"

"Go back to the hall. You've no place here."

"I'm here," she said flatly, "to kill you at need."

The stark words struck Julitta's wrath cold. As she stared, the Scots started forward again, their cries joining in one ululation that lifted the hairs on her nape. She drew and loosed.

Their losses had disciplined the enemy. The ram reached the gate, some of the shield-bearers holding hurdles high to roof its wielders against showering arrows; the rhythmic crashing beat through all the uproar. Heads bobbed along the wall, spears and axes sparked under the sun, the defenders dodged and hacked. Smoke gusted from the village, now a bright ruin. A few saffron-shirted demons capered with blazing brands.

The gate was breaking in jagged fragments, over the beam that barred it; one sidepost was yielding, slanting inward as it slowly broke away near the ground. The smoke thickened. The barn roof was afire where hooting Scots had tossed torches. A boy scrambled along the ridge with a rake, beating and tearing at the thatch in the haze of smoke and sparks. Beasts bellowed, heaving wild-eyed against the flimsy barrier. barrier.

A great groan of anguished timber, and the gate slewed sideways as the post snapped. Howling Scots clawed through the gap. Adam's barricade, thrust inward, yet held breast-high. The ram had jammed in the ruin; crawling under or scrambling over it, they were vulnerable to spears, axes and pitchforks, and beyond it tripped and tangled, wedged by their comrades thrusting behind. Murderous steel reinforced the barricade with bodies. Baldwin's mercenaries held the wall, waiting coolly for heads to lift above it before bouncing up to strike. Half a dozen women lumbered out of the hall with steaming buckets. As the barrier began to waver they swung arcs of glittering water into the press of hairy faces and bare arms. Inhuman squalling ripped through the din, and they ran back for more.

The knight stood in the gap, shield aslant and sword flashing. Adam's vivid head made for him as he straddled the broken gatepost and withstood all blows. Julitta's heart jumped as the blades met. Vaguely she was conscious of screeching and weapon-clangor beyond the hall; then a triumphant yell below jerked her head round. A dozen Scots erupted past the building's corner and into the garth. Half of them raced for the gate; others scattered for the penned cattle and undefended doorways. Julitta, shrieking at her lungs' full pitch for warning, shot her last two arrows as fast as she could draw and loose, Adela's bow sounding in her ear. Three went down before they reached the barricade, where men faced about to meet the others. Adela screamed.

The deaf-mute child stood in the garth, his back to the doorway through which he had strayed, his fair head turning, his hands lifting to ward off soundless nightmare all about him. Voices cried futile warning; round the hall's corner pounded a Scot. His red mouth roared laughter in the beard's

291

black tangle as his spearhead dipped. Adela, her shafts also spent, threw herself down the stair. The spear drove in and swung up, heaving the child high. For an instant his limbs flung abroad, and then hung limp. Adela leaped upon the Scot's shoulders; one hand in his hair jerked back his head for her knife to slash. She sprang clear as he went down in a scarlet welter, and caught up her son.

The cattle were loose, blood and fire in their nostrils, plunging about the garth to hook and trample. Herd-boys yipped at their heels, dogs barked and scurried. Julitta saw a Scot gored and tossed aside, roused from her palsy and darted down to Adela, kneeling in the dirt with her child. She hauled her to the stair, almost knocked off her feet by a bellowing cow that spattered her skirt with foam. At the stairhead Adela sank down with the boy across her knees.

He was dead. Surprise had already gone from his face. Julitta knelt, her arm about the mother's shoulders, and leaned to close his half-open eyes with gentle fingers. Adela shuddered, and raised her own, dry and stricken, to the girl's appalled face.

"He was your half-brother, you know," she said.

Stunned witless, Julitta gaped at her. "You ... you are ...?"

"I bore you," said Eleanor de Scoray bleakly, and gathered close her dead. "Little Charles — my last son — God takes my sons for my sins."

"Ah, no!" Julitta exclaimed quickly, tightening her hold. It was her firm faith that God was more merciful than men; without that trust no one could endure this world. "In pity for his affliction He has taken His innocent home."

"He is gone from me," she answered. The flesh of her face seemed to have sunken on its bones, but she had no tears. She bowed over the dead boy, rocking him in her arms, and Julitta stayed helplessly on her knees beside her with no comfort to offer. A strange quietude enfolded them. It touched her to awareness, and she lifted her head.

The fighting was finished. Even as she looked, the last foe died against the barn with a pitchfork in his vitals. The Scottish knight sprawled across the broken gatepost; boys and dogs were rounding up the scared beasts; wisps of smoke drifted from a black gap in the barn's thatch, but the fire was out. Over the stubble and the waste the Scots were streaming away, beyond bowshot; some of the peasants and mercenaries were already over the wall and briskly cutting throats. One comprehensive glance she gave all that, and then fixed her gaze on Adam's flaming head beside the barricade.

"Go to him," said Adela, shrugging away her arm. Julitta hesitated; this stranger was her mother. The hard eyes read her mind unerringly. "You're not mine," she said with wintry honesty. "I abandoned you. You're his."

Silently she stood up. From the stairfoot she looked back once at the mother embracing her dead, hers in blood but nothing else; then she caught up her skirts and fled straight into Adam's extended arms. She gripped him, pressed to his body, gasped his name until he stopped her mouth with his, holding her so that she could scarcely draw breath. His heart hammered at his ribs, his body shuddered to racking gasps as hers did, but when she drew back her head he was whole; filthy with smoke and sweat, spattered with other men's blood, but unhurt.

"Julitta! What's amiss, dear love?"

"The little boy — Adela's son — a Scot killed him! And — and — Adam, she's my mother!"

He looked sharply down at her, less surprised than she had expected, and freed his hand to cross himself. "God rest the child's soul."

"Adam, did you — did you *know*?"

He shook his head. "I wondered, that day she rebuked you. There's a likeness, and you have her eyes. A suspicion, no more. God pity her, but the child's best out of this world." He gazed across the lessening turmoil at the hunched shape on the stair; from here they could not see the small corpse she held.

Baldwin suddenly dodged under an ox's muzzle and presented himself, his aggravating grin wider than ever. "Adam, you've talents I'd not guessed at." He swiveled an appreciative eye at Julitta. "There's nothing worth looting on their car-

293

casses, but if you'd fancy a Scot's hide to nail up on your gate, my knaves'll pick you a fine hairy trophy and flay it for you."

"Baldwin, go to your wife." Adam nodded at the stair. "They killed her child."

All the color drained from his face to leave it the hue of tallow. "God's Head," he muttered. "The poor little bastard!"

"What had life for him? It's better so."

"Better?" he snarled. "You fool, what d'you know of it? She only married me for his sake; I've naught now to hold her by."

"She needs you —" Julitta began, but he turned on her savagely.

"She'll leave me — she's no reason to stay. Christ in Heaven, she's never pretended to care for me, and she's all the world to me!"

Adam took him by the shoulders and shook him. "Baldwin, there's no greater comfort in grief than love. Go to her!" He thrust him towards the stair. He looked back at Adam, two tears streaking down his cheeks; then he broke into a shambling run. They watched him scramble to his wife's side and take her in his arms; saw her recoil, then suddenly drop her proud head to his shoulder. Together they drew one thankful sigh and turned their backs. Adam pulled Julitta roughly to his side and held her close.

"Adam," she said in a small voice, "I — I cannot feel — I've respect for her, but no love — I cannot feel she's my mother."

"By her own choice she orphaned you. She has no rights in you," he answered grimly. "Did any other hear this avowal?"

"No."

"God send we keep it so. She has brought disrepute on your name these many years. I'll not have it a flagrant scandal."

From a Lorismond's lips that was not without humor, and an unwilling grin tugged her mouth. She reckoned Adela

294

would keep silence, and if Baldwin knew of the kinship he also had maintained commendable discretion. The aftermath of battle was all about them. Serving men were dismantling the barricade, tumbling aside entangled bodies in saffron shirts. When one groaned and lifted a hand, an axe chopped down. Two mercenaries had hauled out the Scottish knight by the heels and were stripping off his hauberk. Peasants ran and shouted beyond the walls, salvaging what they could from their burned homes or gleaning whatever scanty pickings the enemy dead provided. Adam grimaced.

"If they'd had archers or any notion of discipline we'd have been overrun," he commented, and streaked sweat, grime and blood across his filthy brow with a filthier hand. He braced his weary shoulders. "We've this shambles to clear. Get to the hall, Julitta. This is no place for you."

"There'll be work for me," she agreed, and ran. The stairhead was deserted. Only a blotch on the trodden earth showed where the Scot had died. Inside the hall a curious stillness spread outward from a hurdle on the dais. Lady Matilda, Sibylla and the village priest were on their knees beside it. Julitta peered across intervening shoulders, crossed herself and began murmuring prayers. Lady Matilda's wail interrupted before she had finished the first sentence. Gautier had died.

Her uncle's wife saw her and turned on her like a wolf-bitch. "It's your red knave's fault!" she shrieked. "If he'd not set my boy at the post of greatest danger to keep his own traitorous hide safe he'd be alive now!"

"Lady mother, that's not so!" Gilbert protested. Bertille was binding up a bloody arm for him, and he looked harried beyond his wits.

"Why else should he live, and my son die? Where is God's justice that my son is taken from me for that red hound's triumph? Oh, my son, my son!"

Julitta left her to the priest and her distracted son, the greater part of her sympathy overborne by fury for Adam. The Abbess and her nuns were busy among the wounded; every injured man seemed to have at least three women to

295

fuss over him. She searched out Avice, still cowering in a corner, and tried to shake some sense into her, but thankfully relinquished the witless lump of terror to Ivar. Old Lady Cecily surged amid children and little dogs to embrace her and be assured of her dear boy's well-being.

The dear boy strode in, and half the women squeaked. One small girl began to howl. Julitta could scarcely blame her; that her own heart bounded with delight at sight of his purple face, bent nose and bloody garments only gave the measure of how besotted she had grown. Baldwin followed, and she saw at once that all was very well with him. His hard face was oddly at peace.

The bereaved mother screeched at Adam across the bier. "Murderer! You've killed my boy — you set him to be slain, all young and untried —"

Sibylla grabbed her arm, and Gilbert croaked protest. Adam's left eyebrow flicked up; he was younger than Gautier, though only Julitta seemed to recall it. He looked to Gilbert.

"She's — she's distraught — don't —"

He said curtly, "I'm mounting Baldwin and his troop from your stables and riding to Brentborough. The Scots will make for there next."

"No! Thieve our stables empty — Gilbert, it's your duty to seize him and avenge your brother!"

"Lady mother, it was in no way Lord Adam's fault —"

"God's Death, are you a man?" Baldwin's battle-voice overbore all others. "The whelp bungled his blow and that was his ending. But for Lord Adam, you'd all be burned corpses in your household's ashes, you screeching besom! And we don't need your leave to borrow horses; we'll take them!"

"My lord hired you to do his bidding —"

"And not a clipped penny has he paid us yet!" Baldwin retorted, and made for the door. Lady Matilda wept. Gilbert began to bleat, following them outside.

"Lord Adam, I... my mother's great grief... beg you'll not heed... after your valiant defence..."

"Hell's Teeth, I'd not the least regard for any of your household. I fought for the holy nuns and the village folk."

296

He winced. "I... I'd no share in misusing you... and now this debt..."

"It can gall you for your lifetime," Adam answered, and stalked to the stables. The mercenaries were routing out saddles for a makeshift assembly of mounts; Gilbert's and Gautier's destriers, a handful of hacks and the women's palfreys. The two men who had stripped the Scottish knight accosted Adam, and with rough diffidence proffered the dead man's hauberk, helmet and sword, hurriedly scoured.

"If so be as you'd condescend to take it from us, Lord Adam —"

"It being nowise fitting you should peril yourself unmailed, my lord —"

"And who's better entitled than the captain as commanded the fight?"

Adam looked from one to the other. That a pair of mercenaries should voluntarily forgo the only loot of value from the enemy dead was an almost incredible tribute, and Julitta saw that all the troop, surreptitiously listening, concurred heartily. His strained face relaxed, and he smiled at them with such a warmth of gratitude that Julitta bit her lip to hold back tears.

"Hell's Teeth, I'd good men to command! I thank you."

He dived into its rattling folds, and they gave him a cheer and returned zealously to work.

"And that's truth," Adam added to Baldwin as he helped him into the awkward garment. "Without your ruffians we'd never have held the wall." He shrugged his shoulders into it and drew up the hood. It was of the outmoded type, iron rings sewn on leather, that had served the Conqueror's knights a century ago, but it gave adequate protection except for its elbow-length sleeves. He laced up the throat-flap. "Did William admit to some small doubt of his Young King, I wonder, when he left you here?"

"Not of Young Henry. Of me," Baldwin answered, adjusting the swordstrap to Adam's greater height. His shark's grin flashed. "I'd been your guest."

"He never suspected *you* of scruples?"

"A mercenary can't afford them. Now try the shield. Yes,

297

the guige-buckle needs letting out a couple of holes. And my wife was set on helping yours to her desire." His grin widened. "A profitless venture it's been. Being in some sort your father-in-law, I'm bound to uphold you, pay or no pay."

"You'll be paid," Adam promised grimly.

"What?"

"Your passage back to Flanders."

They regarded each other with perfect understanding. Then Baldwin nodded. "My wife's mine. I'm paid. And there's no scope in England for a man of my trade." He turned to yell at his men. "If there's not saddles enough you'll ride bareback, but move, you slow worms!"

"You've a horse for me?" Julitta asked.

"I can't leave you here to be seized for a hostage." Adam joined his hands and tossed her up on to Lady Matilda's sedate black. She checked the hilt of her sleeve knife.

"I never gave a wench a gift repaid me more handsomely," her husband observed gracelessly and swung astride Gilbert's destrier. Her heart bounded to hear the old Adam jest once more.

Ivar came dodging across the garth, and scowled up at him. "I'm coming with you!" he announced belligerently.

"Get yourself across a horse then, and welcome."

As the routiers formed line he ranged up behind Julitta, astride a sturdy pony, and asserted, "My lady's not dismissed me from her service."

"It being understood that you're her man," Adam agreed gravely, "you'll take charge of my stables?"

He scowled again. "Since she's set her fancy on you, aye."

Julitta glanced over her shoulder as the cavalcade passed through the gate. "Avice?" she asked in a low voice.

He grunted. "When I gets any sense out of her, she says all she wants is to stop in t'nunnery and stay a maid for ever, and cries like a leaky bucket." He spat violently. "Wet fish. Lord Adam was right." He glared at Adam's back and fell back to meditate on that culminating wrong.

One of the mercenaries had been killed and another sorely

hurt, so there were fourteen left riding two by two through the ruined gateway, in the quilted leather brigandines and iron caps that had preserved them. They bore eastward along the track to Crossthwaite at a steady run, the dust rising in sun-gilded clouds behind them.

They went through Crossthwaite without slackening pace, shouting warning of Scots and news of Lord Humphrey's slaying to villagers already alarmed by the smoke of Chivingham's burning. They passed and likewise warned two isolated farmsteads, eased to a running walk up the ridge, clattered down the further slope trusting in their horses' sagacity and the righteousness of their cause to preserve their limbs, and gained the lower ford.

Ivar knew it, and guided them across; though thrice as wide, it was less perilous than the upper one, and they suffered no more than a wetting. Through the woods they pounded, their trampling hooves all but drowning the river's brawling, the cavalcade strung out behind Adam and Baldwin. The trees scattered, wide clearings opening. Thin and far away came a cry like a gull's wail. Spurs pricked. At full gallop they stormed out on to the waste before Brentborough as the first yellow-shirted Scots reached the alehouse and smithy.

Adam and Baldwin swung shields from shoulders and drew their swords, the two crossbowmen behind parted to either side and closed in Julitta and Ivar, and the rest in a tight double column thundered after. Some sort of scrimmage was going on at the alehouse door, more saffron demons swarmed whooping across plough and pasture, and from cottages, barns and byres, from fields and gardens the peasants broke and fled. The alehouse leaped to meet them. The cluster of Scots shattered apart, howls rang, Adam's sword swung and jarred. Julitta's palfrey stumbled, squealed, and went on over something yielding. Just outside the alehouse doorway she glimpsed a vast heap of gray homespun. Gunhild had been too unwieldy to run.

Adam brought the line about in a tight half-circle to the village street, the mercenaries keeping it with admirable disci-

299

pline where knights would have broken rank to pursue at their own pleasure. Back they stormed between the cottages as the Scots ran to plunder them, into and over and through the disorderly throng, swords flailing. The man on Julitta's right grunted and folded forward; she leaned to grab his arm, and they galloped stirrup to stirrup, his weight dragging at her hold. A gout of foam or blood spattered her cheek, wet and warm. Again Adam swung his men round and back. A riderless horse broke free and ran wildly.

The peasants had rallied. With wolf-spear, flail, pitchfork and axe they ran to meet them, while the women and children streamed up the hill to the castle. The saffron shirts scattered between the houses, wolves briefly beaten from the flock, while more and more came pelting over the stubble to join them. The villagers were all about the troop, shouting Adam's name and cheering. Julitta secured a better grip on her man's belt; he groaned and clutched the pommel, so she knew he lived. Adam yelled orders through the din, and the line retreated at a steady walk up the slope, the peasants around and among them. A few had snatched up bows. As the Scots loped after them, closing in, first one and then another saw feathers spring in his breast for his last sight on earth. They checked, and then their consuming passion diverted them. Most turned aside to loot the cottages, and only two or three score followed Adam's retreat; yelling, skirmishing, darting in with spears, but never venturing to engage such resolute defence more closely.

The track tilted to the castle. The gallows loomed stark, Odo's body swinging slightly on the rope's end, gulls and crows crying angrily as they circled over its disfigured head. "Open! Open! Let us in!" women were wailing. They huddled with their children by the masonry abutments where the drawbridge's end would descend, but it remained hoisted in their imploring faces, over portcullis and gate. Heads leaned from crenels above. A cracked voice screeched curses at them, but no order issued from any to lower it.

"Mother of God!" Julitta cried incredulously. "Adam, they're refusing succor!"

He jerked his attention from the Scots, and shouted to one of the peasants. "Gyrth! Get them down to Arnisby! We'll hold them off! At his yell the arbalesters halted, while the peasants raced up the hill calling to their families, who scuttled down to meet them. All along the western wall faces watched whitely from crenels, but entry was denied. Lord William would not shelter the folk he claimed to rule.

The men closed about their women and youngsters and started them down towards Arnisby. The Scots, howling warcries in their own tongue, gathered and hurtled at the gap, trying to turn the horsemen's line. Adam yelled again, and the arbalesters spurred after him. Round shields, hairy faces, indecently naked limbs filled Julitta's sight. Steel flashed and clanged, saffron shirts splashed scarlet, half an arm flipped against her saddle bow and lay an instant, fingers half-curled, before it dropped away. She clung grimly to her wounded mercenary. The Scots reeled back, and Adam shouted to his troop to halt. She glanced hastily at the villagers. A few of the enemy had reached them, but the men were fighting them off; as she looked the last broke and ran from the pitchforks.

Down the Arnisby track they moved at a walk, half-turned in saddles to watch the foe, shepherding the peasants between the thickets of gorse and thorn-scrub. A few Scots tried to dodge past among the brakes, but they could not assemble numbers enough to tackle the determined hedge Brentborough men set about their women and children. Unmailed, armed but with spears and long knives, they could not prevail against the ranked mercenaries. Twice Adam halted the withdrawal, and twice the main force sullenly held back.

Ivar had come round to the wounded arbalester's right side and had an arm about him. He drooped limply in their grip, and blood was soaking heavily down his left thigh from under his brigandine. The castle looked down on them, the keep's tawny stone glowing in the noonday sun. Julitta marveled incredulously that her uncle had denied entry to Brentborough folk. Whether from fear of an overwhelming rush of Scots, knowledge of rotten provisions that would not

301

endure a siege, or recognition of Adam in command of Baldwin's troop, he had utterly discredited himself and his rule.

A breathless cheer lifted from the villagers. They were at the bridge. The tanner and his household were toiling across it, stooped under their bundled possessions. Yellow shirts flickering on the crest had alarmed Arnisby from loom and dye vat and cooking fire, and two farm carts had been run up to the bridgehead ready to barricade it. Julitta saw men lugging up timbers and bales of straw. The peasants hastened across to safety. The mercenaries, preserving their admirable order, halted at the bank. Someone called to her to go first, and as she passed through their solid ranks a fierce appreciation filled her for the hard men and the work they had done this day. Excommunicate they might be, damned in this world and to Hellfire everlasting because they killed for hire, but she called out, "God requite you for the lives you have saved, good friends!" As she went she numbered them. They were now eleven.

Many hands reached to help her dismount, to lift down the wounded man and carry him to the baled straw. He died as they laid him down. She crossed herself and prayed with passionate regret. Her lips moving still, she turned to watch the withdrawal. Two by two they turned on to the bridge, and the Scots began to close in, pelting down the track and yelling hideously. Last of all Adam and Baldwin backed to the bridge, fighting off a rush, and then together swung their mounts about and hit the planks at a gallop.

"Now God be praised," Father Simon crowed ecstatically in her ear, "Who sent Lord Adam at our need!"

On her other side a little withered woman, nursing an arm against her breast, sat beside the dead man on the straw bales and rocked back and forth, tears brimming from her eyes. "Gunhild's dead," she croaked, as Julitta stooped over her. "Poor besom took a broom to 'em — too fat to run —"

"I'm sorely grieved," Julitta said. "Let me see —"

"Tweren't bad ale she brewed, but I wouldn't never admit it," Hallgerd regretted. "No, not bad ale. Me arm's broke, m' lady. Owd bones breaks easy and mends hard."

Ivar had splints and strips of cloth before she could call for them. She set the break, aware that the priest was chanting the ninth Psalm; she caught some of the familiar words, "— destroyed the ungodly; Thou has put out their name for ever and ever." The mercenaries were thumping from their mounts, grabbing arbalests from their saddles, setting and loading. As Adam and Baldwin pulled up lathered horses among the waiting throng they formed rank across the bridge and loosed together. The cluster of saffron shirts at its other end disintegrated, leaving four or five behind, and slowly, sullenly retreated up the hill, where Brentborough's smoke bannered along the sky. Still the castle drawbridge remained shamefully raised.

Laughing, weeping, cheering the folk converged on Adam in wild ovation, thronging to kiss his hands, to touch his clothing or his horse, flinging themselves to their knees, holding up small children to look on the face of their young lord, returned from the dead to save his own people. Half-laughing, tears streaking his filthy face, he looked down on them, moved to the heart; then he descended into their rapturous embrace, their darling for his lifetime. He stumbled for words in his halting English.

"My thanks, good folk — enough — let be —"

His face lighted. Through the throng his eyes met Julitta's. Suddenly forceful, he thrust against them, and with instant perception the crowd made way. It was right and fitting that he should heed no other, but in three strides reach his lady who had saved him from his foes, and catch her up in so fervently tender an embrace that women cooed and men sighed. They turned away to mob Baldwin and his bewildered mercenaries, hardened to obloquy and reviling but not to grateful blessings.

20

In the romances, victory was always resoundingly conclusive and the hero had no more to do than seat himself in the place of honor beside his bride at a miraculously-conjured banquet. In real life matters were less tidily disposed. The harried hero, after barricading the bridge, set about putting Arnisby in a defensible condition, lest the Scots should ford the river's upper reaches and come at them from the south. The fishing boats were run down to the water and crammed with women, children, wounded and household goods. Since the fishers and the newer settlement were mostly at odds, it took extreme peril and all Adam's authority to achieve so much cooperation. Young lads with no more sense than to enjoy the adventure scattered sheep over the moor, where inevitably some would be lost to wolves, drove cattle into the woods, and kept a lookout from the high tops and tall trees for yellow shirts, while their fathers smashed loopholes in cottage walls, chopped furze and thorn for barricades and grimly stood guard with whatever weapons they possessed.

Julitta had four wounded arbalesters and three villagers to tend. Beside Gunhild, two men surprised in the fields were certainly dead, and five others were missing. She tried

305

to comfort new-made widows, prayed with the anxious, and condoled with folk who had lost all they owned. Small children screamed and capered and were sick underfoot. Two notorious scolds, already at feud, engaged in a dispute that embroiled a boatful before they were dragged apart.

By mid-afternoon, no Scot having shown himself again, Adam took those mercenaries who were fit to ride and risked revisiting Brentborough. They were away over an hour, and though she told herself severely that she must not cluck over her husband like a mother hen, she thanked God to see his mailed figure appear over the crest at the head of his company. The Scots had gone, and four of the missing villagers had returned, safe and whole. But the village was a gutted desolation, every house plundered and burned, the church a roofless shell, the beasts all driven off. The people must rebuild their existence with nothing in hand but their bare lives, thankful to have been spared for poverty and hardship.

Arnisby opened its doors, finding shelter and beds for all. By the time the sun had dropped behind the hills and their shadow was running eastwards over the steel-bright sea, all was ordered. Adam and Julitta at last could find leisure for their own needs, eagerly provided; hot water, clean clothing, and food. While the weavers vied with each other to assemble a meal worthy of their lord and his heroic followers, he took counsel by the harbor with Baldwin and Wulfstan. Against the horizon's brightness a black water bird drifted with the tide.

"The outlander?" Wulfstan blinked in some bewilderment. "Aye, he's been hanging offshore since he sailed. You wants him, m' lord?"

"Will one of you put out and invite him to the reckoning, as I promised? Take this as a token." He held out the dagger Erling had lent him.

Wulfstan jerked a thumb at his eldest son, regarded his lord with swift comprehension and fumbled for French. "It was him got you away? You wasn't aboard —"

"We were buried in the shingle under the sail," Julitta explained.

He slapped his thigh and roared. "God save him for t' thought!" Then he reverted to his own tongue to admonish his offspring. "Ye slummocky lumps, get to t' outlander afore I skelps t'lugs off'n your gormless heads!"

They sloshed to the nearest boat and piled aboard; whatsoever Lord Adam desired in Arnisby must be his as fast as feet could run and hands engage in providing it. Before the last of the twilight had faded from sea and sky Erling and Hakon had joined the conference at Martin the weaver's table, horns of ale in hand and the meal's bones before them.

"They didn't throw my men outside the gate; we'll have support within," Adam was saying.

"They'll be disarmed," Baldwin pointed out.

"Soon remedied."

"Lord Adam," Martin expostulated, "do you plan to take Brentborough with *eight* men?"

"Seventeen," Erling amended quietly.

"And Wulfstan's fishermen to land us under the cliff. We walk in from behind, surprise the guards and enter the keep."

"The hour before dawn?" Baldwin asked professionally.

"That's the usual choice, and expected. We'll go at curfew."

"But — but folk'll be about —"

"After curfew, when they're settled abed, the duty sergeant makes the rounds with his squad, sees all's in order and posts the guards. We'll wait in the alley between the stables and kennels to smother them peaceably, and then *we* make the rounds in their mail, gather up the guards in turn, and enter the keep. If Lord William and Tusky Gerald aren't abed they'll be addled-drunk, probably both, so we sit on them before they know it."

"You want them alive?"

"There's been killing enough," Adam answered, his weary mouth contracting. "I want no more blood." He glanced down at his hands as if surprised to see them unstained.

Wulfstan cleared his throat and scowled at his sons. "Do

307

we sit in t'boats like shags on a rock and leave outlanders to stand up alongside Lord Adam?" he demanded belligerently. They blinked at him, considered it dubiously, and one by one nodded agreement, "You'll find us handy-like wi' ropes, m' lord, and handier wi' gutting knives."

"It will be remembered." Adam drained his ale-horn and stood up. He met Julitta's grave regard, and smiled at her. "You'll come with me, and wait in the boat." He looked directly at Hakon, who suddenly flushed to his hair roots. "If this venture miscarry and you survive it, I entrust my lady to you."

"My life for hers," Hakon accepted the charge.

"I could devise no better provision for her." He turned to the whole company, now standing. "Good friends all, I thank you. To arms, then; we must be across the river by moonrise."

Julitta sat in the fishing boat's bows and listened to the shuffling of cautious feet dwindling up the hillside. A lop-sided moon squinted over the point, heaved itself clear and floated out into the cloud-streaked sky. Straining, she discerned movement and a faint glimmer of helmets; then that was gone, and there was nothing but the hill face on one hand and the silver estuary on the other. Waves slapped the planking and sucked at the rock. The lame seaman left as anchor-watch muttered curses under his breath. She addressed herself to the Holy Virgin, who had already showed her so much favor, and listened tensely to the wind sighing through grass and bracken.

She had lost count of her prayers, and the moon was shining over the cliffs of Lykewake Bay, when a stone rattled down the hill, and bracken rustled sharply as legs brushed through it. Soft shoes padded and slithered. The seaman silently picked up an oar, no mean weapon in accustomed hands, and her own fingers closed on her dagger's haft. Peering, she sensed movement against the black hillside. Someone stumbled, grunted breathlessly, came scrambling down.

"Sheathe steel!" a familiar voice called softly. "It's Ivar."

Two heads suddenly loomed into the sky. For a heart's beat one shape's resemblance jolted her; then she knew the boy Geoffrey. They came out on the flat rock to which the boat was moored; he stood irresolute a moment, and then at Ivar's gesture climbed aboard the boat rocking as he moved. He uttered a faint yelp and lurched dangerously as his footing shifted under him, then collapsed on to the nearest thwart.

"We ran upon the woeful gosling roaming without his nurse," Ivar was explaining in English, "and Lord Adam bids me bring him down to you safe from harm. Reckon the poor fledgling's had his bellyful o' lordship, by t' way he chucked it thankful-like to Lord Adam and come wi' me meek as a mouse."

"You're not courteous," she rebuked him, but could not refrain from smiling in the dark.

"No word of English in him, m' lady."

The lad lifted his head. "He's calling me a fool," he said petulantly.

"What else?"

"It wasn't my fault! They told me I was rightfully lord —"

"There's proof! Hell's Teeth, did you never ask yourself why such men should trouble to right your wrongs? Do you claim to be so witless an innocent you never guessed you were a pretext for villainy?"

"I didn't know — not until too late — it wasn't my fault!" His voice wavered as though he would weep, and he hunched on the thwart. "I thought it would be so wonderful," he complained, "to be a great lord in the world. To wear fine clothes — feast on rare food and spiced wine — enjoy lovely women — ride out on a tall warhorse — command and be obeyed. All my dreams made real! So — so I looked no further —"

"Bedazzled senseless," Julitta pronounced crisply, and Ivar snorted.

"But it wasn't wonderful at all! Whatever I ordered they

309

overruled. And no feasting or riding out, and all they'd do was drink and quarrel and fornicate with serving wenches. They cheated me!"

There was more asperity than sympathy in Julitta's retort, "You mean they cheated Lord Adam!"

"Then I'm not — are you sure I'm not rightfully —"

"Be honest! You're sure yourself, in your own heart."

He nodded wretchedly. The moonlight touched his brows and nose, cheekbones and chin; he was old Maurice again, weighted with guilt and misery. "And that evil woman — she's never uttered a word of sorrow for her husband, she took your chair, and seized the silks your husband gave you as bride gifts, and ruled like the queen of Hell — and you'll tell me she's my mother? I — I cannot endure — I'll not believe — unless you can prove what befell my father's wife."

"She's dead."

"When? Where?"

Julitta looked up the slope of the headland, and the truth hit her like a club. She knew. "There's only one place she can be," she said slowly, and wondered how anything so obvious could have gone unguessed for eighteen years.

Ivar caught his breath in a little grunt. "M' lady?"

"She never left Brentborough, Ivar. She's still there."

"I suppose you'll find her," Geoffrey said drearily. "The Abbot was right. He said only bastards were hidden away in monasteries, not rightful heirs, and — and I was a fool cozened by scoundrels. I wouldn't believe him. I wanted all they offered, but it's all gone awry."

That was his mother in him, and Julitta did not belittle the force of such envious dreams. Much of this coil had been spun by a woman who wanted more than God had given her.

She had been watching the moon float higher over the cliffs, listening automatically for the curfew before she realized that it would not ring that night; the church bells must be cracked wreckage in the tower's ruins. She listened yet more intently for some yell of discovery or clash of weapons, but heard only uneasy water lipping stone and

310

plank, a scuffle of clothing as someone shifted, the wind whispering and the distant breakers crashing on the headland. Ordinary sounds did not descend so far from the castle, but she comforted herself that battle-clangor must. Yet nightmare visions of Adam empty-eyed and still in the moonlight filled her mind. If he died, her own life would be over too.

"Never fret you, m' lady," Ivar grunted roughly. "About now he'll be kicking your uncle out o' bed."

"God grant it!"

"Don't you doubt it, m' lady. Deadliest thing in a fight ever I seen; fast as a whiplash." He must have recognized the approbation in his own voice, for he added, "I'm *your* man, m' lady, but there'll be no shame in serving young Fire-in-the-thatch — Lord Adam, I mean."

"You'll find it pride," said Julitta.

He looked sharply at her in the moonlight, and nodded. "It's that way, m' lady?" he murmured.

"Yes."

Not long after, a stone skipped high on the hill, and the slither and scrape of feet descended. At last a voice hailed her. "M' lady! T' castle's took! Will you come up?"

At the first word Julitta was on her feet, the boat lurching crazily at her unguarded movement; then she was on the steady rock, hitching her skirts for the climb. The newcomer was hurrying down to meet her, Ivar, Geoffrey and the seaman scrambling up. A pungent odor of fish preceding him proclaimed the messenger's status.

"T' castle's yourn, m' lady: walked in, we did, wi' nowt but a few heads clouted."

A thankful sigh emptied Julitta of dread. Adam had his own again. Only she, who had also known the rootless life of the roads, could guess how much his inheritance meant to him. They were all climbing now; a little further, and their feet found a grassy path and could trot. The fisherman jerked out details as he found breath.

"Took t' sergeant like Lord Adam planned — t' guards on t' gate was his men and joined us joyful — walked into t' guardroom and caught 'em either abed or dicing — sighted

311

t' points at their gizzards and stayed mum as mice. Not a squeak! So we trusses 'em up all on a row, and Lord Adam bids me fetch you."

Torches flared in the bailey, spears and helmets gleamed, and servants gaped outside their huts. Someone raised a cheer at sight of her, and the torchflames lighted welcoming faces everywhere. She was neither surprised nor flattered; they had had two days of her uncle's governance. Adam was not an easy master, but his very defects were more endearing than all Lord William's merits.

Erling waited at the head of the stair to greet and escort her. In the guardroom she received grins from everyone but sulky prisoners. The hall was all confusion in half-light, though someone was lighting torches in wall cressets. Serving men and wenches, roused up from sleep in the floor rushes and huddling disordered garments about them, clustered like sheep. Erling's bulk thrust a way through them for her.

Adam stood on the dais, his helmet under one arm and the mail coif thrust back from his disordered hair. At sight of her his grim face changed; he sprang down impetuously. It still astonished Julitta that she could so affect him. He kissed her on the mouth and set an arm about her, leading her on to the dais. Gerald of Flackness and her uncle, bleary-eyed, half-dressed and incredulously surly, scowled at them. Baldwin lounged alongside, and chuckled maliciously.

"Aye, now comes the reckoning. What's the price, d' you think, of treacherously seizing a neighbor's demense?"

Men erupted from the stairhead in the corner behind them, in their midst Giles and Sweyn the sergeant. They blinked at the torchlight, their state proclaiming to all eyes and noses that they had sojourned two unsavory days in the cells. Adam caught his breath and turned aside to them. Baldwin glanced over his shoulder at him and moved nearer the captives.

"Fit to make even *my* belly spew, tricking that purblind fool with his own wife's bastard. And a gallows-example — your own necks itch?" Gerald snarled at him, but Lord Wil-

312

liam gazed in heavy despair. He grinned evilly at the younger man. "Remembering that you struck Lord Adam in the face, and kicked him, and he with his hands bound? What's the payment for that, or will you grovel on your belly for mercy?"

He slouched his weight on to his left leg, and the swordhilt on that hip jutted temptation. Gerald uttered a strangled sound in his throat and grabbed at it. The metal's rasp startled the hall. The blade swung clear and back. Baldwin turned on his heel, steel ready in his right hand. It drove inside the stroke, under the ribs' arch and up. Gerald's face twisted in a vast astonishment as his blood burst from him. He was dead when he thudded upon the rushes.

"Hell's Teeth! You baited him for that end!"

"Out of a disinterested regard for you, Adam." Baldwin wiped his blade on the dead man's clothing, and grinned jauntily.

"You murdered him unshriven! I ought to hang you out of hand."

Baldwin came closer, bowed to Julitta, and murmured in the undertone all successful scoundrels early cultivate, so that none but she and Adam could hear, "Consider, what more acceptable service could I do my son-in-law?"

Adam's teeth caught his lip. He met his wife's appalled yet appreciative eye, and a reluctant humor tugged the corners of his mouth. "You cutthroat, you've vilely embarrassed me —"

"Better vilely embarrassed now than stabbed in the back six months hence," Baldwin retorted. "He injured you past pardon, so he'd coddle his grudge until death — yours or his."

"Sooner his," Adam candidly admitted, and signaled the nearest men to remove the corpse.

"Call it my step-daughter's dowry," Baldwin muttered in Julitta's ear. "Service comes cheaper than cash, and this has proved a most profitless venture." He patted her unpaternally on the behind, winked into Adam's face of kindling wrath, and mocked them both with his shark's grin. Struggling to suppress laughter in the presence of death, Julitta

313

nipped her husband's arm and felt him suddenly quiver with mirth. He looked down into her eyes, and she recognized the bond of humor and understanding that united them more surely than joy of the flesh.

The dead man had been laid in the wall-chamber that had thrice within a week served this purpose. The hall was bright with torchlight, its confusion brought to order. The servants were herded to its further end, mercenaries and Brentborough men were ranged on guard, and already it took on the aspect of a judicial court. Sweyn at the dais's foot stood to arraign the prisoners, and at his nod William of Chivingham was thrust forward.

He said painfully, "There's a long reckoning." He was beaten, his face sagging into flabby folds and pockets, an old man. "He betrayed us!" he cried, in a kind of anguished croak. "He sold us to the Scots, and my son died!"

"And what was *your* price? Brentborough?"

"No, no, we're not *thieves*! You could have kept it if you'd joined us, but we had to have it one way or another. And there was the boy — your seneschal would open for him — but we meant you no wrong —"

"Only murder? And my faithful servant hanged?"

"All this outcry over a churl!"

"Hell's Teeth, is loyalty so cheap to you?" He looked past him at Constance, standing alone beyond Sweyn as though all had withdrawn from the very touch of her garments.

Defeat had not lessened her. It had released her. She was envy and hate incarnate, staring at Adam and Julitta malevolently for their possession of youth and love and lordship, she who had thrown away all she had to reach for what was not hers. Her face twisted with spite, and she struck recklessly to smirch and hurt.

"Yes, you're well matched, lecher and whore! You'll never know who sires your brats, and she'll never tally your bastards!"

"Speak, and we'll hear you. Spit poison, and it's the cells," Adam replied quietly.

314

"What's to be said?" she answered, casting her contemptuous gaze on Lord William, sunk in grief and despair, and on Geoffrey hesitating by the dais steps. "We should have killed you as you rode in that night."

"That's monstrous!" Geoffrey exclaimed.

"A good plan, but poor tools I had to trust it to, and a green girl tricked them!" Her composure broke. "All plans go awry!" She struck one fist into the other palm. "You've to depend on others, and always they fail you. Bertram was a fool, and Maurice squeamish, and these gutless knaves blathered about their Young King's rights as if seizing Brentborough were a Holy Crusade."

"What was your desire?" Adam asked in the hush.

"To be Lady of Brentborough! All I fought for, schemed for, all I had — and that whey-faced whore's get robbed me of it!"

"Tell the truth!" Geoffrey cried shrilly. "*Are you my mother?*"

She looked at him and shrugged. "It's truth enough that you're Maurice's own son, and that hound his second cousin once removed."

"If you're my mother —" He turned desperately to Julitta. "My father's wife — you said she was dead and you knew where she lay. Prove it! Rightful heir or monster's bastard, in God's Name let me know!"

"Julitta?" Then the questioning in Adam's eyes turned to comprehension; for the first time his mind reached out and picked the thought in hers in that union that would strenghten with their shared years, and his words even echoed her own. "Yes; where else could she be?" He stood up. "Sweyn! A close guard on all three until first light!"

The sky was gray over the lead-gray sea, dimming the moon's last light, when they picked their way over dew-sodden grass, between rocks and gorse clumps, down the headland's side. There were witnesses enough; the prisoners and their guards, Erling and Hakon, Baldwin, Giles, Wulfstan and Ivar, and Father Simon who had passed half the night in the castle. After one false cast in the half-light Julitta

315

found the grassy path where their horses' hoofprints were still plain, though blurred at the edges by rain, and so past the basin from which the rusty stream trickled, to the Roman ruin. All the time her certainty grew surer, so that an eerie thought fastened in her mind that the wronged woman's spirit called on her first lawful successor for justice. They thronged in the doorway, and she glanced once at Constance to see fear breaching her hardihood. Without hesitating she walked to the heap of rubble.

"She lies under these stones."

Men crossed themselves, called on their Saints, flinched back. She stooped to pick up a squared stone and toss it aside. It clattered against the wall, and all started. She turned her head. Not a man budged, but the whites of their eyes glinted uneasily. Then Adam stood beside her.

"*In nomine Patris et Filii et Spiritus Sancti,*" he said softly in the silence, and lifted his token stone. Hakon and Ivar broke from palsy and started to shift them, truly-squared mason's work, of a size for easy handling. Adam's hand closed on Julitta's, and she remembered that the validity of his own tenure was in question. Then she glanced aside at Constance's rigid face, and doubt had no place there. The dawn paled about them. Stones rattled. The lad Geoffrey was shivering, his hands gripped to his breast. Then Hakon checked, a stone in his hands.

"She is here."

Leaning, Julitta saw the double gleam of arm bones, the oblong wrist joints, a fan of fingers. A momentary flinching, and then the two men went furiously at the pile, hurling stones clear until they had uncovered the skeleton. Shreds of cloth clung to the bones, two ropes of dank hair trailed over its ribs, and curled within the bowl of its hips lay the unborn babe's crumbling bones. Hakon stooped, fumbled, rubbed something on his tunic-skirt and held out a blackened silver brooch.

"Lady Bertrade — she always wore it!" Sweyn said hoarsely.

But Adam bent and delicately moved aside hair wisps from the triangular dent crushed into the skull's temple, that all might see it.

"I — I never believed Lord Maurice killed her," Giles muttered.

"Not he," Julitta declared confidently. "It was his leman murdered her."

"No! It was accident — sheer mischance!" Constance protested sharply, and then realized her self-betrayal and caught breath in a gulp. Shocked, comprehending stares turned on her.

"We'll have the truth," Adam commanded quietly. "She surprised you and Lord Maurice here in your guilt."

She looked about her at condemnation and sullenly capitulated. "We were coming away, and there she was in the doorway, holding her horse's bridle and screeching at us. Nothing Maurice could say would pacify her; she was demented with jealousy. A dull plain fool. What had she to squall for? One stupid woman couldn't content Maurice, but she was his wife. She raged that she'd have me out of her household that very hour. Then she fell — it was pure mishap —"

"Don't lie! You struck her down," Julitta corrected her. "I've seen you aid mishap."

"Someone had to quiet her," she justified herself. "Maurice was too soft. And she fell awkwardly — always clumsy, she was — and hit her head on the corner stone. An accident. Her horse took fright at the smell of the blood and bolted, clean over the cliff. I wanted to throw her after it to look like a riding accident, but we heard the grooms following in search of her and all alarmed at the noise of the fall, and it was too late. So he went to meet them and tell them she'd gone into the sea — by God's favor the tide was in — and I dragged her here. Later we buried her under the stones." She shrugged. "But she'd raised talk, and I was over a month gone, so inside the week Maurice had me away to that nunnery to avoid worse scandal."

317

A shocked clucking came from Father Simon. "Murder and adultery! She stands there in mortal sin, unrepentant, while Hell gapes to engulf sinners!"

"Haven't I done penance?" Constance demanded savagely. "All these years — waiting, bound to that thick-witted fool, denied my rightful place? And Maurice — sons I could have borne him in lawful wedlock, and kept out that upstart tourney scavenger! But he was squeamish, vowed he'd confess and denounce me if Bertram died aught but a natural death, and I'd no knowledge of simples. Seventeen barren years in his household, and he never touched me again! And he died first — cheated me! Always I've been cheated!"

Baldwin soberly crossed himself. "She's gallows-ripe," he said.

That was apparently Constance's first intimation that others might not view her expediencies as indulgently as she did herself. She started back; her hands jerked into claws, her bitter stare went from face to face until it fastened full on Julitta's. "All your doing, you little whore! I should have killed you before you wedded!"

Adam stepped between them. Ivar whipped out his dagger. Hakon seized her from behind by the elbows and wrenched her round, thrusting her among the guards, who roused from paralysis to hold her fast. She snarled at them.

"A rope, my lord?" Giles suggested grimly.

Adam looked down at the pale bones stretched on the dark earth, round the condemning faces, at the trapped woman. A gull sailed across the sky, faintly blue now, and shrieked startlingly in the hush. He lifted his head to watch it pass, and Julitta knew all, like her, remembered what the carrion birds had done to Odo's body, laid in the wall-chamber with covered face. Geoffrey whimpered, his hands at his mouth.

"Sweyn!"

"My lord?"

"Take her to the gate and put her out."

Sweyn frowned disapproval and jerked a thumb at the two men who held her. Giles, privileged by his knightly status, said bluntly, "You're as soft as ever Maurice was, my lord."

Constance shrugged free and straightened herself, fair as the coming dawn. "Come, my son!" she invited Geoffrey. "Heart up! There are new ventures for us."

He recoiled. "No! No!" He reached desperate hands to Adam and Julitta. "I'm fruit of adultery and murder — *hers* — let me go back — submit to the abbot and confess my folly —"

"You need not," Adam offered. "I'll provide for you, kinsman. You promised, I think, to do as much for me." A wry smile twitched his mouth.

Geoffrey shuddered. "All I want is to take the vows and never look on a woman again!"

"My own son —" Constance began.

Geoffrey flung to his knees at Adam's feet, clawing at his tunic. Adam put a hand on his shoulder and nodded to Sweyn. The two guards swung her about and forced her away.

"Make for York!" Baldwin advised her, brutally practical. "An army's there, and soldiers aren't fussy." He added, as the blue gown disappeared beyond the broken wall, "In the end, one will cut her throat."

Adam hauled Geoffrey up. "I'll arrange all, lad. Go now with Father Simon." He waited until the priest had led him out, and then turned on William of Chivingham.

That man summoned a scowl, an imitation of past menace. "The victory's yours, and my friends all dead men about you. You've only to kill me, and complete your vengeance."

Adam considered him. In that shadowless light he looked neither victorious nor vengeful, but tired to death. "You'll make reparation for all losses," he began, and then, in sudden revulsion, "Take yourself home, you fool, and contemplate your folly for the rest of your lifetime. I'll reckon myself amply requited." He looked to Baldwin. "See him away, and have someone take up the poor lady's bones."

He caught Julitta's hand and drew her from the ruin, out beyond the tumbled walls and up the hillside until they

319

looked out over the sea. Streaks and feathers of fire floated on the golden sky, and the clouds in the blue zenith flushed pink. Radiance grew behind the horizon's bar.

Brightness too fierce for eye to gaze upon winked at them, grew, became the sun's rim. The gulls wailed about them. The air was gold, and their shadows suddenly flung long and black behind them. Julitta looked up at her husband, who closed his arms upon her. His smile turned all at once to a jaw-cracking yawn.

"All I want is to sleep a week — with you, vixen."